Jo Samjhna Samjho: Love's Last Words

Where Hearts Speak in Silence

This is a work of fiction. Similarities to real people, places, or events are entirely coincidental.

JO SAMJHNA SAMJHO: LOVE'S LAST WORDS

First edition. March 2, 2025.

ISBN: 979-8230079088

Written by Dr Naim Tahir Baig.

Table of Contents

Dr Naim Tahir Baig

Act 1: The Meet-Cute and Initial Connection

Chapter 1: The Tea Party

The autumn breeze carried the scent of jasmine and cardamom through the open windows of Amrita's apartment, where delicate porcelain cups clinked against saucers and muted conversations floated like the steam from freshly brewed chai. It was one of those Sunday afternoons that seemed to stretch into eternity—golden, unhurried, wrapped in the comforting embrace of casual conversation and sweet pastries.

Tauree Sharma stood by the window, her fingers tracing absent patterns on the condensation of her untouched teacup. At twenty-six, she had perfected the art of presence without participation. Her dark eyes, observant and calculating, scanned the room with practiced detachment. She wore a simple cotton kurti in deep maroon—practical, understated, yet elegant enough to avoid drawing attention to the fact that she'd rather be anywhere but here.

"You haven't touched your tea," came Amrita's voice, laced with the gentle concern of a friend who knew too much and too little all at once. "I got that special Darjeeling blend you used to love."

Tauree's lips curved into what she hoped resembled a smile. "Just waiting for it to cool," she lied with practiced ease. The truth was more complicated: today was one of those days when the weight on her chest made even the simple act of swallowing difficult.

"Come meet some of my university friends," Amrita urged, her arm linking through Tauree's with an enthusiasm that brooked no refusal. "They're not nearly as boring as my office colleagues. I promise."

Tauree allowed herself to be guided through the apartment, nodding at appropriate intervals as Amrita introduced her as "my brilliant friend from architecture school." The words slid off her like raindrops on glass. Brilliant. Friend. How easily people assigned labels to relationships, to qualities they perceived but never truly understood. Behind her smile, Tauree felt the familiar hollowness expanding—that peculiar emptiness that had been her constant companion since she was fourteen.

Depression, the doctors called it. Psychopathic tendencies, one particularly forthright therapist had suggested during her second year of university, before Tauree had learned to mask her true nature more effectively. Now, at twenty-six, she had refined her performance to near perfection. She laughed at jokes, asked appropriate questions, and maintained enough friendships to appear normal without the burden of genuine emotional investment.

It was exhausting.

By the time they reached the far corner of the apartment, where a small cluster of people had gathered around a low coffee table, Tauree had already calculated her minimum necessary stay—another forty-five minutes before she could make a graceful exit.

"And this quiet one in the corner is Farrat," Amrita was saying, gesturing toward a young man partially hidden behind an ornate wooden screen. "He teaches literature at the university and writes poetry that will break your heart. Farrat, this is Tauree, my most enigmatic friend."

The man looked up, and Tauree felt a curious ripple of recognition, though she was certain they had never met. There was something in his eyes—dark, like hers, but soft where hers were sharp—that suggested a kindred understanding of pain, though expressed in entirely different languages.

Farrat Mirza wore his vulnerability like a second skin. Where Tauree had built walls, he seemed to have constructed windows—still protected, but allowing glimpses inside. His slender fingers cradled a teacup as if it contained something far more precious than Darjeeling, and the slight furrow between his brows spoke of a man caught in perpetual thought.

"Enigmatic," he repeated, his voice lower and softer than she had expected. "That's quite a burden to place on someone at a tea party."

Something in his tone—gentle mockery tinged with genuine understanding—caught Tauree off guard. For a moment, her carefully constructed mask slipped, and genuine amusement flickered across her features.

"Almost as burdensome as being introduced as a heartbreaking poet," she replied, surprising herself with the ease of the retort.

Farrat's lips curved upward, revealing a smile that transformed his solemn features into something unexpectedly warm. "Touché." He gestured to an empty cushion beside him. "Would you care to sit? I've been told I'm terrible company, but I make up for it by not expecting much conversation."

The honesty in his self-deprecation was refreshing. Without fully understanding why, Tauree found herself settling onto the cushion, her usual calculation momentarily suspended.

"I'm actually terrible company as well," she admitted, the truth slipping out before she could filter it through her usual screen of social niceties. "I came because Amrita threatened to physically drag me here if I refused again."

Farrat's eyes crinkled at the corners. "Ah, so we're both hostages. That's comforting."

A small silence fell between them, but it lacked the awkwardness Tauree had come to expect from initial interactions. Instead, it felt oddly companionable, as if they had mutually agreed to drop the pretense of enjoyment without judgment.

"Your tea is getting cold," Farrat observed after a moment.

Tauree glanced down at her cup, realizing she had been absentmindedly swirling the amber liquid without taking a sip. "I'm not much of a tea drinker," she confessed. "Another social failure to add to my growing list."

"What do you prefer?" he asked, and the simple question carried none of the obligatory politeness she was accustomed to. He seemed genuinely curious, his attention focused solely on her response as if it mattered.

"Coffee. Black. Strong enough to dissolve a spoon," she replied. Then, without planning to elaborate, she added, "It's the only thing that cuts through the fog sometimes."

The words hung between them, more revealing than she had intended. Most people would have shifted uncomfortably or offered platitudes about the weather at such an admission. Farrat did neither.

"The fog," he repeated softly, as if testing the weight of her metaphor. "Yes, I know something about that. Mine feels more like a heavy rainfall, though. Everything muted and distant behind a curtain of water."

Tauree felt something shift inside her—a small crack in the dam she had built to contain her emotions. This stranger with sad eyes and gentle hands had just articulated something she had never fully explained to her numerous therapists.

"How do you manage it?" The question slipped out, unfiltered and raw with a need she rarely acknowledged.

Farrat's gaze drifted toward the window, where the late afternoon light painted the room in hues of gold and amber. "Poetry helps. Teaching. Finding fragments of beauty amid the deluge." His eyes returned to hers. "And sometimes, honest conversations with strangers who understand the weather."

A curious warmth spread through Tauree's chest—not happiness, exactly, but something adjacent to it. Recognition, perhaps. The rare sensation of being seen without judgment.

"I design buildings," she said, offering a piece of herself in return. "Spaces where people can feel... contained. Safe." She paused, realizing she had never articulated this aspect of her work before. "I think I'm trying to build the sanctuary I've always needed."

Farrat nodded, requiring no further explanation. "Creation as shelter. I understand that."

Around them, the tea party continued—laughter bubbling, conversations flowing, the social dance executing its familiar steps. But in their quiet corner, Tauree and Farrat had stepped outside the choreography into something more authentic.

"Would you like to try a different tea?" Farrat asked suddenly. "Amrita has a remarkable collection. There's a jasmine green that's less aggressive than Darjeeling. It might suit you better."

The gesture was small but perceptive—an offering that acknowledged her discomfort without trying to fix her fundamental nature. Tauree found herself nodding.

"I'd like that," she said, and meant it.

Farrat rose gracefully, taking her untouched cup. "I'll be right back."

As she watched him navigate through the clusters of guests, Tauree felt the familiar calculation begin again—the assessment of risk, the measurement of emotional investment, the careful balance of need against vulnerability. Farrat Mirza was dangerous, not because he posed any threat, but because he noticed too much. People who truly saw her rarely stayed.

Yet when he returned moments later with a delicate cup of pale green tea that smelled of summer gardens, she accepted it without hesitation.

"No pressure to finish it," he said, settling beside her again. "But sometimes the ritual of holding warmth between your palms can be its own comfort."

Tauree raised the cup, inhaling the gentle fragrance. "Do you always pay such careful attention to strangers?"

A shadow crossed Farrat's features—brief but unmistakable. "Not anymore," he admitted, and she heard the weight of history in those two words. "I've learned to be more... selective in my attentions."

She recognized the boundary he had just established—the gentle warning that, like her, he carried wounds that had taught him caution. Oddly, this made her more comfortable, not less. There was safety in mutual wariness.

"Yet here you are, fetching tea for a woman who just admitted she doesn't even like it," she observed.

Farrat's smile returned, tinged with self-awareness. "Old habits. I've always been better at caring for others than myself. My friends call it a character flaw."

"And what do you call it?"

"Survival," he said simply.

The honesty of his answer resonated in a chamber of Tauree's heart she had long kept locked. She understood survival—the compromises one made with oneself, the mechanisms that kept the darkness at bay. Her methods differed from his—detachment rather than sacrifice—but the underlying necessity was the same.

"I should warn you," she said, surprising herself again with her candor, "I'm not very good at... this." She gestured vaguely between them. "Connection. I tend to use people as sounding boards for my own thoughts rather than engaging in genuine exchange."

"Is that what you're doing now?" he asked, curiosity rather than judgment in his tone.

Tauree considered this, tilting her head slightly. "Strangely, no. This feels different." She paused, analyzing the unfamiliar sensation. "I think I'm actually interested in your responses."

Farrat laughed—a warm, unexpected sound that drew glances from nearby guests. "Well, that's either the most insulting or the most honest introduction I've ever received. I haven't decided which."

"Both, probably," Tauree admitted, a genuine smile forming on her lips for the first time that afternoon. "I've been told my honesty can be brutal."

"I prefer brutal honesty to gentle deception," Farrat replied, his eyes meeting hers with an intensity that should have made her uncomfortable but somehow didn't. "The former leaves bruises; the latter creates scars."

The poetry in his casual observation reminded her of Amrita's introduction. "Do you really write poetry that breaks hearts?"

A flash of something—embarrassment, perhaps, or old pain—crossed his face. "Amrita exaggerates. I write about broken hearts, which is quite different."

"Including your own?" The question was invasive, and Tauree knew it the moment it left her lips.

Farrat didn't flinch. "Especially my own." He sipped his tea, then added, "It's easier to dissect what you've personally experienced."

Another silence fell between them, but it felt like a conversation in itself—an exchange of unspoken understanding about the nature of pain and its articulation.

Around them, the tea party had reached that golden hour when inhibitions had loosened and laughter came more freely. Someone had put on music—classical ghazals that filled the apartment with melancholy beauty. The juxtaposition of social gaiety against the sorrowful lyrics created a strange dissonance that perfectly matched Tauree's internal landscape.

"Would you read me something you've written?" she asked suddenly. The request was uncharacteristic—she rarely showed interest in others' creative expressions—but something about Farrat's measured words made her curious about the ones he committed to paper.

Surprise flickered across his features, followed by hesitation. "Here? Now?"

"Not necessarily. Another time, perhaps." The implication of future interaction hung between them—an unexpected bridge extending from this afternoon into possibilities beyond.

Farrat studied her for a moment, as if assessing the sincerity of her interest. "I could send you something, if you'd like to give me your number."

The request was casual, without the underlying current of expectation that usually accompanied such exchanges. Tauree found herself reaching for her phone before her usual defenses could intervene.

"I should warn you," Farrat said as they exchanged contact information, "I'm not very good at staying in touch. I tend to disappear into my work and emerge days later, wondering why everyone has given up on me."

Tauree appreciated the disclaimer—a clear setting of expectations that required no emotional reassurance from her. "That works perfectly for me. I dislike obligation in any form."

Something in her blunt statement made Farrat pause, his fingers hovering over his phone screen. "That's... refreshingly straightforward."

"Too straightforward?" she asked, suddenly aware that her candor might have crossed a line.

"No," he replied after a moment's consideration. "Just unexpected. Most people wrap their boundaries in softer packaging."

"I've found that soft packaging tends to tear, leaving everyone confused about where the lines actually are," Tauree said, surprised by how easily she was sharing her philosophy with this stranger.

"A valid point." Farrat slid his phone back into his pocket. "So, explicit boundaries established: I may disappear without warning, and you dislike obligation. Seems like we've laid the groundwork for either a very honest friendship or a spectacular disaster."

The corner of Tauree's mouth twitched upward. "I've found those categories often overlap."

Farrat's expression softened. "Indeed they do."

A comfortable silence settled between them, filled with the ambient sounds of the party—the clink of teacups, the murmur of conversations, the gentle strains of music. For the first time since arriving, Tauree felt the constriction in her chest ease slightly. The tea party would still require another thirty minutes of her time, but the prospect no longer seemed as draining.

"Oh good, you two have met," Amrita's voice broke into their quiet bubble as she appeared beside them, her cheeks flushed with the success of her hosting duties. "I thought you might get along. Both of you live too much in your heads."

Tauree suppressed a flash of irritation at the interruption, at having their nascent connection categorized and labeled by an outside observer. But Farrat merely smiled up at Amrita with genuine affection.

"Your friend is excellent company," he said simply.

"High praise from Farrat," Amrita told Tauree with a conspiratorial wink. "He usually retreats to the balcony after fifteen minutes of social interaction."

"Perhaps I've found a kindred spirit in strategic retreat," Farrat suggested, his eyes meeting Tauree's with quiet understanding.

Something warm and unfamiliar fluttered in Tauree's chest—not quite happiness, but adjacent to it. Recognition, perhaps, or the rare comfort of being understood without explanation.

"Perhaps you have," she agreed softly.

As Amrita was pulled away by other guests, Tauree found herself relaxing into the cushions, her posture less rigid, her grip on her teacup less tense. Beside her, Farrat seemed similarly at ease, his previous guardedness softened into something more approachable.

"Tell me about these buildings you design," he said, genuine interest in his voice. "What makes a space feel safe to you?"

The question was thoughtful, probing beyond surface details into the philosophy that drove her work. Tauree considered it carefully, realizing that few people had ever asked about the emotional underpinnings of her architectural choices.

"Light," she began, surprising herself with the immediacy of her answer. "Natural light, but controlled—filtered through screens or reflected off surfaces to soften its intensity. Clear sightlines, so there are no unexpected corners. Materials that age gracefully, that show their history without falling apart." She paused, aware that she was revealing more about herself than her professional process. "And balance between openness and enclosure—spaces that breathe but still hold you."

Farrat listened with an intensity that made her words feel valuable, his eyes focused on her face as if attempting to read between her carefully chosen phrases. "That's beautiful," he said when she finished. "You're not just building structures; you're creating experiences."

"All architects do that," she deflected, uncomfortable with the perception that reached too close to her hidden motivations. "Some just do it more consciously than others."

"And you're very conscious of it," Farrat observed, not as a question but as a statement of recognition.

Before she could respond, a loud burst of laughter from across the room drew their attention. A group of Amrita's colleagues had engaged in some kind of drinking game involving chai and what appeared to be whiskey, their boisterous energy a stark contrast to the quiet intensity of her conversation with Farrat.

"Would you like to step out onto the balcony?" Farrat asked, noticing her slight wince at the noise. "It's quieter, and the view of the city at sunset is rather remarkable."

The offer was tempting—a respite from the growing cacophony and an extension of their unexpected connection. Yet Tauree hesitated, suddenly aware of how quickly she had lowered her usual defenses with this man. Retreating to a more private setting would signal an investment she wasn't sure she was prepared to make.

"Another time, perhaps," she said, establishing a boundary while acknowledging the possibility of future interaction. "I should actually be leaving soon. I have work to prepare for tomorrow."

If Farrat was disappointed, he didn't show it. Instead, he nodded with understanding that required no explanation. "Of course. Though I hope you'll take me up on the offer someday. Amrita's balcony has inspired some of my better verses."

"I'd like to read those," Tauree said, and meant it.

As if on cue, her phone vibrated with a message—not an actual communication, but a scheduled reminder she had set herself as an exit strategy. She glanced at it, then slipped the device back into her pocket.

"I need to go," she said, rising from the cushion with a grace that belied her internal discomfort. "It was... unexpectedly pleasant talking with you, Farrat."

He stood as well, a gentleman's reflex that spoke of traditional upbringing. "The unexpected pleasures are often the most significant," he replied, his poetic nature evident even in casual conversation. "I hope our paths cross again, Tauree."

The way he said her name—with careful attention to its cadence—sent an odd shiver down her spine. She extended her hand, falling back on formality as a shield against the unfamiliar warmth his presence had evoked.

"Thank you for the tea recommendation," she said as his fingers clasped hers briefly. "It was much better than the Darjeeling."

"Small victories," he said with a slight smile. "Safe journey home."

As Tauree made her way through the apartment, making her excuses to Amrita and saying perfunctory goodbyes to the other guests, she felt Farrat's gaze following her—not intrusive, but attentive, as if committing her to memory. She did not look back, maintaining her composure until she had closed the apartment door behind her.

In the relative quiet of the hallway, Tauree leaned against the wall for a moment, taking inventory of her emotional state. The encounter with Farrat had left her oddly unsettled—not in the depleted way social interactions usually did, but in a manner that felt almost energizing. He had seen glimpses of her true nature and hadn't recoiled. Instead, he had offered understanding without demanding explanation.

It was dangerous, this potential connection. Dangerous because it tempted her toward vulnerability when experience had taught her the safety of detachment. Dangerous because Farrat, with his poet's perception, might see through the carefully constructed persona she presented to the world.

Dangerous because, for the first time in years, Tauree found herself genuinely looking forward to a subsequent interaction with another human being.

As she stepped into the elevator, Tauree made a mental note to analyze this anomaly later, when she could approach it with clinical detachment. For now, she allowed herself the small indulgence of replaying their conversation, of remembering the way understanding had flickered in Farrat's dark eyes when she spoke of fog and sanctuaries.

The elevator doors closed, carrying her downward and away from the tea party, but the echo of Farrat's gentle voice followed her, whispering of poetry yet unread and conversations yet to unfold.

Behind her mask of composure, something fragile and long-dormant stirred—not hope, exactly, but its cautious predecessor: curiosity.

Act 1: The Meet-Cute and Initial Connection

Chapter 2: The First Conversation

Three days after the tea party, Tauree found herself staring at her phone, the notification light blinking with quiet persistence. The message had arrived twenty minutes earlier, but she had deliberately finished her sketch for the community center atrium before allowing herself to check it.

I found this and thought of our conversation. - Farrat

Below the brief text was an image of a poem, handwritten in a slanting, elegant script that spoke of careful consideration rather than hasty scrawl:

The fog descends not with warning
But with familiar silence,
A thief of color and contour,
Leaving only the skeleton of the world
For me to navigate by touch.
Today, I found a match
And struck it against despair
To illuminate not the path forward
But the space I currently inhabit.
Sometimes, that is enough.

Tauree read it twice, then a third time, her finger hovering over the screen. Something in the simple, honest verses resonated with an accuracy that made her chest tighten. The poem articulated her daily struggle—not the dramatic descent into darkness that television portrayed, but the quiet, persistent grayness that made each day an exercise in determined functionality.

She hadn't expected Farrat to contact her, despite their exchange of numbers. In her experience, connections made at social gatherings rarely materialized into anything substantial—a reality for which she was typically grateful. Interaction required energy she preferred to direct toward her work, her carefully constructed routine of productivity that kept the fog at bay.

Yet here was this message, this poem, this unexpected bridge extending from the tea party into her ordered existence. More surprising than the contact itself was the fact that she wasn't immediately calculating an appropriate, distant response. Instead, she found herself contemplating what to say with uncharacteristic care.

After deliberating for longer than she would admit, she typed:

Did you write this? It's strikingly accurate. Though I've never tried striking a match against despair. Sounds dangerous.

His response came quickly, as if he had been waiting:

Yes, last night. Insomnia has its uses. And despair makes an excellent friction surface, in my experience. Would you like to discuss it over that coffee you mentioned? The one strong enough to dissolve a spoon?

Tauree felt herself smiling—a small, private expression in the silence of her apartment. The invitation was direct but undemanding, and his casual reference to their previous conversation created a sense of continuity that felt oddly comforting.

Still, she hesitated. Coffee meant an investment of time, energy, and social capital that she typically reserved for professional obligations. It meant extending this unexpected connection beyond the serendipitous bubble of Amrita's tea party into the structured reality of her daily life.

When and where? she typed before she could overthink it further.

Tomorrow evening, 6 PM? There's a place called Inkwell on Carmichael Street. Their coffee meets your dissolving-spoon standard, and they have a quiet corner where conversation doesn't require shouting.

The suggestion was thoughtful—a time after work hours but not encroaching on the full evening, a place designed for conversation rather than social posturing. Tauree found herself appreciating the consideration behind these choices.

I know it. 6 PM works.

I'll be the one with a book and existential uncertainty. See you then.

The exchange complete, Tauree set her phone aside, surprised by the strange lightness in her chest. It wasn't happiness exactly—that emotion had become so foreign that she wasn't sure she would recognize it—but rather a mild curiosity, an anticipation that momentarily pushed back the persistent gray of her internal landscape.

Returning to her sketch, she found herself adding an unexpected detail to the atrium design—a small reading nook nestled beside the floor-to-ceiling windows, where light would filter through wooden screens to create patterns on the floor. A place for quiet contemplation amid the community space. She stared at the addition, wondering what had prompted it, before setting her pencil down and deciding it was time for sleep.

The following day passed in a blur of client meetings and site visits, the familiar rhythm of professional competence that defined Tauree's existence. She moved through these interactions with practiced precision, her mask of polite engagement firmly in place. Yet beneath this performance, an awareness of the evening's appointment created a subtle undercurrent of anticipation that both irritated and intrigued her.

By 5:45 PM, she was standing outside Inkwell, observing the café through its large windows. The space was exactly as Farrat had described—wooden tables spaced far enough apart for privacy, warm lighting that created pockets of illumination rather than harsh overhead brightness, and a corner section partially screened by bookshelves that offered semi-seclusion without isolation.

And there was Farrat, already seated in that corner, a leather-bound book open before him. He wasn't reading, though—his gaze was directed out the window, his expression pensive in a way that suggested his thoughts were far from the bustling street scene. The evening light caught the angles of his face, highlighting a vulnerability that his composed demeanor at the tea party had partially concealed.

Tauree considered walking away. There was still time to send a message claiming a work emergency, to retreat to the safety of her apartment where emotional complexity could be kept at a manageable distance. She had done it before—abandoned social commitments when the prospect of sustained interaction became too daunting.

But something held her in place. Perhaps it was the memory of how Farrat had acknowledged her dislike of tea without judgment, or how he had listened to her architectural philosophy with genuine interest. Perhaps it was the poem he had sent, with its simple understanding of what it meant to navigate through fog.

Before she could second-guess herself further, she pushed open the café door.

The rich aroma of freshly ground coffee enveloped her as she entered, a sensory welcome that eased some of her tension. Farrat looked up at the sound of the bell, his distracted expression clearing as he spotted her. The smile that transformed his features was neither too eager nor politely distant—just a genuine acknowledgment of her arrival that asked nothing in return.

"You came," he said as she approached, closing his book and rising slightly in his seat—that same old-world courtesy she had noticed at the tea party.

"I said I would," Tauree replied, setting her bag on an empty chair and taking the seat across from him. "Though I did contemplate a strategic retreat about thirty seconds ago."

The honesty slipped out without her usual filter, and she immediately questioned the wisdom of such transparency. Most people would respond with awkward reassurance or subtle offense. Farrat merely nodded.

"I appreciate your resistance to that impulse, then," he said, his tone suggesting he understood the effort involved. "I nearly did the same yesterday when sending you that poem. Vulnerability is not my natural state."

"Yet you write poetry," Tauree observed, "which seems inherently vulnerable."

"Writing allows a certain distance." He traced the embossed cover of his book with long fingers. "The words exist separately from me once they're on the page. Speaking them aloud—or sharing them directly—that's where the real exposure happens."

A server approached before Tauree could respond, and she ordered her usual—black coffee, no sugar, extra shot of espresso. Farrat requested chai with cardamom, an echo of the tea party that seemed fitting somehow.

"So," Tauree said when they were alone again, "do you always share your poetry with strangers you meet at tea parties?"

The question contained a challenge, a probe to understand what made this interaction different, special enough to warrant his reaching out. Farrat seemed to consider it carefully, his expression thoughtful.

"No," he answered finally. "Rarely, in fact. But there was something in how you described the fog..." He paused, searching for words with a poet's precision. "You spoke about it without melodrama or self-pity, just as a condition of existence. I found that refreshing. Most people either deny their darkness or wallow in it."

Tauree felt an unexpected flush of warmth at his assessment. Being seen—truly seen—was rare enough to be disconcerting, but there was something in Farrat's perception that felt more like recognition than exposure.

"Most people prefer the performance of normalcy," she said, her fingers absently arranging the sugar packets on the table into a precise line. "They ask how you are but don't actually want the truth."

"And what is your truth, Tauree?" Farrat asked, the directness of his question softened by the gentleness in his voice.

Their drinks arrived before she could answer, creating a momentary reprieve from the intensity of his inquiry. Tauree wrapped her hands around the warm mug, using the sensation to ground herself in the present moment. The aroma of strong coffee rose in a comforting cloud, familiar and fortifying.

"My truth," she began after taking a sip, the bitter warmth sharpening her focus, "is that I navigate through each day by calculation rather than feeling. I measure the energy required for each interaction, each task, and allocate it carefully because my reserves are limited." She paused, surprised by her own candor. "The fog—depression, the doctors call it—it's always there, varying only in its density. Some days I can see shapes through it; other days, I can barely see my own hands."

Farrat listened without interruption, his attention complete and uncompromised. When she finished, he nodded slowly, his expression suggesting not pity but profound understanding.

"And the psychopathic tendencies?" he asked quietly. "You mentioned those at the tea party, though I wasn't sure if you were being hyperbolic."

Tauree stiffened, caught off guard by his recall of a comment she had made so casually. Most people filtered out such uncomfortable revelations, pretending they hadn't heard or assuming exaggeration. Farrat had done neither.

"That diagnosis was... contested," she said carefully, studying his face for signs of judgment or fear. "But yes, there's a certain emotional detachment, a difficulty connecting with others in conventional ways. I've learned to compensate, to perform the expected responses, but it's exhausting."

"Like wearing a mask that's almost, but not quite, your exact face," Farrat suggested.

The metaphor was so precise that Tauree felt a jolt of recognition. "Yes. Exactly that. Close enough to pass inspection, but never comfortable." She took another sip of coffee. "How did you know?"

A shadow crossed Farrat's features—that same flicker of old pain she had noticed at the tea party. "I recognize the performance," he said after a moment. "Not because I share your specific challenges, but because I've spent years cultivating my own masks. Different reasons, similar mechanisms."

There was a story there, in the careful way he constructed his response, in the deliberate vagueness of "different reasons." But Tauree didn't press. She recognized the boundaries of newly formed trust, the careful dance of revelation and restraint that characterized initial vulnerability.

"And what is your truth, Farrat?" she asked instead, returning his question with equal directness.

He cradled his chai, steam rising between them like a delicate veil. "My truth is that I feel too deeply, not too little," he said, his voice low enough that she had to lean forward slightly to hear him. "I absorb others' emotions like a sponge, often at the expense of my own well-being. I've been called an empath, though I dislike the term for its new-age connotations."

"That sounds exhausting in its own way," Tauree observed.

"It is. Hence the poetry—a controlled release valve." He offered a self-deprecating smile. "And the tendency toward solitude, which Amrita constantly tries to cure me of."

"Is that why you agreed to her tea party? A concession to her social rehabilitation efforts?"

Farrat's laugh was soft but genuine. "Partly. But also because Amrita understands my limitations. She creates environments where I can engage without being overwhelmed—small gatherings, familiar spaces, easy escape routes."

"She did the same for me," Tauree realized aloud. "The invitation specifically mentioned it would be 'just a few close friends.' I didn't realize she was accommodating both of us in different ways."

"Amrita has a gift for seeing people clearly," Farrat said with obvious affection. "She perceives needs that aren't explicitly stated."

Tauree considered this, thinking of how her friendship with Amrita had endured despite her own limited capacity for emotional engagement. Others had gradually dropped away, frustrated by her inconsistent availability and apparent detachment. But Amrita had persisted, adjusting her expectations rather than demanding change.

"She's a better friend than I deserve," Tauree admitted, the honesty uncomfortable but necessary.

"I doubt that's true," Farrat replied, surprising her. "Friendship isn't about deserving. It's about compatibility, about finding people whose jagged edges fit with yours to create something whole."

The poetry in his casual observation made Tauree smile despite herself. "Is that from one of your writings?"

"Not yet," he said, returning her smile. "But it might be now."

A comfortable silence fell between them, filled with the ambient sounds of the café—the hiss of the espresso machine, the gentle murmur of conversations, the occasional clink of ceramic against wood. Unlike the awkward pauses that typically punctuated Tauree's social interactions, this quiet felt companionable, a shared respite from the effort of communication.

"Tell me about your work," Farrat said eventually, redirecting the conversation away from emotional terrain toward the safer ground of professional life. "You mentioned designing buildings at the tea party. What are you working on now?"

The consideration in the question—offering her a chance to regain emotional equilibrium—did not escape Tauree's notice. She found herself describing her current project, a community center in a historically underserved neighborhood, with more enthusiasm than she typically allowed herself to display.

"The challenge is creating a space that feels both accessible and secure," she explained, pulling out her tablet to show him preliminary sketches. "The community has high rates of crime and poverty, so there's a need for safety, but traditional security measures often feel institutional and unwelcoming."

Farrat studied the drawings with genuine interest, his finger tracing the flowing lines of her design. "So you've used transparency as security," he observed. "Clear sightlines, open spaces with defined zones, natural surveillance through strategic placement of windows."

"Yes, exactly," Tauree said, surprised by his immediate grasp of her design philosophy. "Safety through visibility rather than barriers. It's more challenging structurally, but it creates a psychological openness that conventional security design lacks."

"It's beautiful," he said simply. "You've managed to make safety feel like embrace rather than restriction."

The observation was so insightful, so aligned with her unspoken intent, that Tauree felt momentarily exposed—as if Farrat had glimpsed not just her professional process but the emotional underpinnings that drove it. She had always approached architecture as a means of creating the security she struggled to find in human relationships, but few people recognized that subliminal motivation in her work.

"Thank you," she said, the words inadequate for the recognition his comment represented. "What about your work? Teaching literature, Amrita said?"

Farrat nodded, seemingly content with the shift in focus. "Contemporary South Asian literature, primarily, though I also teach a course on poetry across cultures." He spoke about his students with unexpected warmth, describing their insights and growth with a pride that suggested teaching was more than just employment for him.

"I try to create a space where they can engage with difficult emotions through the safety of literary analysis," he explained. "Many of them come from backgrounds where emotional expression is discouraged or regulated along strict cultural lines. Literature offers them a vocabulary for experiences they've never been permitted to articulate."

"A different kind of architecture," Tauree observed, "building spaces with words instead of walls."

Farrat's eyes lit up at the parallel. "I've never thought of it that way, but yes—creating rooms where different thoughts can coexist, corridors that connect disparate ideas, windows that offer new perspectives."

Their conversation flowed with surprising ease after that, moving from work to books to the city's changing landscape. Tauree found herself speaking more freely than she had in years, offering opinions and insights without the careful filtering she typically employed in social settings. Farrat matched her pace, sometimes challenging her perspectives but never in a way that felt confrontational—rather, his questions opened new avenues of thought, invited deeper exploration.

Time slipped past unnoticed until the café owner approached with gentle apology to inform them that closing time had arrived. Tauree glanced at her watch in surprise—it was nearly 10 PM, nearly four hours since she'd arrived.

"I had no idea it was so late," she said as they gathered their belongings. "I've completely disrupted your evening."

"On the contrary," Farrat replied, placing money on the table despite her protest, "you've made it infinitely more interesting than my original plan of grading papers and talking to my plants."

Outside, the night air carried the first hint of autumn chill, and Tauree pulled her light jacket closer. The street was quieter now, the daytime bustle replaced by the subdued energy of evening—occasional taxis, couples walking close together, the distant thrum of music from a restaurant down the block.

"How are you getting home?" Farrat asked, his tone casual but with an undertone of concern that Tauree found more charming than intrusive.

"I'll call a rideshare," she said, reaching for her phone. "My apartment is in Westwood, about fifteen minutes from here."

"Mine's in the opposite direction, in Riverside," Farrat said, mentioning the artistic district known for its converted warehouses and affordable rents. The information was offered without expectation, simply a sharing of personal geography that acknowledged the physical distance between their lives.

A slight awkwardness descended as they stood on the sidewalk, the comfortable intimacy of their café conversation suddenly confronted with the question of what came next. Tauree felt the familiar impulse to retreat, to end the interaction with polite finality and return to the safety of solitude.

But before she could act on it, Farrat spoke. "I enjoyed this, Tauree. More than I expected to, honestly." His honesty was refreshing in its simplicity. "Would it be too forward to suggest we do it again?"

The question was posed without pressure, offered as a genuine inquiry rather than a social obligation. Tauree considered it seriously, weighing the unexpected pleasure of their conversation against her typical reluctance to form ongoing connections.

"I'd like that," she said finally, surprising herself with the truth of it. "Though I should warn you again that I'm not always... available. Emotionally or otherwise."

Farrat nodded, understanding in his eyes. "And I may disappear into work and forget the outside world exists. Between us, we make one functional social being."

The observation startled a laugh from Tauree—a genuine sound of amusement that felt foreign in her throat. "A questionable achievement, but I'll take it."

Her rideshare arrived, creating a natural conclusion to their evening. As she moved toward the car, Farrat made no move to touch her—no handshake, no social hug—respecting the physical boundaries she hadn't explicitly stated but which he seemed to intuit.

"Good night, Tauree," he said simply. "Thank you for the conversation."

"Good night, Farrat," she replied, finding herself oddly reluctant to end the evening. "And thank you for the poem. It... helped. On a day when the fog was particularly dense."

Something flickered in his expression—surprise, perhaps, or pleasure at the knowledge that his words had made a difference. He inclined his head slightly, an acknowledgment that required no verbal response.

As the car pulled away, Tauree found herself looking back, watching Farrat's silhouette grow smaller against the warm lights of the café. An unfamiliar sensation stirred in her chest—not happiness exactly, but something adjacent to it. The recognition of connection, perhaps, or the rare comfort of being understood without explanation.

The fog was still there, a constant companion in her internal landscape. But for the first time in longer than she could remember, Tauree felt as if someone else had stepped into it with her, illuminating not the path forward, but the space she currently inhabited.

And sometimes, that was enough.

Act 1: The Meet-Cute and Initial Connection

Chapter 3: The Midnight Walk

A week had passed since their coffee meeting, and Tauree found herself in an unfamiliar state of anticipation. Each time her phone chimed with a notification, her hand would move toward it with uncharacteristic eagerness before she caught herself, annoyed at this new weakness. Farrat had not contacted her again, and she had not reached out to him—a mutual silence that should have felt comfortable given their established boundaries, yet somehow didn't.

She told herself it was merely intellectual curiosity—an interest in the mind behind the poem he had shared, nothing more. The fog had been particularly dense these past few days, requiring extra coffee and rigorous adherence to her routines to maintain functionality. Work provided the structure she needed, and she immersed herself in the community center project, refining the reading nook she had impulsively added after their first text exchange.

It was nearly midnight on Friday when her phone finally lit up with his name.

Are you awake?

The simplicity of the message made her smile despite herself. Three words that acknowledged the lateness of the hour while leaving space for her to decline engagement without explanation.

Yes, she typed back, equally concise.

His response came quickly: *I'm walking by the river near Alameda Gardens. The night is unexpectedly beautiful. Would you like to join me?*

Tauree stared at the invitation, her rational mind immediately cataloging reasons to decline. It was midnight. The location was at least twenty minutes from her apartment. She had an early meeting with contractors tomorrow. Social interaction required energy she had already depleted through a day of client presentations.

Yet beneath these practical considerations, an unfamiliar impulse stirred—a desire to step outside her carefully structured existence, to experience something unplanned and potentially meaningful.

Why are you walking by the river at midnight? she asked, buying time to process her conflicting impulses.

Insomnia. The words won't come, so I'm searching for them among the reflections on the water. Probably sounds pretentious, but it's the truth.

The honesty in his response resonated with her. How many nights had she paced her own apartment, seeking escape from the persistent buzz of thoughts that prevented rest? How often had she wished for somewhere other than the familiar walls to contain her restlessness?

Before she could overthink it further, she replied: *Text me the exact location. I'll be there in 30 minutes.*

As soon as she sent the message, a wave of anxiety washed over her. This impulsive decision violated her carefully maintained boundaries—the structures she had built to protect her limited energy and emotional resources. Yet the prospect of seeing Farrat again, of continuing their conversation in the quiet intimacy of midnight, held an appeal she couldn't rationally explain.

She changed quickly into jeans and a warm sweater, the practical part of her brain noting the temperature drop that typically accompanied late nights near the river. Her hand hesitated over her medication—the small white pill that sometimes helped when the fog became too thick to navigate. After a moment's consideration, she left it untaken. Tonight, she wanted clarity, even if it came with the sharper edges of unfiltered perception.

The rideshare driver was mercifully silent during the journey, allowing Tauree to prepare herself for the upcoming interaction.

She rehearsed potential conversation topics, calculated the optimal duration for the encounter, and established clear boundaries in her mind about physical proximity and emotional disclosure. The familiar routine of preparation calmed her, creating the illusion of control over an inherently unpredictable situation.

Alameda Gardens was technically closed at this hour, but the riverside path that bordered it remained accessible, a favorite haunt of insomniacs, night joggers, and the occasional poet seeking inspiration in the urban solitude. As the car approached the location Farrat had specified, Tauree spotted him leaning against the stone balustrade that separated the walking path from the gentle slope down to the water.

Even from a distance, there was something compelling about his silhouette against the backdrop of city lights reflected on the river's surface. He stood perfectly still, a rare quality in a world of constant motion, his attention focused on the play of light on water with such intensity that he didn't notice her approach until she was nearly beside him.

"Tauree," he said, turning at the sound of her footsteps, her name spoken with a blend of surprise and pleasure that suggested he hadn't been entirely certain she would come. "You actually came."

"I said I would," she replied, echoing her words from the café with a slight smile. "Though I questioned my sanity several times during the ride here."

Farrat's laugh was soft in the night air. "A reasonable concern when agreeing to meet a virtual stranger by a river at midnight."

"Are we still strangers?" Tauree asked, moving to stand beside him at the balustrade, careful to maintain a comfortable distance. "After four hours of conversation at the café, I'm not sure that definition still applies."

"What would you call us, then?" he asked, genuine curiosity in his tone.

Tauree considered the question, appreciating that he didn't rush to supply his own answer. "Acquaintances seems too formal. Friends feels premature." She paused, searching for the right word. "Fellow travelers, perhaps. Moving in the same direction for a while."

Something in her definition made Farrat smile—a gentle expression that transformed his solemn features. "I like that. Fellow travelers through the fog and the rainfall."

The reference to their respective metaphors for depression created an immediate sense of intimacy, a shared language that bridged the physical space between them. Tauree felt herself relaxing slightly, the anxiety of the impulsive decision receding in the face of his undemanding presence.

"So," she said, gesturing toward the river, "are the words hiding in there somewhere?"

Farrat followed her gaze to where moonlight danced on the rippling surface. "If they are, they're being elusive tonight. I've been working on a poem about disconnection for three days, and every draft feels hollow—like I'm writing about something I've observed rather than experienced."

"Isn't that what writers do? Observe and interpret?"

"Some do," he acknowledged. "But for me, poetry has always been excavation rather than construction—digging into my own experience to find something universal buried within it." He glanced at her, a flash of vulnerability crossing his features. "The problem is that I've been feeling strangely... connected lately. It's disrupting my familiar relationship with isolation."

The implication hung between them—that their recent interactions had contributed to this disruption. Tauree felt a curious blend of satisfaction and alarm at the possibility. She was unaccustomed to having such an impact on another person's emotional landscape.

"Is that why you invited me tonight?" she asked, direct as always. "To understand this disruption?"

Farrat considered her question with the seriousness it deserved. "Partly," he admitted. "But also because when I found myself unable to sleep, walking these paths alone, you were the person I wanted to talk to. That hasn't happened in a very long time."

The honesty in his response created an ache in Tauree's chest—not painful exactly, but a pressure that felt like emotion trying to surface through the protective numbness she typically maintained. She didn't know how to respond to such straightforward vulnerability, so she defaulted to observation.

"It's beautiful here," she said, looking out over the water. "I've lived in this city for six years and never walked this path at night."

Farrat accepted the deflection without comment. "Night transforms familiar landscapes," he said, falling into step beside her as she began to walk. "The absence of detail creates space for imagination."

They moved along the riverside path, their pace unhurried, the sounds of the sleeping city creating a distant backdrop to their footsteps. The air carried the scent of water and stone, with occasional traces of jasmine from the nearby gardens. Overhead, the moon was nearly full, casting enough light to navigate but leaving the spaces between trees shrouded in comfortable darkness.

"Do you do this often?" Tauree asked after a comfortable silence. "Walk at night when you can't sleep?"

"At least twice a week," Farrat replied. "Insomnia has been my companion since childhood. I've learned to use the quiet hours rather than fighting them."

"What happens when it rains?" she asked, thinking of his metaphor for depression—the curtain of water that muted and distanced everything.

A smile tugged at the corner of his mouth. "Then I get wet. There's something purifying about walking in the rain at night—like the city is being rinsed clean, and perhaps I can be too."

Tauree tried to imagine it—Farrat moving through empty streets as water streamed from the sky, seeking not shelter but communion with the elements. The image was surprisingly easy to conjure, fitting what she had come to understand about his nature.

"I stay inside when it rains," she said, offering a piece of herself in return. "I wrap myself in blankets and listen to the sound against the windows. It's one of the few times the fog feels... appropriate. Like the world is matching my internal weather."

Farrat nodded, understanding without need for elaboration. "There's comfort in that congruence. When the external aligns with the internal, it creates a rare harmony."

They reached a small plaza that jutted out over the water, a circular space with stone benches arranged to face the river. By unspoken agreement, they settled onto one of these benches, maintaining the careful distance that had characterized their walk.

Above them, stars pushed through the city's light pollution—not the spectacular canvas of a truly dark sky, but a scattered handful of persistent lights that refused to be entirely dimmed by urban glow. Tauree found herself searching for patterns among them, the familiar childhood game of connecting dots into shapes.

"Do you know the constellations?" she asked, tilting her head toward the sky.

Farrat followed her gaze upward. "Only the obvious ones. Orion. The Big Dipper. My knowledge of the night sky is embarrassingly limited for a supposedly romantic poet."

The self-deprecation in his tone made her smile. "Mine too. I always preferred maps to legends—the precision of cartography over the speculation of mythology."

"That fits," Farrat observed, his voice soft in the night air. "You strike me as someone who values clarity over beautiful uncertainty."

The insight was accurate but incomplete. "I value clarity because uncertainty has rarely been beautiful in my experience," Tauree corrected gently. "It's usually been frightening, or at the very least, exhausting."

Farrat considered this, his profile thoughtful in the moonlight. "That's a fair distinction. I suppose I've had the luxury of finding poetry in uncertainty because my life has otherwise been relatively stable."

"Has it?" Tauree asked, genuine curiosity in her voice. Despite their lengthy conversation at the café, she realized how little she knew about his background, his history, the experiences that had shaped him.

A shadow passed across his features—that same flicker of old pain she had noticed during their previous encounters. "Not always," he said after a moment. "But the instability was... contained. Specific to certain relationships rather than a pervasive condition of existence."

The careful way he framed his response suggested boundaries, areas of experience he wasn't yet ready to explore with her. Tauree respected this reticence, recognizing in it a reflection of her own selective disclosure.

"The fog has been a constant companion since adolescence," she offered instead, sharing her own history as a gesture of reciprocity. "Some days it's so thick I can barely function; other days it's just a slight haze at the edges of perception. But it's always there, coloring how I see the world, how I move through it."

Farrat's attention was complete, his focus on her words rather than formulating his response—a rare quality that made conversation with him so unexpectedly comfortable. When she finished speaking, he nodded slowly.

"Have you found anything that helps?" he asked, the question containing no trace of the patronizing advice-giving that typically followed such disclosures.

"Structure," Tauree replied without hesitation. "Routines. Clear goals and measurable progress. My work, primarily—creating spaces that bring order to chaos." She paused, then added with surprising honesty, "And occasionally, conversations that make me forget the weather for a while."

The implication—that their interactions had provided temporary respite from her persistent depression—hung between them, more vulnerable than she had intended to be. But Farrat received the disclosure with a gentle nod, neither dismissing its significance nor magnifying it into something more than it was.

"I'm honored to provide meteorological distraction," he said, his tone warm with genuine appreciation rather than flirtation.

The gentle humor diffused the intensity of the moment, allowing Tauree to recalibrate emotionally without retreating entirely. She found herself smiling despite the lingering discomfort of vulnerability.

"What about you?" she asked, shifting focus back to him. "What helps when the rainfall becomes too heavy?"

Farrat considered the question seriously, his gaze returning to the river where moonlight created a pathway of silver across the dark water. "Poetry, as you might expect. Teaching—being fully present for my students pulls me out of my own head." He paused, his profile thoughtful in the half-light. "And walking. Moving through the world reminds me that I'm part of it, even when I feel separate."

A comfortable silence fell between them, filled with the ambient sounds of the sleeping city—the distant hum of traffic, the occasional call of a night bird, the gentle lapping of water against stone. Unlike the awkward pauses that typically punctuated Tauree's social interactions, this quiet felt companionable, a shared space that required no verbal filling.

Above them, a wisp of cloud drifted across the moon, momentarily dimming its light before passing on. The breeze carried a hint of autumn chill, and Tauree pulled her sweater closer around her shoulders.

"Are you cold?" Farrat asked, noticing the movement.

"A little," she admitted. "But it's pleasant—clarifying rather than uncomfortable."

He nodded, understanding without offering his jacket or suggesting they leave—respecting her assessment of her own comfort rather than imposing conventional gallantry. The consideration in this small restraint made Tauree unexpectedly grateful.

"Shall we keep walking?" he suggested instead. "Movement tends to generate warmth."

They continued along the river path, their pace unhurried yet purposeful. The conversation flowed with surprising ease, moving from literature to architecture to the peculiar quality of night that invited confidences rarely shared in daylight. Tauree found herself speaking more freely than she had in years, offering opinions and insights without the careful filtering she typically employed in social settings.

"I've always wondered about the architectural significance of bridges," Farrat said as they approached one of the smaller crossings that spanned the river. "They're so explicitly symbolic—physical manifestations of connection."

"Yet they're also boundaries," Tauree observed, professional interest engaged by his observation. "They define where land ends and another territory begins. The same structure that connects also divides."

"Like relationships," Farrat suggested, glancing at her with a poet's perception. "The very agreements that bring people together also establish the terms of their separation."

The insight was unexpectedly profound, touching on Tauree's fundamental ambivalence about emotional connection. She had always viewed relationships as potential threats to her autonomy, demands on her limited emotional resources. Yet Farrat had just articulated a different perspective—that boundaries could be integral to connection rather than opposed to it.

"I've never thought of it that way," she admitted, stepping onto the bridge as she spoke. "I've always seen connection and independence as mutually exclusive."

"Perhaps that's why fog is your metaphor rather than rainfall," Farrat suggested gently. "Fog obscures everything equally—blurs all boundaries until isolation seems like the only clarity. Rain creates distinct patterns, reminds you that separation and connection can coexist."

They had reached the center of the bridge, and Tauree stopped, leaning against the railing to look out over the water. The symbolism of their position wasn't lost on her—suspended between territories, neither here nor there but somewhere in the liminal space between defined states.

"Does poetry always make you this philosophical at midnight?" she asked, deflecting slightly from the emotional resonance of his observation.

Farrat smiled, accepting the shift in tone. "Only when I have a worthy interlocutor. Otherwise, it's just the endless internal monologue of a sleep-deprived academic."

The self-deprecation made her laugh—a genuine sound of amusement that felt unexpectedly free in the night air. "Well, I'm honored to externalize your midnight philosophical ramblings. It's certainly more interesting than my usual insomnia activities of reorganizing my bookshelves by color."

"By color? Not subject or author?" Farrat asked, mock horror in his tone.

"The aesthetics matter," Tauree defended with a smile. "My apartment is designed with specific color harmonies in mind. Books that disrupt the palette get hidden behind more visually compliant volumes."

"The suffering of literature for the sake of interior design," Farrat lamented dramatically. "As a professor of literature, I should be appalled."

"And yet?"

"And yet I find it strangely charming, this prioritization of visual harmony." His smile was warm in the moonlight. "Though I confess my own bookshelves are organized by emotional resonance—a system comprehensible only to me, which drives my more orderly friends to distraction."

The image of Farrat's personal library—books arranged according to an internal emotional logic known only to him—felt unexpectedly intimate, a glimpse into the private world behind his public persona. Tauree found herself wanting to see this space, to understand the organization that reflected his inner landscape.

The realization startled her—this desire to know more, to move beyond the careful boundaries of their current interaction into something deeper. It was precisely the kind of emotional engagement she typically avoided, the investment of attention and interest that depleted her limited resources.

Yet here she was, standing on a bridge at nearly one in the morning, genuinely curious about the bookshelves of a man she had met only twice before. The fog hadn't lifted—it was still there, coloring her perception—but something about Farrat's presence made it seem less isolating, as if he had somehow found a way to step into it with her.

"It's getting late," she said abruptly, suddenly aware of the time and the unprecedented nature of this midnight excursion. "I should probably head home."

If Farrat was surprised by the sudden shift, he didn't show it. Instead, he nodded with that same understanding that required no explanation. "Of course. Can I walk you to a taxi stand, or would you prefer to call a rideshare?"

The consideration in the question—offering assistance without assumption—eased some of Tauree's sudden tension. "I'll call a rideshare," she said, reaching for her phone. "But thank you for the offer."

They walked back the way they had come, their pace slightly brisker now that an endpoint had been established. The comfortable silence of earlier had shifted, carrying a new awareness of time passing, of a connection approaching its temporary conclusion.

As they reached the plaza where they had sat earlier, Tauree's phone indicated her ride was three minutes away. They stood side by side, looking out over the water one last time.

"Thank you for coming," Farrat said quietly. "I know it was an unusual invitation at an unconventional hour."

"Thank you for extending it," Tauree replied, surprising herself with the sincerity in her voice. "It was... unexpectedly peaceful."

Farrat smiled, and in the moonlight, the expression held a quality of genuine pleasure that transformed his solemn features. "High praise from someone who values peace as much as you do."

The observation—that he had recognized her fundamental need for tranquility despite her never explicitly stating it—created that same pressure in Tauree's chest, the sensation of emotion pushing against the protective numbness she maintained. It was disconcerting yet not entirely unpleasant.

"Will you write about this?" she asked suddenly. "The midnight walk, the bridge, the philosophical ramblings?"

"Would you mind if I did?"

The question was unexpected—the idea that he would seek her permission before transforming their shared experience into his art. Most people simply took what they needed from interactions, reshaping them to suit their narratives without consideration for the other's perspective.

"I wouldn't mind," she said after a moment's thought. "As long as you don't mention the color-coded bookshelves. That revelation might damage my professional reputation as a serious architect."

The teasing note in her voice surprised her almost as much as it seemed to delight Farrat, whose laugh rang out softly in the night air.

"Your aesthetic secret is safe with me," he promised solemnly, though his eyes remained bright with amusement.

Headlights appeared at the end of the path—her rideshare arriving with punctual efficiency. The moment of departure had arrived, bringing with it the familiar question of what came next, of how this connection would continue beyond the current interaction.

"I'd like to see you again," Farrat said simply, voicing the unspoken question with characteristic directness. "Perhaps at a more conventional hour next time."

The request was clear but undemanding, offered as a genuine expression of interest without expectation. Tauree considered it seriously, weighing the unexpected pleasure of their midnight walk against her typical reluctance to form ongoing connections.

"I'd like that too," she said finally, the truth of it both surprising and somehow inevitable. "Though I can't promise when I'll have the emotional bandwidth. The fog doesn't operate on a predictable schedule."

"Neither does the rainfall," Farrat replied with understanding. "We can navigate the weather together, when both our skies allow it."

The metaphor—simple yet profound in its acknowledgment of their respective challenges—created a framework for connection that felt manageable to Tauree. Not the constant demand of conventional relationships, but a mutual recognition of limits and possibilities.

"I should go," she said as the car pulled up beside them. "My contractors won't appreciate if I arrive tomorrow having had no sleep."

"Of course." Farrat made no move to touch her—no handshake, no social hug—respecting the physical boundaries she hadn't explicitly stated but which he seemed to intuit. "Sleep well, Tauree. Thank you for sharing the night."

"Good night, Farrat," she replied, finding herself oddly reluctant to end the evening. "Thank you for the invitation. It was... illuminating."

As the car pulled away, Tauree found herself looking back, watching Farrat's silhouette grow smaller against the backdrop of the river. He remained still, watching her departure with that same quiet attention he brought to everything—present without demand, observant without intrusion.

The fog was still there, a constant companion in her internal landscape. But for the first time in longer than she could remember, Tauree felt as if its boundaries had shifted slightly, allowing just enough space for another person to stand beside her within its confines.

As the car turned a corner, taking Farrat out of sight, she leaned back against the seat and closed her eyes. The memory of their conversation remained vivid—the bridge, the moonlight on water, the unexpected comfort of philosophical rambling at midnight. It felt like something to be preserved, a rare moment of connection in a life characterized by strategic isolation.

Tomorrow, the fog might be thicker, the demands of work and routine more pressing. But tonight, for a few hours beside the river, Tauree had experienced a rare sense of peace—not because the fog had lifted, but because someone had been willing to walk through it with her.

And in that simple act of companionship, she had found a clarity that no amount of solitude had ever provided.

Act 1: The Meet-Cute and Initial Connection

Chapter 4: The Art Gallery

Two weeks after their midnight walk, Tauree stood before the full-length mirror in her bedroom, examining her reflection with uncharacteristic scrutiny. She had changed outfits three times already—an unprecedented occurrence for someone who typically approached clothing as a purely functional consideration. Her final selection was still minimalist: straight-cut black trousers, a crisp white button-down shirt with architectural details at the collar, and a single geometric pendant in brushed silver. Professional yet not overly formal, exactly the kind of attire she would wear to meet a client or colleague.

Except this wasn't a professional engagement. It was an art exhibition—specifically, a retrospective on contemporary South Asian artists at the Kareem Memorial Gallery—and she was meeting Farrat there in less than an hour.

The invitation had come unexpectedly, via a text message two days ago:

There's an exhibition at Kareem Memorial this Saturday. Works by several artists I've referenced in my courses. Would you like to join me? 2 PM. No pressure either way.

Tauree had found herself accepting before her usual calculation process could intervene—before she could assess her emotional reserves or weigh the potential drain against the benefits. Something about the way Farrat framed his invitations made them feel less like demands and more like possibilities—doors he was holding open without expectation that she would walk through them.

Now, standing before the mirror, she found herself wondering why this particular engagement had triggered such uncharacteristic indecision about her appearance. She wasn't vain by nature, and certainly not given to the kind of preening self-assessment that many of her female colleagues seemed to find necessary before social events.

"This is ridiculous," she muttered to her reflection, turning away from the mirror with deliberate finality. "It's an art exhibition, not a performance evaluation."

Yet as she gathered her bag and keys, a persistent awareness hummed beneath her practical self-admonishments—a recognition that something had shifted in her response to Farrat, something that made their meetings feel increasingly significant despite her attempts to categorize them as casual encounters between "fellow travelers."

The fog had been relatively thin these past few days, allowing her to function with less effort than usual. She had found herself thinking of phrases from their conversations at unexpected moments—while reviewing blueprints, during her morning coffee ritual, in the liminal space between wakefulness and sleep. Fragments of Farrat's poetry occasionally surfaced in her mind, offering unexpected clarity when the fog threatened to thicken.

It was... unsettling. Not entirely unpleasant, but distinctly outside her carefully structured emotional landscape.

The Kareem Memorial Gallery was housed in a converted textile factory in the arts district—not far from Riverside where Farrat lived, she realized. The building itself was an architectural marvel that Tauree had admired professionally but never visited: original brick walls juxtaposed with steel and glass additions, creating a dialogue between industrial heritage and contemporary design that spoke directly to her aesthetic sensibilities.

As her rideshare approached the gallery, Tauree spotted Farrat waiting on the steps outside, a slim figure in dark jeans and a deep blue kurta, his attention focused on the exhibition catalog in his hands. There was something compelling about seeing him in this context—surrounded by the clean lines and thoughtful spaces of the gallery architecture, his scholarly focus visible even from a distance.

He looked up as she approached, and the smile that transformed his features created an unfamiliar flutter in Tauree's chest—a physiological response she immediately categorized and set aside for later analysis.

"You came," he said, echoing his greeting from the riverside, that same blend of pleasure and mild surprise coloring his voice.

"I said I would," she replied, completing what had become their small ritual of acknowledgment. Then, gesturing toward the building: "I've always wanted to see the interior of this space. The renovation was featured in several architectural journals."

"Then this is perfect," Farrat said, his eyes warming with genuine pleasure at having offered something she valued. "Art and architecture in one experience."

As they entered the gallery, Tauree found herself immediately drawn to the spatial design—the thoughtful flow between exhibition areas, the careful consideration of light and shadow, the way the original structural elements had been preserved and highlighted rather than concealed. She began to comment on these features to Farrat, then caught herself, remembering they were here for the art, not the building.

"Sorry," she said, cutting herself off mid-observation about the clerestory windows. "You didn't invite me here for an architectural critique."

"On the contrary," Farrat replied, surprising her. "I find your perspective fascinating. The way you read spaces is similar to how I read texts—looking for intention, context, the conversation between elements." He gestured toward the soaring ceiling. "Please, continue. I'd like to experience this exhibition through both our lenses."

The invitation—to share her professional perspective without apology—was unexpected but welcome. Most people found Tauree's analytical approach to spaces tedious or overly technical. Even her colleagues tended to prefer emotional responses to architectural precision when outside a work context.

"The architect has created a sequence of compressions and releases," she continued, gesturing to the way the entrance hall narrowed slightly before opening into the main exhibition space. "It creates a subtle rhythm as you move through the gallery—moments of intimacy followed by expansiveness. Notice how your breathing changes as we move from this corridor into the main hall."

Farrat paid close attention as they walked, his awareness focused on the physical experience Tauree was describing. "You're right," he said as they emerged into the larger space. "There's an involuntary exhale, almost like the building is breathing with you."

"Exactly," Tauree confirmed, pleased by his immediate understanding. "Good architecture works with the body's natural responses, not against them. This building is conducting a silent conversation with everyone who enters it."

"Like poetry," Farrat observed, drawing the parallel with quiet conviction. "The best verses create a physical response—a catch of breath, a change in heartbeat—before the mind has fully processed the meaning."

His comparison created a bridge between their professional perspectives, illuminating common ground that Tauree hadn't previously considered. She found herself nodding, unexpectedly energized by this cross-disciplinary dialogue.

They moved into the first exhibition room, where large-scale paintings dominated the walls—vibrant explorations of color and form that immediately commanded attention. Tauree found herself drawn to a particular canvas: deep blues and purples swirling around a central point of white light, creating a vortex that seemed to both pull the viewer in and push outward simultaneously.

"This one speaks to you," Farrat observed, not a question but a recognition.

Tauree nodded, studying the painting with focused attention. "It reminds me of the fog," she said quietly. "But not in a negative way. More like... seeing it from the outside and the inside simultaneously."

Farrat moved beside her, his own gaze tracing the swirling patterns. "I see that," he agreed. "There's a sense of being enveloped but not consumed. Protected rather than trapped."

The precision of his observation—identifying the exact nuance that had drawn her to the piece—created that now-familiar sensation of being truly seen, of having her internal landscape recognized without need for elaborate explanation.

"The artist is Ananya Mehta," Farrat continued, consulting the exhibition guide. "She works primarily with themes of mental landscapes and interior states. This series is called 'Sanctuaries of the Mind.'"

"Appropriate," Tauree murmured, still absorbing the painting's affect. The title resonated with her own architectural philosophy—creating spaces that served as sanctuaries, physical manifestations of the psychological shelter she sought in her designs.

They moved through the exhibition at a measured pace, each offering observations from their particular perspective. Farrat's knowledge of the artists and their cultural contexts provided depth to Tauree's experience, while her spatial awareness highlighted relationships between the works that might otherwise have gone unnoticed.

It was the most intellectually engaging gallery visit Tauree had ever experienced. Usually, she found such outings draining—too many people, too much sensory input, the social pressure to produce appropriate responses to artwork she often found emotionally inaccessible. But with Farrat, the experience was transformative. His quiet presence beside her created a buffer against the usual overwhelm, and their ongoing dialogue provided a framework for processing the visual stimuli in a way that felt manageable rather than exhausting.

In the third exhibition room, they encountered a series of mixed-media installations exploring themes of connection and isolation. One piece particularly caught Tauree's attention: a structure of delicate wire threads stretching between two solid forms, creating a complex web of intersections and empty spaces.

"It makes me think of conversation," she said, circling the installation to view it from different angles. "The spaces between words, how meaning gets constructed in the intervals as much as in the statements themselves."

Farrat's expression brightened with recognition. "Yes, exactly. In poetry, we call it the caesura—the pause or break within a line of verse. Often it's more expressive than the words themselves."

"In architecture, we talk about negative space—the unbuilt areas that give meaning to the constructed elements," Tauree replied, enjoying the parallels between their disciplines. "A room is defined as much by its emptiness as by its walls."

"Like people," Farrat suggested quietly, his gaze meeting hers with unexpected intensity. "Defined as much by what we withhold as what we reveal."

The observation struck Tauree with surprising force, resonating with her own careful management of disclosure and boundary. She had always viewed her selective sharing as a necessary protection, but Farrat's framing suggested something more intentional—that the spaces she maintained around herself might be as meaningful as the aspects she allowed others to see.

Before she could formulate a response, they were interrupted by an animated voice calling Farrat's name. Turning, they saw a young woman approaching—early twenties, vibrant in both dress and manner, her smile wide with recognition.

"Professor Mirza! I thought that was you. What are you doing here?" Then, noticing Tauree, she added with undisguised curiosity, "Oh, hello!"

"Priya," Farrat acknowledged, his expression warming with genuine affection. "I'm here for the exhibition, of course. Several artists we discussed in last semester's Contemporary Visual Culture seminar are featured." Turning slightly, he continued, "This is Tauree Sharma. Tauree, this is Priya Kapoor, one of my most insightful students."

"Former student," Priya corrected with a grin. "I graduated last month, which means I can finally ask you all the personal questions you refused to answer in class." Her attention shifted to Tauree, assessment barely concealed behind her friendly expression. "So, how do you know our enigmatic professor? He never mentions his life outside the university."

There was a teasing familiarity in Priya's manner that suggested a comfortable relationship with Farrat—the kind of easy rapport that sometimes developed between mentor and student when genuine respect existed on both sides. Tauree found herself unexpectedly curious about this dimension of Farrat's life she hadn't yet glimpsed—Farrat the teacher, Farrat the respected professor.

"We met at a mutual friend's gathering," Tauree replied, her usual social mask sliding into place with practiced ease. "I'm an architect. We discovered some interesting intersections between our professional perspectives."

"An architect!" Priya's eyes lit with renewed interest. "That makes perfect sense, actually. Professor Mirza was always making us consider how physical space influences narrative structure. Now I see where that came from."

"I assure you, I was boring students with spatial theory long before I met Tauree," Farrat interjected with gentle humor. "How are the graduate school applications coming along?"

The deflection was subtle but effective, redirecting Priya's attention away from their relationship and toward her own academic future. As the young woman launched into an account of her application process, Tauree observed the interaction with analytical interest. Farrat listened to his former student with genuine attention, asking perceptive questions that demonstrated detailed knowledge of her academic interests and aspirations. His guidance was gentle but precise, offering specific suggestions rather than generic encouragement.

It was a side of him Tauree hadn't seen before—Farrat the mentor, confident in his expertise yet humble in its application. She found herself appreciating this new dimension of his character, the way he directed the spotlight away from himself and toward Priya's potential with such natural ease.

Eventually, Priya checked her phone and exclaimed at the time. "I have to go—I'm meeting friends for a late lunch. It was really nice to meet you, Tauree." Then, with a mischievous smile toward Farrat: "Professor, I expect a full report on what you think of the Mehta installation. It's definitely going to feature in my thesis proposal."

After she departed, a small silence fell between them—not uncomfortable, but marked by a shift in awareness. They had been observed as a pair, their connection now externalized through Priya's curious assessment. Something private had become, however minimally, public.

"She seems very bright," Tauree observed, offering a neutral comment to bridge the moment.

"One of the most promising students I've taught," Farrat confirmed, his pride evident. "Fearless in her thinking, but disciplined in her analysis—a rare combination."

"You clearly made an impression on her," Tauree noted, recalling the young woman's obvious respect beneath her teasing manner.

A flash of self-consciousness crossed Farrat's features. "I try to be the kind of teacher I needed when I was struggling to find my voice," he said simply.

The statement—humble yet revealing—offered another glimpse into his motivations, the values that guided his interactions beyond their immediate connection. Tauree found herself wanting to know more about this aspect of his life, the passion that animated him when he spoke of his students' potential.

"What made you choose teaching?" she asked as they moved into the next exhibition room. "Was it always your plan, or did you come to it through another path?"

Farrat considered the question with characteristic thoughtfulness. "I initially thought I would be a writer exclusively—locked away in some garret, producing verse that would change the world through pure artistic merit." His smile was self-deprecating as he continued, "It took me several years to realize that words gain their power through connection, through being received and interpreted by others. Teaching became a way to facilitate that connection, to help new voices find their own power."

"That's... beautiful," Tauree said, the sincerity in her voice surprising even herself. "Most people I know chose their professions for far more pragmatic reasons."

"Including you?" Farrat asked, genuine curiosity in his tone.

Tauree reflected on the question as they paused before a series of black and white photographs depicting urban landscapes. "Yes and no," she replied finally. "Architecture offered structure, precision, concrete problems with definable solutions—all very appealing to someone struggling with the nebulous nature of depression. But there was also something more..." She searched for the right words. "I wanted to create spaces where people could feel held without being constrained. That desire wasn't entirely rational."

"The most meaningful choices rarely are," Farrat observed. "There's usually a logic beneath the logic, an emotional current guiding the rational decision."

As they continued through the exhibition, their conversation flowed with that same surprising ease Tauree had experienced during their previous encounters. They moved from professional philosophies to favorite books, from childhood memories of significant spaces to the cultural contexts of the artwork surrounding them. Unlike most social interactions, which left Tauree feeling depleted and eager for solitude, this exchange seemed to generate its own energy—each insight building upon the last, each shared perspective opening new avenues of thought.

Near the end of the exhibition, they encountered a small crowd gathered around a particular installation—an immersive piece featuring projected light patterns that responded to viewers' movements. The space was darkened except for these dynamic projections, creating an environment that shifted and flowed as people moved through it.

Tauree hesitated at the edge of the room, her enjoyment of the exhibition suddenly threatened by the prospect of navigating a crowded, sensory-intensive space. Large groups typically triggered her anxiety, the multiple social signals becoming overwhelming to process while maintaining her composed facade.

Farrat noticed her hesitation immediately. "We can skip this one if you prefer," he offered quietly. "Or come back when it's less crowded."

The consideration in his suggestion—acknowledging her discomfort without drawing attention to it or demanding explanation—created that now-familiar warmth in Tauree's chest. He had observed her boundary and respected it without question or judgment.

"Let's come back," she agreed, grateful for the graceful exit he had provided. "There's a small café on the mezzanine level. Would you like to get some tea? Or perhaps actual coffee for me this time?"

"I'd like that," Farrat said, his smile reaching his eyes. "I'm curious to witness this legendary coffee strong enough to dissolve a spoon."

The café was mercifully quiet, most visitors still engaged with the exhibitions below. They found a table near the railing that offered a view of the main gallery floor—a perfect vantage point for people-watching while maintaining comfortable distance from the crowd.

Their beverages arrived—a black coffee strong enough to satisfy even Tauree's standards, and a fragrant masala chai for Farrat. The familiar aroma created a sensory callback to their first meeting at Amrita's tea party, a subtle reminder of the distance they had traveled from strangers to... whatever they were becoming.

"I've been meaning to ask you something," Farrat said after they had settled comfortably into their seats. "The community center you're designing—is it open to the public during the construction process? I'm always looking for real-world examples of spatial theory for my students, and your description of the reading nook particularly intrigued me."

The request—professional rather than personal—still carried an undercurrent of significance. Farrat was asking to see her work, to witness the physical manifestation of the design philosophy she had described to him. It was a different kind of intimacy than emotional disclosure, but no less meaningful.

"It's still mostly structural at this point," Tauree cautioned. "The bones of the building are in place, but none of the finishes or details that will make the space come alive."

"The bones are often the most revealing part," Farrat replied. "Like the underlying structure of a poem before the ornamental language is applied."

Tauree found herself nodding, appreciating once again how easily he translated between their professional vocabularies. "I could arrange a site visit next week, if you're interested. Tuesday afternoon the contractors finish at four, and the site is quiet after that."

"I'd like that very much," Farrat said, genuine enthusiasm in his voice. "My last class ends at three-thirty on Tuesdays."

As they finalized the details, Tauree became aware of a subtle shift in the atmosphere around them. A group of women at a nearby table were glancing in their direction, their expressions a mixture of curiosity and amusement. One leaned toward another, whispering something that caused a suppressed laugh.

Following her gaze, Farrat turned slightly and then stiffened, recognition flickering across his features. "Former colleagues," he explained quietly. "From the university English department."

Before he could elaborate, one of the women approached their table—mid-thirties, stylishly dressed, with an expression of calculated surprise that immediately struck Tauree as performative.

"Farrat Mirza," she exclaimed, her tone warm but her eyes assessing. "What a surprise to find you in a social setting. We were beginning to think you lived in your office."

"Hello, Nisha," Farrat replied, his usual warmth tempered with a restraint Tauree hadn't witnessed before. "It's good to see you. Are you here for the exhibition?"

"Of course. The department practically emptied out for it—though no one expected to find you here, especially not in such charming company." Her gaze shifted to Tauree, expectant.

"This is Tauree Sharma," Farrat said, the introduction revealing nothing about the nature of their relationship. "Tauree, this is Dr. Nisha Lowell, my colleague from the English department."

"Former colleague," Nisha corrected with a smile that didn't quite reach her eyes. "I've moved to the Cultural Studies program, remember? Though I do miss our little literary debates." Turning to Tauree, she continued, "Farrat never mentioned he was seeing anyone. He's quite the mystery man around campus."

The deliberate mischaracterization of their relationship—and the implicit fishing for clarification—was transparent to Tauree, who had navigated far more sophisticated social manipulations in her professional life. She recognized the subtle power play for what it was: an attempt to define her connection to Farrat on terms not of their choosing.

"We share an interest in the intersection of physical and emotional spaces," Tauree replied, her tone pleasant but offering no further details. "The exhibition has been quite illuminating in that regard."

Her response—factual without being forthcoming—seemed to both satisfy and frustrate Nisha, whose smile tightened almost imperceptibly.

"How fascinating," she said, in a tone that suggested it was anything but. "Well, I should return to my group. Lovely to meet you, Tauree. Farrat, don't be such a stranger to the faculty events. We miss your poetic insights."

As she walked away, Tauree noted the subtle tension in Farrat's posture—a restraint that spoke of unspoken history and carefully maintained boundaries. She had seen this physical manifestation of emotional guardedness often enough in her own reflection to recognize it immediately.

"Former colleague but not former friend, I take it," she observed quietly.

Farrat's smile was rueful. "Is it that obvious?"

"Only to someone familiar with the signs of strategic social navigation," Tauree replied. "I've perfected similar maneuvers in my professional circles."

Farrat sighed, his fingers tracing the rim of his teacup. "Nisha and I had a brief... involvement several years ago. It ended poorly—largely my fault, I should add. I withdrew rather abruptly when things became too intense." He glanced up, meeting Tauree's gaze directly. "I told you I was selective in my attentions. What I didn't explain was that it's because I've learned the hard way what happens when I'm not."

The disclosure—straightforward yet clearly difficult—offered context for the boundary he had established during their first meeting, his warning that he had learned to be cautious in his connections. Tauree appreciated both the honesty and the restraint in his explanation—sharing enough to provide clarity without burdening her with excessive detail.

"We all have histories that shape our present boundaries," she said simply. "I appreciate your candor, but no explanation was necessary."

"Nevertheless, I wanted to offer one," Farrat replied, his expression serious. "I value the clarity we've established between us, Tauree. I wouldn't want misunderstanding to cloud it."

The sincerity in his voice created that now-familiar pressure in her chest—the sensation of emotion pushing against the protective numbness she maintained. It was disconcerting yet not entirely unpleasant.

Before she could respond, her phone chimed with a calendar alert—a reminder of an evening client call she had scheduled weeks ago and nearly forgotten in the unexpected pleasure of the afternoon.

"I need to go," she said, checking the time with a frown. "I have a client consultation at six, and I need to review the materials before the call."

"Of course," Farrat replied without hesitation. "Thank you for coming today. I've enjoyed seeing the exhibition through your perspective."

As they gathered their belongings and made their way downstairs, Tauree became aware of eyes following their progress—Nisha and her colleagues, certainly, but also Priya, who had apparently returned and was now watching them with undisguised interest from across the main gallery.

"I believe we've become the subject of speculation," she observed with dry amusement.

Farrat followed her gaze and sighed, though his expression remained more resigned than genuinely troubled. "Academia runs on gossip almost as much as it does on research grants," he said. "By Monday morning, there will be at least three different versions of who you are and what you mean to me circulating through the faculty lounge."

"Does that bother you?" Tauree asked, genuinely curious about his response to this external definition of their still-evolving connection.

Farrat considered the question with characteristic thoughtfulness. "Not the fact of speculation itself," he said finally. "But the reduction it represents—the flattening of something nuanced into something easily categorized and discussed." He glanced at her, uncertainty flickering across his features. "Does it bother you?"

It was a question Tauree would typically have deflected, retreating behind her usual social mask of cool indifference. Yet something in Farrat's genuine concern prompted a more honest assessment.

"I dislike being the object of others' narratives," she admitted. "But in this case, the actual nature of our... friendship... remains private, regardless of external speculation. The essence is unchanged by others' perceptions."

The word "friendship" felt simultaneously inadequate and excessive—too casual for the depth of understanding they had developed, yet too intimate for the careful boundaries they maintained. But Farrat nodded, seeming to understand the imprecision of the label without requiring further clarification.

Outside the gallery, they paused on the steps where he had waited for her arrival just hours before. The late afternoon light bathed the brick facade in a warm glow, creating long shadows that stretched across the plaza before them.

"Tuesday at four, then?" Tauree confirmed, referring to their planned site visit.

"I'll meet you at the community center," Farrat replied with a nod. "Text me the exact address. I'm looking forward to seeing your work in three dimensions."

As her rideshare approached, Tauree found herself unexpectedly reluctant to end their afternoon—a stark contrast to her usual relief at concluding social engagements. Something about Farrat's company had energized rather than depleted her, despite the complex navigation of unexpected social encounters.

"Thank you for today," she said, the words simple but sincere. "It was... illuminating. In multiple ways."

Farrat's smile warmed his features, creating that now-familiar flutter in her chest. "The illumination was mutual, I assure you."

As the car pulled away, Tauree found herself looking back, watching Farrat's figure grow smaller against the backdrop of the gallery. Unlike their midnight parting by the river, he didn't remain still this time—instead raising a hand in farewell, the gesture small but distinct in its acknowledgment of their connection.

The fog was still there, a constant companion in her internal landscape. But now it contained markers, points of reference that hadn't existed before—a midnight bridge, a swirling blue painting, a quiet café overlooking a gallery floor. Small territories within the nebulous gray where another person's presence had created moments of unexpected clarity.

As the car turned a corner, taking the gallery out of sight, Tauree leaned back against the seat and closed her eyes. The memory of their conversation remained vivid—the parallels between poetry and architecture, the shared appreciation of negative space, the quiet understanding in Farrat's eyes when she hesitated at the crowded installation.

Tomorrow, the fog might be thicker, the demands of work and routine more pressing. But today, for a few hours among art and architecture, Tauree had experienced something rare—not just being seen, but being understood. Not just being heard, but being interpreted accurately.

And in that precise translation of her internal landscape into shared understanding, she had found a connection more substantial than any she had known in years.

Act 2: The Build-Up and Growing Tension

Chapter 5: The Long Drive

The invitation came on a Tuesday morning, as unexpected as rain in winter.

I'm driving to the coast tomorrow. A small seaside town called Seaview. There's a poetry reading at sunset, but mostly I need to clear my head. Would you like to join me? No pressure either way.

Tauree stared at Farrat's message, her fingers hovering over her phone screen. It had been three weeks since their visit to the art gallery, followed by his tour of her community center project. Their interactions had settled into a comfortable rhythm—occasional texts sharing observations or fragments of poetry, coffee every week or so when their schedules aligned, a gradual accumulation of shared references and inside jokes that constituted something like friendship.

But this was different. A day trip. Hours in a confined space. The implicit intimacy of a journey undertaken together.

The fog was relatively thin today—more of a haze at the periphery of her vision than the dense cloud that sometimes enveloped her—but still, Tauree's instinct was to decline. Long social engagements depleted her limited emotional resources, and the prospect of being stranded hours from home if the fog suddenly thickened was daunting.

Yet as she formulated a polite refusal, Tauree found herself reconsidering. Their conversations had become one of the few reliable sources of clarity in her otherwise muted existence. When the fog pressed heaviest, she often found herself returning to fragments of Farrat's poetry or recalling observations he'd made that seemed to illuminate her internal landscape with unexpected precision.

What time are you leaving? she typed before she could overthink it further.

8 AM. It's about a three-hour drive. I can pick you up. Or we could meet somewhere if that's more comfortable for you.

The consideration in his suggestion—acknowledging her potential boundaries without making them seem like limitations—was by now familiar but still touching. Farrat consistently offered her options rather than expectations, space rather than pressure.

You can pick me up. I'll text you my address.

As soon as she sent the message, a wave of anxiety washed over Tauree. She had never invited anyone to her apartment, not even Amrita. Her home was her sanctuary, meticulously designed to provide the containment and order she needed to function when the fog was thick. Allowing someone to approach that boundary, even if they didn't cross the threshold, felt like a significant breach of her carefully constructed defenses.

Farrat's response came quickly: *I'll be there at 8. Bring something warm for the evening—the coast gets chilly after sunset. And thank you for trusting me with your address. I understand what that means.*

The acknowledgment—simple but perceptive—eased some of Tauree's anxiety. Once again, Farrat had recognized a boundary without requiring her to articulate it, had honored the significance of what might have seemed to others like a trivial disclosure.

For the rest of the day, Tauree found herself distracted by thoughts of the upcoming journey. She packed and repacked a small bag, deliberating over practical concerns like sunscreen and a light jacket, but also experiencing an unfamiliar flutter of anticipation that made concentration difficult. Eventually, she abandoned her attempts to work on the community center designs and instead spent the evening reorganizing her already immaculate apartment—a ritual that always helped calm her mind when anxiety threatened to overwhelm her.

When she finally went to bed, sleep proved elusive. Tauree lay awake, staring at the patterns of streetlight that filtered through her blinds, mapping the shadows on her ceiling as she had done since childhood. The upcoming journey represented a step outside her carefully controlled existence—a deliberate venture into unpredictability that both terrified and, surprisingly, exhilarated her.

Morning arrived with uncharacteristic clarity. Tauree woke before her alarm, moving through her morning routine with methodical precision. By 7:45, she was waiting by her window, a small backpack at her feet, watching the street below for Farrat's arrival.

His car appeared precisely at eight—a modest sedan in deep blue, not new but well-maintained. There was something reassuring about its unpretentious functionality, so aligned with what she had come to understand about Farrat's practical nature beneath his poetic sensibilities.

Tauree descended to meet him, preferring to intercept his arrival rather than have him approach her door. As she stepped outside, Farrat emerged from the car, his familiar figure a study in contained energy. He wore casual clothes—jeans and a light gray button-down with sleeves rolled to the elbows—but there was a subtle excitement in his movements that Tauree hadn't observed before.

"Good morning," he said, that same smile warming his features as he opened the passenger door. "Thank you for joining me on this impromptu adventure."

"Thank you for the invitation," Tauree replied, settling into the seat with her backpack at her feet. The interior of the car was neat and smelled faintly of sandalwood—clean without being artificially fragrant, comfortable without being luxurious. Like the man himself, Tauree thought.

As they pulled away from her apartment building, a curious sense of liberation washed over her. For the first time in longer than she could remember, Tauree was leaving the familiar geography of her daily existence without a professional purpose or predetermined destination. The sensation was both unsettling and oddly freeing.

"Have you been to Seaview before?" Farrat asked as they navigated through the gradually thinning city traffic.

"No," Tauree admitted. "I don't travel much, except for work. The ocean has always been more of a concept than a reality for me."

"Then this is a perfect first expedition," Farrat said, his tone warm with anticipation. "Seaview is small enough to be manageable but beautiful enough to be worth the journey. The town is built along a natural harbor, with buildings that seem to grow organically from the cliffs. An architect's dream, I would imagine."

The consideration in his observation—linking the destination to her professional interests—created that now-familiar warmth in Tauree's chest. Farrat consistently found ways to build bridges between their separate worlds, to translate experiences into terms that resonated with her particular perspective.

As the city receded behind them, giving way to the more open landscapes of the surrounding countryside, their conversation flowed with surprising ease. They moved from architecture to literature to the peculiar quality of early autumn light that bathed the rolling hills in a golden haze. Tauree found herself speaking more freely than she typically did, offering opinions and insights without the careful filtering she usually employed.

"I've been thinking about what you said at the gallery," Farrat ventured during a comfortable lull in their conversation. "About how people are defined as much by what they withhold as what they reveal."

"That was your observation, not mine," Tauree corrected gently.

"Was it?" Farrat's brow furrowed slightly in concentration. "Perhaps you're right. Our conversations have begun to blend in my memory—your insights triggering mine and vice versa until I can't always recall who said what."

The implication—that their dialogues had become so seamless that ownership of ideas had become fluid—created an unexpected flutter in Tauree's chest. It suggested a level of intellectual intimacy she had never experienced, a merging of perspectives that somehow enhanced rather than threatened her sense of self.

"I've noticed that too," she admitted, watching the landscape flow past her window. "I find myself thinking in your patterns sometimes—considering the poetic implications of spaces or searching for metaphors in ordinary observations."

Farrat glanced at her briefly, surprise and pleasure evident in his expression. "That might be the nicest thing anyone has ever said to me," he said quietly.

The sincerity in his voice created a moment of charged silence between them—a recognition of something significant passing between them, an acknowledgment that their connection had evolved beyond casual friendship into something more profound, if still undefined.

Tauree turned toward the window, using the passing scenery to ground herself as she processed this realization. The landscape had changed dramatically as they drove—urban density giving way to suburbs, then farmland, and now the first rolling hills that signaled their approach to the coastal region. The transformation mirrored her internal journey over the past months, from isolated stasis to this unexpected motion toward...what, exactly?

"Would you mind if I played some music?" Farrat asked, sensing perhaps her need for a shift in focus.

"Not at all," Tauree replied, grateful for his intuitive understanding.

The sound system came to life with the gentle strains of classical ghazals—the same style of music that had played at Amrita's tea party where they first met. The melancholy beauty of the vocals filled the car, creating a contemplative atmosphere that perfectly complemented the increasingly dramatic landscape outside.

"This reminds me of the day we met," Tauree observed, the memory vivid despite the months that had passed. "Amrita was playing ghazals at her tea party."

"You remember that detail?" Farrat asked, genuine surprise in his voice.

"I remember most details," Tauree said with a small shrug. "It's both a blessing and a curse. Useful professionally but sometimes overwhelming personally."

"An architect's eye combined with a perfect memory," Farrat mused. "No wonder your designs have such precision. You're essentially carrying entire buildings in your mind, down to the smallest detail."

The observation—accurate but framed as admiration rather than oddity—made Tauree smile despite herself. Most people found her attention to minute details strange or obsessive, but Farrat consistently reframed her differences as strengths, her peculiarities as valuable perspectives.

As they continued driving, the road began to wind more dramatically, cutting through hills that grew steadily taller until they became proper mountains. The vegetation changed too—becoming more rugged and wind-sculpted as they approached the coast. Occasionally, through gaps in the terrain, Tauree caught glimpses of blue horizon where sea met sky, each sighting sending a small thrill of anticipation through her.

"We're getting close," Farrat said, noticing her attentiveness to these first views of the ocean. "Another twenty minutes or so."

The road narrowed as it descended toward the coast, twisting through a forested valley before emerging suddenly onto a promontory that offered their first unobstructed view of Seaview. Farrat pulled into a small lookout area, allowing them to pause and absorb the vista before continuing.

"Oh," Tauree breathed, the sound escaping involuntarily as she took in the scene below.

The town was exactly as Farrat had described—a collection of buildings that seemed to grow organically from the cliffs, arranged in tiers that descended toward a natural harbor where fishing boats bobbed alongside more recreational vessels. The architecture was a fascinating blend of practical maritime functionality and whimsical adaptations to the dramatic terrain. Colors that might have seemed garish elsewhere—deep blues, bright whites, warm terracottas—worked in perfect harmony against the backdrop of sea and stone.

"It's beautiful," she said simply, her professional appreciation for the design merging with a more visceral response to the natural beauty of the setting.

"I thought you might see it that way," Farrat replied, satisfaction evident in his voice. "The first time I came here, I immediately thought of how you would appreciate the way the buildings relate to the landscape—neither dominating nor submitting to it, but engaging in a kind of dialogue."

The comment—revealing that he had thought of her in her absence, had viewed a new place partly through her perspective—created that now-familiar pressure in Tauree's chest, the sensation of emotion pushing against the protective numbness she typically maintained.

They continued down into the town, the road growing narrower as it wound between buildings that seemed to lean toward each other across the street, creating intimate corridors of space that opened occasionally into small plazas or viewpoints. Farrat navigated with the confidence of familiarity, eventually parking near a small inn overlooking the harbor.

"I thought we might have lunch here before exploring," he suggested as they exited the car. "The seafood is remarkable, and the view from their terrace is worth experiencing."

The inn was clearly historic—its stone walls weathered by generations of sea air, its wooden beams darkened with age. Inside, the space was surprisingly bright, with windows positioned to capture maximum light and frame specific views of the harbor below. They were led to a table on the terrace, where the autumn sun created a pocket of warmth protected from the sea breeze by clever architectural positioning.

"This is perfect," Tauree said as they settled into their seats. The terrace offered an ideal vantage point to observe both the natural and built environment of Seaview—the way shops and homes had been adapted to the steep terrain, the informal public spaces created where streets widened unexpectedly, the relationship between the working harbor and the more touristic areas.

"I'm glad you think so," Farrat replied, his expression warm as he watched her take in the surroundings. "I've always found this place restorative. There's something about the constant motion of the sea against the permanence of the cliffs that puts my own concerns into perspective."

Their lunch arrived—locally caught fish prepared simply but perfectly, accompanied by vegetables that tasted of sun and sea air. The food was unpretentious but deeply satisfying, much like the town itself. As they ate, their conversation flowed easily between observations about the architecture, the quality of light on the water, and the various types of boats in the harbor below.

"You mentioned a poetry reading at sunset," Tauree said as they finished their meal. "Is that the purpose of your visit, or just a fortunate coincidence?"

A shadow passed across Farrat's features—brief but unmistakable. "A bit of both," he admitted. "I come here periodically when I need space to think. The poetry reading happened to align with this particular visit, which seemed... significant somehow."

There was more to the story than he was sharing—Tauree could sense it in the careful way he constructed his response, in the momentary tension around his eyes. But she didn't press. She recognized the boundaries of newly formed trust, the careful dance of revelation and restraint that characterized their evolving connection.

"And what are you needing space to think about?" she asked instead, keeping her tone light despite the potential weight of the question.

Farrat's gaze met hers, a flash of vulnerability crossing his features before he glanced out toward the horizon. "The usual poet's dilemmas—where words come from, why they sometimes desert us, what responsibility we bear for how they're received." He paused, then added with unexpected directness: "And more personally, how to navigate connections when past experience has taught caution."

The implication hung between them—that their relationship was part of what he was contemplating during this coastal retreat. Tauree felt an unfamiliar flutter of anticipation mixed with apprehension. This wasn't the fog's usual chill, but something warmer and more complex.

"I understand that dilemma," she said quietly. "It's not so different from my own."

Farrat nodded, a small smile softening his features. "I thought you might. We're approaching from opposite directions, perhaps, but facing similar questions."

The acknowledgment—that they were engaged in parallel internal journeys—created a moment of profound connection between them, a recognition that transcended the need for further explanation.

After lunch, they spent the afternoon exploring the town on foot. Farrat proved to be an excellent guide, showing Tauree not just the obvious attractions but the hidden corners that revealed Seaview's authentic character—a tiny bookshop wedged between larger buildings, its interior a labyrinth of shelves reaching to the ceiling; a craftsman's workshop where local materials were transformed into objects both beautiful and useful; a small community garden terraced into the cliffside, where elderly residents tended plants while exchanging gossip.

Throughout their wanderings, Tauree found herself increasingly aware of Farrat's physical presence beside her—the way he moved with careful deliberation through narrow spaces, the unconscious grace with which he gestured when explaining something that excited him, the subtle shifts in his expression that revealed his emotional response to different environments. She had always been observant of physical details, but this heightened awareness of another person's embodied existence was unfamiliar and slightly disconcerting.

As the afternoon progressed toward evening, they made their way to a small cove slightly removed from the main harbor. A modest structure that appeared to be a repurposed boathouse stood at the edge of the beach, its weathered wooden exterior softened by climbing roses that somehow thrived despite the salt air.

"This is where the poetry reading will be held," Farrat explained as they approached. "It's a local tradition—once a month when the weather allows. Anyone can read, though there are usually a few regular contributors who anchor the event."

"Will you be reading?" Tauree asked, curious about this aspect of Farrat's life she had yet to witness firsthand.

His expression grew slightly self-conscious. "I've been invited to. The organizer is a former student who now lives here. But I haven't decided yet." He glanced at her, uncertainty flickering across his features. "Would it bother you if I did?"

The question surprised Tauree—both the content and the implicit value it placed on her comfort. "Why would it bother me?"

Farrat considered his response carefully, his gaze drifting toward the sea. "Poetry is intimate—especially the kind I tend to write. It reveals more than casual conversation ever could." He turned back to her, his expression serious. "Our connection has been built on a certain kind of selective sharing. Poetry doesn't always respect those boundaries."

The observation struck Tauree with its accuracy. They had indeed constructed their relationship on carefully controlled disclosure—each offering precisely what they felt capable of revealing while respecting the other's need for emotional space. Poetry, with its raw honesty and emotional intensity, might indeed disrupt that delicate balance.

"I'd like to hear you read," she said after a moment's consideration. "I've only experienced your words on the page so far. I'm curious about how they sound in your voice."

Relief and something like pleased surprise crossed Farrat's features. "Then I'll consider it," he said simply.

They continued walking along the beach, the sand cool beneath their feet as the late afternoon sun began its descent toward the horizon. The tide was going out, revealing tide pools where small marine creatures carried on their complex lives in miniature oceans. Tauree found herself crouching to examine these ecosystems, fascinated by the architectural ingenuity of the shells and structures created by their inhabitants.

"You're smiling," Farrat observed as he knelt beside her to investigate a particularly vibrant anemone. "It suits you."

Tauree touched her face reflexively, surprised to find that he was right. The expression felt unfamiliar, as if her features had assumed a configuration they rarely practiced. "I suppose I am," she acknowledged. "This place is... remarkable."

"It's more than the place," Farrat suggested gently. "It's you allowing yourself to experience it without reserve."

The observation—perceptive and slightly challenging—made Tauree glance up sharply. Farrat met her gaze steadily, neither apologizing for the insight nor pressing it further. She considered his words, recognizing their truth. For once, she wasn't filtering her experience through the usual protective layers of detachment and analysis. She was simply present, responsive to the beauty around her in a way she rarely permitted herself to be.

"Perhaps you're right," she conceded, returning her attention to the tide pool. "It's easier here, somehow. Away from familiar contexts and expectations."

"That's why I come," Farrat said, his voice soft as the waves that lapped at the shore nearby. "Distance provides perspective—on others, but more importantly, on ourselves."

As sunset approached, people began to gather at the boathouse—a diverse collection of individuals that seemed to reflect the eclectic nature of the town itself. There were obviously local residents, fishermen still in their work clothes, shopkeepers Tauree recognized from their afternoon explorations. But there were also visitors like themselves, drawn by the promise of poetry against the backdrop of sea and setting sun.

Inside, the boathouse had been transformed into a simple performance space—rows of mismatched chairs facing a small platform where a single microphone stood, framed by a large window that perfectly captured the western sky. Strings of small lights had been hung from the rafters, creating a warm, intimate atmosphere that contrasted beautifully with the growing drama of the sunset visible through the windows.

They found seats near the back, where Tauree could observe both the performers and the audience without feeling exposed. As they settled in, a woman approached Farrat, her expression lighting with recognition.

"Professor! You came!" Her enthusiasm was genuine but not overwhelming. "Will you be reading tonight? I've saved a slot for you, just in case."

"Maya, good to see you," Farrat replied warmly. "This is Tauree Sharma. Tauree, Maya Patel was one of my first graduate students. She's now Seaview's librarian and the organizer of these gatherings."

Maya extended her hand to Tauree with a friendly smile. "Any friend of Professor Mirza is welcome here. Has he told you he's something of a legend at these readings? People still talk about the poem he shared last spring."

Farrat looked slightly embarrassed by this revelation. "I think that's an exaggeration."

"It's really not," Maya insisted before turning back to the matter at hand. "So, will you read tonight?"

Farrat glanced at Tauree, a subtle request for final confirmation. When she nodded slightly, he turned back to Maya. "Yes, I have something I could share."

"Wonderful!" Maya exclaimed. "I'll put you toward the end, if that's alright. People will want to hear you, but we like to give newer voices the less intimidating early slots."

After Maya moved on to greet other arrivals, Tauree turned to Farrat with curious amusement. "A legend, are you? You failed to mention that part."

"An extreme overstatement," Farrat replied, though a hint of color had risen to his cheeks. "I've only read here a few times, when I happened to be visiting."

Before Tauree could tease him further, the event began. Maya welcomed everyone with warm simplicity, explaining the format—each reader would have five minutes, with brief musical interludes between every few performers.

The quality of the poetry varied widely, as one might expect from such an open forum. There were earnest beginners whose passion outweighed their technique, weathered locals whose plainspoken verses captured the rhythms of coastal life, and a few more polished practitioners whose work showed evidence of serious study and practice. Throughout, the audience was attentive and supportive, offering encouragement through their focused silence and appreciative applause.

As the reading progressed, Tauree found herself increasingly aware of Farrat beside her—the subtle shifts in his posture as he leaned forward during particularly moving recitations, the almost imperceptible nods when a phrase especially resonated, the way his fingers occasionally twitched as if physically responding to the cadence of the words. She had always known he loved poetry, but witnessing his embodied response to it revealed the depth of that connection in a way their conversations never had.

Outside, the sun continued its descent, the sky transforming from blue to gold to deepening shades of orange and pink. The light that filtered through the windows took on an almost supernatural quality, bathing the simple interior of the boathouse in a warm glow that seemed to enhance the intimate atmosphere of shared creativity.

Finally, Maya returned to the microphone. "For our final reading tonight, we're honored to welcome back Professor Farrat Mirza, whose words have moved many of us during his previous visits. Professor?"

As Farrat rose from his seat, Tauree felt an unexpected flutter of anticipation in her chest. She had read his poetry, had discussed it with him at length, but had never heard him perform it in his own voice, with his own cadence and emphasis. It felt, suddenly, like she was about to witness something profoundly personal—a different kind of intimacy than they had yet shared.

Farrat moved to the front with understated grace, his tall figure silhouetted against the spectacular sunset now visible through the window behind him. He adjusted the microphone slightly, then looked out over the audience with calm composure.

"Thank you for the kind welcome," he began, his voice taking on a quality Tauree hadn't heard before—slightly deeper, more resonant, as if accessing a different register of himself. "I'd like to share something I've been working on recently. It's called 'The Long Drive.'"

Tauree felt a jolt of surprise at the title—so directly referencing their day together. She hadn't realized he had been writing about this experience, though perhaps she should have anticipated it given his tendency to process his life through verse.

Farrat paused, taking a breath that seemed to center him, then began:

"Distance unspools between us like ribbon,
Measuring not separation but the strange geometry
Of two people occupying the same space
While traveling at identical speeds.
The road offers its own linguistics—
Each curve a comma, each straight stretch
A sentence where thoughts complete themselves
Before the next turn interrupts with new terrain.
You watch the landscape with architect's eyes,
Finding structure in the scattered arrangement of trees,
Purpose in the placement of weathered fence posts.

I envy this ability to read order from chaos.
My own gaze keeps returning to the rearview mirror,
Where your profile is framed against passing scenery—
A composition constantly changing yet somehow fixed,
Like a word whose meaning shifts with each usage
But remains essentially itself.
What am I looking for in these glances?
Perhaps confirmation that presence
Is not merely physical occupation of adjacent space
But something more permeable, a shared atmosphere
Where separate weathersystems briefly merge.
The fog you carry and the rainfall I navigate
Creating, momentarily, a climate unique to us—
Neither dispersing the other,
But together forming something
Neither could produce alone."

He paused, his gaze lifting toward the back of the room where Tauree sat perfectly still, her breath caught in her chest. For a moment, their eyes met across the crowded space—a connection so direct and unguarded that she felt physically affected by it, as if a current had passed between them. Then he continued, his voice softening slightly:

"I have driven this road before,
Have watched this same sun trajectory toward horizon,
Have witnessed these identical waves pattern the shore.
Yet nothing is the same when filtered through
The knowledge of your perception beside me.
This, perhaps, is what we rarely admit about connection—
That it fundamentally alters not just how we relate to others
But how we experience the world itself.
The long drive is never about reaching a destination.
It is about creating a temporary universe,

Contained within the moving capsule of shared attention,
Where time measures itself not in minutes or miles
But in revelations exchanged like currency,
Each disclosure a tender offering
That cannot be redeemed elsewhere."

As Farrat finished, the boathouse remained silent for a suspended moment—a collective held breath before applause erupted, more enthusiastic than for any previous reader. Tauree found herself clapping automatically, though her mind was still processing the profound vulnerability of what she had just witnessed.

The poem had exposed not just Farrat's feelings about their connection but his perception of her internal landscape, his understanding of her fog and how it intersected with his rainfall. More startling still was how accurately he had captured the transformative effect of their relationship—how each had begun to experience the world partly through the other's perspective.

Farrat made his way back through the audience, accepting quiet compliments with modest nods, his gaze fixed on Tauree as he approached their seats. When he reached her, he paused, uncertainty flickering across his features—the first time she had seen him truly apprehensive about her response.

"That was..." Tauree began, then faltered, struggling to find words adequate to the complexity of her reaction. "You wrote that today? During our drive?"

"Parts of it had been forming for weeks," Farrat admitted, reclaiming his seat beside her. "But yes, much of it came together as we drove. Something about seeing you in that context—experiencing something new, away from our established patterns—crystallized what I had been trying to articulate."

Around them, the event was concluding, people gathering their belongings and forming conversation clusters as they prepared to depart. But Tauree barely registered this activity, her attention entirely focused on the man beside her and the words he had just shared.

"Was it too much?" Farrat asked quietly when she didn't immediately continue. "I debated whether to read it, knowing you would recognize yourself in it."

"No," Tauree said, surprising herself with the certainty in her voice. "It wasn't too much. It was..." She searched for the right word, settling finally on the simplest truth. "It was beautiful. And more accurate than I would have expected, given how carefully I've tried to maintain my boundaries."

Relief softened Farrat's features, followed by a smile that reached his eyes. "Poets don't observe boundaries the way architects do," he said, a gentle teasing in his tone. "We're always peeking around corners and peering through windows we probably shouldn't."

The metaphor—so aligned with her professional vocabulary yet twisted slightly to reveal his different approach—made Tauree smile despite the emotional intensity of the moment. "Clearly I've been too preoccupied with structural integrity to notice my privacy being poetically invaded."

Their shared laughter eased the tension, creating a bridge across the newly revealed depth of their connection. As they rose to join the departing audience, Tauree felt a curious lightness in her chest—not the absence of the fog, which remained a constant presence in her internal landscape, but a sense that it had somehow become more navigable in the light of Farrat's perception.

Outside, darkness had fallen completely, the last traces of sunset fading from the western sky. The temperature had dropped significantly, and Tauree was grateful for the warm jacket she had packed at Farrat's suggestion. Above them, stars were beginning to emerge—far more visible here than in the city, their ancient light creating patterns across the vast darkness.

"Are you hungry?" Farrat asked as they walked back toward the town center. "There's a small restaurant near the harbor that stays open late. Or we could begin the drive back, if you're tired."

The question contained no assumption, no preference disguised as inquiry. As always, Farrat was offering options rather than expectations, space rather than pressure. The consistent consideration in these small moments—the accumulation of choices freely given rather than obligations imposed—had become one of the foundations of their connection.

"I'm not ready to leave yet," Tauree admitted, surprising herself with the truth of it. Despite the emotional intensity of the evening, she felt no urgent need to retreat to solitude, no desperate requirement for the sanctuary of her apartment. "Dinner would be nice."

The restaurant Farrat suggested turned out to be perfect—a small establishment overlooking the harbor, its windows reflecting the lights of boats gently bobbing on the night-darkened water. Inside, the atmosphere was warm and unpretentious, with wood-paneled walls hung with maritime artifacts and photographs documenting the town's history.

They were seated at a corner table that offered both privacy and a view of the harbor—an ideal vantage point for conversation after the revelations of the poetry reading. As they settled in, Tauree found herself studying Farrat with renewed attention, trying to reconcile the man across from her with the poet who had so precisely articulated the nuances of their evolving connection.

"You're looking at me differently," Farrat observed after they had ordered, his perception as acute as ever.

"I'm trying to understand how you see me," Tauree admitted, the honesty easier in the wake of his poetic vulnerability. "Your poem captured aspects of my experience I've never articulated, even to myself."

Farrat considered this, his expression thoughtful. "Poetry often accesses understanding that precedes conscious recognition," he said. "I don't always know what I perceive until I find the words for it. Sometimes the writing reveals connections my conscious mind hasn't yet assembled."

"That's both fascinating and slightly terrifying," Tauree observed. "To discover what you know only after you've expressed it."

"It can be," Farrat agreed with a small smile. "Especially when what's revealed contradicts what you thought you understood about yourself." He paused, his gaze meeting hers directly. "Which happens more frequently than I care to admit."

The implication hung between them—that his growing connection to her had challenged some aspect of his self-perception, had revealed contradictions between his established patterns and his current experience. Tauree recognized the sentiment with startling clarity, having experienced similar disruptions to her carefully constructed understanding of her own emotional landscape.

"I know something about that," she said quietly. "My response to... this... hasn't aligned with my usual patterns. It's been disconcerting."

"This," Farrat repeated, the single word encompassing the complex, undefined nature of their relationship. "We've been careful not to name it, haven't we?"

"Names create expectations," Tauree replied. "Boundaries. Definitions that might not fit the actual experience."

"True," Farrat acknowledged. "But they also provide clarity, a shared understanding of what's being built." His smile turned self-deprecating. "The architect in you might appreciate more precise blueprints for this construction project we've undertaken."

The metaphor—drawing on her professional vocabulary to illustrate their personal situation—was so perfectly aligned with how they had come to communicate that Tauree found herself smiling despite the seriousness of the conversation.

"Perhaps," she conceded. "But I've come to appreciate the value of organic development—structures that respond to the terrain rather than imposing rigid forms upon it."

"Then we continue as we have been," Farrat suggested. "Allowing this connection to define itself through experience rather than preconception."

Their food arrived—seafood again, but prepared differently than their lunch, emphasizing different flavors and textures while maintaining the essential character of locally sourced ingredients. As they ate, their conversation shifted to lighter topics—observations about the poetry reading, reflections on the town's unique architecture, memories of other coastal experiences from their separate pasts.

Yet beneath this easier exchange ran a current of deeper awareness—a recognition that something significant had transpired between them, that Farrat's poem had articulated emotional truths they had previously circled without directly acknowledging.

As they finished their meal, Tauree found herself unexpectedly reluctant to end the evening. The prospect of the return journey—three hours in the darkness with only the ribbon of highway before them—held a peculiar appeal rather than the usual dread of extended social engagement. Perhaps it was the relative simplicity of car conversation, where silence could exist comfortably alongside speech, or perhaps it was simply that she wasn't yet ready to leave this temporary universe they had created, as Farrat had called it in his poem.

"Shall we head back?" Farrat asked as they settled their bill, his tone neutral, offering the question without attachment to a particular answer.

"Yes," Tauree replied, though a part of her wished to extend their stay in this place where different rules seemed to apply, where the fog that typically clouded her perception had temporarily thinned to reveal unexpected clarity. "It's getting late, and we both have work tomorrow."

Outside, the night had deepened, the temperature dropping further to create a crisp clarity in the air. The streets of Seaview were quiet now, most establishments closed for the evening, the resident population retired to their homes while the day visitors had long since departed. Their footsteps echoed slightly as they walked back toward where Farrat had parked the car, the sound emphasizing the intimate emptiness of the town after dark.

As they approached the vehicle, Tauree paused, turning to look back at the harbor one last time. The moon had risen while they were dining, its light creating a silvery path across the water—not unlike the one she and Farrat had observed during their midnight walk by the river months ago. The parallel struck her with unexpected force, a reminder of how their relationship had evolved while maintaining its essential character.

"I'd like to come back here someday," she said, the words emerging without premeditation.

Farrat, who had stopped beside her, nodded. "It's the kind of place that rewards repeated visits. Different seasons transform it entirely—the winter storms are particularly dramatic."

The implication—that future visits together were a possibility, that their connection might extend beyond the current moment into a shared future—hung between them, neither acknowledged nor denied. It was characteristic of how they had come to relate, this careful balance between recognition and restraint, potential and patience.

The drive back began in comfortable silence, both of them absorbed in their own reflections as the coastal road wound its way back toward the mountains that separated Seaview from the inland regions. The car's headlights carved a tunnel of visibility through the darkness, the beams occasionally catching the reflective eyes of night creatures watching from the roadside vegetation.

"May I ask you something personal?" Farrat said eventually, his voice quiet in the darkness of the car.

"You can ask," Tauree replied, her standard response to such requests—an acknowledgment that questions were permitted while reserving the right to decline answering.

"In your apartment—the one place that's entirely yours, designed to your exact specifications—what's your favorite feature? The element that provides the most comfort or satisfaction?"

The question wasn't what Tauree had expected—not a probe into her past or her feelings about their evolving relationship, but something both more intimate and less threatening. A window into her private domain that requested only what she was willing to reveal.

"The light," she answered after a moment's consideration. "I designed a series of skylights and light wells that track the sun's movement throughout the day. No matter what time it is, natural light enters the space at an angle that creates specific patterns on the walls and floors." She paused, unsure whether to share the deeper significance of this feature. "When the fog is particularly thick—internally, I mean—those patterns of light provide a kind of... anchoring. A reminder that there's still illumination, even if my perception of it is muted."

Farrat nodded, his profile thoughtful in the dim glow from the dashboard. "Thank you for sharing that," he said simply, no additional questions pushing for further disclosure, no platitudes diminishing the significance of her revelation.

"What about you?" Tauree asked, surprising herself with the reciprocal inquiry. "What's your favorite feature of your home?"

The smile that curved Farrat's lips was visible even in the low light. "My bookshelves," he replied without hesitation. "Not just for their contents, though those are precious to me, but for the particular way I've arranged them. Along one entire wall of my living room, floor to ceiling, organized in that system incomprehensible to anyone but me that I mentioned before."

"Emotional resonance, you called it," Tauree remembered.

"Yes. Books that create similar internal landscapes are shelved together, regardless of genre or author or time period. It creates some strange neighbors—ancient philosophy beside contemporary fiction, poetry sharing space with scientific journals—but it makes perfect sense to my particular mind."

The image was so quintessentially Farrat that Tauree found herself smiling. "I'd like to see that someday," she said, the words slipping out with unexpected ease.

"I'd like to show you," he replied, the simple response carrying layers of meaning that neither felt compelled to analyze in the moment.

As they continued their journey, the road beginning its ascent into the mountains, their conversation flowed with that same surprising ease Tauree had experienced throughout the day. They moved from architecture to literature to the peculiar quality of memory that transformed experiences even as it preserved them. Outside, the landscape changed from coastal scrub to denser forest, the trees occasionally giving way to reveal spectacular views of the moonlit terrain below.

"Will you share more of your poetry with me?" Tauree asked during a comfortable lull, the question prompted by the lingering impact of his reading at the boathouse.

Farrat glanced at her briefly, surprise evident in his expression before he returned his attention to the winding road. "If you'd like," he said, a hint of uncertainty in his voice. "Though I should warn you—most of it is not as... optimistic as what I shared tonight."

"I wouldn't expect it to be," Tauree replied, understanding the implication. "Depression isn't known for inspiring cheerful creative expression."

"No," Farrat acknowledged with a small smile, "though it does tend to produce more interesting art than contentment. There's a reason most great literature isn't about people having a pleasant day where nothing significant happens."

The observation—wryly accurate and gently self-deprecating—made Tauree laugh, the sound unexpectedly free in the confines of the car. "True. My most innovative architectural solutions have emerged from navigating particularly dense fog, not from moments of uncomplicated clarity."

"We make use of our weather systems, however challenging they might be," Farrat mused, the metaphor they had established for their respective forms of depression now a comfortable shorthand between them. "The rainfall may soak me to the skin, but it also nourishes what I try to grow."

The road grew steeper and more winding as they approached the mountain pass that marked the highest point of their journey. Farrat navigated the hairpin turns with careful attention, his hands sure on the steering wheel, his focus intensifying in response to the more demanding terrain. Tauree found herself watching him in these moments of concentration—the slight furrow between his brows, the set of his jaw, the subtle adjustments of his posture as he anticipated each curve. There was something compelling about this physical manifestation of his focus, so different from the more contemplative presence she typically observed in him.

"Tell me about your past relationship," she said suddenly, the question emerging without premeditation. "The one you mentioned briefly after we encountered your colleague at the gallery."

Farrat's hands tightened slightly on the steering wheel, though his expression remained composed. "That's quite a shift in conversation," he observed mildly.

"You don't have to answer," Tauree replied, immediately regretting the impulsive inquiry. "It was an invasive question."

"No, it's a fair one," Farrat said after a moment's consideration. "Especially given what I shared in my poem tonight." He fell silent for a short time, gathering his thoughts as he navigated a particularly sharp turn. When he spoke again, his voice was measured but honest.

"Her name was Leila. We met at a literary conference five years ago—both presenting papers on different aspects of diasporic literature. The connection was immediate and intense, intellectually and otherwise." He paused, a shadow crossing his features. "I was emerged from a period of profound isolation. The rainfall, as we've come to call it, had been particularly heavy for several years. Leila was brilliant, passionate, and seemingly undeterred by my melancholy tendencies."

The road straightened temporarily, allowing Farrat to relax his posture slightly as he continued. "For a while, it was transformative. She drew me out of myself, insisted on engagement with the world in ways I had been avoiding. But her approach to connection was... all-encompassing. She wanted complete access—to my thoughts, my creative process, my emotional landscape—without recognizing that sometimes I needed spaces that were solely mine."

"Boundaries," Tauree supplied, understanding immediately.

"Yes," Farrat nodded. "Or the lack thereof. When I tried to establish them—to create some protected territory within the relationship—she perceived it as rejection. The more she pushed, the more I withdrew, until we were caught in a cycle that brought out the worst in both of us."

He navigated another curve before continuing, his voice quieter now. "The end was not my proudest moment. After months of increasingly desperate attempts to make her understand my need for occasional solitude, I simply... disappeared. Canceled my classes for a week, turned off my phone, and drove to a cabin in the mountains where no one could reach me. When I returned, I ended the relationship without adequate explanation or closure."

"And she's still at the university," Tauree observed, connecting this history to their encounter with Nisha at the gallery.

"No, Nisha wasn't Leila," Farrat clarified. "Nisha came after—a brief, ill-considered attempt to prove to myself that I could engage without repeating the same pattern. It failed for different but equally instructive reasons." He glanced at Tauree, his expression apologetic. "I'm not presenting a particularly favorable picture of myself, I realize."

"You're presenting an honest one," Tauree replied, appreciating the straightforward accountability in his recounting. "We all have failures of courage or clarity in our histories."

"What about you?" Farrat asked after a moment, the reciprocal question offered without expectation. "You mentioned a past relationship at the tea party, I believe. Something that contributed to your wariness of emotional attachment."

The reference to their first meeting—his precise recall of a detail she had mentioned only in passing months ago—didn't surprise Tauree. Farrat's attention to such nuances had become one of the constants in their evolving connection. Still, she considered her response carefully, weighing how much to reveal about a chapter of her life she rarely discussed.

"His name was Vikram," she began, her gaze fixed on the road ahead. "We met during my final year of architecture school. He was brilliant, charismatic—the kind of person who filled any room he entered. I was... flattered by his attention. Someone like him, choosing someone like me, seemed improbable enough to be significant."

The memories surfaced with uncomfortable clarity—Vikram's dazzling smile, his intense focus when he decided something was worth his attention, the way he made everything feel more vibrant simply by his participation in it. For a young woman struggling with chronic depression and emotional detachment, his vitality had seemed like a lifeline.

"The relationship moved quickly," she continued, her voice steady despite the discomfort of recollection. "Too quickly, in retrospect. Within months, we were living together, making plans for our futures. He spoke about us as a unit, a partnership that would conquer the architectural world together."

Farrat remained silent, giving her space to tell the story at her own pace, his attention evident but undemanding. The road began to descend now, having crested the mountain pass, the curves less sharp but the descent requiring its own kind of careful navigation.

"I tried so hard to be what he wanted," Tauree said, the admission more difficult than she had anticipated. "To match his energy, his sociability, his seemingly boundless capacity for engagement. But the fog doesn't lift just because someone shines a bright light at it. If anything, the contrast makes the grayness more apparent."

She paused, organizing the painful memories into a coherent narrative. "Eventually, he grew frustrated with what he called my 'emotional unavailability.' He started seeking that connection elsewhere—first professionally, then personally. When I discovered his infidelity, his defense was that I had 'forced' him to look elsewhere by being 'fundamentally incapable of real intimacy.'"

The words still carried a sting, years later—not because she had loved Vikram enough for his betrayal to break her heart, but because his assessment had tapped into her deepest fears about her own capacity for human connection.

"He wasn't entirely wrong," she admitted, her honesty matching Farrat's earlier accountability. "I was emotionally unavailable in the ways he needed. But rather than acknowledging the fundamental incompatibility, he made it about my deficiency—something I needed to 'fix' in order to be worthy of love."

"That's cruel," Farrat said quietly, the first interruption to her narrative. "And profoundly unfair."

"Perhaps," Tauree conceded. "Though I've come to see it as more misguided than malicious. He genuinely couldn't comprehend a different model of connection—one that respected differences rather than trying to erase them."

Farrat nodded, understanding evident in his expression. "We tend to universalize our own needs, assuming everyone experiences connection in the same way we do. It takes a certain kind of awareness to recognize that other patterns might be equally valid, just different."

The observation—insightful and free from judgment—created that now-familiar warmth in Tauree's chest. Farrat consistently found ways to reframe her experiences in terms that validated rather than pathologized her differences, that recognized value in her particular way of moving through the world.

"After Vikram," she continued, "I retreated into work and solitude. It seemed safer, more reliable. Until..." She trailed off, unsure how to complete the thought without moving into territory that felt too vulnerable, too revealing.

"Until?" Farrat prompted gently when she didn't continue.

"Until recent events suggested other possibilities," Tauree finished, the deliberate vagueness both a boundary and an acknowledgment of the significance of their evolving connection.

Farrat received this partial disclosure with a small nod, neither pressing for greater specificity nor dismissing the implied importance of their relationship. The restraint in his response—the space he consistently gave her to define the terms of her own revelations—had become one of the cornerstones of their connection.

They fell into a comfortable silence as the car continued its descent from the mountains, the road gradually straightening as they approached the foothills that would eventually give way to the more populated regions nearer the city. Outside, the landscape had transformed again—the dense mountain forests thinning to reveal scattered settlements, occasional lights marking human habitation in the otherwise dark terrain.

"Thank you," Farrat said eventually, breaking the silence. "For sharing that with me. And for coming today. Both have meant more than I can adequately express, even with all my supposed facility with words."

"Thank you for inviting me," Tauree replied, surprising herself with the depth of sincerity in her voice. "It's been... unexpectedly meaningful."

The simple exchange—honest without being effusive, acknowledging significance without inflating it—felt characteristic of how they had come to communicate, this careful balance between recognition and restraint that defined their evolving connection.

As they approached the outskirts of the city, the road widening and traffic increasing even at this late hour, Tauree found herself contemplating the day's journey—not just the physical distance traveled, but the emotional territory they had traversed together. From the moment Farrat had picked her up that morning to this quiet return in darkness, something had shifted between them, a deepening of understanding that couldn't be easily categorized or contained.

The fog remained, as it always did—that persistent gray filter through which she experienced the world. But something had changed in how she navigated within it. The map of her internal landscape now contained new markers, reference points that hadn't existed before. Farrat's perception of her, so accurately articulated in his poem, had somehow altered her perception of herself—not erasing the fog, but providing new ways to orient within it.

When they finally reached her apartment building, Farrat pulled to a gentle stop at the curb, turning off the engine to create a moment of stillness after the hours of motion. For a few seconds, neither spoke, the silence between them comfortable yet charged with unspoken awareness.

"Would you like to come up for coffee?" Tauree asked suddenly, the invitation as surprising to herself as it clearly was to Farrat, whose expression registered momentary shock before settling into careful neutrality.

"It's late," he said gently, the response clearly intended to give her an easy retraction if the offer had been impulsive rather than deliberate.

"It is," Tauree acknowledged, appreciating his consideration but unexpectedly certain of her invitation. "But I'd like to show you the skylights I mentioned. The moon creates particularly interesting patterns at this hour."

Farrat studied her face, as if ensuring the invitation was genuine before responding. "Then yes," he said simply. "I'd like that very much."

As they ascended to her apartment—first in the elevator, then down the hallway to her door—Tauree felt a curious absence of the anxiety that had accompanied her earlier decision to share her address with Farrat. Instead, there was a sense of rightness in this progression, a natural extension of the trust that had been building between them through months of careful, considerate interaction.

Her apartment, when she unlocked the door and led him inside, was exactly as she had left it that morning—immaculately ordered, every object in its designated place, the space a physical manifestation of her need for structure and clarity. Yet seeing it now through Farrat's eyes, she found herself noticing details differently—the careful curation of colors, the strategic positioning of furniture to create flow between spaces, the subtle integration of natural and artificial light sources.

"This is beautiful," Farrat said as he entered, his gaze moving appreciatively over the design elements that defined the space. "It feels exactly like you—precise without being cold, structured without being rigid."

The observation—so aligned with how she had intended the space to feel—created that now-familiar pressure in Tauree's chest, the sensation of being truly seen, of having her intentions recognized without elaborate explanation.

"Look up," she suggested, gesturing toward the ceiling where the skylights she had described created geometric apertures in the otherwise solid surface.

Farrat tilted his head back, his expression transforming with quiet wonder as he observed the patterns of moonlight streaming through the carefully positioned openings, creating pools of silvery illumination on the walls and floors. The light moved across the surfaces in a choreographed dance determined by the precise angles of the skylights, the time of night, the season of the year.

"It's like a calendar made of light," he said softly, understanding immediately the architectural and emotional intention behind the design. "A physical manifestation of time passing, of consistency within change."

"Yes," Tauree confirmed, once again struck by how easily he translated between their vocabularies, how precisely he grasped the underlying purpose of her aesthetic choices. "When the fog is particularly thick, it helps to have these reminders that patterns still exist, that order continues even when my perception of it is compromised."

Farrat nodded, his attention still on the play of light across the walls. "Poetry serves a similar function for me," he said. "The patterns of meter and rhyme, the predictable structures of certain forms—they create architecture for feelings that might otherwise seem formless and overwhelming."

The parallel—so perfectly aligned with how they had come to understand each other's disciplines—made Tauree smile despite the seriousness of the observation. Once again, they had found common ground in the space between their different approaches to the world.

"I'll make coffee," she said, moving toward the kitchen area that opened off the main living space. "Make yourself comfortable."

As she prepared the coffee—the ritual familiar and grounding—Tauree was acutely aware of Farrat's presence in her home, the way he moved through the space with respectful curiosity, examining the books on her shelves, the art on her walls, the architectural models displayed on various surfaces. Unlike most visitors, who tended to touch objects without permission or ask intrusive questions about her design choices, Farrat's exploration was considerate—looking closely but not handling, noting details but not demanding explanations.

When she returned with two mugs of coffee, she found him standing by the window that offered a view of the city lights spread out below. The reflection of his figure against the glass created a curious doubling effect—Farrat both present in her space and projected against the broader urban landscape beyond, a visual metaphor for how he had come to exist both within her private world and within the larger context of her life.

"Your coffee," she said, extending one of the mugs toward him.

Farrat turned, accepting the offering with a small smile of thanks. "Strong enough to dissolve a spoon?" he asked, referencing her description from their first meeting.

"Of course," Tauree confirmed, pleased by his recall of this detail. "I wouldn't serve anything less, especially at this hour."

They settled onto the minimalist sofa that faced the window, the city view creating a backdrop for their conversation. The coffee was indeed strong, its bitterness cutting through the fatigue of the long day with bracing efficiency. For a few moments, they sat in comfortable silence, each absorbing the simple pleasure of shared quiet after hours of interaction.

"I've been thinking about what you said in the car," Farrat ventured eventually. "About recent events suggesting other possibilities."

Tauree felt a momentary tension, uncertain whether she was prepared to articulate more explicitly what she had deliberately left vague during their drive. But Farrat continued before she could respond, his tone thoughtful rather than pressing.

"I've experienced something similar," he said, his gaze directed toward the city lights rather than at her, offering a kind of privacy within their proximity. "A recalibration of what I thought was possible, given my particular... weather patterns."

The metaphor—their established shorthand for the depression that colored both their experiences—created an immediate sense of shared understanding. Tauree found herself nodding, though Farrat wasn't looking at her to see the gesture.

"The rainfall doesn't stop," he continued, his voice soft in the quiet apartment. "But I'm finding that sharing the weather with someone who understands its patterns makes it less isolating. Less all-encompassing."

The observation struck Tauree with its precision, articulating exactly what she had been experiencing but struggling to define. The fog remained a constant presence in her internal landscape, but something about Farrat's perception of it—his acceptance without attempt to disperse it, his recognition of its patterns without judgment of its persistence—had fundamentally altered how she related to her own condition.

"Yes," she said simply, the single word containing multitudes of acknowledgment. "Exactly that."

Farrat turned toward her then, his expression serious yet gentle. "I don't want to misinterpret," he said carefully. "Or to project my own experience onto yours. But if we are indeed observing similar phenomena, I think it's worth acknowledging explicitly."

The directness of his approach—characteristic yet still somewhat unexpected—created a moment of suspended possibility between them. Tauree found herself at a threshold of sorts, aware that her response would define something essential about the nature of their evolving connection.

"I agree," she said after a moment's consideration, matching his directness with her own. "Though I'm not sure I have adequate language for it yet. My usual vocabulary feels insufficient for this particular... architectural challenge."

The slight smile that curved Farrat's lips acknowledged her attempt at their shared metaphorical language. "Perhaps we don't need complete blueprints yet," he suggested. "Just a general agreement about the kind of structure we're attempting to build."

"And what kind is that, in your view?" Tauree asked, genuinely curious about his perception of their relationship's emerging form.

Farrat considered the question with characteristic thoughtfulness, his gaze returning to the city lights beyond the window as he formulated his response. "Something with room for both connection and solitude," he said finally. "A design that respects our individual boundaries while creating shared spaces where we can meet as equals. Not a conventional dwelling, perhaps, but one uniquely suited to our particular needs."

The description—architectural in its specificity yet poetic in its implications—resonated deeply with Tauree's own unspoken vision for what might be possible between them. Not the all-consuming merger that Vikram had demanded, nor the complete access that had overwhelmed Farrat in his relationship with Leila, but something more carefully calibrated to their respective requirements for both intimacy and independence.

"That sounds... structurally sound," she said, her tone warmer than the technical language might suggest. "A design worth developing further."

Farrat's smile deepened, reaching his eyes with genuine pleasure at her response. "I think so too," he said simply.

They fell into another comfortable silence, the moment of explicit acknowledgment giving way to quiet contemplation of its implications. Outside, the moon had shifted position, changing the patterns of light that streamed through Tauree's skylights. The new configuration created different geometries on the walls and floors—still ordered, still beautiful, but adapted to the changing conditions of the night.

"It's late," Farrat observed eventually, though his tone suggested no urgency to depart. "I should probably go and let you rest. We both have work tomorrow."

"Yes," Tauree agreed, though she felt an unfamiliar reluctance to end the evening, to return to her usual solitude after the day's shared experiences. "Thank you for driving. And for sharing your poetry. And for..." She paused, searching for words adequate to encompass all that had transpired between them. "For navigating this weather system with me."

Farrat nodded, understanding all that remained unspoken in her simple gratitude. "Thank you for joining me," he replied, the words equally simple but laden with similar depth. "For being willing to explore unknown territory without a complete map."

As she walked him to the door, Tauree found herself contemplating how to conclude the evening—the social rituals of farewell suddenly complex in light of the day's revelations. Before she could overthink it, Farrat solved the dilemma by extending his hand, the gesture offering connection without presumption.

"Until next time," he said as their hands met, his touch warm and firm without being possessive.

"Until next time," Tauree echoed, the promise of future interaction both comforting and exciting in its implicit continuity.

After he had gone, Tauree moved to the window, watching as Farrat emerged from her building and returned to his car. As he drove away, she felt an unfamiliar fullness in her chest—not happiness exactly, but something adjacent to it. Recognition, perhaps, or the rare comfort of being understood without explanation.

The fog was still there, a constant companion in her internal landscape. But now it contained new landmarks, reference points that hadn't existed before—a coastal town bathed in sunset light, a poem that articulated what she had never found words for, patterns of moonlight across her apartment walls shared with someone who understood their significance.

As she prepared for sleep, moving through her nightly routine with habitual precision, Tauree found herself unexpectedly at peace with the day's developments. The careful boundaries she had maintained for years had been adjusted, not demolished—expanded to include new possibilities without sacrificing the essential protections she needed.

Tomorrow, the fog might be thicker, the demands of work and routine more pressing. But tonight, for a few hours in a seaside town and on the long drive home, Tauree had experienced something rare—not just being seen, but being understood. Not just being heard, but being interpreted accurately.

And in that precise translation of her internal landscape into shared understanding, she had found a connection more substantial than any she had known before—a foundation upon which something new and unexpected might be built, if they continued to navigate their weather systems together with the same care and consideration that had brought them this far.

Act 2: The Build-Up and Growing Tension

Chapter 6: The Rainy Afternoon

Two weeks after their day trip to Seaview, the sky above the city had transformed from clear autumn blue to a threatening slate gray. Tauree stood at the window of her office, watching dark clouds gather with unusual speed and density. The weather forecast hadn't mentioned rain, which meant she'd left her umbrella at home—an oversight she now regretted as the first heavy drops began to strike the glass with increasing intensity.

"Looks like it's going to be a downpour," commented her colleague Maya, pausing at Tauree's door with a stack of blueprints. "Did you bring an umbrella?"

"No," Tauree replied, mentally recalculating her evening plans. She had intended to walk the fifteen blocks to the community center site to check on some recent modifications to the reading nook. Now that would have to wait. "I'll probably just stay until it passes."

Maya glanced at her watch. "It's already past six. Those clouds look like they're settling in for the night. You might want to grab a taxi before everyone else has the same idea."

Before Tauree could respond, her phone chimed with a notification. Farrat's name appeared on the screen, the first communication from him since their return from Seaview. The timing was curious—almost as if the gathering storm had somehow conjured him into her thoughts.

Caught in the downpour near Armstrong Building. Taking refuge at Serendipity Café on Elmwood. If you're nearby and similarly stranded, they have excellent chai and surprisingly good poetry books on their shelves.

Tauree felt an unexpected flutter in her chest as she read the message. The Armstrong Building was less than three blocks from her office. The invitation—couched as casual information rather than expectation—was characteristic of how Farrat consistently offered connection without pressure.

Since their return from Seaview, Tauree had found herself in a state of unaccustomed confusion. The day trip had altered something fundamental between them, shifting their carefully constructed friendship into territory that remained undefined but undeniably different. Farrat's poem, his gentle acknowledgment of the growing significance of their connection, his presence in her apartment—all had created a new intimacy that both exhilarated and terrified her.

She had spent the past two weeks alternating between analyzing their interactions with clinical detachment and avoiding the subject altogether by immersing herself in work. She had neither initiated contact nor responded to the soft silence that had fallen between them—not out of disinterest, but out of an uncertainty that felt dangerously close to vulnerability.

Now, watching the rain transform from scattered drops to sheets of water cascading down her window, Tauree found herself composing a reply before her usual calculations could intervene.

Coincidentally just three blocks away at my office. Will head there shortly. I may arrive resembling a drowned architect.

His response came immediately: *I'll have a towel and coffee waiting. The strong, spoon-dissolving kind.*

As Tauree gathered her things, she found herself smiling at the reference to their ongoing joke about her coffee preferences. This was the pattern they had established—small callbacks to previous conversations, a growing lexicon of shared references and inside jokes that created a sense of continuity between their interactions, no matter how much time had passed between them.

"I've changed my mind," she said to Maya, who was still hovering near her door. "I'm going to brave the storm."

"Really?" Maya looked surprised, familiar enough with Tauree's meticulous planning and aversion to discomfort to recognize how unusual this decision was. "Must be something important."

"Just coffee," Tauree replied, her tone deliberately casual as she slipped on her light jacket, knowing it would provide minimal protection against the deluge outside.

Maya's raised eyebrow suggested she didn't entirely believe this explanation, but she didn't press further. "Well, good luck out there. It's really coming down."

That proved to be an understatement. The moment Tauree stepped outside the building's protective awning, the rain hit her with physical force—cold, insistent, and utterly drenching. Within seconds, her carefully styled hair was plastered to her skull, water streaming down her face and neck, her light jacket becoming a sodden, useless weight against her skin.

Most people would have turned back, surrendering to the elements and choosing the dry safety of their office over such discomfort. But something propelled Tauree forward—a determination that surprised even herself. Three blocks in the pouring rain was objectively unpleasant, yet she found herself moving with purpose through the storm, navigating around puddles that were rapidly becoming small lakes at each intersection.

By the time she reached Serendipity Café, Tauree was thoroughly soaked, her shoes squelching with each step, her clothes clinging uncomfortably to her body. The café's warmly lit interior, visible through steamed-up windows, appeared like a beacon of civilization amidst the primal force of the storm. She pushed open the door, bringing a gust of wind and water with her that made several patrons look up in alarm.

And there was Farrat, rising from a corner table, his expression shifting from anticipation to amused concern as he took in her waterlogged appearance. Unlike Tauree, he appeared to have been caught only in the initial stages of the downpour—his clothes showed evidence of dampness but not the complete saturation that she had achieved in her three-block journey.

"You weren't exaggerating about the drowned architect," he said, approaching with a clean cloth napkin he'd apparently requested in preparation for her arrival. "Here, this isn't quite a towel, but it might help a bit."

"Thank you," Tauree replied, accepting the napkin gratefully and dabbing at her face. Water was still dripping from her hair, creating a small puddle at her feet. "I seem to have brought half the storm inside with me."

"It suits you, oddly enough," Farrat observed with a slight smile. "There's something poetic about someone who designs shelters being temporarily at the mercy of the elements."

The observation—perceiving meaning in what most would see as mere discomfort—was so characteristic of Farrat that Tauree found herself smiling despite her bedraggled state. "I'm not sure my current appearance would convince potential clients of my ability to create waterproof structures," she remarked dryly.

"On the contrary," Farrat countered, gesturing toward their table where two steaming mugs waited. "It demonstrates your commitment to field research. No one understands the value of shelter like someone who has recently lacked it."

As they settled at the table, Tauree became aware of her surroundings in a way her rain-dashed entrance had prevented. Serendipity Café was unlike the sleek, modernist coffee shops that dominated the downtown area. Instead, it seemed to have emerged from another era entirely—warm wood paneling, mismatched but comfortable furniture, and walls lined with bookshelves containing what appeared to be a thoughtfully curated collection of volumes rather than decorative props.

The space created a curious sense of containment without confinement—exactly the quality Tauree strived for in her architectural designs. The layout encouraged interaction without forcing it, with tables positioned to allow conversation while maintaining personal space. Small reading lamps created pools of warm light throughout the room, allowing each table to exist in its own intimate atmosphere while remaining part of the collective environment.

"I've never been here before," Tauree admitted, wrapping her cold hands around the mug Farrat had pushed toward her. The coffee was indeed as strong as she preferred, its aroma cutting through the lingering chill that clung to her despite the café's warmth. "It's lovely."

"I discovered it by accident last year during another unexpected storm," Farrat explained. "It's become something of a sanctuary when the weather drives me indoors during my walks. The owner is a former literature professor who decided books and coffee were more satisfying than departmental politics."

As if summoned by this mention, an elderly man approached their table—tall and thin with a shock of white hair and bright, intelligent eyes behind wire-rimmed glasses. "Farrat, good to see you again," he said warmly before turning curious eyes toward Tauree. "And you've brought a friend who appears to have had a close encounter with our unexpected tempest."

"Professor Abrams," Farrat acknowledged with evident respect. "This is Tauree Sharma, a brilliant architect and fellow appreciator of strong coffee. Tauree, this is Malcolm Abrams, owner of this remarkable establishment and former chair of Comparative Literature at the university."

"Pleased to meet you," Tauree said, extending a hand that she realized too late was still damp from the rain.

Malcolm Abrams took it without hesitation, his grip firm despite his advanced age. "Any friend of Farrat's is welcome here, especially one sensible enough to brave the elements for good coffee and conversation." He gestured toward her sodden state with a sympathetic smile. "I might have something that would help. One moment."

He disappeared through a door behind the counter, returning moments later with a soft, oversized cardigan in deep burgundy. "My office gets chilly in winter, so I keep this handy," he explained, offering it to Tauree. "You're welcome to borrow it while your jacket dries. Pneumonia would be an excessive price to pay for coffee, even ours."

The unexpected kindness caught Tauree off guard. Her typical response to such offers was polite refusal—maintaining boundaries, avoiding obligations. But something about the genuine concern in the old professor's eyes made her accept with a simple "Thank you" as she slipped off her wet jacket and wrapped the borrowed cardigan around her shoulders. The wool was soft with age and carried a faint scent of pipe tobacco and old books—comforting in its scholarly associations.

"I'll have Eliza bring over some of our ginger tea as well," Malcolm added. "Best thing for warding off chills. Farrat can vouch for its medicinal properties."

After he had gone, Tauree raised an eyebrow at Farrat. "You seem to have established quite a rapport here."

"Malcolm has been kind to me," Farrat acknowledged with a small nod. "When I first discovered this place, I was in a particularly difficult period. The rainfall, as we've come to call it, was especially heavy. I spent hours here, reading or just sitting, and he never once made me feel I was taking up space better used by paying customers who wouldn't nurse a single cup of tea all afternoon."

The admission—a glimpse into Farrat's life before they met—created that now-familiar pressure in Tauree's chest, the sensation of emotion pushing against the protective numbness she typically maintained. It was one thing to discuss their respective forms of depression in abstract terms, another to envision Farrat seeking refuge in this warm space during his darkest moments.

"It feels like a place that would understand that need," she observed, glancing around at the other patrons—a mixture of students with laptops, elderly individuals reading newspapers, and a few pairs engaged in quiet conversation. No one seemed hurried or anxious about claiming their small piece of the shared space.

"It does," Farrat agreed. "Malcolm has a theory that good cafés serve the same function in modern society that sacred spaces did in earlier times—places of sanctuary where ordinary rules of commerce and competition are temporarily suspended in favor of contemplation and community."

A young woman approached with a small teapot and an additional cup, setting them down with a friendly nod before withdrawing. The ginger tea released a spicy, warming aroma as Farrat poured some for Tauree, who accepted it with gratitude. The first sip spread heat through her still-chilled body, the ginger providing a pleasant burn that complemented rather than competed with her coffee.

Outside, the storm had intensified further—rain lashing against the windows in rhythmic waves driven by an increasingly powerful wind. The sound created a percussive backdrop to their conversation, emphasizing the contrasting warmth and stillness of their shelter.

"So," Farrat said after they had both spent a moment appreciating their respective beverages, "how have you been these past two weeks? The community center project progressing well?"

The question was casual but carried undercurrents of genuine interest and, perhaps, an acknowledgment of the silence that had stretched between them since their return from Seaview. It offered Tauree an easy entry point into conversation without immediately addressing the more complex aspects of their evolving relationship.

"The structure is nearly complete," she replied, grateful for the familiar professional territory. "We've encountered some challenges with the reading nook—the angle of the skylights needed adjustment to create the optimal light patterns throughout the day. I was actually planning to check on the modifications this evening before the rain intervened."

"Serendipitous intervention, then," Farrat observed with a small smile. "Though I admit I've been hoping for an opportunity to continue our conversation from Seaview. The one we began in your apartment, about the structure we might be building together."

The directness of his reference—bringing their unspoken connection immediately into focus rather than circling it gradually—was unexpected but not unwelcome. Tauree had spent two weeks analyzing that conversation from every angle, and still felt unprepared for its continuation. Yet something about the storm raging outside, the borrowed warmth around her shoulders, and the cocoon-like quality of the café created a space where such vulnerability seemed less threatening.

"I've been thinking about that too," she admitted, her fingers tracing the rim of her teacup. "Though I haven't reached any definitive conclusions."

"Neither have I," Farrat replied, the honesty in his voice creating a bridge between them. "Which is unusual for me. Normally I process experiences through writing—transform them into metaphor and image until they become something I can understand. But this..." He gestured subtly between them. "This has resisted that translation."

"Because it's still evolving," Tauree suggested, the insight emerging before she had fully formulated it. "Still taking shape. Like a building in the early stages of construction, when the foundations are laid but the final form remains fluid."

Farrat nodded, appreciation for the metaphor evident in his expression. "Yes, exactly. And perhaps that's as it should be. Some processes can't be rushed without compromising structural integrity."

The reference to her professional vocabulary—her concern for sound construction and proper sequence—created that familiar sense of being truly seen, of having her particular perspective honored rather than overlooked. It was this quality in Farrat that had first drawn her to him at Amrita's tea party, this capacity to meet her where she was rather than demanding she translate herself into more conventional terms.

"I do know one thing," Tauree said after a moment's consideration. "The past two weeks have been... different. Even when we weren't in direct communication, I found myself thinking about our conversations, considering how you might interpret various experiences I encountered."

"I've had the same experience," Farrat admitted, a hint of wonder in his voice. "Yesterday I was grading papers, and I found myself wondering how you would perceive the architectural metaphors in a particular poem. Not just as a passing thought, but with enough specificity that I actually made notes to share with you when we next spoke."

The revelation—that he had anticipated future conversations, had actively prepared for them even during their silence—created an unexpected warmth in Tauree's chest, different from the physical heat of the tea and coffee. This was the essence of what had begun to transform between them: not just enjoyment of each other's company, but the integration of each other's perspectives into their separate lives.

"That's not something I'm accustomed to," she said quietly. "In my experience, relationships have typically been compartmentalized—existing in specific contexts and times, but not permeating the spaces between encounters."

"For me as well," Farrat agreed. "Though in my case, it was usually the opposite problem—previous relationships tended to flood all areas of my life, leaving no room for independent thought or experience. This feels... different. Present without being consuming."

Outside, a particularly loud crack of thunder punctuated his observation, as if the elements themselves were responding to the significance of this shared recognition. The lights in the café flickered briefly before stabilizing, causing a momentary hush in the ambient conversation before it resumed at a slightly higher volume, nervous laughter dispersing the tension.

"The storm has moved directly overhead," Farrat observed, glancing toward the windows where rain continued to lash with undiminished force. "We might be here for a while."

The prospect—extended time in this warm space while nature raged outside—created none of the usual anxiety Tauree associated with unplanned social encounters. Instead, she felt a curious sense of liberation, as if the storm had temporarily suspended the usual rules governing her carefully structured existence.

"I don't mind," she said, surprising herself with the ease of the admission. "This is... nice. Unexpected, but nice."

Farrat's smile warmed his features, reaching his eyes in a way that created that now-familiar flutter in Tauree's chest. "I think that might be our unofficial motto," he suggested lightly. "'Unexpected, but nice.' It seems to characterize most of our encounters."

The observation was so accurate that Tauree found herself laughing—a genuine sound of amusement that felt unexpectedly free in the ambient noise of the café. "Starting with Amrita's tea party," she agreed. "I certainly didn't expect to find myself in a substantive conversation about emotional weather patterns when I reluctantly agreed to attend."

"Nor did I expect to be discussing architectural theory with a woman who organized her bookshelves by color rather than content," Farrat countered with a teasing light in his eyes.

"You're never going to let me forget that, are you?" Tauree asked, mock indignation in her tone.

"Never," Farrat confirmed solemnly, though his eyes still danced with amusement. "It's too perfect an encapsulation of how practical concerns and aesthetic sensibilities merge in your approach to the world."

The observation—elevating what might have been a simple quirk into a meaningful expression of her character—was characteristic of how Farrat consistently reframed her differences as valuable perspectives rather than oddities to be corrected. It was this quality, perhaps more than any other, that had allowed their connection to deepen despite her usual wariness of emotional entanglement.

As they continued talking, the conversation flowing with that same surprising ease Tauree had experienced during their previous encounters, she became aware of a subtle shift in the quality of light around them. The storm outside had transformed the afternoon into premature evening, and Malcolm or one of his staff had begun lighting candles on each table—small flames in glass holders that created pools of golden illumination throughout the space.

The effect was both practical and atmospheric—providing light during the storm's darkness while enhancing the café's sense of intimate shelter. Around them, other patrons had settled into this altered reality, some reading by candlelight, others engaged in hushed conversations that seemed to have deepened with the changing ambiance.

"This reminds me of power outages during monsoon season when I was a child," Farrat observed, his face softened in the candlelight. "My grandmother would gather the family in her kitchen, light candles, and tell stories until the electricity returned. Sometimes I found myself hoping the power would stay off just a little longer, so the stories could continue."

The memory—offered without calculation or obvious purpose—provided another glimpse into the experiences that had shaped him. Tauree found herself unexpectedly moved by the image of a young Farrat absorbed in his grandmother's tales by candlelight, finding joy in what others might have experienced as mere inconvenience.

"My experience was quite different," she offered in return, the exchange of personal history becoming more natural with each interaction. "Power outages meant my father would become irritable about work disruptions, and my mother would fret about food spoiling in the refrigerator. I learned to retreat to my room with a flashlight and building blocks, creating structures that didn't require electricity to function properly."

"Young Tauree, already solving architectural problems by candlelight," Farrat observed with a smile. "I can imagine you completely absorbed in construction while chaos reigned elsewhere in the house."

"It was my first lesson in creating sanctuary," Tauree acknowledged, the insight emerging as she spoke. "Finding ways to establish order and purpose regardless of external circumstances."

"Like your skylights," Farrat noted, drawing the connection to her apartment's design. "Creating predictable patterns of light even as conditions change outside."

"Yes," Tauree confirmed, once again struck by how easily he translated between her experiences and their broader implications. "Consistency within change, as you called it that night."

The reference to his visit to her apartment—the culmination of their day trip to Seaview—created a momentary intensity between them, a shared recollection of the boundaries that had been carefully crossed and the possibilities that had been acknowledged, if not fully explored.

Before either could address this directly, a flash of lightning illuminated the entire café with stark clarity, followed almost instantly by a deafening crack of thunder that suggested the bolt had struck dangerously close by. The lights went out completely this time, plunging the space into darkness except for the small candles on each table.

There was a collective gasp from the other patrons, followed by nervous laughter and the glow of cell phone screens being activated around the room. Malcolm's voice came from near the counter, calm and reassuring: "Nothing to worry about, folks. The generator will kick in for essential services in a moment. In the meantime, enjoy the atmospheric enhancement to your coffee experience."

As if on cue, a few emergency lights came on, providing minimal illumination to the café's main pathways while leaving the individual tables in their pools of candlelight. The effect was oddly magical—transforming an unexpected power outage into something that felt intentional and intimate.

Tauree found herself studying Farrat's face in this new lighting, the flickering flame emphasizing different aspects of his features than she had noticed before—the curve of his cheekbone, the thoughtful set of his mouth, the way his eyes reflected the small fire between them. Without the café's ambient noise—the espresso machine, the background music, the hum of conversation amplified by electric lights—their table felt like an island of stillness amid the storm's continued assault outside.

"Are you all right?" Farrat asked, noticing her intense observation.

"Yes," Tauree replied, slightly embarrassed at being caught staring. "Just...noticing how different familiar things appear in altered light."

"An apt metaphor for much of human experience," Farrat observed, his voice gentle in the muted atmosphere. "Especially relationships. The same person viewed through different circumstances often reveals entirely new facets."

The observation struck Tauree with unexpected force—not just for its general truth, but for its specific application to their evolving connection. She had indeed seen different aspects of Farrat through their various encounters—his scholarly focus at the gallery, his poetic vulnerability at Seaview, his quiet attentiveness during their midnight walk. Each context had illuminated different facets of his character, creating a composite understanding that was both more complex and more complete than any single interaction could provide.

"I've been thinking about what you said in your poem," she said suddenly, the candlelit intimacy somehow making it easier to approach topics that might have felt too vulnerable in ordinary circumstances. "'The long drive is never about reaching a destination. It is about creating a temporary universe, contained within the moving capsule of shared attention.'"

Farrat looked surprised that she had memorized his words so precisely, but nodded for her to continue.

"I've never been particularly skilled at creating those 'capsules of shared attention,'" Tauree admitted. "The fog makes it difficult to maintain that kind of focus on another person, to remain fully present rather than partially withdrawn. But with you..." She paused, searching for words adequate to the complexity of her experience. "With you, it happens without deliberate effort. The attention flows naturally, consistently finding its level like water."

The metaphor wasn't precisely what she wanted, but Farrat's expression suggested he understood what she was trying to articulate—that quality of unforced connection that had characterized their interactions from the beginning, the ease with which they had established a shared vocabulary across their different disciplines and experiences.

"I know exactly what you mean," he said quietly. "There's a concept in poetry called 'natural cadence'—the rhythm that emerges not through technical adherence to meter, but through the organic flow of thought finding its most authentic expression. That's how our conversations feel to me—not constructed according to social convention, but flowing according to genuine interest and understanding."

The parallel—drawing on his professional vocabulary to illuminate her experience—mirrored how she had come to think of their connection, each consistently translating their separate worlds into terms the other could access and appreciate.

A comfortable silence fell between them, filled with the ambient sounds of the storm outside and occasional murmurs from other tables. The power outage had created a curious intimacy throughout the café, strangers speaking in hushed tones as if sharing a collective experience rather than merely occupying the same space. Phones had largely been put away, their harsh blue glow seeming intrusive in the warm orange light of candles.

When Malcolm approached their table again, he carried a tray with fresh coffee and what appeared to be a small plate of pastries. "On the house," he said with a warm smile. "Power outages call for sugar and caffeine, in my experience. And it appears you two might be settling in for a while, given the weather reports."

"Weather reports?" Farrat inquired, accepting the offerings with a grateful nod.

"My old radio in the back room still works," Malcolm explained. "They're saying this storm system has stalled over the city—likely to continue well into the night with possible flooding in low-lying areas. Public transportation is already disrupted in some neighborhoods."

The news should have alarmed Tauree—her carefully structured routine disrupted, her apartment potentially inaccessible for hours, her evening plans thoroughly derailed. Yet she found herself experiencing a curious calm, as if the storm had created a suspension of ordinary concerns, a parenthesis in which different rules applied.

"Thank you for letting us know," she said to Malcolm. "And for your hospitality. This is exactly where I'd choose to be stranded during a storm."

The older man's smile deepened, creating a web of lines around his eyes that spoke of a lifetime of genuine expressions rather than polite facades. "High praise from an architect who designs sanctuaries," he observed, his perceptiveness reminding Tauree that he was, after all, a former literature professor—trained to read between lines and discern patterns in human behavior.

After he had gone, Farrat regarded Tauree with gentle curiosity. "You're remarkably calm about being potentially stranded. That doesn't align with what I know of your preference for structure and predictability."

The observation—accurate but offered without judgment—created an opportunity for Tauree to examine her own unexpected response to the situation. Why wasn't she more concerned about the disruption to her careful routines? Why didn't she feel the usual anxiety that accompanied unplanned social encounters?

"I think it's because this feels like a true shelter," she said after a moment's reflection. "Not just from the physical storm, but from the usual pressures and expectations. There's nowhere else to be, nothing else to do but remain present in this moment. It's..." She searched for the right word. "Liberating."

Farrat nodded, understanding evident in his expression. "Imposed limitations sometimes create unexpected freedom. When choices are reduced by external circumstances, the burden of constant decision-making is temporarily lifted."

"Yes, exactly," Tauree agreed, appreciating once again how precisely he grasped the nuances of her experience. "And in this particular case, being stranded in a warm café with good coffee, interesting books, and..." She hesitated briefly before continuing, "And good company doesn't feel like a hardship."

The small acknowledgment—that his presence was a feature rather than a bug in this unexpected situation—created a moment of quiet connection between them. Farrat's smile in response held a quality of genuine pleasure that transformed his solemn features, reaching his eyes with warmth that seemed to match the candle's glow between them.

As the evening progressed, their conversation flowed with that same surprising ease Tauree had experienced during their previous encounters. They moved from architecture to literature to the curious psychology of people during storms—how shared experiences of natural phenomena often temporarily dissolved social barriers and created communities among strangers.

Around them, the café had indeed developed a curious sense of collective identity, with people at different tables occasionally sharing observations or offers of assistance. A woman with an engineering background helped Malcolm stabilize a wobbly bookshelf that the earlier thunder had dislodged. A group of students shared their portable battery packs with an elderly couple who needed to contact worried family members. The young barista, Eliza, moved through the space with additional candles and periodic updates from Malcolm's radio.

"This is what I was trying to capture in the community center design," Tauree observed, watching these interactions with professional interest. "That quality of individual purpose within collective space, private experience within shared environment."

"It's working remarkably well here," Farrat noted, following her gaze around the room. "Though I suspect Malcolm has been cultivating this particular community for years through subtle curation of space and experience."

"Like any good architect of social environments," Tauree agreed, her appreciation for the café deepening as she recognized the intentional design elements underlying its apparently organic atmosphere.

As if summoned by their discussion, Malcolm appeared again at their table, this time with a leather-bound book tucked under his arm. "I thought you might appreciate this, Farrat," he said, placing it on the table between them. "Given your interest in the intersection of architectural and poetic space. It's not commercially available—a small press publication from a colleague at the university who explores spatial theory through verse."

Farrat accepted the book with evident interest, opening it carefully to reveal pages of text arranged in unusual geometric patterns, the poems themselves forming architectural shapes on the page. "This is remarkable," he said, genuine appreciation in his voice. "Thank you for thinking of it."

"I had a feeling you two might appreciate it," Malcolm replied with a knowing smile before moving on to check on other patrons.

As Farrat carefully turned the pages, Tauree leaned closer to examine the innovative interplay between form and content. The poems were arranged to physically embody their subjects—a sonnet about a tower stretched vertically up the page, a meditation on horizons spread in a thin line across the width, a reflection on spiraling thoughts curved in an Archimedean pattern that drew the eye inward.

"This is fascinating," she said, professional interest thoroughly engaged. "It's using the physical space of the page as an additional dimension of meaning, not just as a neutral container for text."

"Exactly," Farrat agreed, his expression animated with intellectual excitement. "The spatial arrangement becomes part of the poem's statement, inseparable from the words themselves." He glanced up at her, a new connection forming in his eyes. "Not unlike how your architectural designs incorporate emotional meaning into physical structure—the skylights that track time, the reading nook that creates intellectual intimacy within community space."

The parallel—drawing their separate professional worlds together once again—created that familiar sense of being truly understood, of having her work perceived not just in technical terms but in its deeper emotional intentions.

They spent the next hour exploring the book together, each bringing their particular expertise to the interpretation of these poems that existed somewhere between literature and visual art, between emotional expression and spatial theory. Their heads bent close over the pages, voices lowered to maintain the intimate atmosphere created by candlelight and storm, they created their own small universe of shared attention—exactly the "capsule" Farrat had described in his poem at Seaview.

Outside, the storm continued unabated, rain lashing against the windows in sheets driven by wind that occasionally rose to howling intensity before subsiding into steady, determined percussion. The café had adjusted to its power-limited state, with Malcolm and his staff providing regular refreshments and updates on the weather situation. Some patrons had departed during brief lulls in the downpour, while others had settled in for extended stays, creating makeshift workspaces or reading nooks at their candlelit tables.

It was nearly ten o'clock when Malcolm approached again, his expression apologetic. "I hate to interrupt, but I've just heard that they're closing several main roads due to flooding, including the one that would take you toward Westwood," he said, addressing Tauree.

"If you're planning to return home tonight, you might want to make arrangements soon, before options become even more limited."

The news brought Tauree abruptly back to practical considerations. Her apartment was indeed in Westwood, on higher ground but accessed through areas that were apparently now flooded. The fog—which had retreated to the barest hint at the periphery of her awareness during the evening's unexpected intimacy—threatened to descend again as she contemplated the disruption to her carefully structured existence.

"Thank you for letting me know," she said to Malcolm, her mind already calculating alternatives. She could try to find a hotel room, though those would likely be in high demand given the circumstances. She could attempt to navigate around the closures, though driving in such conditions would be both difficult and potentially dangerous.

Before she could pursue these thoughts further, Farrat spoke, his tone careful and unthreatening. "My apartment is in Riverside, which is on higher ground and in the opposite direction from the worst flooding. You'd be welcome to use my guest room until the roads clear." He paused, then added with characteristic consideration, "No pressure or expectation, of course. Just an option to consider."

The offer hung between them—simple yet laden with potential significance. Staying in Farrat's home would cross another boundary in their evolving relationship, creating a new level of intimacy beyond the controlled contexts of cafés, galleries, and even their day trip to Seaview. Even their brief time in her apartment after returning from the coast had been carefully limited, a specific moment rather than an extended stay.

Yet as Tauree considered the prospect, she found herself experiencing more curiosity than apprehension. Farrat's home—with its emotionally organized bookshelves and the other personal touches she had yet to discover—represented a dimension of him she had glimpsed only through his descriptions. The opportunity to see this private space, to understand more directly the environment he had created for himself, held an unexpected appeal.

"That's very kind," she said carefully. "Are you certain it wouldn't be an imposition?"

"Not at all," Farrat replied, his expression open and unguarded. "The guest room is already prepared—a habit from my university days when colleagues would sometimes need accommodation during conferences. And I suspect we could continue our exploration of architectural poetry in more comfortable circumstances than these, pleasant as they have been."

The reference to their shared intellectual engagement—framing the invitation in terms of continuing their conversation rather than any more personal motivation—was characteristic of how Farrat consistently offered connection without pressure, space without expectation.

"I'd appreciate that," Tauree said finally, the decision feeling simultaneously momentous and entirely natural. "Thank you."

The simple exchange—offer and acceptance—created a subtle shift in the atmosphere between them, an acknowledgment of another threshold crossed in their evolving relationship. Yet there was no awkwardness in it, no sense of boundaries being breached rather than mutually adjusted. Instead, there was a curious rightness to the progression, as if the storm had merely accelerated a natural trajectory already in motion.

Malcolm, who had tactfully stepped away during their brief exchange, returned with their bill and what appeared to be a small package wrapped in waxed paper. "For your journey," he explained, handing the package to Farrat. "Some of Eliza's ginger cookies. Best defense against stormy weather, in my experience."

"You're very kind," Farrat replied, accepting both the package and the bill with a grateful nod. "This evening has been an unexpected pleasure, despite—or perhaps because of—the weather's intervention."

"Sometimes the universe conspires to create exactly the conditions we need, if not necessarily those we might have planned," Malcolm observed with the quiet wisdom of someone who had witnessed many such "serendipitous" convergences over the years. "Safe travels, and I hope to see you both again under less dramatic circumstances."

As they prepared to leave, Tauree suddenly remembered the borrowed cardigan still draped around her shoulders. "I should return this," she said, beginning to remove it.

"Keep it for now," Malcolm insisted with a gentle wave of dismissal. "The storm hasn't finished with us yet, and you'll need it more than my office will tonight. You can return it on your next visit."

The assumption of future connection—that she would return to this place that had so unexpectedly become significant—created a small glow of warmth in Tauree's chest. In the span of a single stormy evening, she had acquired not just a new favorite café but a sense of belonging within its particular community.

Farrat had prepared for their departure with practical efficiency, borrowing a large umbrella from Malcolm's collection near the door and positioning it to create maximum coverage as they stepped out into the still-raging storm. The rain hit the canvas with such force that it created a continuous roar above their heads, the sound making conversation nearly impossible as they hurried toward the small parking structure where Farrat had left his car.

Even with the umbrella, they were both damp by the time they reached the vehicle—nothing like Tauree's drenched arrival at the café, but enough to make the car's interior feel like blessed sanctuary when they finally closed the doors against the elements. For a moment they sat in silence, listening to the rain hammer against the roof and windows, creating a cocoon of sound that emphasized their separation from the world outside.

"Well," Farrat said finally, a hint of amusement in his voice as he turned the key in the ignition, "this certainly qualifies as 'unexpected, but nice.' Though 'adventurous' might be a more accurate description at this point."

The reference to their earlier conversation—finding humor in the dramatic escalation of their simple coffee meeting into an overnight arrangement—eased any potential awkwardness the situation might have created. Tauree found herself smiling despite the discomfort of damp clothes and disrupted plans.

"At least we're not attempting to navigate this in separate vehicles," she observed as Farrat carefully backed out of the parking space. "I'm not sure my architectural training included sufficient preparation for flood management."

"Whereas my literary background is full of epic floods," Farrat countered with a small smile. "Though most end with dramatic transformations of the landscape and social order, which seems excessive for a spring storm."

Their banter continued as Farrat navigated the rain-slicked streets with careful attention, taking a circuitous route that avoided the main areas of flooding. The windshield wipers worked at maximum speed, barely maintaining visibility against the relentless downpour. Occasionally they would pass emergency vehicles, lights flashing as crews dealt with fallen trees or stranded motorists, stark reminders of the storm's serious impact beyond their personal experience of it.

As they drove, Tauree found herself contemplating the curious trajectory that had brought her to this moment—sitting in Farrat's car in the middle of a historic storm, heading toward his apartment for an unplanned overnight stay. None of it aligned with her usual patterns of careful planning and emotional distance. Yet instead of anxiety, she felt a strange sense of rightness about the situation, as if the storm had merely accelerated a process that was already underway, revealing a truth that might have taken much longer to acknowledge under ordinary circumstances.

The rain created sheets of silver in the headlights, transforming the familiar city into something otherworldly—a landscape of water and reflection where solid forms seemed to dissolve and reconstitute themselves with each sweep of the wipers. It reminded Tauree of how she had described her depression to Farrat during their first real conversation: the fog that made even familiar territories difficult to navigate, that blurred the boundaries between objects and obscured the path forward.

Yet tonight, despite the literal manifestation of obscured vision all around them, Tauree felt an unusual clarity. Perhaps it was the contrast between external chaos and internal calm, or perhaps it was simply Farrat's steady presence beside her, navigating the storm with the same thoughtful attention he brought to their conversations. Whatever the cause, the fog that typically colored her perception had receded to the barest hint at the periphery of her awareness, allowing her to experience the moment with rare immediacy.

"We're almost there," Farrat said as they turned onto a quieter street lined with what appeared to be converted industrial buildings. "Riverside was originally warehouse district before artists and academics discovered its potential for affordable living spaces with architectural character."

The area was indeed distinctive—brick buildings with large windows and interesting architectural details that spoke of their industrial heritage, now softened by the addition of small gardens, artistic touches, and warm lighting that created an impression of creative community rather than commercial utility.

They pulled into a small private lot behind one of these buildings, a three-story brick structure with large arched windows that suggested it might once have been a factory or workshop of some kind. Farrat parked in a numbered space near a side entrance, then turned to Tauree with a small smile.

"Welcome to my humble abode," he said, gesturing toward the building. "Though I should warn you—the bookshelves really are as chaotically organized as I described. Enter at your own psychological risk."

The gentle self-deprecation—acknowledging her architectural precision while preparing her for his more organic approach to organization—made Tauree smile despite the renewed anticipation she felt at entering Farrat's private domain. "I'll try to restrain my urge to reorganize by author and subject," she promised solemnly.

The dash from car to building was brief but thoroughly drenching, the rain still falling with undiminished intensity as they hurried through puddles that had formed in the uneven pavement of the old lot. Inside, a small vestibule led to a stairwell with the building's original iron railings still intact, though now painted a deep blue that complemented the exposed brick walls.

"I'm on the top floor," Farrat explained as they began to climb. "The stairs are worth it for the light and the view—though neither is particularly impressive at the moment, given the weather."

By the time they reached the third floor, Tauree was keenly aware of her disheveled state—hair damp from the rain, borrowed cardigan slightly rumpled, and shoes that had seen far too much water for one evening. Yet there was something liberating about this temporary abandonment of her usual composed appearance, as if the storm had granted permission to exist in a less controlled state.

Farrat unlocked a heavy wooden door at the end of the hallway, stepping aside to allow Tauree to enter first with a gesture that managed to be courteous without being overdone. As she stepped across the threshold, Tauree felt a curious sense of crossing more than a physical boundary—entering not just Farrat's apartment but a new phase of their relationship, one defined by a deeper level of trust and mutual understanding.

The space that greeted her was simultaneously exactly what she had expected and full of surprising details she could never have anticipated. The apartment was indeed a converted industrial space, with high ceilings, exposed brick walls, and large windows that would normally provide excellent natural light. The open floor plan created a sense of continuous flow between functional areas—living room transitioning to dining area to kitchen without hard boundaries, yet each space clearly defined by thoughtful arrangement of furniture and subtle shifts in lighting.

And there, dominating one entire wall just as Farrat had described, were the bookshelves—floor to ceiling, filled with volumes arranged in a pattern that would indeed be incomprehensible to anyone but their owner. Tauree could immediately see what he had meant about "emotional resonance" guiding the organization; books of wildly different sizes, ages, and apparent subjects sat beside each other, creating juxtapositions that would make a conventional librarian shudder but clearly made perfect sense to Farrat's particular mind.

"Please, make yourself comfortable," Farrat said, closing the door behind them. "I'll get you a towel and show you to the guest room so you can change into something dry."

As he disappeared down a hallway, Tauree took the opportunity to observe the space more carefully, her architect's eye cataloging details that revealed aspects of Farrat's character beyond what their conversations had disclosed. The furniture was an eclectic mix of pieces chosen clearly for comfort rather than adherence to any particular style, yet the overall effect was harmonious rather than chaotic. Original artwork hung on the walls—not expensive pieces, but items selected with evident care for their emotional impact rather than decorative function.

What struck her most, however, was the thoughtful arrangement of light sources throughout the space. Unlike the harsh overhead lighting common in converted industrial buildings, Farrat had created a system of layered illumination—floor lamps, desk lights, small fixtures highlighting specific shelves or artwork. The effect was remarkably similar to what Tauree herself tried to achieve in her designs: light that created a sense of both intimacy and spaciousness, that defined areas without rigidly separating them.

"You're analyzing my lighting design," Farrat observed with gentle amusement as he returned with a fluffy towel and what appeared to be neatly folded clothing. "I can practically see the professional assessment happening behind your eyes."

"It's impressive," Tauree admitted, accepting the towel gratefully. "Most people default to overhead lighting in spaces like this, which creates harsh shadows and flattens the architectural features. You've created layers that enhance rather than compete with the original structure."

"High praise from a professional," Farrat said with a small smile. "Though I can't claim any formal knowledge—just years of reading in various lights and developing strong opinions about which conditions best serve different types of texts."

The explanation—linking his design choices to his literary life rather than any architectural theory—was so characteristic of Farrat that Tauree found herself smiling despite her damp discomfort. Even in this most practical of matters, his approach emerged from his particular relationship with words and ideas, just as her own designs grew from her understanding of emotional responses to physical space.

"The guest room is this way," Farrat continued, gesturing toward the hallway from which he had emerged. "There's an attached bathroom with everything you should need. And I've put out some clothes that might work as temporary replacements while yours dry—just a T-shirt and sweatpants, nothing fancy, but they're clean and dry."

The consideration in these preparations—anticipating her needs without being asked—created that now-familiar warmth in Tauree's chest. Farrat's thoughtfulness manifested not in grand gestures but in these small, practical kindnesses that showed genuine attention to another's comfort and dignity.

The guest room, when he showed her into it, continued the theme of thoughtful simplicity that characterized the rest of the apartment. A comfortable-looking bed with crisp linens, a small desk near the window, a reading lamp positioned for optimal illumination, and a chair that invited relaxation without demanding it. The space was neither sterile nor overly personal—a perfect balance that welcomed without imposing, exactly the quality Tauree strived for in her own architectural designs.

"I'll let you get settled," Farrat said, placing the folded clothes on the bed. "Take your time. When you're ready, I'll be in the kitchen. I thought some hot tea might be appropriate after our adventure in the elements."

After he had gone, closing the door quietly behind him, Tauree stood for a moment simply absorbing the space. There was something profoundly telling about how Farrat had designed this room intended for others—the careful attention to comfort without presumption, the provision of necessities without clutter, the creation of a space that could temporarily belong to whoever occupied it rather than constantly reminding them of their visitor status.

The bathroom continued this theme of thoughtful hospitality—clean towels arranged neatly, basic toiletries provided discretely on a small shelf, lighting that was practical without being harsh. Tauree took a quick shower, washing away the chill of the rain and the subtle tension of navigating unfamiliar social territory. The hot water restored both physical comfort and emotional equilibrium, allowing her to process the evening's unexpected developments with greater clarity.

When she emerged, dressed in Farrat's borrowed clothes (which were predictably too large but soft with age and surprisingly comfortable), she felt a curious blend of vulnerability and ease. There was something quietly intimate about wearing someone else's clothing, about carrying their scent and feeling the fabric that normally touched their skin against her own. Yet there was also a surprising comfort in it—as if temporarily adopting Farrat's external trappings created a bridge between their separate experiences, a physical manifestation of the mental territory they had begun to share.

She found Farrat in the kitchen as promised, his back to her as he attended to something on the stove. The domestic scene—so different from their usual coffee shop or gallery encounters—created a momentary pause in Tauree's approach, a recognition of how dramatically the storm had accelerated the natural evolution of their relationship.

"That smells wonderful," she said, announcing her presence as she moved to lean against the kitchen counter.

Farrat turned, a small smile warming his features as he took in her appearance in his borrowed clothes. "It's just a simple chai," he replied, returning his attention to the pot he was stirring. "My grandmother's recipe. She insisted it had medicinal properties beyond mere warmth and comfort, though I suspect that was primarily to encourage its consumption among reluctant children."

"The clothes are very comfortable," Tauree said, addressing the unspoken observation in his glance. "Thank you."

"They look better on you than they do on me," Farrat replied with a lightness that prevented the comment from feeling too personal or weighted. "I've put your things in the dryer. They should be ready by morning."

The simple domestic exchange—focused on practical matters of comfort and clothing—helped ease any potential awkwardness in their new context. This was not a romantic scenario but simply two friends navigating unexpected circumstances with mutual consideration and respect.

As Farrat poured the steaming chai into mugs, Tauree found herself drawn to the large windows that dominated the living area. The storm continued unabated outside, rain streaming down the glass in rivulets that distorted the city lights beyond into abstract patterns of color and movement. There was something mesmerizing about watching the elements from this position of secure shelter—another example of the contrast between external chaos and internal calm that had characterized the entire evening.

"It's beautiful, in its way," Farrat observed, joining her at the window and offering one of the mugs. "The transformation of the familiar into something temporarily unrecognizable."

"Like seeing through the fog," Tauree replied, accepting the chai gratefully. "Everything still exists, but its edges and boundaries are altered, requiring new methods of navigation."

"Exactly," Farrat agreed, his gaze moving between the storm-obscured view and Tauree's profile. "Though tonight, the external weather seems to have created unusual clarity rather than confusion—at least in my experience."

The observation—quietly acknowledging the significance of their evolving connection without demanding response—created a moment of gentle intensity between them, a recognition that transcended the need for elaborate explanation.

"In mine as well," Tauree admitted after a moment's consideration, the honesty easier in this storm-encapsulated space where ordinary rules seemed temporarily suspended. "Perhaps it's the contrast—internal clarity against external chaos, instead of the reverse."

Farrat nodded, understanding without need for further elaboration. This had become one of the hallmarks of their connection—the ability to grasp the essence of each other's experience without requiring exhaustive articulation, to recognize the underlying patterns in each other's thought without demanding constant translation.

They moved to the comfortable seating area near the bookshelves, the arrangement of furniture creating a natural conversation space without forcing proximity. The chai was indeed remarkable—complex with spices and subtle sweetness, warming in a way that went beyond mere temperature to create a sense of well-being that spread from physical to emotional domains.

"May I ask you something?" Farrat inquired after they had both spent a moment appreciating the beverage. "About your experience of the fog?"

"You can ask," Tauree replied, her standard response to such requests—acknowledging that questions were permitted while reserving the right to decline answering.

"When we first discussed our respective forms of depression," Farrat continued, his tone thoughtful rather than probing, "you described the fog as varying in density but always present. Has that remained consistent throughout your life, or have there been periods where it lifted completely?"

The question was surprisingly specific—not a general inquiry about her condition but a precise exploration of its particular manifestation. Tauree considered it carefully, appreciating that

Farrat had framed it without presumption or pity, simply seeking to understand her experience more accurately.

"There have been brief moments," she said finally, her gaze directed toward the storm beyond the windows rather than at Farrat. "Usually associated with intense focus on a particular project or problem—a state of flow where my attention is so completely absorbed that the fog temporarily recedes from awareness. But it never disappears entirely, and it always returns when the focus breaks."

"And in interpersonal contexts?" Farrat asked, the question gentle but direct. "Has connection with others ever created similar moments of clarity?"

This was the more complex question—the one that probed beyond professional experience into the more vulnerable territory of relationships. Tauree took a sip of chai, using the moment to organize her thoughts.

"Not historically," she admitted, surprising herself with the candor of her response. "In fact, social interactions typically thickened the fog rather than dispersing it—the effort of performance, of translating between my internal experience and conventional expression, usually depleted rather than replenished my resources."

She paused, aware that she was approaching the boundary of what she typically disclosed about her emotional landscape. Yet something about the storm encasing them in this temporary universe, about the genuine attention in Farrat's expression, encouraged her to continue.

"Recently, however, there have been... exceptions to that pattern," she said quietly. "Conversations that somehow align with rather than oppose the fog's currents. Connections that require less translation, less performance."

The implication hung between them—that their relationship represented one such exception, that Farrat's particular way of engaging with her had somehow bypassed the usual barriers that separated her from genuine connection with others.

"I've had a similar experience with the rainfall," Farrat acknowledged, matching her vulnerability with his own. "Historically, relationships intensified rather than alleviated it—either because I absorbed others' emotional states too completely, or because maintaining appropriate boundaries required such vigilance that I exhausted myself in the process."

He glanced toward the window, where actual rain continued to lash against the glass with undiminished force. "The metaphor becomes almost too literal on a night like this," he observed with a small smile. "But yes, there have been recent exceptions to that pattern as well. Connections that somehow coexist with the rainfall rather than either drowning in it or attempting to dam it."

The parallel acknowledgment—that each had found in the other a rare exception to their usual experience of relationships—created a moment of profound connection between them. Neither needed to explicitly state what they both clearly recognized: that something unusual and valuable had developed between them, something that honored rather than ignored their respective challenges while creating space for genuine understanding to emerge.

Outside, a particularly loud crack of thunder punctuated this silent recognition, as if the elements themselves were responding to the significance of the moment. The lights flickered briefly but remained on, the building's old but solid construction providing steady shelter against the storm's assault.

"Your bookshelves are even more fascinating than you described," Tauree said after a moment, deliberately shifting toward lighter territory. "I'm trying to decipher the organizational logic, but I suspect it would require intimate knowledge of your reading history to fully comprehend."

Farrat accepted the transition with evident appreciation for its timing, his expression warming with genuine enthusiasm for the subject. "Would you like the guided tour? It won't make the system less idiosyncratic, but it might at least illuminate the method behind the apparent madness."

"I'd like that very much," Tauree replied, recognizing the invitation for what it was—not just an explanation of book arrangement, but a window into Farrat's internal landscape, the particular way his mind organized and connected ideas across conventional categories.

What followed was one of the most fascinating hours of Tauree's life. As Farrat led her through his bookshelves, explaining the emotional and intellectual connections that had guided his unusual cataloging system, she gained insight not just into his reading habits but into the unique architecture of his mind. Books were grouped not by genre or author or time period but by the particular quality of thought they provoked, the emotional terrain they explored, the questions they raised rather than the answers they provided.

"These all create the same sensation of vertigo at the edge of understanding," he explained, indicating a shelf that contained everything from advanced physics to mystical poetry to experimental fiction. "Not confusion exactly, but the specific feeling of recognizing that you're encountering something just beyond your current capacity to fully comprehend—like standing at a great height and feeling simultaneously terrified and exhilarated by the vastness below."

The description was so precise, so perfectly aligned with a sensation Tauree had experienced but never articulated, that she found herself nodding in immediate recognition. "I know exactly what you mean," she said. "It's how I felt when I first encountered certain architectural theories that fundamentally challenged my understanding of space and form."

"Exactly," Farrat confirmed, his expression lighting with the pleasure of being understood. "It's not about the subject matter at all, but about the particular quality of mental and emotional experience the work creates."

As they continued around the room, Farrat occasionally pulling down specific volumes to illustrate a point or share a particularly significant passage, Tauree found herself deeply moved by the experience. This was a different kind of intimacy than she had anticipated—not the physical proximity that overnight stays typically suggested, but a profound sharing of mental and emotional landscape, a guided tour through the territories that had shaped Farrat's particular way of understanding the world.

The storm provided a constant backdrop to their conversation, rain still hammering against the windows and occasional thunder punctuating their exchanges. But within the apartment, a different kind of weather had developed—a warm intellectual engagement that created its own microclimate of shared attention and mutual discovery.

Eventually, they settled back onto the comfortable seating, their discussion having evolved from specific books to broader questions of how different minds organize and process information. The conversation flowed with that same surprising ease Tauree had experienced during their previous encounters, moving between architecture and literature to psychology and philosophy with a natural fluidity that required no forced transitions or explanations.

"It's getting late," Farrat observed eventually, glancing at the clock with evident surprise at how much time had passed. "And it's been quite a day for both of us."

The observation—gentle but practical—acknowledged the reality of physical fatigue without diminishing the intellectual and emotional engagement they had shared. Once again, Farrat was creating space without pressure, offering options rather than expectations.

"Yes, it has," Tauree agreed, feeling the weight of the day's events settling into her awareness as the observation drew attention to the late hour. The initial dash through the rain to Serendipity Café seemed to have happened days rather than hours ago, so much had transpired between then and now.

"The guest room should have everything you need," Farrat continued, rising from his seat with that same considerate attention to her comfort that had characterized the entire evening. "But please let me know if there's anything else that would make you more comfortable."

"Thank you," Tauree said, the simple words encompassing gratitude for far more than just the practical hospitality he had offered. "For everything. This evening has been... unexpected, but quite remarkable."

"The best experiences often are," Farrat replied with a small smile, acknowledging the reference to their earlier characterization of their relationship. "Unexpected, but nice. Though in this case, 'nice' seems inadequate for the particular quality of conversation and connection."

The slight correction—elevating their standard phrase to acknowledge the special significance of the evening—created a moment of gentle intensity between them, a recognition that something valuable and rare had transpired amid the unlikely circumstances created by the storm.

As Tauree prepared for sleep in the thoughtfully appointed guest room, she found herself in an unfamiliar state of calm reflection rather than anxious analysis. The fog remained, as it always did—that persistent gray filter through which she experienced the world. But tonight it had thinned to a translucent veil rather than an obscuring cloud, allowing a clarity of perception and emotion that felt both unfamiliar and deeply right.

Outside, the storm continued its assault on the city, rain and wind and occasional thunder creating a symphony of elemental forces against which human structures could offer only temporary shelter. Yet within those shelters—within this particular space that Farrat had created and now shared—a different kind of weather prevailed. Not the fog of isolation nor the rainfall of overwhelming emotion, but something new and unnamed that honored both while creating its own distinct climate.

As Tauree drifted toward sleep, lulled by the rhythm of rain against the windows and the lingering warmth of chai and conversation, she found herself contemplating the curious trajectory that had brought her to this moment. From reluctant attendance at Amrita's tea party to this storm-mandated stay in Farrat's home, each step had seemed both unexpected and somehow inevitable—a path discovered only through the walking of it, a connection defined not by external labels but by the particular quality of understanding that had developed between them.

Tomorrow the storm would pass, roads would clear, and ordinary routines would resume. Yet Tauree knew with quiet certainty that something fundamental had shifted during this rainy afternoon and evening, something that could not be undone or forgotten once the skies cleared. Like the city itself, transformed temporarily by the deluge but permanently altered in subtle ways by its passage, their relationship had entered new territory—unmapped but full of possibility, challenging but rich with potential discovery.

With this thought, she surrendered to sleep, the sound of rain against the windows merging with dreams in which fog and rainfall somehow coexisted, creating not confusion but a new kind of clarity born from the meeting of different weathers, different ways of moving through the world that had found, against all expectation, a way to navigate together.

Act 2: The Build-Up and Growing Tension

Chapter 7: The Festival

The morning after the storm dawned with unexpected clarity, as if the night's deluge had not just cleared the streets but somehow purified the very air above the city. Tauree woke in Farrat's guest room, momentarily disoriented by the unfamiliar patterns of light playing across walls that were not her own. The events of the previous evening came back to her in a gentle wave—the rain-soaked dash to Serendipity Café, the candlelit conversations during the power outage, the drive through flooded streets to Farrat's apartment, and the remarkable hours spent exploring his emotionally organized bookshelves.

She lay still for a moment, assessing her internal weather. The fog was there, as always, but it remained the thin translucent veil of the night before rather than the thick cloud that often greeted her mornings. Something about the unexpected disruption to her routine—or perhaps the particular quality of connection she had experienced with Farrat—had temporarily altered her usual patterns, creating a space of unusual clarity within her typically muted perception.

The smell of coffee drifted through the apartment, rich and inviting. Tauree rose, finding her clothes from the previous day neatly folded outside her door—dry now, though bearing the slight rumpling that came from machine rather than air drying. She changed quickly, folding Farrat's borrowed clothes with precise care before making her way toward the kitchen.

Farrat stood by the large windows, a mug in his hand, contemplating the transformed city below. The storm had indeed passed, leaving behind a landscape washed clean, colors more vibrant against the backdrop of cleared skies. He turned at the sound of her approach, a smile warming his features.

"Good morning," he said. "I hope you slept well. The roads are clearing, according to the morning news, though there's still significant flooding in some areas."

"I did, thank you," Tauree replied, accepting the mug of coffee he offered—strong and black, just as she preferred. The small consideration—that he had remembered and prepared for her particular taste—created that now-familiar warmth in her chest. "Your guest room is remarkably comfortable."

"I'm glad," Farrat said simply. "There's bread for toast, or I can offer eggs if you'd prefer something more substantial."

The domestic exchange—focused on practical matters of morning routines—helped ease any potential awkwardness in this new context. They had crossed another threshold in their evolving relationship, yet there was no sense of boundaries being breached rather than mutually adjusted. Instead, there was a curious rightness to the progression, as if the storm had merely accelerated a natural trajectory already in motion.

As they shared a simple breakfast at Farrat's kitchen counter, watching the city gradually return to its normal rhythms below, conversation flowed with that same surprising ease Tauree had experienced during their previous encounters. They discussed the storm's impact, the quality of light on freshly washed buildings, the way crisis often revealed unexpected aspects of community and connection.

"There's something I wanted to mention," Farrat said eventually, his tone shifting slightly to indicate a change in subject. "The university hosts an annual cultural festival next weekend—music, art, food, various performances. It's actually quite remarkable—less academic than you might expect, more a genuine celebration of diverse creative expressions."

He paused, a hint of self-consciousness in his expression. "I've been asked to do a reading at one of the poetry events. Nothing as intimate as Seaview, a much more structured affair. But I thought...if you were interested, you might enjoy experiencing different aspects of the festival as well. Several architectural departments contribute installations, and the music is genuinely worth hearing."

The invitation hung between them—another opportunity to extend their connection beyond its established patterns, to witness each other in different contexts and surroundings. Tauree considered it carefully, weighing her usual reluctance to attend crowded events against her growing curiosity about the different facets of Farrat's life she had yet to observe.

"I'd like that," she said finally, the truth of it surprising even herself. "Though I should warn you, large gatherings typically exhaust me rather quickly."

"We could approach it strategically," Farrat suggested, understanding immediately the nature of her concern. "The festival spans the entire campus, with events spread throughout the day. We could create a selective itinerary, focusing on specific events with breaks for quiet and recovery between them. No obligation to stay for any particular duration."

The consideration in his proposal—acknowledging her limitations without treating them as flaws to be overcome—was characteristic of how Farrat consistently made space for her particular needs within their shared experiences. He never demanded that she conform to conventional patterns of social engagement, instead finding ways to adapt circumstances to accommodate her requirements for structure and periodic retreat.

"A strategic approach sounds perfect," Tauree agreed. "And I am curious to hear you read in a more formal setting. Your performance at Seaview was..." She paused, searching for words adequate to the complexity of that experience. "Illuminating."

A slight color rose in Farrat's cheeks at the reference to his poem about their day trip—the piece that had so directly addressed the evolving significance of their connection. "This will be different," he said. "Less personal, more academic in context. But perhaps still interesting, in its way."

Their planning was interrupted by Tauree's phone, which chimed with a message from her office. Several client meetings had been rescheduled due to storm-related disruptions, requiring her immediate attention to calendar adjustments. The practical demands of professional life asserting themselves felt like a return to familiar territory after the unusually intimate interlude created by the storm.

"I should go," she said, finishing her coffee with reluctance. "The office will be in chaos today, with everyone trying to reorganize around yesterday's disruptions."

"Of course," Farrat replied, rising to clear their breakfast dishes with unaffected ease. "I'll drive you, if that would help. The public transportation system may still be compromised."

The offer—practical rather than possessive—maintained the balance they had established throughout their evolving connection. Farrat consistently provided options rather than expectations, support without demand. It was this quality, perhaps more than any other, that had allowed Tauree to gradually adjust her boundaries without feeling threatened or overwhelmed.

The drive to her office was companionable, their conversation flowing naturally between reflections on the previous evening and more practical considerations about the week ahead. As they navigated streets still bearing evidence of the storm's passage—fallen branches, occasional standing water, cleanup crews working to restore order—Tauree found herself contemplating the curious parallel between the city's transformation and her own internal landscape. Both had experienced an unexpected disruption that had temporarily altered familiar patterns, both were now returning to normal function while subtly changed by what had transpired.

When they reached her office building, Farrat pulled into a loading zone near the entrance, putting on his hazard lights to indicate a brief stop. The moment of parting carried a subtle weight—the transition from the intimate space created by the storm back into their separate professional worlds.

"Thank you," Tauree said simply. "For everything. The shelter, the conversation, the—" She paused, searching for a word that could encompass the particular quality of connection they had shared. "The weather reports," she finished with a small smile, referencing their metaphorical language for their respective forms of depression.

Farrat's answering smile reached his eyes, warming with recognition of the reference. "Any time," he replied. "Though perhaps next time we could arrange it without requiring a historic storm as catalyst."

"I'd like that," Tauree said, the simple affirmation feeling significant in its unqualified directness.

As she exited the car, there was no awkward moment of determining the appropriate farewell gesture—no social hug, no handshake, no physical contact that might complicate the careful balance they maintained. Instead, there was simply an exchange of smiles, a silent acknowledgment of something valuable shared and something more awaiting future exploration.

"I'll send you details about the festival," Farrat said. "You can decide which events interest you most, and we can plan accordingly."

"Perfect," Tauree replied. "I look forward to it."

As she watched his car pull away, rejoining the flow of traffic that was gradually returning to normal volume and rhythm, Tauree experienced none of the usual relief that typically accompanied the conclusion of extended social engagement. Instead, there was a curious sense of continuation—as if their connection remained active even in physical separation, a conversation merely paused rather than concluded.

The week that followed unfolded with a familiar rhythm of professional demands and structured routines. Tauree immersed herself in the community center project, working closely with contractors to refine the reading nook that had become the heart of the design. The fog fluctuated in its density—thicker on some days than others, occasionally receding to that unusual translucency she had experienced the morning after the storm. She found herself increasingly aware of these variations, more attuned to the subtle weather patterns of her internal landscape.

Farrat's messages arrived at thoughtful intervals—never demanding immediate response, always offering something of substance rather than mere social maintenance. He sent a detailed program of the university festival, annotated with personal recommendations and practical notes about crowd density, acoustic quality, and optimal viewing positions for various events. There were occasional fragments of poetry he encountered in his reading, observations about architecture he noticed during his walks, and once, a photograph of an unusual cloud formation that resembled the organizational pattern of his bookshelves.

Each communication felt like a continuation of their ongoing conversation, a bridge extending across the physical distance between their separate lives. Tauree found herself responding with similar offerings—a sketch of the refined reading nook design, a passage from an architectural theory text that had resonated with their discussions of space and meaning, a wry observation about her colleagues' post-storm coffee consumption rates.

By the time the weekend of the festival arrived, they had established a detailed itinerary that balanced Tauree's need for structure and periodic retreat with their shared interests in various events. The schedule included Farrat's reading, selected musical performances, a visit to the architectural installations, and—most importantly—designated breaks in quiet spaces where Tauree could recover from the social stimulation.

They arranged to meet at a small café on the edge of campus—a strategic choice that allowed Tauree to approach the festival gradually rather than being immediately immersed in its full intensity. As she walked from the parking area on that bright Saturday morning, she could already hear distant music and the ambient sounds of celebration drifting across the university grounds.

Farrat was waiting at an outdoor table, his tall figure immediately recognizable even from a distance. He wore dark jeans and a deep green button-down shirt—more formal than his usual casual attire, a concession perhaps to his later role as performer rather than merely spectator. He rose as she approached, that same smile warming his features, reaching his eyes with genuine pleasure at her arrival.

"You came," he said, echoing their now-familiar greeting ritual.

"I said I would," Tauree replied, completing the exchange with a small smile of her own. "Though I reserve the right to strategic retreat if the crowds become overwhelming."

"Absolutely," Farrat agreed without hesitation. "I've actually scouted several potential sanctuary spaces while walking the grounds this morning. The library's rare book reading room is practically deserted, and there's a small courtyard behind the humanities building that seems to exist in a different acoustic universe from the rest of campus."

The consideration in this preparation—that he had actively sought out places where she might find respite if needed—created that now-familiar warmth in Tauree's chest. Farrat consistently demonstrated understanding of her particular needs without treating them as limitations to be overcome or accommodated with reluctance. Instead, he incorporated them into their shared planning as natural factors to be addressed, no different from checking the weather before a picnic or confirming opening hours before visiting a museum.

They began with a visit to the architectural installations, strategically scheduled early while the crowds were still relatively thin. Graduate students from the university's design program had created a series of temporary structures throughout the central campus, each exploring different relationships between form, function, and human experience. Some were purely conceptual—exercises in theoretical space that privileged idea over usability. Others were remarkably practical—elegant solutions to specific environmental or social challenges.

Tauree moved through the exhibition with professional interest, her analytical mind engaging with the technical aspects of each design while also observing the emotional responses they evoked in visitors. Farrat walked beside her, occasionally offering observations from his literary perspective—noting how certain structures created narratives through their spatial progressions, how others evoked particular emotional states through their manipulation of light and shadow.

"This one reminds me of your community center reading nook," he observed, pausing before a small pavilion designed to create a contemplative space within the busy festival environment. "The way it's simultaneously open to the surrounding context yet creates a distinct psychological territory within it. A boundary that connects rather than separates."

The parallel—drawing on their shared vocabulary of architectural and emotional space—was characteristic of how they had come to communicate, each consistently translating between their separate disciplines to create bridges of understanding. Tauree found herself nodding in agreement, appreciating both the technical accuracy and the deeper resonance of his observation.

"The student has a good grasp of graduated transitions," she noted, examining the subtle shifts in material and proportion that guided visitors from the exterior environment into the more contained interior space. "Though I would have adjusted the overhead plane to create more variation in the quality of light."

As they continued through the exhibition, Tauree became aware of a gradual increase in the festival's energy around them. More people filled the pathways, music from various performance stages created an overlapping soundscape, and the scents of diverse foods from the international booths began to permeate the air. The stimulation level was rising, though still within manageable parameters for her particular sensitivities.

"Are you ready for some music?" Farrat asked, attentive as always to her changing state. "Or would you prefer one of those sanctuary breaks we scheduled?"

"Music, I think," Tauree replied after a moment's internal assessment. "Though perhaps from the periphery rather than the center of the audience."

They made their way to one of the smaller performance areas, where a chamber ensemble was preparing to play a program of contemporary compositions. Farrat guided them to a spot at the edge of the gathering, partially shaded by a large oak tree that provided both physical and psychological shelter from the increasing crowd. The position was perfect—close enough to appreciate the music fully, yet with an open path for retreat if needed.

The music itself was unexpectedly moving—complex without being inaccessible, emotionally resonant without becoming sentimental. Tauree found herself drawn into the intricate conversations between instruments, the way themes were introduced, developed, and transformed through the composer's careful orchestration. Beside her, Farrat listened with similar attention, his expression revealing a depth of engagement that matched her own.

During a particularly beautiful passage—a cello line that seemed to speak directly to some unnamed longing—Tauree glanced at Farrat and found him already looking at her, a curious intensity in his expression. For a moment, they held each other's gaze, the music creating a bridge between them more direct than words could have achieved. Then, with a small smile that acknowledged the shared experience, they both returned their attention to the performance.

After the concert concluded, they made their way to one of the designated sanctuary spaces Farrat had identified—the small courtyard behind the humanities building. The transition was perfectly timed, as Tauree could feel the first edges of overstimulation beginning to press against her consciousness, the fog threatening to thicken in response to the accumulated sensory input of the morning.

The courtyard was indeed remarkably peaceful—a small, enclosed garden with stone benches arranged around a simple fountain. The walls of the surrounding buildings blocked most of the festival noise, creating an acoustic oasis where conversation could proceed without competition from external sources. They settled onto one of the benches, the gentle sound of water providing a soothing backdrop to their exchange.

"How are you finding it so far?" Farrat asked, his tone carrying genuine interest rather than polite social inquiry.

"Better than I expected," Tauree replied honestly. "Your strategic planning has made a significant difference. Being able to engage selectively rather than attempting to absorb everything at once changes the experience entirely."

"I'm glad," Farrat said simply. "It's a fine balance—participating enough to appreciate what the festival offers while respecting your particular response to stimulation. Not unlike my own relationship with certain kinds of social environments."

The observation—drawing a parallel between their different but related challenges—created that sense of mutual recognition that had become foundational to their connection. They were indeed approaching from opposite directions, as Farrat had noted during their day trip to Seaview, but facing similar questions about how to navigate a world whose default settings often failed to accommodate their particular needs.

They spent half an hour in the quiet courtyard, their conversation flowing with that same surprising ease Tauree had experienced during their previous encounters. They discussed the architectural installations, the emotional landscapes evoked by the music, and the curious sociology of festival environments—how they temporarily suspended ordinary social conventions while imposing their own distinct rules of engagement.

As they prepared to rejoin the festival, Farrat glanced at his watch. "My reading is in about an hour," he said. "There's a small food court near the humanities stage where we could get lunch before then, if you're hungry."

"That sounds perfect," Tauree agreed, feeling genuinely restored by their period of retreat.

The food court turned out to be a collection of international vendors representing cuisines from around the world—a global village contained within the university grounds. The diversity of options was impressive, though potentially overwhelming in its abundance of choice. Without discussion, they fell into a natural division of labor: Farrat navigated the various stalls to gather their selections while Tauree secured a table at the periphery of the seating area, where they could observe the festival activity without being directly immersed in it.

As they shared dishes from Lebanon, Japan, and Ethiopia—a multicultural feast that somehow worked in harmonious combination—Tauree found herself increasingly aware of a subtle shift in Farrat's demeanor. A thoughtful tension had entered his expression, a slight furrow between his brows that suggested he was mentally preparing for his upcoming performance.

"Are you nervous about the reading?" she asked, the directness characteristic of their communication.

Farrat considered the question with his usual thoughtfulness. "Not nervous exactly," he replied. "But definitely conscious of the transition required—from private individual to public performer. It always takes a certain mental adjustment, a shift in how I relate to both the words and the audience."

"Like adapting to different acoustic environments," Tauree suggested, drawing a parallel to musical performance that seemed to resonate with his experience.

"Exactly," Farrat agreed, appreciation for the metaphor evident in his expression. "Different spaces require different presentations of the same essential material. What works in the intimate setting of Seaview would feel inauthentic in the more formal academic context."

"Will you be reading published work or new material?" Tauree asked, genuinely curious about this aspect of his creative life she had glimpsed only briefly during their coastal trip.

"Some of each," Farrat replied. "The organizers requested certain pieces that appeared in a university literary journal last year, but I've included some newer work as well. Though nothing quite as..." He paused, searching for the right word. "Nothing quite as personally revelatory as what I shared at Seaview."

The reference to his poem about their day trip—"The Long Drive" with its direct exploration of their evolving connection—created a moment of shared recollection between them. Tauree could still recall specific lines from that piece, the precision with which he had articulated the transformative effect of their relationship, how each had begun to experience the world partly through the other's perspective.

"That makes sense," she acknowledged. "Different contexts, different aspects of the work. Like how I might present a design differently to contractors than to clients or community stakeholders."

"Precisely," Farrat said, his expression warming with the familiar pleasure of being understood. "Each audience requires its own particular framing, its own vocabulary of engagement."

As they finished their meal and began making their way toward the humanities stage where Farrat's reading would take place, Tauree found herself increasingly curious about this aspect of his life she was about to witness. She had heard him read in the intimate setting of the Seaview boathouse, had discussed his poetry in detail during their various conversations, but had not yet seen him in his professional context as an academic and recognized literary figure.

The humanities stage had been set up in a natural amphitheater—a gently sloping lawn that created excellent sightlines to the elevated platform where performances would take place. A substantial crowd had already gathered, larger than Tauree had anticipated for a poetry reading. She recognized some faces from the art gallery—Farrat's former colleagues and students, members of the university community who clearly knew his work and had come specifically to hear him.

"I should go prepare," Farrat said as they reached the periphery of the audience. "There's a spot over there, beneath that Japanese maple, that should offer good viewing while remaining outside the densest part of the crowd. Would that work for you?"

Once again, his consideration of her particular needs manifested in practical attention to detail rather than general concern. He had identified a specific location that would allow her to engage with the performance without being overwhelmed by the surrounding audience, had created space for her participation on terms that respected her sensitivities.

"Perfect," Tauree confirmed, genuinely appreciating both the suggestion and the understanding behind it. "I'll be fine. Go prepare for your reading."

As Farrat moved toward the staging area, Tauree made her way to the spot he had indicated. The Japanese maple did indeed create a perfect vantage point—its spreading branches offering dappled shade against the afternoon sun, its position providing clear views of the stage while maintaining a comfortable distance from the more densely packed central audience. She settled onto the grass, noticing how the tree's canopy created a natural frame for the stage, enhancing rather than obstructing her experience of the upcoming performance.

Several other poets read before Farrat, their styles and subjects varying widely—from intensely personal confessional verse to more experimental linguistic explorations. The audience received each with respectful attention, though Tauree noticed a subtle shift in energy when the emcee announced Farrat's name, a perceptible increase in anticipation that suggested his work was particularly valued within this community.

When Farrat stepped onto the stage, Tauree was struck by a curious transformation in his presence. The quiet, thoughtful man with whom she had shared coffee and conversation seemed to expand slightly, occupying the public space with a calm authority that commanded attention without demanding it. His posture straightened, his voice took on that quality she had noticed at Seaview—slightly deeper, more resonant, accessing a different register of himself for the performance context.

"Thank you for the kind welcome," he began, adjusting the microphone with practiced ease. "I'll be reading a selection of poems exploring the relationship between internal and external landscapes—how our perception shapes the territories we inhabit, and how those territories, in turn, influence our understanding of ourselves."

The theme—so aligned with their ongoing conversations about fog and rainfall, about emotional and physical architecture—created an immediate connection between this public performance and their private exchanges. Farrat hadn't mentioned this framing during their earlier discussions of his reading, and Tauree wondered if it represented a recent crystallization of ideas they had been developing together through their dialogues.

The first poem explored the concept of thresholds—those transitional spaces between defined territories that were neither fully one thing nor another. Farrat's voice gave each word precise weight and rhythm, his pacing creating a sense of gradual movement through the conceptual landscape he was describing. The piece resonated strongly with Tauree's architectural sensibilities, her professional attention to how humans experience transitions between different types of spaces.

As the reading continued, Tauree found herself increasingly absorbed in both the content of the poetry and the particular quality of Farrat's performance. There was nothing showy or theatrical about his presentation—no dramatic gestures or artificial intensity—yet he commanded complete attention through the authentic engagement he brought to each piece. The words seemed to emerge not just from his voice but from some deeper source of connection to their meaning, a embodied understanding that transcended mere recitation.

The final poem was introduced with a slight shift in Farrat's tone, a barely perceptible hesitation that suggested particular significance.

"This last piece is new," he said, "still finding its final form. It explores how we create internal architectures to house our experiences—structures of meaning that both contain and shape our understanding of what we've lived."

As he began to read, Tauree immediately recognized elements that echoed their conversations about her architectural approach and his poetic one—the parallel ways they created order from chaos, meaning from experience. Though the poem contained no direct references to their relationship, its exploration of how different minds might create bridges between their separate perceptual worlds carried unmistakable resonances of their evolving connection.

The audience responded with the most enthusiastic applause of the afternoon, several listeners rising to their feet in appreciation. Farrat acknowledged this response with a modest nod, his public persona maintaining that perfect balance between confidence and humility that Tauree had observed in his private interactions as well. He thanked the audience simply, then stepped away from the microphone, transitioning smoothly from performer back to private individual as he left the stage.

Tauree remained beneath the Japanese maple, processing both the content of the poetry and her emotional response to witnessing this dimension of Farrat's life. She had always known he was respected in academic and literary circles—their encounter with his former student at the art gallery had made that clear—but experiencing directly the impact of his work on others created a new appreciation for the public aspect of his identity she had previously encountered only through his personal disclosures.

"What did you think?"

The voice came from beside her, and Tauree turned to find Priya, the former student they had met at the art gallery, settling onto the grass nearby. Her expression held genuine curiosity mixed with a hint of knowing amusement, as if she had deliberately sought out Tauree among the dispersing audience.

"It was remarkable," Tauree replied honestly. "The way he constructs relationships between abstract concepts and lived experience is quite profound."

"That's one of his gifts," Priya agreed with evident admiration. "Making philosophical inquiries feel personally relevant, finding the universal in the specific. Though I noticed something different in today's reading—especially that final piece."

"Oh?" Tauree responded, careful to maintain neutral interest despite her internal alertness to this observation from someone who clearly knew Farrat's work well.

"There's a new quality to the work," Priya elaborated, her perception clearly extending beyond casual appreciation to more analytical engagement. "His earlier poetry often examined connection from a position of careful distance—observing rather than participating. This new piece feels more...embedded in the experience it describes. As if he's writing from within rather than about."

The assessment was surprisingly insightful, aligning with what Tauree had observed in the evolution of Farrat's poetry from the fragments he had shared with her over the months of their acquaintance. There was indeed a shift occurring in his relationship to his subject matter, a move from observational distance toward more direct engagement that paralleled changes in how he approached their evolving connection.

"I'm not familiar enough with his earlier work to make that comparison," Tauree replied, a technical truth that avoided either confirming or denying Priya's observation. "But the poem was certainly powerful in its exploration of how we structure meaning."

Priya studied her with renewed interest, clearly noting the careful neutrality of her response. "Well, as his former student, I've read everything he's published, attended all his local readings. And I've never heard him dedicate a public performance to the relationship between internal and external landscapes—which happens to be exactly what you two were discussing at the gallery when I interrupted you."

The directness of the observation—connecting their private conversation to his public presentation—created a moment of unexpected vulnerability. Tauree felt exposed, not by anything she had done or said, but by the perceptible influence their connection had exerted on Farrat's creative work, visible now to others with sufficient context to recognize the patterns.

Before she could formulate a response that neither confirmed nor denied this connection, she spotted Farrat making his way through the dispersing crowd toward them. He moved with that same understated confidence she had observed on stage, accepting brief congratulations from audience members with gracious nods but continuing purposefully in their direction.

"Priya," he acknowledged as he reached them, his tone warm but slightly cautious as he noted her presence beside Tauree. "I didn't know you were attending the festival."

"I wouldn't miss your reading, Professor," Priya replied with genuine enthusiasm. "Especially since the department newsletter hinted you might be sharing new work. Which was absolutely worth hearing, by the way. Particularly that final piece about internal architectures."

"Thank you," Farrat said simply, his gaze moving between Priya and Tauree with a hint of uncertainty about the nature of their interaction. "I hope I'm not interrupting an important conversation."

"Not at all," Priya assured him, rising from the grass with a quick, graceful movement. "I was just sharing my critical appreciation with your friend here, who was kind enough to humor my analytical tendencies." She glanced at her phone, then added, "And now I'm actually late for meeting friends at the international dance performance. It was good seeing you both again."

With a wave and a knowing smile, she departed, leaving Tauree and Farrat in a moment of curious adjustment—their private connection having been observed and commented upon, if indirectly, by someone who knew enough to recognize its influence on his creative work.

"She's perceptive," Tauree observed as Farrat settled onto the grass beside her, the simple statement acknowledging what had transpired without requiring elaboration.

"Extremely," Farrat agreed with a small sigh. "One of her greatest strengths as a student, and occasionally a challenge in more personal contexts." He glanced at Tauree, a hint of concern in his expression. "I hope she wasn't too intrusive with her observations."

"Not at all," Tauree assured him. "Just enthusiastically analytical about your work. It was actually rather interesting to hear her perspective on how your poetry has evolved."

A flash of self-consciousness crossed Farrat's features. "I should have mentioned that the theme of today's reading was inspired by our conversations," he said. "It wasn't a deliberate omission—more that the connection seemed so natural to me that I didn't think to articulate it explicitly."

"No explanation was necessary," Tauree replied, the simple reassurance reflecting their established pattern of giving each other space without demanding constant disclosure. "The work stands on its own, regardless of its inspirations. And it was beautiful, Farrat. Truly."

The sincerity in her voice created a moment of quiet connection between them, an acknowledgment of something valuable shared through his creative expression. Farrat's smile warmed his features, reaching his eyes with genuine pleasure at her response to his work.

"Thank you," he said simply. "That means a great deal, coming from someone who understands so precisely the relationships between structure and meaning, between form and emotional experience."

As they sat beneath the dappled shade of the Japanese maple, the festival continuing around them with its vibrant energy and diverse expressions, Tauree found herself contemplating the curious evolution of their connection. From that first reluctant conversation at Amrita's tea party to this moment of shared creative resonance, each interaction had built upon the last, creating a relationship unlike any she had previously experienced—neither demanding complete merger nor maintaining rigid separation, but establishing a permeable boundary across which genuine understanding could flow in both directions.

"What would you like to experience next?" Farrat asked, after they had spent a comfortable interlude processing the reading and its aftermath. "There's an international dance performance that sounds remarkable, or we could visit the visual arts exhibition, or perhaps you'd prefer one of our scheduled sanctuary breaks to recover from the morning's stimulation."

The consideration in the question—offering options rather than expectations, space rather than pressure—remained one of the constants in their evolving relationship. Farrat consistently created room for her particular needs without treating them as limitations to be overcome or accommodated with reluctance. It was this quality, perhaps more than any other, that had allowed Tauree to gradually adjust her boundaries without feeling threatened or overwhelmed.

"Actually," she said, surprising herself with the suggestion that formed, "I think I'd like to experience some of the festival food areas again. The international offerings were quite remarkable, and I've always found cultural exploration through cuisine to be less overwhelming than some other forms of engagement."

"I know exactly the section we should visit next, then," Farrat replied, his expression brightening with enthusiasm. "There's a collection of street food vendors from across South Asia that a colleague mentioned was particularly authentic. If you're interested in cultural expressions through food, it would be a perfect next experience."

They made their way through the festival grounds, navigating the increasing crowds with careful attention to maintaining comfortable space around them. Farrat seemed to have an intuitive sense of how to create pathways through the busiest areas, guiding Tauree along less congested routes without being obvious or protective about the accommodation.

The South Asian street food section was indeed a remarkable cultural experience—a collection of vendors offering regional specialties from across India, Pakistan, Bangladesh, and Sri Lanka. The aromas alone created an immersive sensory experience, a complex layering of spices and cooking techniques that spoke to centuries of culinary tradition and innovation.

They approached the exploration methodically, Farrat occasionally providing historical or cultural context for particular dishes based on his academic knowledge of the region's literature and history. Tauree found herself genuinely enjoying the process of selecting small portions from various vendors, creating a progressive tasting menu that allowed them to experience a remarkable diversity of flavors and techniques.

As they shared a particularly delicious chicken kathi roll from a Bengali vendor, Tauree noticed a small crowd gathering near a central area where some kind of demonstration appeared to be taking place. The energy felt different from the more structured performances they had witnessed earlier—more participatory, with people being invited from the audience to join whatever was happening at the center.

"What's going on there?" she asked, curious despite her usual wariness of crowd dynamics.

"Ah," Farrat replied, following her gaze. "That would be the folk dance demonstrations. Each hour they feature traditions from a different region, teaching simple steps to anyone who wishes to participate. I believe this session is focused on Punjabi bhangra, which is particularly energetic and joyful."

As if to confirm his explanation, the sound of dhol drums suddenly filled the air—a driving, infectious rhythm that seemed to physically affect those who heard it. People were clapping along with the beat, and at the center of the gathering, instructors demonstrated basic movements that audience members attempted to follow with varying degrees of success and abandon.

"Would you like to observe from a distance?" Farrat asked, noting her attention to the gathering. "There's a good vantage point over there where we could see without being drawn into participation."

The consideration in his suggestion—assuming her preference for observation over participation—was characteristic of how he consistently respected her boundaries without making her feel limited by them. Yet today, something about the infectious energy of the music, the joyful abandon of the participants, and perhaps the gradual accumulation of positive experiences throughout the day created an unexpected impulse in Tauree.

"Actually," she said, surprising herself as much as Farrat, "I think I might like to try it. Not at the center of the crowd, of course, but perhaps at the periphery where we could join without being too surrounded."

Farrat's expression registered momentary surprise before warming into genuine pleasure at her unexpected interest. "Are you sure? There's no obligation at all."

"I'm not sure at all," Tauree admitted with a small laugh that felt unexpectedly free. "Which is precisely why I think I should try it. I rarely experience spontaneous impulses, especially in crowded public settings. It seems... significant."

Farrat nodded, understanding immediately the importance of what she was describing—not just a casual interest in dance but a rare moment of the fog lifting enough to allow genuine spontaneity, an unplanned response to present circumstances rather than careful calculation of risks and benefits.

"Then we should definitely honor the impulse," he said, offering his hand to help her rise from their seated position. "And I promise a strategic retreat the moment it feels overwhelming."

They approached the dance area carefully, finding a spot at the outer edge of the gathering where they could participate without being enclosed by the crowd. The instructors were demonstrating simple bhangra steps—energetic movements with emphasis on shoulder and arm positions, rhythmic stomping that connected dancers directly to the earth beneath them. The motions were structured enough to be learnable but expressive enough to allow personal interpretation.

Tauree watched carefully, her architect's eye analyzing the patterns of movement, the relationship between individual expression and collective harmony. Beside her, Farrat began to follow along with the instructions, his movements surprisingly fluid for someone whose physical presence she had always experienced as thoughtfully contained. There was a subtle grace in how he interpreted the steps, an unself-conscious joy that revealed yet another dimension of him she hadn't previously witnessed.

Taking a deep breath, Tauree began to attempt the movements herself—tentatively at first, focusing on the technical aspects of foot placement and arm position. The rhythm of the dhol provided a clear structure, a framework within which expression could safely occur.

Gradually, as she grew more comfortable with the basic patterns, she found herself responding more directly to the music itself, her body finding natural ways to interpret the driving beat.

"You're a natural!" Farrat observed, his expression bright with genuine delight at her participation. "The movements suit you."

"It's just applied physics," Tauree replied with mock seriousness, though she couldn't suppress the smile that rose in response to his encouragement. "Momentum, balance, rhythmic coordination—all very scientific."

Farrat laughed, the sound mixing with the music around them. "Of course. Purely technical consideration of mass and motion. Nothing at all to do with joy or expression."

As they continued following the instructor's lead, moving through increasingly complex sequences while maintaining their comfortable position at the periphery, Tauree found herself experiencing a rare moment of unselfconscious presence. The fog had receded to the barest hint at the edges of her awareness, allowing an unusual immediacy of experience—the sensation of movement, the collective energy of the crowd, the expression of something vital and ancient through contemporary bodies.

More surprising still was the awareness of connection with Farrat through this shared physical experience. Their previous interactions had been primarily intellectual and emotional, expressed through conversation and selective disclosure. This was different—a parallel engagement with rhythm and movement, a synchronization of response to the same external stimulus that created a new dimension to their evolving relationship.

The dance session lasted only about fifteen minutes, the perfect duration for maintaining energy without exhausting participants. As the music concluded and the crowd began to disperse, Tauree found herself slightly breathless but remarkably energized—a different quality of stimulation than what she typically experienced in social settings, more invigorating than depleting.

"That was..." She paused, searching for words adequate to the unexpected quality of the experience. "That was not what I expected."

"In a positive way, I hope?" Farrat asked, studying her expression with attentive interest.

"Definitely positive," Tauree confirmed. "Though I'm not sure I can articulate exactly why. Something about the structured spontaneity of it—the clear framework that still allows for personal expression. Not unlike good architectural design, now that I think about it."

Farrat nodded, his expression reflecting appreciation for the parallel she had drawn. "Dance and architecture are both arts of defined space and human movement through it," he observed. "Both create experiences that are simultaneously physical and emotional, technical and expressive."

As they moved away from the dance area, finding a quieter spot to recover from the energetic engagement, Tauree found herself contemplating this unexpected highlight of the festival experience. In planning their day, she had anticipated enjoying the architectural installations and Farrat's poetry reading, had prepared herself to manage the challenges of crowds and stimulation. What she hadn't anticipated was discovering this new capacity for spontaneous engagement, this ability to participate rather than merely observe when conditions aligned properly.

"I think I understand now why you included dance in our potential itinerary," she said as they settled onto a bench beneath the shade of a large elm tree. "Despite my never having expressed interest in it."

"Did I?" Farrat asked, seeming genuinely unsure about this detail of their planning.

"Yes, it was on your annotated program, marked as 'optional but potentially interesting from an architectural perspective—human bodies creating temporary spatial patterns.'"

Farrat smiled at her precise recall of his notes. "Well, it seems my intuition was better than my conscious reasoning. I honestly didn't expect you'd want to participate, but I thought the patterns might interest you as an observer."

"Your intuition often perceives possibilities I haven't recognized in myself," Tauree observed, the insight emerging as she spoke. "Not in a presumptuous way, but in how you create space for options beyond what I might typically choose."

The observation—acknowledging his role in gradually expanding her range of experiences—created a moment of gentle intensity between them. Farrat's expression softened, a hint of vulnerability crossing his features.

"I try to be careful with that," he said quietly. "To offer without expecting, to create openings without pressure to enter them. After my experiences with Leila and others, I became acutely aware of how easily invitation can become expectation, how subtle the line between encouraging and demanding can be."

"You navigate it beautifully," Tauree assured him, the simple compliment carrying the weight of genuine appreciation. "Which is why I find myself trying things I wouldn't attempt with others. The space you create feels... safe. Even when the activities themselves might not be."

Farrat's smile warmed his features, reaching his eyes with genuine pleasure at her assessment. "That might be the most meaningful feedback I've ever received," he said simply.

As the afternoon progressed toward evening, they continued their strategic navigation of the festival, balancing periods of engagement with necessary retreats to quieter spaces. They visited the visual arts exhibition, where student work displayed a remarkable range of techniques and perspectives. They listened to traditional music from Central Asia, the unfamiliar tonal patterns creating an almost meditative experience of attentive listening. Throughout, they maintained that careful balance between participation and observation, stimulation and recovery that allowed Tauree to enjoy the event without becoming overwhelmed by it.

The final scheduled event of their day was an outdoor film screening set to begin as sunset approached—an international selection of short films to be projected against the white wall of the humanities building. The setting was perfect for comfortable viewing—an open lawn where attendees could spread blankets at whatever distance felt appropriate, creating natural spacing between groups without formal separation.

Farrat had come prepared with a small blanket, which he spread on a gentle slope that offered excellent sightlines to the projection area while maintaining comfortable distance from other viewers. As they settled onto this temporary territory, the day's accumulated experiences created a pleasant weariness in Tauree—not the depleted exhaustion she typically associated with extended social engagement, but a satisfied fatigue that spoke of meaningful activity and genuine connection.

"How are you feeling?" Farrat asked, attentive as always to her changing state throughout the day. "Has it been too much? We could still make a graceful exit before the films begin."

"I'm actually doing remarkably well," Tauree replied, somewhat surprised by the accuracy of this assessment. "Tired, certainly, but not in the way I usually experience after social events. This feels more like... productive exhaustion. Like after completing a challenging design project."

"I know exactly what you mean," Farrat said, nodding in recognition. "The satisfaction of having engaged fully with something meaningful, rather than the depletion that comes from performing social rituals that serve no deeper purpose."

As darkness gradually descended and more people gathered for the screening, soft lights illuminated the pathways around the viewing area while leaving the central space in strategic darkness for optimal projection. The effect was both practical and atmospheric—providing safety while enhancing the cinematic experience. Tauree found herself appreciating the thoughtful design, the careful balance between functional necessity and aesthetic experience.

The films themselves were diverse in both content and technique—experimental animations from Japan, a documentary about traditional craft preservation in Peru, a narrative piece exploring family relationships in Nigeria. Each offered a window into different human experiences, different ways of perceiving and representing the world. Between selections, Tauree and Farrat exchanged observations in quiet voices, their ongoing conversation enhancing rather than distracting from the viewing experience.

During the final film—a poetic exploration of urban architecture in Barcelona that seemed particularly selected to appeal to Tauree's professional interests—she became aware of a subtle shift in their physical proximity. Whether through gradual adjustment over the course of the screening or a more deliberate repositioning, they were now sitting close enough that their shoulders occasionally brushed when either moved. The contact was minimal but undeniably present, creating a new dimension of connection beyond their usual intellectual and emotional engagement.

More surprising than the proximity itself was Tauree's response to it. Rather than feeling invaded or overwhelmed, she experienced a curious comfort in this modest physical connection—a natural extension of the understanding they had developed through months of careful conversation and selective disclosure. There was no expectation in the contact, no demand for escalation or reciprocation, simply a quiet acknowledgment of shared territory, both physical and emotional.

As the credits rolled on the final film and gentle applause spread through the audience, neither moved immediately to increase distance. Instead, they remained in that position of casual contact as they discussed the film's artistic merits and technical achievements, its particular approach to documenting architectural space and human movement within it.

"The filmmaker had an excellent eye for how light transforms structural elements throughout the day," Tauree observed. "Almost like your apartment with its carefully positioned lamps—creating different experiences of the same physical space through strategic illumination."

"I was thinking the same thing," Farrat replied, glancing at her with that now-familiar pleasure of shared perspective. "Though I was connecting it to your community center design—how the reading nook changes character as the light shifts through your precisely positioned skylights."

The parallel observations—each referencing the other's private space rather than focusing exclusively on the film—created a moment of quiet recognition between them. Their evolving relationship had indeed reached a point where each other's environments had become reference points for understanding new experiences, where the territories they had shared had begun to influence how they perceived the world beyond their direct connection.

Around them, the audience was dispersing gradually, some lingering to discuss the films while others headed toward the festival's evening music events or began making their way toward campus exits. The day was concluding, the structured itinerary they had planned now complete, yet neither seemed in particular hurry to declare the experience finished.

"Would you like to get some tea before heading home?" Farrat suggested as they finally rose from their blanket, his movements unhurried as he folded the fabric with precise care. "There's a small café at the edge of campus that should be relatively quiet compared to the festival proper. A gentle transition back to ordinary reality."

The invitation—offering continuation without assumption—maintained that careful balance they had established throughout their evolving connection. Farrat consistently created space for her to determine the parameters of their engagement, to set boundaries based on her current capacity rather than external expectations or conventional patterns.

"I'd like that," Tauree replied, the simple affirmation feeling natural rather than calculated. "A gradual decompression sounds perfect."

As they walked through the festival grounds toward the campus periphery, Tauree found herself reflecting on the unexpected richness of the day's experiences. She had anticipated enjoying certain aspects of the festival—the architectural installations, Farrat's poetry reading—while enduring others as necessary components of the social contract. What she hadn't expected was discovering new capacities within herself, new possibilities for engagement that emerged when conditions aligned properly.

The dance participation remained particularly significant in her mind—that rare moment of spontaneous response to present circumstances rather than careful calculation of risks and benefits. Something about the combination of Farrat's consistent respect for her boundaries, the festival's inherent permission for experimental behavior, and perhaps her own gradual evolution through their months of connection had created space for this unexpected expression.

The café Farrat had suggested proved to be exactly as he had described—a small establishment at the campus edge, far enough from the festival's main activities to offer relative quiet while still carrying some of the day's energy in its atmosphere. They found a table near the window, where they could observe the gentle flow of pedestrians against the backdrop of early evening, the festival lights creating pools of color and activity in the distance.

Their tea arrived—a fragrant jasmine for Tauree, a spiced chai for Farrat—creating another sensory bridge to their first meeting at Amrita's tea party. The parallel struck Tauree with unexpected force, a recognition of how far they had traveled from that initial reluctant conversation to this moment of comfortable shared reflection.

"What are you thinking?" Farrat asked, noting her contemplative expression.

"About trajectories," Tauree replied, the architect's vocabulary emerging naturally. "How certain points of origin lead to destinations that couldn't have been anticipated from the starting position."

"Like your decision to attend Amrita's tea party despite your reluctance," Farrat suggested, immediately grasping the reference in her abstract observation.

"Exactly," Tauree confirmed, appreciation for his perceptiveness creating that familiar warmth in her chest. "If someone had described today's experiences to me then—participating in Punjabi dance, spending hours at a crowded festival, feeling energized rather than depleted by the engagement—I would have dismissed it as completely implausible."

"Yet here we are," Farrat said simply, the statement acknowledging not just their physical presence in the café but the remarkable evolution of their connection over the intervening months.

"Here we are," Tauree echoed, the simple affirmation containing recognition of something significant achieved, something neither could have predicted yet both had somehow helped create through their careful, consistent respect for each other's particular needs and boundaries.

As they continued talking, their conversation flowing with that same surprising ease Tauree had experienced since their first genuine exchange, she found herself experiencing an unusual clarity of perception—not just of Farrat across the table, but of their evolving relationship and her own changing response to it. The fog remained, as it always did, but it had thinned to a translucent veil rather than an obscuring cloud, allowing her to see with rare precision the terrain they had traversed together.

From that first reluctant conversation at Amrita's tea party to their midnight walk by the river, from the art gallery visit to their impulsive day trip to Seaview, from the storm-mandated stay in Farrat's apartment to this day of strategic festival navigation—each interaction had built upon the last, creating a relationship unlike any she had previously experienced. Neither demanding complete merger nor maintaining rigid separation, they had established permeable boundaries across which genuine understanding could flow in both directions.

More remarkable still was how this connection had begun to transform her experience beyond their direct interactions—how moments of spontaneity now occasionally emerged through the fog's usual careful calculation, how her architectural designs had evolved to incorporate more organic elements alongside her preference for precise structure, how her tolerance for improvisational experiences had gradually expanded without compromising her fundamental need for clarity and order.

"I have something for you," Farrat said suddenly, interrupting her reflections as he reached into his messenger bag. "I wasn't sure when the right moment would be to share it, but this seems appropriate somehow."

He withdrew a small, carefully wrapped package and placed it on the table between them. The paper was simple but elegant—a deep blue with subtle pattern that revealed itself only at certain angles, secured with a slim silver ribbon that spoke of attention to aesthetic detail without excessive ornamentation.

"This isn't—" He paused, a hint of uncharacteristic uncertainty crossing his features. "This isn't meant to create any obligation or expectation. It's simply something that made me think of you, that seemed to belong in your possession rather than mine."

The carefulness of his preface—emphasizing the gift's freedom from hidden demands—was characteristic of how he consistently created space for her autonomy within their connection. Even in this gesture of giving, he was ensuring her ability to receive without feeling burdened by implicit expectation.

"Thank you," Tauree said simply, accepting the package with genuine appreciation for both the tangible offering and the thoughtful spirit behind it.

She unwrapped it with precise care, preserving the paper and ribbon rather than tearing them away—a habitual neatness that reflected her broader approach to order and structure. Inside was a book, but not the typical commercial publication she might have expected. This was clearly a limited edition art piece—a slender volume bound in simple cloth with an embossed geometric pattern that created texture rather than image.

The title, embossed in silver on the cover, read simply: "Intersections: Poetry and Architecture." Opening it carefully, she discovered an extraordinary collaboration between a poet and an architect—each page presenting a poem alongside architectural drawings that responded to the verse not through literal illustration but through parallel exploration of similar themes in different vocabularies.

"It's remarkable," she said, genuinely moved by the thoughtfulness of the selection. "Where did you find it?"

"There's a small press run by the university arts department," Farrat explained. "They produce limited edition collaborations between different creative disciplines. When I saw this particular volume during a department event last month, it immediately made me think of our conversations about the parallels between poetry and architecture, about how both create experiences that exist at the intersection of physical and emotional space."

The precision of his selection—finding something that so perfectly captured the particular quality of their ongoing dialogue—created that now-familiar pressure in Tauree's chest, the sensation of being truly seen, of having her specific interests and perspectives recognized and valued.

"This is..." She paused, searching for words adequate to express her appreciation without falling into conventional platitudes. "This is perfectly aligned with how we've been thinking together. Thank you, Farrat. I'll treasure it."

The simple sincerity in her voice created a moment of quiet connection between them, an acknowledgment of something valuable shared beyond the physical gift itself. Farrat's smile warmed his features, reaching his eyes with genuine pleasure at her response.

As they finished their tea and prepared to conclude their day together, the comfortable silence that fell between them carried none of the awkwardness that typically characterized such transitions in Tauree's experience. There was no anxiety about appropriate farewell gestures, no calculation of what signals might be conveyed through particular words or actions. Instead, there was a shared understanding that what had developed between them would continue to evolve at its own natural pace, guided by mutual respect rather than external expectations or conventional patterns.

Outside the café, the evening had fully settled over the campus, the festival lights creating a colorful glow against the darkening sky. They stood for a moment on the sidewalk, neither immediately moving toward departure nor suggesting further extension of their time together.

"Thank you for today," Tauree said simply. "For the strategic planning that made it possible, and for the space to discover unexpected possibilities within it."

"Thank you for trusting the process," Farrat replied, his expression warm with genuine appreciation. "For being willing to navigate unfamiliar territory without requiring a complete map in advance."

The exchange—acknowledging each other's contributions to the day's success—created a perfect balance of recognition, neither diminishing their individual agency nor ignoring their mutual influence on the experience they had shared.

As they finally moved toward their separate vehicles, Tauree carrying her precious book carefully in hand, she felt none of the usual relief that typically accompanied the conclusion of extended social engagement. Instead, there was a curious sense of continuation—as if their connection remained active even in physical separation, a conversation merely paused rather than concluded.

The fog was still there, a constant companion in her internal landscape. But now it contained new landmarks, reference points that hadn't existed before—a poetry reading that bridged public and private understanding, a spontaneous dance at the periphery of a crowd, a book that captured in tangible form the particular quality of their ongoing dialogue about space and meaning.

As she drove home through the quiet evening streets, Tauree found herself contemplating not just the day's experiences but the broader trajectory of change they represented. The careful architect of precise spaces was learning, gradually and with appropriate caution, to incorporate more organic elements into her designs—both the literal structures she created professionally and the more abstract architectures of her engagement with the world.

The fog might never lift completely—that persistent gray filter would likely remain a constant feature of her internal landscape. But she was discovering new ways to navigate within it, new points of reference that allowed orientation even when visibility remained limited. And in Farrat, she had found a fellow traveler who neither demanded the fog disperse nor pretended it didn't exist—who simply offered to walk alongside her through its varying densities, sharing his own rainfall in an exchange of understanding that had created, somehow, a microclimate uniquely their own.

Tomorrow would bring a return to work and routine, to the carefully structured existence that provided necessary stability. But Tauree knew with quiet certainty that something had shifted during this festival day, something that could not be undone or forgotten once ordinary patterns resumed. Like the city transformed by the storm weeks earlier, she had been temporarily altered by unexpected experiences but permanently changed in subtle ways by their passage through her life.

With this thought, she felt an unfamiliar sense of anticipation rather than anxiety about what might develop next—a willingness to discover the continuing evolution of this connection that honored boundaries while creating new possibilities, that respected difference while establishing genuine understanding across it. Not fog lifting, perhaps, but fog becoming navigable in ways she had never previously imagined possible.

Act 2: The Build-Up and Growing Tension

Chapter 8: The Threshold

Three weeks after the university festival, Tauree stood in the nearly completed community center, watching as late afternoon sunlight filtered through the skylights she had designed. The reading nook—that carefully crafted space of intellectual intimacy within community—was finally manifesting as she had envisioned it. The contractors had executed her specifications with unusual precision, creating the exact quality of light she had calculated would transform throughout the day, marking time with shifting patterns across the walls and floors.

"It's exactly right," she murmured to herself, a quiet satisfaction warming her voice as she watched dust motes dance in the slanting sunbeams.

The community center project had been her primary focus for months, the concrete manifestation of her architectural philosophy—creating spaces that served as sanctuaries, physical expressions of the psychological shelter she sought in her designs. Now, with completion merely weeks away, she could finally see how the theoretical had become tangible, how her vision had transformed into a reality that others could experience.

She walked slowly around the reading nook, observing how the space changed from different angles, how the careful positioning of shelves and seating created both openness and intimacy, connection and privacy. It was a physical embodiment of the balance she had been exploring in her personal life as well—the permeable boundaries that allowed genuine understanding to flow without compromising individual integrity.

Her phone chimed with a notification. Farrat's name appeared on the screen, the timing unexpected yet somehow perfectly aligned with her thoughts. Since the festival, their communication had settled into a comfortable rhythm—messages shared without expectation of immediate response, observations offered as connections occurred rather than social obligation.

Finally finished grading essays. Considering celebrating with coffee at Serendipity. Would you like to join if you're free? Malcolm asked after you last time I was there. No pressure either way.

The invitation—characteristically offering connection without demand—created that now-familiar warmth in Tauree's chest. Three weeks had passed since they had spent time together in person, though their conversation had continued through thoughtfully timed messages and occasional phone calls. Work had consumed both of them—final examinations for Farrat, completion deadlines for Tauree—creating a natural pause in their physical proximity while their intellectual and emotional connection continued to develop.

She glanced around the community center, mentally assessing what remained to be done before she could justifiably conclude her day. The contractors had left an hour ago, the site supervisor having provided a detailed update on the week's progress. Her notes were complete, her observations documented, her follow-up items listed for Monday's meeting. There was no practical reason to remain, only the aesthetic pleasure of witnessing her design in this particular quality of late afternoon light.

Just finishing at the community center. Could meet you at Serendipity in about 30 minutes. The reading nook is finally manifesting as intended.

His response came almost immediately: *Perfect timing. Looking forward to hearing about it. Will secure a quiet corner and that spoon-dissolving coffee you prefer.*

As Tauree gathered her things and prepared to leave the site, she found herself contemplating the curious evolution of their connection over the past months. From that first reluctant conversation at Amrita's tea party to their midnight walk by the river, from the impulsive day trip to Seaview to their strategic navigation of the university festival—each interaction had built upon the last, creating a relationship that honored difference while establishing genuine understanding across it.

More remarkable still was how this connection had begun to influence her professional work. The community center design had evolved during their acquaintance, incorporating more organic elements alongside her preference for precise structure. The reading nook in particular had been refined through their conversations about the intersection of physical and emotional space, about how environments could both contain and transform human experience.

The book Farrat had given her at the festival—that extraordinary collaboration between poet and architect—had become a reference point for her recent design decisions. She had kept it on her desk at the office, occasionally opening to specific pages when seeking inspiration for particularly challenging aspects of the project. Her colleagues had noticed the shift in her approach, though none had directly commented on it, perhaps sensing that the evolution was still in process, still finding its final form.

Outside, the October afternoon was drawing toward evening, the quality of light shifting toward the golden hour that photographers prized for its warm illumination. Tauree walked to her car, her mind moving between professional satisfaction with the day's progress and a quieter anticipation of seeing Farrat again after these weeks of primarily textual connection.

The drive to Serendipity Café brought her through familiar neighborhoods now transformed by autumn colors—trees lining the streets displaying vibrant reds and golds against the backdrop of urban architecture. The seasonal transition seemed an appropriate metaphor for her own ongoing transformation, a gradual shift from one state to another that maintained essential character while displaying new qualities of color and light.

As she approached the café, memories of the storm-driven evening that had brought her there months ago surfaced with unexpected clarity—the rain-soaked dash through flooded streets, the candlelit conversations during the power outage, the subsequent drive to Farrat's apartment and his remarkable bookshelves organized by emotional resonance rather than conventional categorization. What had begun as an unplanned disruption had evolved into a significant marker in their developing relationship, a threshold crossed that had altered subsequent interactions in subtle but meaningful ways.

Serendipity appeared much as she remembered it—warm wood paneling, mismatched but comfortable furniture, walls lined with thoughtfully curated books. The atmosphere remained that perfect balance of intellectual engagement and physical comfort, of community and individuality that she strived to create in her own architectural designs.

Farrat was already there, settled at a corner table illuminated by one of the café's characteristic reading lamps. He was bent over a book, his profile outlined against the warm glow, the familiar posture of scholarly concentration that she had come to associate with him. As if sensing her arrival, he looked up, his expression immediately warming as their eyes met across the space.

"You came," he said, rising slightly as she approached the table, completing their now-traditional greeting ritual.

"I said I would," Tauree replied, settling into the chair opposite him. She noted the two mugs already waiting—a strong black coffee for her, what appeared to be a spiced chai for him. The consideration in this preparation—anticipating her arrival, remembering her preference—created another moment of that quiet warmth that had become characteristic of their interactions.

"How goes the battle with undergraduate essays?" she asked, wrapping her hands around the coffee mug with appreciation for its heat against the slight autumn chill that clung to her fingers.

"Finally concluded," Farrat replied with a small sigh that held both relief and lingering exhaustion. "Eighty-seven papers on contemporary diasporic literature, ranging from genuinely insightful to creatively plagiarized from obscure internet sources."

"That explains the celebration," Tauree observed with a smile, noting the slight shadows beneath his eyes that suggested recent late nights.

"Indeed. Academic freedom comes with the price tag of periodic grading marathons." His smile returned, reaching his eyes despite the evident fatigue. "But enough about my paperwork purgatory. Tell me about the community center—the reading nook is manifesting as intended?"

The genuine interest in his question—specific rather than general, referencing her exact message rather than offering vague politeness—was another quality that had drawn Tauree into increasingly deep conversation with him. Farrat consistently demonstrated actual attention to her words and thoughts, building their exchanges on substantive engagement rather than social performance.

"It is," she confirmed, a hint of professional pride warming her voice. "The contractors finally aligned the skylights exactly as specified in the design. The light patterns move across the walls and floors precisely as I calculated they would—marking time through the day while creating different qualities of illumination for different types of engagement with the space."

"Like your apartment," Farrat observed, drawing the connection to her personal design. "Creating consistency within change, a reliable framework that accommodates temporal variation."

"Yes," Tauree agreed, once again appreciating how quickly he grasped the underlying intention of her work. "Though the community center version is more complex—designed to serve multiple users with different needs and preferences, rather than a single inhabitant whose patterns are known and predictable."

"A technical challenge with profound human implications," Farrat noted, his expression thoughtful. "Creating a space that provides both structure and flexibility, that guides without constraining, that offers sanctuary without isolation."

The observation—articulating precisely the philosophical core of the project—created that now-familiar sense of being truly understood, of having her work perceived not just in technical terms but in its deeper emotional intentions.

"That's it exactly," she confirmed. "The entire center aims to achieve that balance, but the reading nook is where the principle is most clearly expressed. It's designed to function as a threshold space—neither fully public nor completely private, permitting both community and solitude depending on how it's utilized."

"A physical manifestation of the boundaries we've been discussing in our relationship," Farrat suggested, the parallel emerging with characteristic perceptiveness. "Permeable rather than rigid, defined yet adaptable."

The observation created a moment of quiet intensity between them—a recognition that their ongoing conversation about connection and separation, about fog and rainfall, had indeed influenced the physical expression of Tauree's architectural philosophy. What had begun as abstract discussion had gradually transformed into concrete design elements, theory becoming practice through their shared exploration of these concepts.

"I hadn't explicitly made that connection," Tauree admitted, though as soon as he articulated it, the parallel seemed obvious. "But you're right. The evolution of the reading nook design coincides precisely with the development of our... friendship."

The slight hesitation before the word "friendship" reflected her ongoing uncertainty about how to categorize their relationship. It remained neither conventional romance nor typical friendship, neither formally defined nor casually dismissible. It existed in that same threshold space she had created in the community center—a territory with flexible boundaries that permitted multiple forms of engagement without requiring rigid classification.

"Speaking of thresholds," Farrat said after a moment, his tone shifting slightly to indicate a change in subject, "I've been invited to participate in a literary retreat next month—a small gathering of poets and writers at a lake house about three hours from the city. Four days of workshops, readings, and creative exchange." He paused, a hint of uncharacteristic hesitation crossing his features. "The invitation includes a 'plus one' option, for partners or close connections who might appreciate the environment even if not participating in the formal literary aspects."

The implication hung between them—not quite an invitation yet, but the opening of a possibility. Unlike their previous shared experiences, which had lasted hours rather than days, this would represent an extended period of proximity, a significant expansion of their typical pattern of connection.

"It sounds interesting," Tauree replied carefully, neither accepting nor declining what had not yet been explicitly offered. "What kind of environment is it? Rustic cabins or more formal accommodations?"

"Somewhere between," Farrat explained, seeming to appreciate her focus on practical details rather than emotional implications. "The main house is quite substantial—a renovated lodge with private rooms and excellent light. There are also a few separate cabins for those who prefer more solitude. The setting is remarkable—situated on a small lake surrounded by forest, about a mile from the nearest neighbors. Very peaceful, especially in November when the summer residents have departed."

He paused, then added with characteristic consideration: "Each participant has a private room, regardless of whether they come alone or with someone. There's no assumption of shared accommodations."

The clarification—addressing potential concerns about boundaries and privacy without requiring her to voice them—was typical of how Farrat consistently created space for her autonomy within their evolving connection. He provided information that allowed informed decisions without pressure toward particular outcomes.

"Would I be expected to participate in the literary aspects?" Tauree asked, continuing to explore practical considerations before addressing the underlying question of whether she would attend.

"Not at all," Farrat assured her. "Many participants bring partners or friends who use the time for their own projects or simply enjoy the setting while the formal workshops proceed. There are shared meals and evening readings that everyone attends, but the daytime activities are quite flexible."

Tauree considered the possibility, weighing her typical reluctance toward extended social engagements against her growing curiosity about this dimension of Farrat's life she had glimpsed during his reading at the university festival. The prospect of four days in close proximity to others would normally have triggered immediate refusal, yet she found herself genuinely contemplating the invitation.

"When is it exactly?" she asked, mental calendar already calculating project deadlines and professional commitments.

"November 10th through 14th," Farrat replied. "Thursday through Monday. I understand if it's not possible with your work schedule."

The dates coincided with the community center's official opening, which could not be rescheduled or delegated. The project that had consumed months of her professional attention, that had evolved alongside her relationship with Farrat, required her presence for its culmination.

"I can't," she said, genuine regret coloring her voice. "The community center opening is that weekend. As lead architect, I need to be present for the official events and the initial operational period to address any issues that might arise."

"Of course," Farrat acknowledged immediately, no hint of disappointment or pressure in his response. "That's a crucial moment for a project you've invested so much in. It would be inappropriate to miss it."

The simple acceptance—recognizing the legitimacy of her professional commitment without attempting to negotiate or diminish its importance—reinforced what Tauree had come to value most about their connection. Farrat consistently honored her boundaries and obligations as valid in themselves, not merely as obstacles to his preferences.

"I would have been interested," she added, wanting to acknowledge the invitation's appeal despite its impossibility. "The setting sounds remarkable, and I'm curious about this aspect of your creative life."

"There will be other opportunities," Farrat assured her, his smile genuine despite the declined invitation. "The retreat happens twice yearly, and there are similar events throughout the year. When the timing aligns better with your schedule, the invitation remains open."

The easy deferral—accepting present limitations while maintaining future possibilities—created none of the usual tension

Tauree associated with declined social invitations. There was no subtle guilt-inducement, no implication that her priorities were misaligned, simply a recognition of practical reality and an unforced continuation of their connection.

"Thank you," she said simply, the words encompassing appreciation for both the invitation and the grace with which he accepted her decline. "I'd like to hear about it when you return—what you presented, how the environment influenced the work."

"I'd like that too," Farrat replied, his expression warming with the prospect of future exchange. "I've been working on a new sequence of poems exploring threshold spaces—those territories that exist between defined categories, that permit multiple modes of being simultaneously. Your community center reading nook has been a significant influence on the developing work."

The revelation—that her architectural design had directly influenced his creative writing—created a moment of profound connection between them. Just as his poetic perspective had gradually shaped her approach to spatial design, her architectural vision was informing his literary explorations. Their separate disciplines were increasingly engaged in dialogue, each transforming the other through this ongoing exchange of perspectives.

"I'd be very interested to read those when they're ready to be shared," Tauree said, genuine curiosity in her voice. "The concept of threshold spaces has been central to my recent thinking about both architecture and... personal boundaries."

The slight hesitation before "personal boundaries" reflected her ongoing caution about directly addressing the nature of their evolving relationship. Even after months of deepening connection, Tauree remained careful about explicit emotional disclosure, preferring to approach such territory through the more comfortable vocabularies of architecture and spatial theory.

"They're still finding their form," Farrat said, understanding evident in his expression. "But I'd value your perspective when they're ready for outside eyes. Your architectural insight often reveals dimensions of the work I hadn't consciously recognized."

As their conversation continued, flowing with that same surprising ease Tauree had experienced since their first genuine exchange, she found herself contemplating the curious trajectory that had brought them to this moment. What had begun as reluctant attendance at a social obligation had evolved into a connection that was gradually transforming both her professional work and her understanding of her own capabilities for engagement.

The fog remained, as it always did—that persistent gray filter through which she experienced the world. But it had become increasingly navigable, its patterns more predictable, its effects less isolating. Not because Farrat had somehow dispelled it, but because he had been willing to acknowledge its reality while still engaging with the person who existed within its confines.

Outside, the autumn evening had deepened, streetlights illuminating falling leaves that danced in the slight breeze. Inside Serendipity, the atmosphere had shifted subtly as day patrons departed and evening visitors arrived—students with laptops and textbooks, couples seeking quiet conversation, solitary readers creating private worlds in public space. Malcolm moved through the café with unobtrusive attention, refreshing beverages, adjusting lighting, maintaining that perfect balance between community and individuality that characterized the establishment.

"How is your apartment project progressing?" Farrat asked, shifting to a topic they had discussed in their recent messages. "The renovation of the prewar building in the historic district?"

"Challenging but fascinating," Tauree replied, grateful as always for his precise recall of her professional activities. "The structural elements are extraordinary—craftsmanship you simply don't see in modern construction. But the existing layout reflects dated assumptions about how spaces should function. The challenge is honoring the historical integrity while creating environments that serve contemporary needs."

"Another type of threshold," Farrat observed, the connection emerging with characteristic perceptiveness. "Existing between past and present, preservation and innovation."

"Exactly," Tauree confirmed, once again appreciating how quickly he grasped the conceptual core of her work. "Finding the balance between honoring what came before and creating what needs to exist now. Too much deference to history creates a museum rather than a living space. Too much emphasis on current trends produces something that will feel equally dated in another generation."

"Like the literary canon," Farrat suggested, drawing a parallel to his own discipline. "The ongoing negotiation between established works and emerging voices, between preservation of cultural foundations and incorporation of new perspectives."

The comparison—revealing similar tensions within their separate fields—created another bridge between their professional worlds, another point of connection across their different areas of expertise. This had become a defining quality of their relationship: the discovery of underlying patterns that transcended surface differences, the recognition of shared principles expressed through distinct vocabularies.

As their conversation continued, moving between professional projects and philosophical considerations, practical challenges and theoretical frameworks, Tauree became aware of a subtle shift in the quality of their exchange. There was an increasing comfort in their intellectual intimacy, a deepening trust in how each received and engaged with the other's perspectives. What had begun as careful navigation of separate territories had evolved into a shared exploration, a collaborative investigation of ideas that belonged to neither exclusively but emerged from their particular dialogue.

"I've been meaning to ask you something," Farrat said during a natural pause, his tone shifting slightly to indicate a change in subject. "The book I gave you at the festival—'Intersections: Poetry and Architecture'—has it proven useful in your work? I noticed you mentioned it in relation to the community center design."

"Extraordinarily so," Tauree confirmed, genuine appreciation warming her voice. "It's become a reference point for certain design challenges—not as a source of direct solutions, but as a reminder of how different vocabularies can address similar questions from complementary angles. I've kept it on my desk at the office."

"I'm glad," Farrat said simply, though his expression revealed deeper pleasure at hearing his gift had found meaningful integration into her professional life. "The collaboration between those particular artists seemed to capture something essential about our ongoing conversations."

"It did," Tauree agreed. "Though our dialogue has evolved beyond what they explored in that volume. We've developed our own vocabulary at the intersection of architecture and poetry, our own way of translating between structural and verbal expression."

The observation—acknowledging the unique character of their intellectual exchange—created a moment of quiet recognition between them. They had indeed constructed something distinctive through their months of conversation, a shared framework for understanding that borrowed from both their disciplines while belonging exclusively to neither.

The café had grown quieter as evening deepened, many patrons departing for dinner plans or other activities. Malcolm approached their table with unobtrusive courtesy, offering to refresh their beverages if they wished to stay longer. The interaction carried none of the subtle pressure to vacate that often characterized service establishments during busy periods—only genuine hospitality that valued their presence rather than merely their consumption.

After Malcolm had departed with their orders for fresh drinks, Farrat's expression grew slightly more serious, a hint of deliberate consideration entering his features. "There's something I've been contemplating," he said, his tone thoughtful. "Related to our ongoing exploration of boundaries and connection."

Tauree felt a momentary tension, uncertain of the direction this might take but attentive to the shift in his demeanor. "Yes?" she prompted when he didn't immediately continue.

"We've spent these months developing a relationship that exists in a threshold space—neither conventional friendship nor traditional romance, neither casual acquaintance nor formal partnership. This has suited our particular needs for both connection and autonomy, for both shared understanding and personal space."

He paused, organizing his thoughts with characteristic care. "I've been wondering if we might benefit from more explicit discussion of what this connection means to each of us—not to constrain it with rigid definition, but to ensure our understanding remains aligned as it continues to evolve."

The suggestion—approaching directly what they had largely addressed through metaphor and parallel—created a moment of vulnerability between them. Tauree felt the fog threatening to thicken in response to this potential emotional exposure, the habitual withdrawal that typically protected her from such intimate terrain. Yet something in Farrat's careful framing—his emphasis on mutual understanding rather than unilateral declaration—kept the haze from solidifying into an impenetrable barrier.

"What prompted this consideration?" she asked, neither refusing the conversation nor immediately embracing it, seeking context before commitment.

"Two things," Farrat replied, his candor characteristic of their established communication. "First, my invitation to the literary retreat revealed an implicit assumption I hadn't previously articulated—that our connection might naturally extend into more extended shared experiences, into territories we haven't yet explored together. Second, some comments from colleagues at the university suggested they've drawn conclusions about the nature of our relationship based on limited observations at the festival and elsewhere."

He held up a hand slightly, forestalling potential concern. "I'm not suggesting we need to define ourselves for others' benefit or conform to external expectations. Only that it might be valuable for us to ensure our own understanding remains aligned as circumstances present new possibilities and challenges."

Tauree considered his explanation, appreciating both its honesty and its respect for her agency in the conversation. Farrat wasn't demanding disclosure or commitment, merely suggesting that their evolving connection might benefit from more direct acknowledgment alongside their comfortable metaphorical framework.

"That seems reasonable," she said after a thoughtful pause. "Though I confess I'm not entirely sure how to approach such a discussion. My experience with... significant relationships has been limited and not particularly successful, as I've mentioned previously."

"Mine as well," Farrat acknowledged with a small smile that held both self-deprecation and genuine reflection. "Though perhaps our shared awareness of past missteps creates useful caution rather than merely fear. We've both learned the cost of assumptions in relationships, the importance of clear understanding alongside emotional connection."

Their refreshed beverages arrived—another perfectly brewed coffee for Tauree, a different tea selection for Farrat. The brief interruption provided a welcome moment to gather thoughts, to consider how to approach this threshold they were contemplating crossing together—from implicit to explicit understanding, from metaphorical to direct acknowledgment.

"Perhaps we could begin with what works in our current arrangement," Tauree suggested as Malcolm withdrew, her architect's mind naturally seeking structural foundation before addressing decorative elements. "The aspects of our connection that feel valuable and sustainable, that we would want to preserve as we move forward."

"An excellent approach," Farrat agreed, visible appreciation for her pragmatic framing. "For me, one essential quality has been the space we create for each other's separate existence—the recognition that connection doesn't require constant presence or performative togetherness. There's room for solitude without implying rejection or disinterest."

"Yes," Tauree confirmed, immediate recognition of this core value. "The absence of expectation that we must conform to conventional patterns of interaction. The understanding that retreating to process experience independently doesn't diminish the connection but actually sustains it."

"Exactly," Farrat said, nodding with the familiar pleasure of aligned perspective. "Another crucial element for me has been intellectual engagement without competitive positioning. The genuine interest in each other's disciplines and perspectives, the exploration across categorical boundaries without need to establish superiority or dominance."

"The collaborative aspect," Tauree added, developing the observation. "How our separate professional vocabularies have begun to inform each other, creating something distinctive in the exchange rather than merely parallel tracks of individual development."

They continued in this vein, identifying the essential qualities that had made their connection valuable to each of them—the precise balance of disclosure and privacy, the comfort in both silence and speech, the absence of artificial timelines or external benchmarks for progression. The conversation flowed with that same surprising ease Tauree had experienced throughout their relationship, even as it ventured into terrain they had previously navigated primarily through metaphor and parallel.

"There's something else," Tauree said eventually, approaching what felt like a significant threshold in her own capacity for disclosure. "Something I've observed but haven't explicitly acknowledged."

Farrat's attention focused with that characteristic quality of genuine interest without demand, creating space for her to proceed at her own pace.

"The fog," she continued, referencing their established metaphor for her depression, "has become more... navigable since we've known each other. Not because it's fundamentally changed its character or permanently lifted—I don't believe that's how clinical depression functions, at least not in my experience. But because our particular mode of connection doesn't require its absence or denial to function effectively."

She paused, organizing thoughts that felt both vulnerable and important to articulate. "Previous relationships demanded performance of conventional emotional responses that were often inaccessible to me, creating a cycle of inadequacy and withdrawal. This connection we've established doesn't require me to be something other than what I am—it accommodates the fog rather than expecting its dispersal."

The disclosure—more direct than her typical approach to emotional territory—created a moment of quiet intensity between them. Farrat's expression reflected both recognition and careful consideration, receiving her words with the attentiveness she had come to trust over their months of acquaintance.

"I've had a similar experience with the rainfall," he replied, matching her vulnerability with his own. "Not that it has ceased—the melancholy still moves through me in its familiar patterns. But our connection hasn't required either submerging you in it or pretending it doesn't exist. There's a particular freedom in being neither defined by it nor obligated to hide it, in having it acknowledged as part of my landscape without becoming the entire terrain."

The parallel acknowledgment—that each had found in the other a rare acceptance of their particular mental weather—created a profound moment of connection between them. Not the manufactured intensity of conventional romance, but something more sustainable and authentic: the recognition of having discovered a relationship that accommodated rather than denied their individual realities.

"So perhaps what we're defining," Tauree suggested, "is not so much a category for our connection as the particular qualities that make it valuable to each of us. The specific balance of autonomy and intimacy, of independence and mutual influence that allows both of us to function authentically while still engaging meaningfully."

"Yes," Farrat agreed, appreciation evident in his expression. "Less about finding an existing label and more about acknowledging the unique characteristics of what we've constructed together. A custom architecture rather than a standard floor plan."

The architectural metaphor—drawing on her professional vocabulary to illuminate their personal situation—created a natural bridge between abstract emotional territory and more concrete conceptual framework. This had become a hallmark of their communication: the translation between different domains of understanding, the creation of shared language from their separate disciplinary foundations.

Outside, the autumn evening had fully settled into night, the café windows now reflecting interior light rather than admitting external illumination. Time had passed without either monitoring its progression, another characteristic of their interaction—that quality of unselfconscious presence that contrasted with Tauree's usual hyperawareness of duration during social engagements.

"It's getting late," she observed, noting the changed atmosphere both inside and outside the café. "We've been here longer than I realized."

"Time moves differently in good conversation," Farrat replied with a small smile. "Another quality worth acknowledging in our particular connection—that neither feels compelled to watch the clock, to measure interaction against external schedules rather than internal rhythms."

The observation—identifying yet another valuable aspect of their relationship—brought them full circle to their original purpose: articulating what made their connection distinctive and meaningful. They had not arrived at a conventional label or category, had not forced their evolving relationship into predetermined parameters. Instead, they had begun to create a shared vocabulary for understanding its particular character, its unique balance of qualities that served both their separate needs and their mutual engagement.

"Should we continue this conversation at another time?" Farrat suggested, respecting the implicit conclusion in her acknowledgment of the hour. "Perhaps after you've had opportunity to reflect on what we've discussed so far?"

The offer—creating space for individual processing rather than demanding immediate resolution—was characteristic of how he consistently honored her needs within their interactions. No expectation of performance or immediate reciprocity, simply recognition that significant insights often required time to develop fully.

"I think that would be valuable," Tauree agreed, genuine appreciation in her voice. "This has been... illuminating. But I would benefit from some time to consider the implications more thoroughly."

"Of course," Farrat said simply, no hint of disappointment or pressure in his response. "There's no artificial timeline for understanding, no external benchmark for when such recognition should occur."

As they prepared to leave, gathering belongings and settling their bill, Tauree found herself contemplating the curious evolution they had begun to articulate. What had started as reluctant attendance at a social obligation had developed into something neither could have anticipated—a connection that existed in that threshold space between defined categories, that permitted multiple modes of engagement simultaneously, that honored difference while establishing genuine understanding across it.

Outside, the autumn night was clear and cool, stars visible despite the city's ambient light. They stood for a moment on the sidewalk, neither immediately moving toward departure nor suggesting further extension of their time together.

"Thank you for initiating this conversation," Tauree said, recognizing the courage it had required to approach directly what they had primarily addressed through metaphor. "It was more comfortable than I anticipated."

"Thank you for engaging with it so thoughtfully," Farrat replied, his expression warm in the gentle illumination from the café windows. "For bringing your architectural perspective to what might otherwise have remained nebulous emotional territory."

The exchange—acknowledging each other's contributions to their evolving understanding—created a perfect balance of recognition, neither diminishing their individual agency nor ignoring their mutual influence on the experience they had shared.

As they finally moved toward their separate vehicles, Tauree felt none of the usual relief that typically accompanied the conclusion of extended social engagement. Instead, there was that now-familiar sense of continuation—as if their connection remained active even in physical separation, a conversation merely paused rather than concluded.

The fog was still there, a constant companion in her internal landscape. But it contained new landmarks, reference points that hadn't existed before—a direct acknowledgment of its presence alongside the recognition that it need not prevent meaningful connection, a shared vocabulary for understanding its patterns without requiring its permanent dispersal.

As she drove home through the quiet streets, Tauree found herself contemplating not just the evening's conversation but the broader trajectory it represented. They had approached a significant threshold together—from implicit to explicit understanding, from metaphorical to direct acknowledgment—and had begun to cross it with the same careful attention to balance that had characterized their entire relationship.

The fog might never lift completely—that persistent gray filter would likely remain a constant feature of her internal landscape. But she was discovering new ways to navigate within it, new points of reference that allowed orientation even when visibility remained limited. And in Farrat, she had found a fellow traveler who neither demanded the fog disperse nor pretended it didn't exist—who simply offered to walk alongside her through its varying densities, sharing his own rainfall in an exchange of understanding that had created, somehow, a microclimate uniquely their own.

Tomorrow would bring a return to work and routine, to the final preparations for the community center opening that would prevent her joining Farrat at the literary retreat. But Tauree knew with quiet certainty that something had shifted during this evening's conversation, something that could not be undone or forgotten once ordinary patterns resumed. They had begun to articulate what had previously existed only in practice, had started to create a shared vocabulary for the particular architecture of connection they had built together.

With this thought, she felt an unfamiliar sense of anticipation rather than anxiety about what might develop next—a willingness to continue exploring the unique territory they had discovered between them, to keep building something that honored boundaries while creating new possibilities, that respected difference while establishing genuine understanding across it. Not fog lifting, perhaps, but fog becoming increasingly navigable through the careful construction of landmarks they could both recognize and trust.

Act 2: The Build-Up and Growing Tension

Chapter 9: The Distance

The morning after their illuminating conversation at Serendipity Café, Tauree woke to a text message from Farrat:

I realized on my drive home last night that we crossed an important threshold together. Whatever comes next, I wanted to express my gratitude for your willingness to engage so directly with what has typically remained in the realm of metaphor between us. Rest well, architect of both spaces and understanding.

The message carried none of the anxious need for immediate response that typically characterized morning-after communications in Tauree's limited experience with relationships. Instead, it felt like a gentle acknowledgment of their shared journey, a marker placed at the threshold they had begun to cross together without demanding she rush to join him on the other side.

She read it twice, then set her phone aside to complete her morning routine—the structured sequence of activities that helped anchor her days regardless of the fog's density. Only after her shower, coffee, and brief review of the day's scheduled tasks did she compose a response:

The conversation proved more clarifying than destabilizing—unusual in my experience of emotional territory. Perhaps because we approached it with architectural precision rather than romantic abstraction. I find myself contemplating the particular balance we've constructed together with both analytical appreciation and something adjacent to contentment. Thank you for initiating that exploration.

The exchange complete—neither overcommunicative nor artificially restrained—Tauree turned her attention to the day ahead.

The community center project demanded focus as it entered its final phase before opening, with countless details requiring her oversight to ensure the actual implementation aligned with her carefully crafted vision.

Yet as she reviewed contractor reports and material selections, her mind occasionally returned to their conversation at Serendipity—the careful articulation of what made their connection valuable to each of them, the recognition of how it had begun to transform their separate professional approaches, the acknowledgment of that curious microclimate they had created between fog and rainfall where both could exist without overwhelming the other.

For the first time in her experience, discussing the nature of a relationship had created clarity rather than confusion, had illuminated rather than obscured the terrain they were navigating together. Perhaps because they had approached it as a collaborative investigation rather than a negotiation of competing desires, as an architectural problem of balance and structure rather than an emotional contest to be won or lost.

The week that followed maintained their established rhythm of thoughtful but undemanding communication. Farrat sent occasional messages about his preparations for the literary retreat, sharing fragments of the threshold poems he was developing and observations about how architectural concepts were informing his creative process. Tauree responded with updates on the community center's progress, reflections on threshold spaces in her current designs, and questions about how certain literary techniques might translate into spatial experience.

Neither pushed for more explicit definition of what had been acknowledged at Serendipity, neither retreated from the directness they had established. It was as if they were allowing that conversation to settle, to find its natural place within the evolving structure of their relationship without forcing its immediate application.

Ten days after their café meeting, Tauree stood in the nearly completed community center, supervising the installation of the final elements in the reading nook. The contractors had executed her specifications with remarkable precision, creating exactly the quality of light and space she had envisioned—a threshold territory that existed between public and private, between structured learning and organic discovery.

"It's really something special, Ms. Sharma," commented Miguel, the project foreman who had been skeptical of certain design elements when first presented with the plans months ago. "Never seen anything quite like it. Not just architecturally, I mean—though that's impressive too. But the feeling it creates... hard to describe."

"Threshold space," Tauree said, the term emerging naturally from her recent conversations with Farrat. "Neither one thing nor another exclusively, but a territory that permits multiple modes of engagement simultaneously."

Miguel nodded, understanding without requiring elaborate explanation. "Exactly that. My daughter's studying literature at the community college—she'd love this space. Mind if I bring her by after the official opening? She writes poetry, spends hours in the public library looking for quiet corners that don't quite exist there."

"I think that would be appropriate," Tauree replied, unexpectedly moved by this connection between her architectural vision and the specific human need it might serve. "The space was designed for precisely that purpose—supporting creative thought within community context."

As Miguel moved away to direct his crew in the final adjustments to the bookshelves that lined one wall of the reading nook, Tauree found herself contemplating this unexpected moment of connection. The barrier between professional detachment and emotional engagement had grown increasingly permeable in recent months, allowing her to recognize more directly the human impact of her work without becoming overwhelmed by it.

Like so many aspects of her life lately, this evolution seemed connected to her relationship with Farrat—to the particular quality of understanding they had developed together, to how his perception of her work had gradually influenced her own experience of it. Not a dramatic transformation that denied her fundamental nature, but a subtle shift in how she navigated within the fog's persistent presence.

Her phone vibrated with an incoming call—not a text, which was their usual mode of communication. Farrat's name appeared on the screen, creating a momentary flutter of surprise. They rarely spoke by phone, preferring the thoughtfulness of written exchange or the direct presence of in-person conversation.

"Hello," she answered, moving toward a quieter corner of the building where construction sounds wouldn't overwhelm the call.

"Tauree," Farrat's voice carried an unusual tension that immediately caught her attention. "I apologize for calling rather than texting. I've encountered an unexpected situation and wanted to speak directly."

"What's happened?" she asked, professional efficiency automatically engaging in response to his evident concern.

"Nothing catastrophic," he assured her quickly. "But potentially complicated. Remember my former colleague Nisha, whom we encountered at the art gallery?"

"Yes, of course." The memory was precise—the calculated intervention, the deliberate mischaracterization of their relationship, the subtle power play that Tauree had recognized and deflected.

"She's been appointed as the new co-director of the literary retreat I mentioned," Farrat explained, his voice carrying a careful neutrality that suggested managed emotion beneath. "I've just learned this from the organizer, who assumed I already knew. Apparently, the previous co-director had a medical emergency, and Nisha was asked to step in due to her experience with similar events."

"I see," Tauree replied, immediately grasping the implications. "That creates a potentially uncomfortable dynamic for your participation."

"Yes," Farrat confirmed. "And it also changes the nature of the invitation I had considered extending to you, had the timing aligned with your schedule. The situation would be more complex than I'd originally anticipated."

The careful phrasing—acknowledging the invitation he had been contemplating without implying it had been formally offered and rejected—was characteristic of how Farrat consistently created space for her agency within their evolving connection. Even in this moment of unexpected complication, he was maintaining that fundamental respect for boundaries and clarity they had established.

"Would you prefer to withdraw from the retreat?" Tauree asked, focusing on practical considerations rather than emotional implications—an approach that often helped clarify complex situations.

"I'm considering it," Farrat admitted. "My initial impulse was to cancel immediately. But professionally, it represents an important opportunity. Several publishers and journal editors will be present, and I had planned to share the threshold poems that have emerged from our conversations about architecture and perception."

"Those are strong pieces," Tauree observed, recalling the fragments he had shared in recent weeks. "Significant both creatively and conceptually."

"Thank you," Farrat said, genuine appreciation warming his voice despite the underlying tension. "That's part of my dilemma. Withdrawing means losing an opportunity to present work that feels important, not just personally but potentially to others engaging with similar questions about spaces of transition and perception."

Tauree considered this carefully, her analytical mind naturally seeking structural solutions to emotional challenges. "What specifically concerns you about Nisha's involvement? The personal history between you, or how she might interpret or influence your current situation?"

The question created a brief silence—not discomfort, but thoughtful consideration. This had become characteristic of their communication: the space to process complex questions without requiring immediate response, the recognition that some inquiries deserved careful reflection rather than reflexive answer.

"Both, I suppose," Farrat replied eventually. "Though not equally. The personal history is uncomfortable but manageable—we've maintained professional courtesy when required by university functions. What concerns me more is the potential for misinterpretation or complication of current circumstances."

His careful avoidance of directly referencing their relationship, using instead the more neutral "current circumstances," struck Tauree as significant. Even in this private conversation, Farrat was respecting the unfinished nature of their exploration, the threshold they had approached but not yet fully crossed in defining what existed between them.

"You're concerned she might draw conclusions or make assumptions about our connection based on limited information," Tauree suggested, completing the thought he had left implicit.

"Yes," Farrat confirmed, relief evident in his voice at her precise understanding. "And given her position as co-director, those assumptions could create uncomfortable dynamics beyond just personal awkwardness. The retreat is meant to be a space of creative focus and professional development. Unnecessary complications would undermine that purpose."

"I understand," Tauree said, appreciating both the practical and emotional dimensions of his concern. "Would my unavailability to attend simplify the situation? Without my physical presence, there would be less immediate basis for speculation or misinterpretation."

"Potentially," Farrat acknowledged. "Though knowing Nisha, even the mention of a significant connection might prompt questions. And I don't want to create a situation where I feel compelled to either minimize what exists between us or define it in terms that don't accurately reflect its particular nature, especially when we ourselves are still articulating that understanding."

The observation struck Tauree with unexpected force—not just for its insight into the immediate dilemma, but for what it revealed about Farrat's approach to their relationship even in her absence. He was unwilling to diminish its significance for social convenience, yet equally unwilling to force it into conventional categories that would misrepresent its actual character. The integrity of this position, the respect it demonstrated for what they were building together, created that now-familiar warmth in her chest.

"I appreciate that perspective," she said, her voice carrying more emotion than she typically allowed in professional settings. She glanced around, ensuring the construction workers remained focused on their tasks rather than her conversation. "It aligns with what we discussed at Serendipity—the importance of honoring the particular nature of our connection rather than conforming to external expectations."

"Exactly," Farrat agreed, evident relief in his tone at her understanding. "Which brings me back to the question of whether to attend at all. Part of me feels it would be simpler to withdraw, to avoid the entire complexity. But that also means allowing these external circumstances to dictate professional opportunities and creative presentation."

Tauree recognized the subtle request beneath his explanation—not for her to make the decision, but to engage with the problem as a shared consideration rather than his individual dilemma. This too felt significant: he wasn't merely informing her of a situation but inviting her perspective as someone whose interests were also implicated, however indirectly.

"If the retreat represents a significant professional opportunity," she said after careful consideration, "withdrawing entirely seems to grant undue influence to circumstances that should remain peripheral. Perhaps there's an architectural solution to this social challenge."

"An architectural solution?" Farrat repeated, curiosity evident in his voice.

"Yes," Tauree continued, professional confidence engaging as she approached the problem through her disciplinary lens. "In design, when elements must coexist that have potential for negative interaction, we create strategic separation while maintaining necessary connection. Controlled points of engagement within a broader system of thoughtful distancing."

"That's remarkably applicable," Farrat observed, understanding immediately the parallel she was drawing. "Suggesting I participate in the formal aspects of the retreat—the workshops, readings, professional networking—while limiting social engagement to what's professionally necessary."

"Exactly," Tauree confirmed. "Maintaining presence in essential territories while minimizing exposure in optional ones. The literary equivalent of designing distinct functional zones within a unified structure."

"A threshold approach to social navigation," Farrat summarized, appreciation evident in his voice. "Present but selectively engaged, participating without full immersion."

"It would allow you to present the threshold poems in their intended professional context without unnecessary complications," Tauree concluded. "While preserving both your creative opportunity and the integrity of our developing understanding."

The silence that followed carried none of the tension of their earlier exchange—instead, it held the quality of shared recognition they had experienced so often in their conversations, that moment when disparate perspectives aligned to create unexpected clarity.

"Thank you," Farrat said finally. "For approaching this as a design challenge rather than merely an emotional dilemma. It provides a framework for navigation that honors both professional necessity and personal integrity."

"Architects specialize in creating structures that accommodate complex human needs while minimizing potential conflicts," Tauree replied, a hint of wry humor entering her voice. "Though we typically apply these principles to physical spaces rather than social dynamics."

"The principles translate remarkably well," Farrat observed. "Perhaps another territory where our professional vocabularies can inform each other's practice."

As they concluded their conversation, agreeing to speak again after Farrat had formally responded to the retreat organizer, Tauree found herself contemplating this unexpected development with analytical interest rather than emotional distress. Unlike previous experiences where relationship complications had triggered anxiety and withdrawal, this situation had engaged her problem-solving capacity, had invited collaborative resolution rather than individual retreat.

The construction sounds around her gradually reclaimed her attention as she ended the call, the immediate demands of the community center project requiring her professional focus. Yet as she moved through the building, reviewing installation details and addressing contractor questions, a part of her mind continued processing the conversation with Farrat and its broader implications.

They had encountered their first significant external complication—a situation that had potential to disrupt the carefully balanced connection they had established. Rather than destabilizing that connection, however, the challenge had seemingly strengthened it, had invited application of their shared vocabulary to a practical problem, had demonstrated the resilience of what they were building together.

This realization carried its own significance—not just for the immediate situation with the literary retreat, but for the evolving architecture of their relationship. They were developing not only shared understanding but shared methods for navigating complications, strategies for maintaining balance when external forces threatened to disrupt it.

The fog remained present, as always, but it had not thickened in response to this unexpected complexity. Instead, Tauree found herself moving through it with unusual clarity, her perception sharpened rather than dulled by the engagement with Farrat's dilemma. It was as if their collaboration had created a new pathway through her typically clouded emotional terrain, a route that engaged her analytical strengths rather than demanding conventional emotional responses she found difficult to access.

Three days later, Tauree stood in her office reviewing the final documentation for the community center opening scheduled for the following weekend. Everything was proceeding according to plan—the construction complete, the furnishings installed, the operational systems tested and verified. After months of intensive work, her vision had been successfully translated into physical reality, creating exactly the balance of community and sanctuary she had intended.

Her phone chimed with a notification, Farrat's name appearing on the screen. They had exchanged brief messages since their conversation about the literary retreat, but nothing substantial—each engaged with their respective professional demands, maintaining connection without requiring constant communication.

Update on the retreat situation: I've decided to attend, implementing our architectural approach to social navigation. The organizer was understanding about my limited availability for social aspects, framing it as a focus on creative work rather than community engagement. I'll present the threshold poems on Saturday evening. Would you be interested in reviewing the final sequence before I depart on Thursday? Perhaps coffee tomorrow if your schedule permits. No pressure either way.

The message maintained their established pattern of offering connection without expectation, creating space for her response based on current capacity rather than obligatory reciprocation. Tauree checked her calendar, noting a relatively light schedule the following afternoon as contractors completed final preparations at the community center.

Tomorrow works well. Serendipity at 3:00? Looking forward to seeing the completed sequence.

His response came quickly: *Perfect. I'll bring the complete manuscript and spare you my initial readings. Some pieces benefit from revision before performance.*

The slight self-deprecation—acknowledging the difference between draft and refined presentation—created a small smile as Tauree set her phone aside and returned to her documentation review. There was something increasingly comfortable about these exchanges, a natural rhythm that had developed without conscious effort or explicit negotiation. They had found a way of communicating that honored both her need for space and his capacity for expression, that created connection without demanding constant maintenance.

The following afternoon found her arriving at Serendipity precisely at three, the familiar warmth of the café welcoming her as she stepped through the door. Unlike the storm-driven evening that had first brought her here, today was clear and mild—perfect autumn weather that colored the city with golden light and vibrant foliage. The contrast struck her as she scanned the interior, looking for Farrat among the scattered patrons.

He wasn't there yet—unusual, as he typically arrived early for their meetings. Tauree selected a quiet corner table, positioned to view both the entrance and the café's interior while maintaining comfortable distance from other customers. She ordered her usual strong black coffee, settling in with architectural journals to review while waiting.

Twenty minutes passed without Farrat's arrival or any message explaining his delay. This departure from established pattern created a curious sensation in Tauree—not anxiety exactly, but a disruption of expectation that triggered attentiveness. Farrat was meticulously punctual, his respect for agreed timing being one of the many small considerations that had allowed their connection to develop despite her typical wariness of social unpredictability.

She sent a simple text: *Everything alright?*

No response came, increasing the subtle tension she was experiencing. After another ten minutes, she decided to call—something she rarely initiated, preferring the controlled pace of written communication. The call went directly to voicemail, suggesting his phone was either turned off or unable to connect.

Now genuine concern began to emerge. This wasn't merely a social inconvenience but a significant deviation from established patterns that suggested something unusual had occurred. Tauree considered her options methodically, as she approached all problems: wait longer at the café, return to her office, attempt other methods of contact.

As she deliberated, the café door opened to admit not Farrat but a familiar figure from the university festival—Priya, his former student who had analyzed his poetry with such perceptive insight. The young woman scanned the interior with apparent purpose, her expression brightening when she spotted Tauree in the corner.

"I thought I might find you here," Priya said, approaching with a directness that suggested urgency beneath her casual manner. "Professor Mirza asked me to find you."

"Is everything alright?" Tauree asked, professional composure maintaining despite the unexpected development.

"Mostly," Priya replied, settling into the chair opposite without waiting for invitation. "He's at the university medical center. Nothing life-threatening," she added quickly, noting Tauree's expression. "He fainted during a faculty meeting about an hour ago. Probably just exhaustion and low blood sugar according to the nurse, but they're running tests to be certain."

"I see," Tauree said, processing this information with outward calm despite the unexpected concern it triggered. "How did you know to find me here?"

"He regained consciousness almost immediately," Priya explained. "First thing he said was that he needed to contact you about your meeting at Serendipity. His phone was damaged when he fell—screen shattered completely. He asked if I would find you and explain what happened, since he couldn't message you himself."

The explanation aligned with what Tauree knew of Farrat—his consideration for commitments, his dislike of unexcused absences or unexplained changes to plans. Even in a medical situation, he had prioritized ensuring she wasn't left wondering about his absence, had found a way to communicate despite the technical failure of his phone.

"Thank you for delivering the message," Tauree said, gathering her belongings with efficient movements. "Which medical center, specifically?"

"University Health on Westlake Avenue," Priya replied, watching Tauree's preparations with evident curiosity. "They're keeping him for observation and tests. I can give you a ride if you'd like—my car's just outside."

"That's not necessary," Tauree responded automatically, her habitual independence engaging before she fully considered the practical efficiency of the offer. Then, recognizing this reflexive resistance to assistance, she reconsidered. "Actually, that would be helpful if it's not an inconvenience. I took public transportation here."

"No problem at all," Priya assured her, rising from the chair with the energetic movement Tauree remembered from their previous encounters. "I was heading back to campus anyway. The professor was pretty insistent that I find you—seemed more concerned about missing your meeting than about his own condition."

"That sounds characteristic," Tauree observed, following Priya toward the exit after leaving payment for her barely-touched coffee. "Consideration for others often supersedes self-concern in his priorities."

"Exactly," Priya agreed as they stepped into the autumn afternoon. "It's what makes him such an exceptional teacher, though sometimes a frustrating friend. He notices everyone's needs except his own until they become impossible to ignore."

The casual insight into Farrat's character from someone who knew him in a different context created a moment of unexpected connection between the two women as they walked toward Priya's car. Tauree found herself curious about this perspective—how Farrat appeared to those who encountered him in his professional capacity rather than the more personal territory they had explored together.

"Has this happened before?" she asked as they settled into the compact vehicle. "The fainting episode, I mean."

"Not that I know of," Priya replied, navigating smoothly into traffic. "Though there are rumors among graduate students about a period several years ago when he canceled classes unexpectedly and was absent from campus for over a week. When he returned, he looked like he hadn't slept the entire time. But that's just academic gossip—I was an undergraduate then and didn't know him personally yet."

Tauree recognized the timeline immediately—it aligned with what Farrat had shared about his relationship with Leila, how he had "disappeared" when the emotional demands became overwhelming, retreating to a cabin in the mountains before returning to end the relationship. Hearing this external confirmation of his personal disclosure created an unexpected sense of validation, a reinforcement of the authenticity that had characterized their evolving connection.

"The faculty meeting where he collapsed," Tauree said, shifting focus from past to present, "do you know what it concerned?"

"End-of-term scheduling, budget allocations, the usual administrative tedium," Priya replied with the dismissive tone of someone who found such matters irrelevant to genuine academic pursuit. "Though there was apparently some tension about the literary retreat he's attending next week. Something about co-director appointments and programming changes."

"I see," Tauree said, making the connection immediately to the situation Farrat had described involving Nisha. It seemed the complication extended beyond personal history into professional territory, creating additional stress beyond what he had initially anticipated.

"Do you know what caused the tension specifically?" she asked, careful to maintain neutral interest rather than revealing particular knowledge of the situation.

"Not exactly," Priya admitted. "Though Professor Lowell—that's Dr. Nisha Lowell from Cultural Studies—was apparently quite vocal about certain participants and their qualifications. The department gossip suggests there's history there beyond academic disagreement, but no one seems to know details."

The implications were clear enough—Nisha had been using her position as co-director to question Farrat's participation in the retreat, creating professional challenges on top of the personal complexity they had already identified. No wonder the situation had created sufficient stress to potentially contribute to his physical collapse, especially if combined with the typical end-of-term workload and preparation for the retreat itself.

They arrived at the University Health Center, a modern building attached to the main medical complex that served both the campus community and the surrounding neighborhood. Priya led the way through the institutional corridors with the confident navigation of someone familiar with the layout, bringing them to a registration desk where she explained the purpose of their visit.

"Professor Mirza is in observation room 3B," the receptionist informed them after checking her computer. "Dr. Winslow is currently with him. You can go back, but you may need to wait if they're conducting tests."

"Thank you," Tauree replied, professional courtesy automatic despite the unfamiliar environment and unexpected circumstances.

"I should head to my seminar," Priya said, glancing at her watch. "Would you like me to stay and show you the way to the observation area?"

"That's not necessary," Tauree assured her, noting the clearly marked directional signs throughout the facility. "Thank you for your assistance. Please don't be late to your academic commitments on my account."

"Tell the professor I hope he feels better soon," Priya said as she prepared to depart. Then, with a suddenly more serious expression: "And make sure he actually rests. He's terrible at self-care when there's work to be done or others to consider."

"I'll convey the message," Tauree promised, recognizing the genuine concern beneath the young woman's direct manner.

As Priya departed with a quick wave, Tauree made her way toward the observation area, following the institutional signage through corridors that exhibited the typical healthcare environment—efficient but impersonal, functional without warmth. Her mind continued processing the information she had gathered, connecting Farrat's fainting episode with the retreat complications and his general tendency to prioritize others' needs above his own wellbeing.

She located room 3B and paused outside, hearing voices in conversation beyond the partially closed door. One was recognizably Farrat's, though it carried an unusual weariness beneath his typical measured cadence. The other belonged to a woman, her tone professionally neutral with underlying authority—presumably Dr. Winslow mentioned by the receptionist.

"—simply a recommendation to reduce stress and ensure adequate rest and nutrition," the doctor was saying as Tauree approached. "The tests show no underlying condition beyond the obvious physical exhaustion and mild dehydration. But these episodes can be warning signs that your current patterns are unsustainable."

"I understand," Farrat replied, his voice carrying that quality of respectful attention Tauree had observed in his interactions with experts across fields. "The timing is unfortunate with end-of-term responsibilities and the retreat next week, but I'll make appropriate adjustments."

"I'd recommend canceling non-essential commitments entirely," the doctor countered, her tone firming slightly. "Your body has given you a clear signal that it requires recovery time. Modifying activities may not be sufficient if the underlying stressors remain present."

"Some commitments represent professional opportunities that won't recur," Farrat explained, his voice revealing careful navigation between acknowledgment of medical advice and assertion of personal priorities. "But I understand your recommendation and will implement meaningful changes, not merely cosmetic adjustments."

Tauree hesitated outside the door, reluctant to interrupt what seemed an important medical conversation. As she considered whether to wait in a nearby sitting area, the doctor's voice rose slightly as if concluding the discussion.

"I'll note your response in the chart, Professor Mirza. The discharge papers will include specific recommendations for nutrition, hydration, and stress management. I strongly encourage you to follow them, even when they conflict with your professional commitments or personal inclinations."

The door opened fully then, revealing a middle-aged woman in a white coat who paused briefly upon seeing Tauree in the hallway.

"Are you here for Professor Mirza?" the doctor asked, professional assessment evident in her quick visual evaluation.

"Yes," Tauree replied simply, offering no elaboration on the nature of their connection.

"He's being discharged shortly," Dr. Winslow informed her. "Make sure he actually rests tonight instead of returning to work. The body doesn't negotiate when it reaches its limits—it simply enforces them, as he discovered this afternoon."

"I understand," Tauree said, professional seriousness matching the doctor's tone.

With a brief nod, Dr. Winslow continued down the corridor, leaving Tauree to enter the observation room where Farrat sat on the edge of an examination bed. He was dressed in his usual clothes, though they appeared somewhat rumpled, presumably from the fall and subsequent medical attention. His complexion was paler than usual, with subtle shadows beneath his eyes suggesting the exhaustion the doctor had referenced.

"Tauree," he said, genuine surprise crossing his features before warming into evident pleasure at her arrival. "You didn't need to come. I hoped Priya would simply explain my absence so you wouldn't be left wondering."

"She delivered your message," Tauree confirmed, moving into the room with measured steps that respected the potential vulnerability of his current state without expressing excessive concern. "And offered transportation, which seemed practical given the circumstances."

"Thank you for coming," he said simply, the words carrying deeper appreciation than their brevity might suggest. "I apologize for disrupting our plans. The timing of this... episode was remarkably inconvenient."

"Medical events rarely consult one's calendar before manifesting," Tauree observed, a hint of wry humor entering her voice as she settled onto a chair near the examination bed. "Though I suspect the timing isn't entirely coincidental, given what Priya mentioned about tensions regarding the literary retreat."

A flash of recognition crossed Farrat's features—not surprise that she had made the connection, but acknowledgment that she had already gathered relevant information and drawn appropriate conclusions. This had become characteristic of their interaction: the assumption of perceptiveness rather than the need for elaborate explanation, the recognition of each other's analytical capabilities without requiring demonstration.

"The situation has become more complex than I initially described," he admitted, running a hand through his already disheveled hair in a gesture of uncharacteristic discomposure. "Nisha has taken her co-director role as an opportunity to question my participation entirely, suggesting my work lacks the 'contemporary relevance' the retreat aims to showcase. The debate became rather heated in today's faculty meeting, immediately before my... undignified collapse."

"Hardly undignified to respond physiologically to sustained stress," Tauree countered, her tone matter-of-fact rather than consoling. "The body has its own architectural integrity, which asserts itself when structural limits are approached. No different from materials in a building responding to excessive load."

The parallel—drawing on her professional vocabulary to normalize his experience rather than pathologize it—created a visible shift in Farrat's expression, a relaxation of tension he might not have recognized he was carrying.

"An architectural perspective on physical collapse," he said, a small smile warming his features despite his evident fatigue. "Somehow more reassuring than the conventional medical framework of 'listening to your body' and other vague directives."

"Both approaches have validity," Tauree acknowledged. "But one uses the language of failure while the other recognizes natural systems of protection activating as designed. I prefer the latter framing, particularly in this instance."

A nurse appeared at the doorway with discharge papers and final instructions, interrupting their conversation. Tauree stepped back while the medical professional reviewed recommendations for rest, hydration, and follow-up care, noting Farrat's attentive reception of information despite his evident eagerness to depart the clinical environment.

Once the formalities were complete and they were alone again, Farrat rose from the examination bed with careful movements that suggested persistent lightheadedness beneath his composed exterior.

"May I offer transportation?" Tauree asked, practical assistance rather than anxious hovering. "I assume you don't have your car, given the circumstances of your arrival."

"That would be very helpful," Farrat acknowledged with characteristic directness. "Though I hate to impose further on your afternoon, which has already been significantly disrupted."

"No imposition," Tauree assured him, gathering her bag and the discharge papers the nurse had left. "I'll call a rideshare that can take us to your apartment. Unless you need to return to campus for any reason?"

"No," Farrat replied, visible relief suggesting the thought of returning to the university held little appeal after the day's events. "My essential materials are in my messenger bag, which a colleague brought to the medical center. Everything else can wait until tomorrow."

As they made their way through the medical facility toward the exit, Tauree noticed Farrat's careful pace and slightly unsteady gait—subtle indicators that his physical condition remained compromised despite the professional composure he maintained. Without comment or excessive attention, she adjusted her own movements to remain beside him, creating unobtrusive support without drawing attention to his temporary vulnerability.

Outside, autumn sunlight cast long shadows across the medical center plaza, the late afternoon light golden against the institutional architecture. Tauree guided them to a bench while she arranged for transportation on her phone, allowing Farrat to rest without explicitly suggesting he needed to do so.

"The threshold poems," he said suddenly as they waited, "were what I wanted to share with you today. The completed sequence that emerged from our conversations about architectural and emotional transitions. I brought the manuscript to Serendipity."

"We can reschedule that review," Tauree replied, practical prioritization automatic in her response. "Your recovery takes precedence over literary consultation."

"Of course," Farrat acknowledged. "But I would still value your perspective before the retreat, if timing permits. The poems represent something significant in my recent work—a direct engagement with the intersection of physical and emotional space that has developed through our ongoing dialogue."

There was something in his tone—not merely professional interest in feedback, but a deeper significance attached to sharing this particular creative expression. Tauree recognized it immediately: these poems represented a manifestation of their shared exploration, a creative articulation of the territory they had been navigating together. His desire to share them before the retreat carried meaning beyond literary consultation.

"Perhaps I could review them this evening," she suggested, a solution emerging that respected both his creative priorities and the medical advice for rest. "After you're settled at home. I could collect takeout on the way, ensuring appropriate nutrition without requiring food preparation on your part."

The offer—practical assistance framed without emotional excess—created visible relief in Farrat's expression. "That would be ideal, if it doesn't impose too significantly on your schedule. I have no other commitments this evening, having cleared my calendar for our original meeting at Serendipity."

"No imposition," Tauree assured him as their rideshare arrived at the curb. "I'll simply relocate our planned conversation to a more appropriate venue given the circumstances."

The drive to Farrat's apartment proceeded in comfortable silence, each processing the day's unexpected developments without requiring immediate discussion. Tauree arranged for the car to stop at a restaurant near his building—a Mediterranean place they had ordered from during the storm months earlier, which offered nutritious options aligned with the medical recommendations in the discharge papers.

Farrat's apartment welcomed them with familiar warmth when they finally arrived, the converted industrial space maintaining that perfect balance of intellectual engagement and physical comfort that Tauree had noticed during her first visit. The floor-to-ceiling bookshelves organized by emotional resonance rather than conventional categorization, the carefully positioned lighting that created layers of illumination throughout the open plan, the comfortable furniture arranged to permit both conversation and solitary reading—all elements that reflected Farrat's particular way of inhabiting space.

"Please make yourself comfortable," he said as they entered, his movements still carrying that careful deliberation that suggested persistent physical fragility beneath his composed exterior. "I need a moment to change into something less... institutional."

He disappeared down the hallway toward his bedroom, leaving Tauree to arrange their takeout containers on the kitchen counter with methodical precision. She located plates and utensils with ease, remembering their placement from her previous visit during the storm—a small detail that struck her as significant in its normalcy, this accumulated knowledge of another's private space that developed through repeated interaction.

When Farrat returned, he had changed into more comfortable clothing—loose-fitting pants and a soft sweater in deep blue that somehow made him appear simultaneously more relaxed and more vulnerable. His hair was damp, suggesting he had splashed water on his face or perhaps taken a quick shower to remove the institutional atmosphere of the medical center. The effect was a visible reset, a transition from patient back to person that Tauree recognized as both physical and psychological necessity.

"That smells wonderful," he observed, approaching the kitchen with more natural movement than he had displayed at the medical center. "I didn't realize how hungry I was until this moment. Apparently collapsing dramatically in front of one's colleagues creates quite an appetite."

The self-deprecating humor—acknowledging the situation without dwelling on its potential seriousness—created a small smile on Tauree's face as she finished arranging their meal on plates rather than eating directly from containers. The small civility seemed important somehow, a restoration of dignity after the vulnerability of medical circumstances.

"The discharge papers emphasized protein and complex carbohydrates," she noted, indicating the selections she had made. "Hummus, grilled chicken, roasted vegetables, brown rice. Medical recommendations executed in culinary form."

"Perfect," Farrat said with genuine appreciation. "And remarkably thoughtful. Thank you, Tauree. Not just for the food, but for..." He paused, searching for words adequate to encompass the day's unexpected developments. "For responding to this situation with such practical consideration. Many would have defaulted to either excessive concern or awkward distance."

"Those responses serve emotional needs of the responder rather than practical needs of the situation," Tauree observed, her analytical perspective automatic yet accurate. "Neither seemed particularly useful in this context."

They settled at the kitchen counter rather than moving to the more formal dining table, the casual arrangement creating exactly the right balance of connection and independence for their meal. Conversation flowed easily despite the unusual circumstances, touching on the community center's approaching completion, Farrat's department politics beyond the retreat controversy, and the changing autumn light that transformed the city's architecture each afternoon.

Neither directly addressed the medical episode or its potential implications until they had finished eating and moved to the more comfortable seating area near the bookshelves. Tauree noticed Farrat's movements had become more natural with proper nutrition and hydration, his color gradually returning to normal as the physical deficits that had triggered his collapse began to correct themselves.

"The threshold poems are here," he said, retrieving a slim leather portfolio from his messenger bag. "If you're still willing to review them this evening. I understand completely if you'd prefer to reschedule, given the day's unexpected developments."

"I'd like to see them," Tauree replied with genuine interest. "If you're not too fatigued for substantive discussion."

"Actually, I find I'm experiencing that peculiar energy that sometimes follows physical collapse," Farrat admitted. "As if the body, having enforced its limits through dramatic means, now wishes to demonstrate its resilience through equally dramatic recovery. I suspect a crash will follow, but for now, I'm quite capable of literary conversation."

He opened the portfolio and extracted a slim manuscript, the pages neatly typed with occasional handwritten annotations in the margins—evidence of the revision process that transformed initial inspiration into refined expression. The title page read simply "Thresholds" with Farrat's name below and a dedication: "For T.S., who illuminated the architecture of transition."

The simple acknowledgment—neither excessive in its emotional declaration nor diminished to professional formality—created that now-familiar warmth in Tauree's chest, a recognition that their ongoing dialogue had directly influenced his creative work in ways he was willing to publicly acknowledge.

"May I?" she asked, extending her hand toward the manuscript.

"Please," Farrat replied, passing it to her with a gesture that carried both offering and vulnerability—the particular quality of trust required to share creative work before its final form had been established.

Tauree began reading with the focused attention she brought to architectural plans or structural calculations, her analytical mind engaging with the organizational principles of the poetic sequence before responding to its emotional content. The collection comprised twelve poems arranged in a deliberate progression, beginning with physical thresholds—doorways, windows, bridges—before transitioning to more abstract territories of perception and relationship.

What struck her immediately was how accurately Farrat had captured the particular quality of threshold spaces she had articulated in her architectural designs—that curious territory that existed between defined categories, that permitted multiple modes of engagement simultaneously, that created transition without requiring rigid boundary. His poetic vocabulary had translated her spatial concepts into emotional exploration, expanding the framework they had developed together into new expressive territory.

The central poem in the sequence, titled simply "Nook," directly referenced the community center reading space she had designed, using its architectural features as metaphors for the psychological shelters humans created within social contexts:

Light filters through strategic apertures,
Neither fully revealing nor completely concealing
The territory where thought assumes physical form.
Here, in this constructed pause between public and private,
Words breathe differently—
Shaped by communal air yet intimate in their reception,

Each syllable finding its particular architecture
Within the shared shelter of attention.
I have searched for such spaces all my life:
Territories that permit both solitude and connection,
Where boundaries exist not as barriers
But as necessary definition of what might otherwise
Remain formless and therefore uninhabitable.
What you have built in physical form,
I attempt in language—
A structure that shelters without confining,
That guides without determining,
That acknowledges weather without surrendering to storm.

The final lines carried such direct acknowledgment of their shared metaphorical framework—the fog and rainfall that characterized their respective forms of depression—that Tauree felt momentarily exposed, as if a private conversation had suddenly been projected into public space. Yet the reference remained sufficiently abstract that only someone familiar with their particular dialogue would recognize its specific application, creating exactly the balance of disclosure and privacy that had characterized their evolving relationship.

She continued reading, noting how each subsequent poem built upon the foundation established by its predecessors, creating a cumulative exploration of threshold experiences that culminated in the final piece. This concluding work, titled "Microclimate," addressed directly the particular territory they had discovered between them—neither fully merged nor completely separate, a space where different weather patterns could coexist without overwhelming each other.

As she finished the manuscript, Tauree found herself experiencing an unfamiliar emotional response—not the analytical appreciation she typically brought to creative work, but something more visceral and immediate. The poems had articulated aspects of her experience she had never fully expressed, had captured the particular quality of connection they had established in language that felt precisely adequate to its complexity.

"These are..." she began, then paused, searching for words that would convey genuine response without defaulting to generic praise. "These represent something significant, Farrat. Not just artistically accomplished, though they certainly are that, but conceptually illuminating. You've translated spatial theory into emotional territory in ways I hadn't anticipated but immediately recognize as accurate."

"Thank you," he replied, genuine appreciation warming his voice. "That's precisely what I hoped to achieve—not merely aesthetic engagement but conceptual expansion. The dialogue between architectural and poetic perspectives has proven remarkably generative for my creative process."

"The final poem," Tauree observed, returning to the manuscript's concluding piece, "addresses our particular... weather systems more directly than your previous work. Is that intentional progression or evolutionary development?"

"Both, I think," Farrat acknowledged with characteristic thoughtfulness. "The sequence naturally moves from external to internal thresholds, from physical to emotional territories. But there's also been an evolution in my willingness to engage directly with what exists between us, rather than approaching it primarily through metaphor and parallel."

The observation aligned precisely with what they had discussed at Serendipity—that progression from implicit to explicit understanding, from metaphorical to direct acknowledgment of their evolving connection. The poetic sequence had tracked this same trajectory, culminating in more direct engagement with what had previously remained in the realm of suggestion and implication.

"And you'll present these at the retreat?" Tauree asked, returning to practical considerations from their more abstract exploration.

"Yes, though likely not the complete sequence given time constraints," Farrat explained. "I'll select representative pieces that establish the conceptual framework while respecting the formal parameters of the reading."

"Will you include 'Microclimate'?" she asked, curiosity genuine about how he would navigate the increasing directness of the later poems in a public setting, particularly given Nisha's presence and the complications she represented.

Farrat considered this thoughtfully, his expression revealing the careful calculation such decisions required. "I'm inclined to include it," he said finally. "Not as provocation or unnecessary revelation, but because it represents the culmination of the conceptual exploration. Without it, the sequence lacks its natural resolution, its architectural completion, if you will."

The architectural reference—drawing on her professional vocabulary to illuminate his creative decision—created that familiar sense of genuine dialogue between their separate disciplines, of translation across domains that had become characteristic of their connection.

"I agree," Tauree said after considering his reasoning. "The piece stands on its own artistic and conceptual merits, regardless of any personal elements that informed its creation. To exclude it for external considerations would compromise the integrity of the complete work."

Relief visibly relaxed Farrat's features, suggesting her perspective on this matter carried particular significance beyond mere literary feedback. "That was my assessment as well," he confirmed. "Though I wanted your perspective given the... increasingly direct engagement with what we've been exploring together."

A comfortable silence fell between them, filled with the ambient sounds of the apartment building and distant city traffic beyond the large windows. Outside, evening had fully settled, transforming the industrial-style space with that particular quality of urban night—soft darkness interrupted by distant lights, the glow of surrounding buildings creating an archipelago of illumination against the darkness.

"How are you feeling?" Tauree asked eventually, practical concern reasserting itself as she noticed subtle signs of returning fatigue in Farrat's posture and expression. "The discharge papers emphasized adequate rest following the episode."

"Increasingly aware that today's medical adventure was not merely dramatic inconvenience but genuine physical warning," he admitted with characteristic honesty. "The initial recovery energy is fading, leaving rather insistent reminders that my body successfully made its point about limits and boundaries."

"Then perhaps we should conclude our literary consultation," Tauree suggested, professional efficiency engaging in service of his wellbeing. "The poems are excellent, Farrat. They will represent your work admirably at the retreat, regardless of organizational complications or personal history with certain participants."

"Thank you," he said simply, the words encompassing appreciation for both her literary assessment and her practical consideration of his current limitations. "Not just for the feedback, but for... adapting to today's unexpected developments with such remarkable flexibility. Your capacity to maintain presence within changing circumstances continues to impress me."

The observation struck Tauree with unexpected force—not because it was particularly profound, but because it recognized an evolution in her behavior she hadn't fully acknowledged herself. Historically, unexpected disruptions to carefully structured plans had triggered anxiety and withdrawal, had thickened the fog until navigation became nearly impossible. Yet today's dramatic deviation from anticipated events had engaged her problem-solving capacity rather than her retreat mechanisms, had invited adaptation rather than abandonment.

"It surprised me as well," she admitted, the honesty easier in this space they had created between them where direct acknowledgment had gradually replaced metaphorical distance. "Typically, such significant disruption to expected patterns would have triggered... different responses."

"The flexibility wasn't at the expense of your fundamental nature," Farrat observed with characteristic perception. "You approached the disruption architecturally—assessing structural needs, implementing practical solutions, maintaining essential integrity while adapting formal expression. Not a compromise of your particular way of being, but its application to unexpected circumstances."

The insight—recognizing adaptation without fundamental change, evolution within consistent character—created that now-familiar sense of being truly seen, of having her particular nature understood without requiring elaborate explanation.

As Tauree prepared to leave, gathering her belongings and ensuring the kitchen was returned to its original order, she found herself contemplating the curious trajectory of this unexpected day. What had begun as a planned meeting to review literary work had transformed into medical assistance and home visitation, yet the essential purpose had still been fulfilled—the threshold poems had been shared and discussed, their significance acknowledged by both creator and recipient.

"Will you be alright this evening?" she asked as they moved toward the door, practical concern without excessive hovering. "The discharge papers emphasized monitoring for recurring symptoms."

"I'll be fine," Farrat assured her. "The university health service will call to check on me later, and I have neighbors who have been alertded to the situation. All necessary precautions without unnecessary anxiety."

The balance he struck—acknowledging legitimate concern without amplifying it into drama—was characteristic of how he consistently created space for both practical care and emotional composure. No dismissal of genuine risks, but no indulgence in their exaggeration either.

At the door, they paused in that familiar moment of transition that had characterized so many of their partings—the threshold between connection and separation, between shared experience and individual processing. Usually, this moment carried a comfortable ambiguity, neither requiring physical contact nor actively avoiding it, each reading the other's current capacity for such engagement without requiring explicit negotiation.

Tonight, however, Tauree felt an unfamiliar impulse toward concrete expression of the concern and connection she had experienced throughout this unexpected day. Without overthinking the gesture, she reached out and briefly clasped Farrat's hand—a simple touch that conveyed genuine acknowledgment without demanding elaborate response.

"Rest well," she said simply. "I'll check on you tomorrow."

"Thank you," Farrat replied, his fingers returning the brief pressure of hers before releasing, the contact neither extended beyond its natural conclusion nor shortened by discomfort. "For everything."

As Tauree made her way down the hallway toward the stairs, she found herself contemplating this small but significant gesture and what it represented in their evolving connection. Physical contact had rarely featured in their relationship, both maintaining careful attention to the other's boundaries in this domain as in others. Yet tonight's brief handclasp had felt neither intrusive nor performative—simply an appropriate expression of the particular quality of concern she had experienced, translated into physical form as naturally as their ideas had been translated between architectural and poetic vocabularies.

Outside, the autumn night was clear and cool, stars visible despite the city's ambient light. Tauree paused on the sidewalk, allowing herself a moment to process the day's unexpected developments before arranging transportation home. The fog remained present, as always, but it had maintained that unusual translucency that had characterized her perception in recent months, allowing her to navigate complex emotional terrain without becoming disoriented or overwhelmed.

Something was shifting in her experience—not dramatically or suddenly, but with the gradual persistence of natural evolution. The careful architect of precise spaces was learning, incrementally and with appropriate caution, to navigate territories that couldn't be completely planned or controlled. Not by abandoning her fundamental nature, as Farrat had so accurately observed, but by applying its strengths to new domains, by finding architectural solutions to emotional challenges.

As she finally arranged for a rideshare and began her journey home, Tauree found herself contemplating the threshold poems and their exploration of spaces that existed between defined categories. She and Farrat were creating just such a territory in their evolving relationship—neither conventional friendship nor traditional romance, neither casual acquaintance nor formal partnership. A custom architecture designed to accommodate their particular needs for both connection and autonomy, for both shared understanding and personal space.

The fog might never lift completely—that persistent gray filter would likely remain a constant feature of her internal landscape.

But she was discovering new ways to navigate within it, new points of reference that allowed orientation even when visibility remained limited. And in Farrat, she had found a fellow traveler who neither demanded the fog disperse nor pretended it didn't exist—who simply offered to walk alongside her through its varying densities, sharing his own rainfall in an exchange of understanding that had created, somehow, a microclimate uniquely their own.

Tomorrow would bring return to routine, to the final preparations for the community center opening and the professional demands of project completion. But something had shifted during this unexpected day, something that could not be undone or forgotten once ordinary patterns resumed. They had crossed another threshold together—from metaphorical to physical expression, from planned engagement to spontaneous adaptation—and had found, once again, that what lay beyond was neither threatening disaster nor miraculous transformation, but simply the next territory in their ongoing exploration, another space where different weathers could coexist without overwhelming each other.

Three days passed before Tauree saw Farrat again. Their communication continued through messages and a brief phone call, each respecting the other's professional demands while maintaining connection. He reported gradual recovery from the fainting episode, having implemented the medical recommendations with characteristic thoroughness—proper nutrition, adequate hydration, strategic rest periods between necessary academic obligations.

The community center consumed Tauree's attention almost completely during this period, the approaching opening ceremony requiring innumerable small decisions and adjustments that only she could authorize. The reading nook was finally complete, exactly as she had envisioned it—a threshold space within the larger architecture that permitted both community and solitude, both structured learning and organic discovery.

On the afternoon before Farrat's departure for the literary retreat, they arranged to meet at the community center—his suggestion, offered with characteristic consideration for her demanding schedule. "I'd like to see the completed reading nook before I leave," his message had explained. "Both to understand the physical manifestation of what inspired the threshold poems and to wish you well before your opening weekend. No pressure if timing doesn't permit."

Tauree had arranged for him to visit during a quiet period when contractors had completed their day's work but before the cleaning crew arrived for final preparations. The building would be empty except for them, allowing for unhurried observation without the distractions of other people or activities.

She waited near the main entrance, watching through glass doors as Farrat approached across the plaza that fronted the community center. His movements had returned to their natural rhythm, showing no lingering effects of the medical episode that had disrupted their plans days earlier. He carried his messenger bag, presumably containing the threshold poems and other materials for the retreat, and walked with that quality of attentive presence she had observed since their first genuine conversation—aware of his surroundings without being distracted by them, engaged without being scattered.

"You came," she said as she opened the door, completing their now-traditional greeting ritual.

"I said I would," Farrat replied, a small smile warming his features as he stepped into the building. Then, glancing around at the soaring entryway with its carefully positioned skylights and welcoming proportions: "This is remarkable, Tauree. The quality of light alone is extraordinary—the way it guides movement without forcing it, suggests pathways without demanding them."

The immediate engagement with the architectural essence of the space—seeing not just its physical form but its emotional intention—created that familiar sense of being truly understood, of having her work perceived not merely in technical terms but in its deeper purposes.

"Thank you," she said simply. "It's gratifying to see the design fully realized after months of existing only in plans and models. Come, I'll show you the reading nook. It's in the northeast corner, where morning light creates particularly interesting patterns across the floor and walls."

She led him through the building, noting with professional satisfaction how his movement responded naturally to the architectural cues she had designed—the subtle variations in ceiling height that created different qualities of space, the strategic positioning of visual anchors that drew attention toward intended focal points, the careful transitions between public and more intimate areas.

"You've created a genuinely democratic space," Farrat observed as they moved through the main gathering area. "Accessible without being simplified, sophisticated without being exclusive. That's remarkably difficult to achieve in public architecture."

"That was precisely the intention," Tauree confirmed, pleased by his perception of this core principle. "To create environments that invite engagement without requiring specific educational or cultural background to navigate successfully. Architecture that communicates directly through spatial experience rather than relying on learned codes or references."

They reached the reading nook, and Tauree paused at its threshold, allowing Farrat to experience the space on its own terms before she explained its design principles. The area was defined by subtle changes in floor material and ceiling height rather than walls or partitions, creating psychological boundaries without physical separation from the surrounding environment.

Bookshelves lined one wall, their height deliberately varied to create different qualities of enclosure and exposure. Comfortable seating was arranged in configurations that permitted both solitary reading and small group discussion, each position carefully calculated to provide both prospect (view of approaching others) and refuge (sense of backing and protection) as environmental psychology suggested was optimal for human comfort.

Most striking, however, was the quality of light. Skylights positioned with mathematical precision allowed natural illumination to enter at carefully calculated angles, creating patterns across the floor and walls that would shift throughout the day, tracking time through abstract choreography of light and shadow. The effect was simultaneously practical and poetic—functional illumination that also created aesthetic experience.

"It's exactly as you described," Farrat said quietly, moving into the space with evident appreciation. "A threshold territory that exists between defined categories, that permits multiple modes of engagement simultaneously. Architecture as poetry made physical."

"That's a generous interpretation," Tauree replied, though his assessment resonated with her own understanding of what she had created. "Though the influence of our conversations about thresholds and transitions is certainly present in the final design."

Farrat continued exploring the space, noting details with the same attentive perception he brought to literary analysis—the careful positioning of lighting fixtures that would complement natural illumination after sunset, the acoustic properties that created gentle separation from surrounding areas without complete isolation, the subtle color variations that defined different functional zones within the overall territory.

"Your poem captured it with remarkable accuracy," Tauree observed, recalling the piece titled "Nook" from his threshold sequence. "The quality of 'constructed pause between public and private' where 'words breathe differently' is precisely what I hoped to achieve in the physical design."

"The correspondence between our separate vocabularies continues to fascinate me," Farrat replied, settling onto one of the reading chairs as if testing its proportions and positioning. "How architectural principles and poetic concepts often describe the same essential human experiences through different linguistic frameworks."

Tauree joined him, taking a seat positioned at right angles to his—close enough for comfortable conversation while maintaining independent sightlines to the surrounding space. This careful balance of connection and autonomy had become characteristic of their physical positioning during conversations, each intuitively finding arrangements that honored both shared attention and individual perspective.

"How are you feeling about the retreat?" she asked, shifting from architectural appreciation to his immediate future. "Has the medical episode affected your planned participation?"

"I've modified the schedule somewhat," Farrat explained. "Declining some optional activities to ensure adequate rest between essential commitments. The reading of the threshold poems remains the primary focus, with necessary preparation and professional networking maintained while reducing purely social engagements."

"The architectural approach to social navigation we discussed," Tauree observed with a small smile, recalling their conversation about managing Nisha's presence at the event.

"Exactly," Farrat confirmed. "Controlled points of engagement within a broader system of thoughtful distancing. Though the medical episode provided convenient justification for such selectivity without requiring elaborate explanation."

"A tactical advantage emerging from unfortunate circumstances," Tauree noted with characteristic pragmatism.

"Indeed," Farrat agreed. "Though I would have preferred to discover such strategic solutions without dramatic physical collapse as catalyst."

Their conversation continued, moving between the community center design, the approaching opening ceremony, and practical considerations for the retreat. Throughout, Tauree noticed a subtle shift in their interaction—a comfortable directness that had gradually replaced the more careful navigation of their early acquaintance. Not a dramatic transformation, but an incremental evolution toward more explicit acknowledgment of what existed between them.

As evening approached, signaled by changing light patterns through the skylights Tauree had so carefully positioned, they began moving toward the building's exit. Farrat would depart for the retreat early the following morning, while Tauree remained in the city for the community center opening that represented the culmination of months of professional focus.

"I wish I could attend the opening," Farrat said as they reached the main entrance. "To witness the community's first engagement with what you've created here. It represents something significant in architectural philosophy, not merely functional design."

"Thank you," Tauree replied, genuine appreciation warming her voice. "Though I understand the retreat's timing couldn't be adjusted to accommodate my professional schedule. These intersections of opportunity and obligation rarely align perfectly."

"Perhaps that's appropriate," Farrat observed with characteristic thoughtfulness. "Each pursuing our separate professional directions while maintaining connection across the distance. Another form of threshold navigation—neither completely merged nor entirely separate."

The observation struck Tauree with its accuracy—this was indeed another manifestation of the particular balance they had established, another territory where boundaries existed not as barriers but as necessary definition of what might otherwise remain formless. Their separate professional worlds continued to develop along their natural trajectories, neither compromised nor distorted by their evolving relationship, yet increasingly informed by the ongoing dialogue between architectural and poetic perspectives.

"I'd like to hear about the retreat when you return," she said as they stepped outside into the early evening light. "How the threshold poems were received, whether the architectural approach to social navigation proved effective."

"I'd like that too," Farrat replied, his expression warming with anticipation of future exchange. "And I look forward to hearing about the community center opening—how actual users engage with the spaces you've designed, whether they discover the intended experiences or create unexpected ones."

They had reached that familiar moment of transition that characterized their partings—the threshold between connection and separation, between shared experience and individual processing. Usually, this carried a comfortable ambiguity, each reading the other's current capacity for engagement without requiring explicit negotiation.

Today, however, Farrat paused more deliberately than usual, his expression reflecting careful consideration before he spoke.

"May I share something before I leave?" he asked, his tone suggesting the question was genuine rather than rhetorical. "A thought that has been developing since our conversation at Serendipity and crystallized during my recent... medical adventure."

"Of course," Tauree replied, curiosity genuine about what had prompted this more formal approach to disclosure.

"I've been contemplating what we discussed about the particular nature of our connection," Farrat began, his words carefully chosen yet flowing naturally. "The unique balance we've established between autonomy and intimacy, between independence and mutual influence. And I've realized something that perhaps should have been obvious earlier, but sometimes the closest patterns are the most difficult to recognize."

He paused briefly, organizing thoughts with characteristic precision before continuing.

"What we've constructed together—this custom architecture of relationship that honors both connection and separation—isn't merely an accommodation of our respective limitations or challenges. It's a genuinely preferable arrangement, a more authentic expression of relationship than conventional models that demand either complete merger or rigid distance."

The insight struck Tauree with unexpected force—not because it was particularly surprising, but because it articulated something she had felt but not fully expressed. Their careful navigation of boundaries, their thoughtful creation of shared territory, their gradual development of mutual understanding across different perceptual frameworks—these weren't compromises necessitated by their respective forms of depression, but positive developments that honored more fundamental aspects of their individual natures.

"Yes," she said simply, the word carrying recognition beyond its brevity. "It's not a temporary accommodation until something more conventional becomes possible, but a deliberate architecture designed for sustainable habitation."

"Exactly," Farrat confirmed, visible pleasure at her immediate understanding. "Not a relationship defined by what it lacks or avoids, but by what it actively creates and maintains—this particular balance that permits both genuine connection and necessary solitude, both shared understanding and independent perception."

The clarity of this mutual recognition—this explicit acknowledgment of what they had been building together—created a moment of profound connection between them. Not the manufactured intensity of conventional romance, but something more substantial and authentic: the awareness of having discovered a form of relationship that served both their separate needs and their shared exploration.

"I wanted to articulate this before leaving," Farrat continued, "not as demand for response or commitment, but as explicit recognition of what has been implicitly developing between us. The threshold poems attempt to capture this in creative form, but sometimes direct statement serves where metaphor might permit ambiguity."

"I appreciate the directness," Tauree replied, her own capacity for explicit acknowledgment having evolved alongside their relationship. "It provides structural clarity without imposing rigid definition—another characteristic of good architecture."

The architectural reference—returning to her professional vocabulary in this moment of emotional significance—created a small smile of recognition between them, an acknowledgment of how consistently they translated between their separate disciplines, finding shared language in the space between their different expertise.

As evening settled more fully around them, the community center's exterior lighting activating automatically in response to declining natural illumination, they finally moved toward departure—Farrat to his final preparations for the retreat, Tauree to her remaining tasks before the opening ceremony.

"I'll message you when I arrive at the retreat tomorrow," Farrat said, maintaining their established pattern of undemanding communication.

"I'll check in about the opening on Saturday," Tauree replied, completing the exchange with similar attention to balanced connection.

This time, their parting included no physical contact, no repetition of the handclasp that had marked their previous farewell. Yet somehow the absence felt neither like retreat nor rejection—simply another expression of their particular understanding, another recognition that connection didn't require constant physical manifestation to remain authentic and meaningful.

As Tauree watched Farrat walk away across the plaza, his figure gradually blending with the evening shadows, she found herself contemplating the curious evolution they had articulated together. What had begun as reluctant attendance at a social obligation had developed into something neither could have anticipated—a relationship that existed in that threshold space between defined categories, that permitted multiple modes of engagement simultaneously, that honored difference while establishing genuine understanding across it.

The fog remained present, as always, that persistent gray filter through which she experienced the world. But it had become increasingly navigable, its patterns more predictable, its effects less isolating. Not because Farrat had somehow dispelled it, but because he had been willing to acknowledge its reality while still engaging with the person who existed within its confines.

As she turned back toward the community center, her professional focus reasserting itself after this brief personal interlude, Tauree carried with her a quiet certainty about the particular architecture they were constructing together. Not a conventional structure built according to social expectation or romantic tradition, but a custom design created through careful attention to both individual needs and mutual possibilities, a space where different weathers could coexist without overwhelming each other.

Tomorrow would bring separation—physical distance as each pursued their separate professional commitments. But the connection they had established would continue across that distance, neither diminished by absence nor dependent on constant presence. Another threshold territory to navigate, another opportunity to discover how their particular understanding might adapt to changing circumstances while maintaining its essential character.

The community center doors closed behind her with a soft sound of mechanical precision, returning her attention to the immediate demands of final preparations before the opening ceremony. Yet even as she moved through the building with professional efficiency, noting last details that required adjustment and confirming arrangements for the weekend's events, a part of her mind remained engaged with what she and Farrat had recognized together:

That what existed between them wasn't merely accommodation of limitation, but active creation of possibility. Not compromise, but innovation. Not settling for less, but discovering something different—a relationship architecture designed precisely for their particular ways of being in the world, a custom structure that permitted both connection and solitude, both shared understanding and independent perception.

A threshold space, uniquely their own.

Act 2: The Build-Up and Growing Tension

Chapter 10: The Reunion

Four days without Farrat created an unexpected space in Tauree's carefully structured existence. Though their physical meetings had never been daily occurrences, his absence at the literary retreat generated a curious awareness of distance that transcended mere geography. As she moved through the final preparations for the community center opening, she found herself mentally composing observations she would share upon his return, collecting moments that would bridge the temporary separation they had agreed was professionally necessary for them both.

The community center opening proceeded with meticulous precision, exactly as she had planned through months of detailed preparation. City officials delivered appropriately brief speeches, community stakeholders expressed predictably enthusiastic appreciation, and the assembled crowd moved through the spaces with the mixture of curiosity and celebration such events typically generated. Tauree navigated these interactions with practiced professional composure, addressing questions about design elements and architectural choices with the clear, technical explanations that had become her signature communication style in public contexts.

Only once during the ceremony did she experience an unexpected moment of emotional connection to the proceedings. As Miguel, the project foreman who had initially been skeptical of certain design choices, arrived with his daughter—a literature student who wrote poetry—Tauree found herself watching their introduction to the reading nook with unusual attentiveness. The young woman's expression as she encountered the threshold space Tauree had created—that territory between public and private, between structured learning and organic discovery—carried a quality of immediate recognition that transcended the usual polite appreciation.

"It's exactly what I've been trying to describe to my professor," the girl told her father, unaware that Tauree stood within earshot. "A space that exists between categories, that permits different modes of engagement simultaneously. Like the best poems—structured enough to create meaning but open enough to allow personal interpretation."

The observation—so precisely aligned with what Tauree and Farrat had discussed about threshold spaces—created an unexpected tightness in her chest. Here was direct evidence that her architectural vision could translate across different perceptual frameworks, could speak to others who navigated the world through entirely different disciplinary vocabularies. It was one thing to experience this recognition with Farrat, whose particular sensitivity and attention had created a unique channel of understanding between them. It was quite another to witness it in a stranger who had no knowledge of the conversations that had informed the design.

Later that evening, as the crowds departed and the community center settled into the quiet that would become its nighttime character, Tauree remained behind, wanting to experience the spaces without the distortion of ceremonial attention or public performance. She made her way to the reading nook, settling into one of the carefully positioned chairs that offered both prospect and refuge, and observed how the artificial lighting interacted with the architectural elements now that natural illumination had faded.

She had designed this transition with meticulous attention—how the space would transform from day to evening, maintaining its essential character while adapting to changing conditions. The effect was exactly as she had envisioned: warm pools of light creating intimate territories within the larger environment, shadows defining boundaries without constructing barriers, illumination guiding without demanding.

It was in this moment of professional satisfaction, of quiet recognition that her vision had been successfully realized, that she found herself reaching for her phone. The impulse to share this experience with Farrat emerged without calculation or deliberation—a natural extension of how their separate professional lives had gradually become reference points for each other, territories of individual focus that nevertheless permitted moments of shared recognition.

The message she composed maintained their established balance of specific observation without excessive elaboration:

The community center opening proceeded as planned. Currently experiencing the reading nook in evening conditions—the artificial lighting creates exactly the threshold quality we discussed, defining territories without imposing boundaries. The daughter of the project foreman recognized the space as "existing between categories" without prompting, suggesting the architectural intention translates across different perceptual frameworks. I hope the retreat is providing similar confirmation of your threshold poems.

She sent it without overthinking the content or timing, then returned her attention to the space around her. Unlike her usual careful monitoring for response, she set the phone aside, allowing whatever reply might come to arrive in its own time rather than becoming the focus of her attention. This too represented an evolution in her communication patterns—the capacity to initiate connection without requiring immediate reciprocation, to extend an observation without attaching expectation to its reception.

The fog remained present, as always, that persistent gray filter through which she experienced the world. But tonight it held a peculiar quality of transparency, as if the successful realization of her architectural vision had temporarily clarified the medium through which she perceived her surroundings. Not fog lifting exactly, but fog becoming sufficiently translucent that details emerged with unusual precision.

She remained in the reading nook for nearly an hour, observing how the space functioned in this quieter, more intimate condition. Different than the public performance of the opening ceremony, this was the environment's true test—how it would serve those seeking refuge within community, connection within independence. The proportions, the lighting, the acoustics, the carefully calculated relationships between elements—all functioned exactly as intended, creating that balance of structure and flexibility she had envisioned from the beginning.

When she finally rose to leave, her phone still showed no response from Farrat. This created no anxiety or concern, only a recognition that their separate professional commitments required different patterns of attention and availability. He had mentioned the scheduled reading of his threshold poems would occur Saturday evening—the same time as her community center opening. Their parallel professional culminations, occurring simultaneously but in separate locations, seemed an appropriate manifestation of the particular relationship they had been building: connected yet independent, influenced without being merged.

As she gathered her belongings and prepared to depart, Tauree found herself contemplating this curious evolution in her response to silence. Earlier in her life, unanswered messages had triggered immediate retreat, a defensive withdrawal based on the assumption of rejection or disinterest. Now she experienced a different quality of interpretation—not anxious projection of negative possibilities, but simple recognition that communication occurred within contexts that sometimes permitted immediate exchange and sometimes required delayed response.

This shift didn't represent dramatic transformation of her fundamental nature, as Farrat had so accurately observed during his medical episode. She hadn't suddenly developed conventional emotional responses or abandoned her careful approach to social engagement. Rather, she had discovered new applications of her existing strengths—architectural solutions to relationship challenges, structural approaches to interpersonal navigation.

The community center locked securely behind her, its security systems activating with mechanical precision as she departed. Tomorrow would bring further professional obligations—post-opening assessments, initial operational adjustments, documentation of how actual usage aligned with or deviated from designed intention. But tonight she had witnessed the successful realization of a vision that had evolved alongside her relationship with Farrat, had seen how their conversations about threshold spaces had influenced and enriched her architectural approach without compromising its essential integrity.

The fog might never lift completely—that persistent gray filter would likely remain a constant feature of her internal landscape. But she was discovering new ways to navigate within it, new points of reference that allowed orientation even when visibility remained limited. And in Farrat, she had found a fellow traveler who neither demanded the fog disperse nor pretended it didn't exist—who simply offered to walk alongside her through its varying densities, sharing his own rainfall in an exchange of understanding that had created, somehow, a microclimate uniquely their own.

Sunday morning brought clear autumn skies and a message from Farrat, waiting on her phone when she woke:

Last night's reading proceeded despite organizational complications. The threshold poems were received with unexpected enthusiasm, particularly by those with architectural backgrounds who recognized the spatial concepts translated into emotional terrain.

"Microclimate" generated significant discussion about territories that exist between conventional categories. A publisher expressed interest in the complete sequence. Nisha maintained professional distance, though her review notes referenced "excessive abstraction" and "retreat from emotional directness." I found myself unexpectedly grateful for the physical separation that allowed the work to stand on its own merits without personal history complicating its reception. Congratulations on your community center opening—the recognition you described confirms what I've always appreciated about your work: its ability to communicate complex concepts through direct spatial experience.

The message carried that quality of specific detail and thoughtful reflection that characterized their communication—information about significant developments without excessive elaboration, personal observation without emotional demand. Tauree read it twice, appreciating both the content and the particular balance it maintained between professional report and personal connection.

As she prepared for the day ahead, moving through her morning routine with habitual precision, she composed a response that maintained their established pattern:

I'm pleased the threshold poems found receptive audience despite organizational complications. The architectural translation works in both directions, it seems—my spatial concepts into your emotional exploration, your poetic frameworks into my structural approach. Publisher interest represents appropriate recognition of the work's significance beyond our particular dialogue. I look forward to hearing more details upon your return. The community center continues its transition from designed intention to lived experience today as regular operations begin.

The exchange complete—neither overcommunicative nor artificially restrained—Tauree turned her attention to the day ahead. The first true operational day of the community center would provide critical data about how actual users engaged with the spaces she had designed, whether they discovered the intended experiences or created unexpected ones. This represented the ultimate test of architectural vision: not the ceremonial opening with its predictable appreciation, but the ordinary use that would reveal whether the design truly served its intended purpose.

She arrived at the community center mid-morning, after regular weekend programming had begun. Unlike the previous day's formal events, today's activities represented natural community engagement—children's reading groups in the main gathering space, adult education classes in the learning studios, informal social interaction in the café area. Tauree moved through these environments with professional attentiveness, observing patterns of use and interaction without disrupting them through obvious examination.

The reading nook had attracted several occupants, each engaging with the space in slightly different ways. An elderly man sat in the corner position she had designed specifically for solitary reading, his position utilizing the carefully calculated balance of privacy and connection she had intended. A pair of teenage girls occupied the small discussion area, their conversation animated but contained within the acoustic boundaries created by ceiling height and material selection. A middle-aged woman alternated between reading and observing the activity in the main area, her position at the threshold between spaces allowing precisely the dual engagement Tauree had envisioned.

This successful realization of design intention created a quiet satisfaction that transcended mere professional pride. The spaces were functioning as genuine environments for human experience, not merely as architectural statements or technical achievements. People were discovering and utilizing the particular qualities she had incorporated—the threshold territories, the balanced relationships between elements, the subtle guidance that permitted choice without requiring it.

As she continued her observation, moving between different areas of the building with unobtrusive attention, Tauree's phone vibrated with another message from Farrat:

Departing retreat early due to unexpected schedule change—final workshop canceled when presenter became ill. Should arrive back in city by late afternoon. Would you be available for coffee this evening? I'd like to share retreat observations and hear more about community center reception while both experiences remain fresh. Serendipity at 7:00? No pressure either way.

The invitation—characteristic in its offering of connection without expectation—created that now-familiar warmth in Tauree's chest. Their planned reunion had been accelerated by circumstances neither could have anticipated, creating an opportunity for exchange while their parallel professional culminations remained immediate rather than filtered through memory and reflection.

She checked her schedule—the community center observation could reasonably conclude by late afternoon, with documentation and analysis continuing tomorrow. The prospect of sharing her architectural experiences while they remained immediately accessible, and hearing Farrat's literary observations before they became retrospective, held genuine appeal beyond mere social engagement.

Serendipity at 7:00 works well. Looking forward to comparing notes on our respective professional territories while impressions remain immediate.

As she sent the response, Tauree recognized another subtle evolution in her communication patterns—the expression of genuine anticipation without calculation or performance. Unlike her typical careful assessment of social engagement as obligation to be managed, this interaction carried a quality of authentic interest that required no professional justification or logical framework to validate it.

The remainder of her observation period at the community center proceeded with focused attention, her professional perspective cataloging patterns of use and interaction with methodical precision. Yet beneath this analytical approach, an awareness of the evening's planned conversation created a parallel current of reflection—which elements would translate most effectively into their shared vocabulary of threshold spaces, what observations might contribute to their ongoing exploration of territories that existed between defined categories.

By late afternoon, she had completed her professional assessment, documenting key observations and identifying minor adjustments that might enhance the spaces' functionality without compromising their essential character. The community center was operating exactly as she had intended—not with rigid adherence to predetermined patterns, but with the flexible responsiveness to actual human needs that had been central to her design philosophy.

As she departed, exchanging brief professional acknowledgments with the operational staff who would maintain the environment in her absence, Tauree felt a curious satisfaction that transcended mere project completion. The community center represented not just successful execution of architectural vision, but embodiment of concepts that had evolved through her conversations with Farrat—ideas about threshold spaces and perceptual frameworks that had gradually transformed her approach without fundamentally altering its essential character.

She returned to her apartment with sufficient time to transition from professional observation to evening meeting, changing from the more formal attire the community center opening had required to simpler clothing that reflected her personal aesthetic rather than professional presentation. The shift was subtle but significant—movement from public performance to more authentic self-expression, from designed impression to genuine presence.

The autumn evening had brought earlier darkness as the season progressed, street lights already illuminating the city as she walked toward Serendipity. Unlike their storm-driven meeting months earlier, tonight was clear and cool, perfect weather for walking the moderate distance rather than arranging transportation. The rhythm of movement through urban space created a welcome transition between her day's professional focus and the approaching conversation, a physical manifestation of the shift between separate territories they navigated together.

Serendipity Café welcomed her with familiar warmth—the wood paneling, mismatched but comfortable furniture, and walls lined with thoughtfully curated books creating that perfect balance of intellectual engagement and physical comfort she had appreciated since her first visit. The space remained that ideal combination of community and individuality, of connection and independence that aligned so precisely with her architectural philosophy.

Farrat was already there, seated at what had become their usual corner table illuminated by one of the café's characteristic reading lamps. Unlike their previous meeting, which had been disrupted by his medical emergency, tonight he appeared rested and attentive, his expression warming immediately as their eyes met across the space.

"You came," he said, rising slightly as she approached the table, completing their now-traditional greeting ritual.

"I said I would," Tauree replied, settling into the chair opposite him. She noted the two mugs already waiting—a strong black coffee for her, what appeared to be a spiced chai for him. The consideration in this preparation—anticipating her arrival, remembering her preference—created another moment of that quiet warmth that had become characteristic of their interactions.

"How was the remainder of your retreat?" she asked, wrapping her hands around the coffee mug with appreciation for both its heat and the thoughtfulness it represented.

"Productive despite the organizational complications," Farrat replied, his expression reflecting careful assessment rather than simple categorization. "The threshold poems generated more significant response than I had anticipated, particularly from those who recognized the architectural concepts translated into emotional exploration."

"Including the publisher who expressed interest?" Tauree asked, recalling this detail from his earlier message.

"Yes," Farrat confirmed. "A small but respected literary press specializing in cross-disciplinary work. The editor was particularly drawn to how the sequence navigates territories between defined categories, creating experiences that exist simultaneously in multiple frameworks rather than requiring exclusive classification."

"That's precisely what I hoped to achieve with the community center reading nook," Tauree observed, the parallel emerging with natural ease. "A space that permits different modes of engagement without demanding selection between them."

"How was the public response to that element of the design?" Farrat asked, genuine interest evident in his expression. "Your message mentioned the project foreman's daughter recognizing its threshold quality without prompting."

"That was merely first confirmation," Tauree replied, satisfaction warming her voice as she described the day's observations. "Today I witnessed actual usage patterns that aligned precisely with design intention—different individuals utilizing the same environment for varied purposes simultaneously without conflict or compromise. The threshold quality functioning exactly as conceived, creating territories that permit both connection and independence, both structured engagement and organic discovery."

As they continued sharing their parallel professional experiences—Farrat's literary presentation and subsequent discussions, Tauree's architectural realization and observed functionality—a familiar pattern emerged in their exchange. Each translated aspects of their separate disciplines into terms the other could access and appreciate, creating bridges between territories that might otherwise remain disconnected. The threshold poems and reading nook became reference points for understanding how similar concepts could manifest through different expressive forms, how spatial and verbal frameworks could address the same essential human experiences.

"And Nisha's presence?" Tauree asked eventually, recalling the organizational complication that had created potential tension in the retreat context. "Did the architectural approach to social navigation prove effective?"

"Remarkably so," Farrat acknowledged, a hint of surprise in his tone suggesting the strategy had exceeded his expectations. "The controlled points of engagement within a broader system of thoughtful distancing created precisely the balance required—professional interaction without unnecessary personal complication. Her review notes referenced 'excessive abstraction' and 'retreat from emotional directness,' but the criticism remained within appropriate academic parameters rather than extending into more personal territory."

"The structural solution to social challenge functioning as intended," Tauree observed with quiet satisfaction. "Creating necessary separation while maintaining essential connection."

"Exactly," Farrat agreed, appreciation for her architectural framing evident in his expression. "Though I found myself surprisingly grateful for a different aspect of the situation than I had anticipated."

"Oh?" Tauree prompted, curiosity genuine.

"The physical separation between us," Farrat explained, his tone thoughtful rather than dramatic. "Not because I wished for your absence, but because it allowed the threshold poems to stand entirely on their own merits, to be received without extraneous associations or assumptions based on observed connection between creator and inspiration."

The observation struck Tauree with unexpected force—not because it suggested diminished significance of their relationship, but because it acknowledged the value of independence within connection, of separation as positive quality rather than mere absence of proximity. This had become central to their evolving understanding: that distance need not represent disconnection, that periods of separate development strengthened rather than threatened their particular balance.

"I experienced something similar with the community center," she acknowledged, the parallel emerging as she considered his observation. "There was value in observing how others engaged with the spaces without my explaining the design intentions or theoretical foundations. Seeing actual usage patterns emerge organically rather than in response to architectural explanation."

"The creations functioning independently of their creators," Farrat suggested, the insight characteristic of their shared explorations. "While still carrying the essential qualities that emerged from our ongoing dialogue about threshold territories."

As their conversation continued, flowing with that same surprising ease Tauree had experienced throughout their relationship, Malcolm approached their table with the unobtrusive attention that characterized his café management. The elderly former professor carried a small plate of pastries, which he set between them with a warm smile.

"On the house," he said simply. "To celebrate your respective professional achievements. Farrat mentioned the publisher's interest in his threshold poems, and I noticed the community center opening was featured in today's paper."

The gesture—acknowledging both their separate accomplishments and their shared presence—created a moment of unexpected connection among the three of them. Malcolm had become, without deliberate intention, a witness to the evolution of their relationship, from that storm-driven evening months earlier to this quiet celebration of parallel professional developments.

"Thank you, Malcolm," Farrat replied with genuine appreciation. "Not just for the pastries, but for creating this environment where such conversations can develop naturally."

"Sanctuary spaces are increasingly rare," the former professor observed with the quiet wisdom of his years. "Territories that permit both intellectual engagement and emotional authenticity, both connection and contemplation. I merely attempt to maintain one small example in an otherwise fragmented world."

After he had departed with a gentle nod, Tauree found herself considering his description—"sanctuary spaces" that permitted seemingly contradictory experiences to coexist without conflict. It aligned precisely with what she and Farrat had been exploring through their separate disciplines and shared dialogue, this possibility of territories that existed between conventional categories, that honored difference while establishing connection across it.

"We've been constructing something similar, haven't we?" she observed, the insight emerging without premeditation. "Not just in our professional work—the threshold poems and reading nook—but in the particular relationship we've established. A sanctuary space that permits both connection and independence, both shared understanding and separate development."

"Yes," Farrat agreed, his expression reflecting the same recognition her words had articulated. "A territory designed according to our specific needs and capacities rather than conventional expectations or predetermined patterns. Architecture in the broadest sense—creating structures that accommodate authentic human experience rather than demanding conformity to existing templates."

The clarity of this mutual understanding—this explicit acknowledgment of what they had been building together—created a moment of profound connection between them. Not manufactured intensity or dramatic declaration, but quiet recognition of something valuable constructed through careful, consistent attention to balance and integrity.

As their conversation continued, moving between professional developments and personal reflections, Tauree became aware of a subtle shift in the quality of their exchange. The careful navigation of early acquaintance had gradually evolved into more direct engagement, the metaphorical frameworks that had initially facilitated communication now complemented by explicit acknowledgment of what existed between them.

Not that metaphor had been abandoned—their shared vocabulary of threshold spaces and weather patterns remained valuable tools for understanding complex emotional terrain. But these frameworks now existed alongside more direct expression, creating multiple layers of communication that reflected the particular architecture of their relationship.

When Malcolm approached again much later, gently informing them of the café's approaching closing time, Tauree realized with surprise how many hours had passed without either monitoring the clock. This too had become characteristic of their interactions—that quality of unselfconscious presence that contrasted with her usual hyperawareness of duration during social engagements.

"Walk you home?" Farrat suggested as they gathered their belongings and prepared to depart. The offer carried no expectation or implication beyond its literal meaning—simple extension of their conversation through shared movement rather than sudden conclusion at the café door.

"I'd like that," Tauree replied, the acceptance natural rather than calculated. "The evening is pleasant for walking."

Outside, the autumn night had deepened, stars visible in the clear sky despite the city's ambient light. They moved together through the quiet streets, their pace unhurried, conversation continuing with that same easy flow that had characterized their exchange throughout the evening.

"I've been thinking about what you shared before I left," Farrat said as they approached the halfway point between Serendipity and Tauree's apartment. "About what we've constructed together being a deliberate architecture rather than temporary accommodation."

"Yes," Tauree acknowledged, recalling their conversation outside the community center days earlier.

"It represents something significant," Farrat continued, his tone thoughtful rather than dramatic. "Not just personally for us, but conceptually for understanding relationship itself. The possibility that connection need not require conformity to predetermined patterns or conventional categories."

"A threshold approach to relationship," Tauree suggested, drawing on their shared vocabulary. "Creating territories that permit multiple modes of engagement simultaneously, that honor difference while establishing genuine understanding across it."

"Exactly," Farrat confirmed, appreciation for her architectural framing evident in his expression. "And I've been considering how to develop this understanding beyond our particular experience—perhaps through critical essays that expand the threshold poems into more explicit theoretical exploration."

The prospect—extending their shared insights into broader intellectual territory—created that familiar sense of collaborative possibility that had characterized their relationship from the beginning. Not merging their separate professional domains, but identifying connections between them that might illuminate both more completely.

"That aligns with some architectural writing I've been contemplating," Tauree observed, the parallel emerging with natural ease. "Expanding the community center design principles into more explicit theoretical articulation of threshold spaces in public architecture."

"Parallel explorations of the same conceptual territory through different disciplinary lenses," Farrat suggested, the insight characteristic of their shared thinking. "Not collaboration in the conventional sense of producing single work together, but complementary development that permits both connection and independence."

As they continued walking, the conversation flowing between professional possibilities and personal reflections, Tauree found herself experiencing an unusual clarity of perception—not just of Farrat beside her, but of their evolving relationship and her own changing response to it. The fog remained, as it always did, but it had thinned to a translucent veil rather than an obscuring cloud, allowing her to see with rare precision the terrain they had traversed together.

From that first reluctant conversation at Amrita's tea party to their midnight walk by the river, from the art gallery visit to their impulsive day trip to Seaview, from the storm-mandated stay in Farrat's apartment to their strategic navigation of the university festival—each interaction had built upon the last, creating a relationship unlike any she had previously experienced. Neither demanding complete merger nor maintaining rigid separation, they had established permeable boundaries across which genuine understanding could flow in both directions.

When they finally reached her apartment building, they paused at the entrance in that familiar moment of transition that had characterized so many of their partings—the threshold between connection and separation, between shared experience and individual processing. Unlike earlier occasions, however, tonight carried a quality of continuation rather than conclusion, of conversation paused rather than terminated.

"May I suggest something?" Farrat asked, his tone maintaining that careful balance between offering and expecting that had become foundational to their connection.

"Of course," Tauree replied, curiosity genuine.

"Given our respective professional developments and continuing exploration of threshold concepts," he began, his words flowing with characteristic precision, "perhaps we might establish a more regular pattern of exchange? Not to impose structure where organic development has served well, but to create intentional space for dialogue amid our separate obligations."

The suggestion—offering continuity without demanding constancy—reflected exactly the balance they had established throughout their relationship: connection that respected independence, proximity that honored distance.

"What did you have in mind?" Tauree asked, neither accepting nor declining until the proposal had been fully articulated.

"Perhaps a weekly meeting," Farrat suggested. "Not as rigid obligation that creates anxiety if circumstances prevent it, but as consistent intention that establishes rhythm without requiring perfect adherence. A structural framework flexible enough to accommodate our separate professional demands while creating reliable points of connection."

The architectural framing—structure that permitted flexibility rather than imposing rigidity—resonated with Tauree's professional sensibility and personal inclination. Unlike conventional relationship progression with its implicit expectations of increasing time commitment and reduced independence, this proposal acknowledged their particular need for both connection and solitude, both shared exploration and separate development.

"An architectural solution to relationship navigation," she observed, appreciation warming her voice. "Creating defined space for engagement without compromising individual territory."

"Exactly," Farrat confirmed, evident pleasure at her immediate understanding. "Not conventional 'dating' with its predetermined patterns and implicit destinations, but custom architecture designed for sustainable habitation according to our particular needs and capacities."

The clarity of this mutual recognition—this explicit acknowledgment of what they were building together—created another moment of profound connection between them. Not manufactured intensity or dramatic declaration, but quiet appreciation of something valuable constructed through careful, consistent attention to balance and integrity.

"I think that would work well," Tauree said finally, the decision emerging from genuine consideration rather than social obligation. "Perhaps Wednesdays at Serendipity? The midweek timing creates natural breathing room around professional deadlines that typically cluster toward weekends."

"Perfect," Farrat agreed, his expression reflecting appreciation for her practical consideration. "Structural intention without rigid demand. A framework that supports connection without requiring conformity to conventional patterns."

As they prepared to conclude their evening, Tauree found herself contemplating the curious evolution they had articulated together. What had begun as reluctant attendance at a social obligation had developed into something neither could have anticipated—a relationship that existed in that threshold space between defined categories, that permitted multiple modes of engagement simultaneously, that honored difference while establishing genuine understanding across it.

This time, their parting included a brief clasp of hands—that simple gesture of connection that had emerged during Farrat's medical episode now incorporated into their natural expression. Neither performative nor constrained, the contact lasted exactly as long as felt appropriate to them both, neither extended beyond its natural conclusion nor shortened by discomfort.

"Until Wednesday, then," Farrat said as their hands separated, the words carrying anticipation without demand.

"Until Wednesday," Tauree echoed, completing their exchange with similar attention to balanced connection.

As she entered her apartment building and Farrat continued his walk home through the autumn night, Tauree carried with her a quiet certainty about the particular architecture they were constructing together. Not a conventional structure built according to social expectation or romantic tradition, but a custom design created through careful attention to both individual needs and mutual possibilities, a space where different weathers could coexist without overwhelming each other.

The fog remained present, as always, that persistent gray filter through which she experienced the world. But something had shifted in how she navigated within it—not dramatic transformation or sudden clarity, but gradual evolution in her relationship to its varying densities. She had discovered new landmarks within the familiar gray, reference points that allowed orientation even when visibility remained limited.

Tomorrow would bring return to professional focus, to the continued documentation and analysis of the community center's actual usage, to the architectural writing she had been contemplating about threshold spaces in public design. But tonight she carried with her this recognition of parallel development—how her professional work and personal connection with Farrat had evolved alongside each other, each influencing without determining the other's trajectory.

As she moved through her apartment, the skylights she had designed tracking moonlight across walls and floors with mathematical precision, Tauree found herself experiencing an unfamiliar sense of confirmation—not just of her architectural vision successfully realized, but of her capacity for connection that honored rather than compromised her fundamental nature. The careful architect of precise spaces had discovered that the same principles that guided her professional work could structure personal territory as well, creating relationships with the same thoughtful balance of containment and expansion, of guidance and freedom that characterized her physical designs.

With this thought, she surrendered to the quiet of her carefully designed sanctuary, the space that had gradually incorporated aspects of her evolving understanding with Farrat without losing its essential character as refuge from external demands. Like the community center reading nook they had discussed so extensively, her apartment represented successful realization of architectural vision—a threshold space that permitted multiple modes of engagement simultaneously, that created shelter without confinement, that acknowledged weather without surrendering to storm.

The fog might never lift completely—that persistent gray filter would likely remain a constant feature of her internal landscape. But she was discovering that fog need not prevent navigation, that limited visibility could accommodate meaningful progress if the terrain contained sufficient landmarks to permit orientation. And in Farrat, she had found a fellow traveler who neither demanded the fog disperse nor pretended it didn't exist—who simply offered to walk alongside her through its varying densities, sharing his own rainfall in an exchange of understanding that had created, somehow, a microclimate uniquely their own.

A threshold space, deliberately constructed, uniquely theirs.

Act 3: The Resolution and Bittersweet Conclusion

Chapter 11: The Final Walk

Wednesday evening came with an unexpected clarity—one of those rare autumn days when the air seems purified by the season's transition, colors more vibrant against the backdrop of approaching winter. Tauree stood before the full-length mirror in her bedroom, a ritual that had once been foreign to her methodical nature but had gradually become part of her preparation for meetings with Farrat. Unlike her earlier overthinking about appearances, tonight's consideration was more deliberate—an acknowledgment that what she wore represented a choice about how she wished to present herself in this particular moment, not anxiety about external judgment.

She settled on a simple outfit that reflected her architectural sensibilities—clean lines, subtle textures, neutral colors with a single element of deep burgundy that added warmth without demanding attention. Professional without being formal, personal without being casual. A deliberate threshold between categories, she thought with a small smile at how thoroughly their shared vocabulary had permeated even these private considerations.

Their weekly meetings at Serendipity had continued for two months now, establishing a rhythm that balanced structure and flexibility exactly as Farrat had suggested. When professional obligations occasionally required rescheduling, they adjusted without drama or disappointment, the framework supporting connection without demanding conformity to rigid expectations. The arrangement had proven remarkably effective—creating reliable points of engagement without compromising the independence that remained essential to them both.

In the intervening weeks, their professional lives had developed along parallel tracks that occasionally intersected through their ongoing dialogue. Farrat's threshold poems had been accepted for publication by the literary press that had expressed interest during the retreat, with a scheduled release the following spring. Tauree's architectural writing on threshold spaces in public design had been commissioned for a respected industry journal, her community center project having attracted attention beyond local recognition.

Yet something had shifted in recent days—a subtle tension emerging beneath their established patterns, a sense of approaching transition that neither had directly addressed. Tauree had noticed it first in Farrat's increasingly thoughtful silences, moments when his typical attentiveness seemed directed inward rather than toward their shared conversation. She had observed similar patterns in herself—a growing awareness that their careful balance had reached a point where evolution of some kind seemed necessary, though the direction remained unclear.

Tonight felt significant somehow, though nothing explicit had been stated. Perhaps it was simply the changing season, the sense of natural transition that autumn brought to the external world mirroring their internal landscape. Or perhaps it was something more specific—an intuition that the threshold territory they had so carefully constructed was approaching another boundary that would require deliberate navigation.

The fog remained present, as always, that persistent gray filter through which Tauree experienced the world. But it had evolved from an obscuring cloud into a more translucent medium, its density varying but its fundamental character now familiar enough to navigate with increasing confidence. She had learned to recognize its patterns, to anticipate its thickening and thinning without being defined by either state. And in Farrat, she had found someone who neither demanded its dispersal nor pretended it didn't exist—who simply acknowledged its reality while engaging with the person who existed within its confines.

As she gathered her keys and prepared to leave for Serendipity, Tauree found herself contemplating the curious architecture they had constructed together over these months. Not a conventional relationship built according to social prescription, but a custom design created through careful attention to both individual needs and mutual possibilities. A space where different weathers could coexist without overwhelming each other, where fog and rainfall created a microclimate uniquely their own.

The walk to Serendipity took her through familiar neighborhoods now transformed by deepening autumn—trees nearly bare, their structural forms revealed as foliage surrendered to seasonal change. The metaphor wasn't lost on her: how certain essential qualities became more visible when decorative elements fell away, how fundamental architecture emerged more clearly in transition. Perhaps this was what she sensed in their evolving connection—not dissolution but revelation, the underlying structure becoming more apparent as initial novelty gave way to sustained engagement.

Serendipity Café welcomed her with its characteristic warmth, the ambient sounds of quiet conversation and gentle music creating that perfect balance of community and individuality she had come to appreciate. Malcolm nodded from behind the counter, his acknowledgment carrying the understated recognition of a regular patron whose preferences were known without requiring explanation.

Farrat wasn't at their usual corner table—unusual, as he typically arrived early to secure their preferred location and order their customary beverages. Tauree glanced around, momentarily disoriented by this disruption to established pattern, before spotting him near the entrance. He stood as she approached, his expression carrying that same thoughtful quality she had observed in recent meetings—attentive yet somehow distant, present yet partially elsewhere.

"I thought we might try something different tonight," he said instead of their usual greeting ritual. "The evening is unusually mild for November, and there's something I'd like to show you. Would you be willing to take a walk instead of staying here?"

The suggestion—altering their established pattern without abandoning it entirely—created a moment of subtle tension in Tauree. Change, even minor, typically triggered calculation and caution in her approach. Yet she found herself nodding without the usual internal debate about disrupted expectations.

"Where are we going?" she asked, practical consideration rather than resistance.

"The river path," Farrat replied, the location immediately significant to them both. "Near where we took our midnight walk months ago. There's a particular quality of light at this time of evening that I think you might appreciate—the way it interacts with water and stone creates an architectural experience that words struggle to capture."

The reference to their earlier encounter—one of the first significant connections they had established—carried unmistakable weight. Not just casual variation to their routine, but deliberate return to territory that held shared meaning. Tauree recognized the significance but couldn't yet interpret its specific intention, creating a curious blend of anticipation and uncertainty.

"I'd like that," she said simply, the truth of it surprising even herself.

They left Serendipity together, Malcolm's knowing glance following them as they departed without their usual extended stay. The city streets gradually gave way to quieter paths as they approached the riverside, their conversation flowing with characteristic ease despite the changed circumstances. They discussed Farrat's final revisions to the threshold poems before publication, Tauree's documentation of the community center's evolving usage patterns, the curious intersection of their professional vocabularies that continued to create unexpected insights for them both.

Yet beneath this familiar exchange ran a current of unspoken awareness—that something beyond routine adjustment was occurring, that this particular walk represented transition of some kind. Neither addressed it directly, allowing the conversation to maintain its natural rhythm while the meaning of their altered pattern remained temporarily suspended between them.

The river appeared before them as they rounded a final bend in the path, its surface transformed by evening light into a complex interplay of reflection and absorption. Unlike their midnight walk months earlier, when darkness had rendered the water a mysterious void occasionally illuminated by moonlight, tonight the setting sun created a dynamic canvas of color and movement—oranges and golds shifting across the rippling surface, shadows deepening to purple where bridges interrupted the light's passage.

"It's beautiful," Tauree observed, her architect's eye immediately engaged by the interaction of natural and constructed elements—how the river's organic flow contrasted with the geometric precision of the bridges, how light revealed relationships between forms that remained hidden in other conditions.

"I discovered it by accident last week," Farrat explained as they continued along the riverside path. "I was walking home from campus along an unfamiliar route and happened to pass this stretch just as the sun was setting. It struck me as something you would appreciate—the temporal architecture of light and water, structure revealed through transition."

The consideration in this observation—noticing environmental qualities she would value, preserving the experience to share rather than merely appreciating it individually—created that familiar warmth in Tauree's chest. After months of connection, Farrat still approached their exchanges with that quality of genuine attention and thoughtful offering that had initially drawn her into deeper conversation with him.

They walked in comfortable silence for a while, the path gradually leading them toward the small plaza where they had sat during their midnight encounter. The circular space with stone benches arranged to face the river seemed both familiar and transformed by the different quality of light—the same structural elements now revealing completely different experiential qualities.

"I've been thinking," Farrat said as they settled onto the same bench they had occupied months earlier, his tone shifting slightly to indicate a change from their casual conversation. "About thresholds and transitions, about how certain territories exist between defined states rather than fully embodying either."

Tauree recognized immediately that they had reached the purpose of this altered meeting pattern, the reason for returning to this particular location rather than maintaining their established routine at Serendipity. Something significant was approaching—not a casual observation but a deliberate engagement with their evolving connection.

"As have I," she acknowledged, creating space for whatever he wished to express without presuming its specific direction.

Farrat turned slightly to face her more directly, his expression serious yet gentle, carrying none of the dramatic intensity conventional relationships might demand for significant moments. "The particular architecture we've constructed together over these months has been remarkable—this balance of connection and independence, of shared understanding and separate development.

It has permitted exploration that neither conventional friendship nor traditional romance would have accommodated, has created possibilities that predetermined categories would have precluded."

Tauree nodded, recognizing the precise articulation of what they had often discussed—the custom design they had created through careful attention to both individual needs and mutual possibilities.

"Yet I find myself approaching another threshold," Farrat continued, his voice carrying that quality of thoughtful precision she had come to associate with his most significant disclosures. "Not away from what we've established, but toward what it might evolve into if we choose to continue its development. And before attempting that crossing, I wanted to ensure alignment in our understanding of both current territory and potential direction."

The architectural framing—threshold, territory, direction—reflected how thoroughly their shared vocabulary had become integrated into their communication, how consistently they translated emotional landscape into spatial terms that honored precision without sacrificing meaning.

"I've sensed a similar transition point," Tauree acknowledged, her own perception aligning with his observation. "A recognition that our careful balance has reached a stage where evolution seems both possible and necessary, though its specific form remains undefined."

Relief visibly relaxed some tension in Farrat's posture—not dramatic transformation but subtle indication that her perception matched his own, that they were indeed approaching the same threshold from compatible directions.

"The question becomes," he said after a moment's consideration, "whether that evolution maintains our established principles while expanding their application, or whether it requires fundamental reconsideration of the architecture itself."

The distinction struck Tauree as precisely the core issue—not whether change was occurring, but whether it represented development within existing framework or reconstruction according to different parameters. Her architectural mind immediately engaged with this conceptual challenge, approaching personal territory through professional vocabulary.

"In structural terms," she offered, "there's significant difference between adaptive reuse that honors original integrity while accommodating new function, and demolition that creates space for entirely new construction. Both have validity in appropriate contexts, but they represent fundamentally different relationships to existing conditions."

"Exactly," Farrat agreed, appreciation for her architectural framing evident in his expression. "And I find myself firmly in the adaptive reuse category—valuing what we've constructed too deeply to consider its demolition, yet recognizing that static preservation without functional evolution leads to eventual obsolescence."

The clarity of this mutual recognition—this aligned understanding of both current situation and preferred approach to its development—created a moment of profound connection between them. Not manufactured intensity or dramatic declaration, but quiet appreciation of something valuable that deserved thoughtful evolution rather than either rigid preservation or complete reconstruction.

"So the question becomes," Tauree suggested, continuing their architectural exploration of emotional territory, "what functional adaptations might allow continued habitation while accommodating evolving needs? What structural modifications permit development without compromising essential integrity?"

Around them, the evening light continued its gradual transition, the sun's position shifting to create new patterns of illumination across the river's surface. The temporal architecture Farrat had wanted to share with her—this interaction of natural elements through transitional conditions—provided perfect environmental context for their conversation about evolution and adaptation.

"I've been considering several possibilities," Farrat replied, his tone maintaining that careful balance between offering and imposing that had become foundational to their connection. "Each representing different degrees of adaptation while preserving core principles."

"Such as?" Tauree prompted, genuine curiosity engaging with this exploration of potential futures.

"The most conservative adaptation," Farrat began, architect discussing design options with respected colleague rather than romantic partner proposing relationship escalation, "would maintain our current pattern while gradually increasing its frequency or duration—perhaps twice-weekly meetings rather than once, or extended conversations that occasionally include shared activities beyond our established contexts."

Tauree nodded, appreciating both the specific suggestion and the manner of its presentation—options offered for consideration rather than expectations demanding response.

"A moderate adaptation," he continued, "might include more deliberate integration of our separate professional territories—perhaps collaborative writing that explores the intersection of architectural and poetic approaches to threshold spaces, or joint presentations that demonstrate complementary perspectives on shared concepts."

This possibility created immediate intellectual engagement for Tauree—not primarily emotional response but genuine professional interest in potential collaboration that would respect their separate disciplines while identifying meaningful connections between them.

"And more significant adaptation?" she asked, completing the structural analysis they were constructing together.

Farrat paused briefly, organizing thoughts with characteristic precision before responding. "Would involve more fundamental reconsideration of how our separate territories interact—not merging them completely, which would compromise the independence that remains essential to us both, but creating more consistent overlap between them. Shared experiences that extend beyond our current pattern while maintaining necessary boundaries."

The careful non-specificity of this description—avoiding conventional terms like "dating" or "relationship" with their predetermined expectations—reflected their established approach to connection. Not forcing experience into existing categories, but creating custom architecture designed for their particular needs and capacities.

"And your assessment of these options?" Tauree asked, neither accepting nor declining any specific proposal until their exploration had been fully articulated.

"I find myself drawn toward moderate adaptation with elements of the more significant approach," Farrat replied after thoughtful consideration. "Maintaining our essential balance while allowing more deliberate development of both intellectual collaboration and personal connection. Not dramatic reconstruction of what exists between us, but thoughtful evolution that acknowledges changing conditions without abandoning fundamental principles."

The river before them had transformed again as the sun approached the horizon, shadows lengthening across the water's surface while remaining light concentrated into more intense color. Not complete transition from day to night, but that threshold period where elements of both coexisted in temporary balance—dusk, neither fully light nor completely dark, a liminal territory that existed between defined states.

"What are your thoughts?" Farrat asked, his question creating genuine space for her perspective rather than merely seeking confirmation of his own.

Tauree considered carefully, approaching this significant threshold with the same analytical precision she brought to architectural challenges. Not emotional reaction or social performance, but genuine assessment of both current conditions and potential development.

"I agree that moderate adaptation seems most appropriate," she said finally, her decision emerging from actual consideration rather than obligation or avoidance. "Preserving what functions effectively while allowing thoughtful evolution where beneficial. The intellectual collaboration particularly appeals to me—creating work that could exist independently while drawing from our shared exploration of threshold concepts."

Relief and pleasure visibly transformed Farrat's expression—not dramatic emotion but genuine appreciation that their separate assessments had arrived at compatible conclusions. This had become characteristic of their connection: the discovery of aligned understanding without requiring identical perspective, of shared direction emerging from independent consideration.

"And regarding the personal aspects of potential adaptation?" he asked, the question direct without being demanding.

Tauree appreciated the clarity of his inquiry—no assumption that professional collaboration automatically included personal development, no presumption that her interest in one domain necessarily extended to the other. This continued respect for her agency and boundaries, even in moments of potential transition, represented exactly what she valued in their established architecture.

"I'm open to thoughtful expansion there as well," she acknowledged, her honesty easier in this space they had created between them where direct engagement had gradually replaced metaphorical distance. "Though with characteristic caution about maintaining necessary independence within developing connection."

"Of course," Farrat agreed immediately, no disappointment or pressure in his response. "The principle of balanced autonomy remains essential—not compromise of fundamental requirements but evolution that respects their continued importance."

As they sat together in the deepening dusk, the conversation flowing between specific possibilities and broader principles, Tauree found herself experiencing an unusual clarity of perception—not just of Farrat beside her, but of their evolving relationship and her own changing response to it. The fog remained, as it always did, but it had thinned to a translucent veil rather than an obscuring cloud, allowing her to see with rare precision the terrain they had traversed together and the potential paths that lay ahead.

From that first reluctant conversation at Amrita's tea party to their midnight walk by this very river, from the art gallery visit to their impulsive day trip to Seaview, from the storm-mandated stay in Farrat's apartment to their strategic navigation of the university festival—each interaction had built upon the last, creating a relationship unlike any she had previously experienced. Neither demanding complete merger nor maintaining rigid separation, they had established permeable boundaries across which genuine understanding could flow in both directions.

And now they approached another threshold together—not dramatic transformation or sudden clarity, but gradual evolution in their carefully constructed architecture. Not abandoning what they had built, but adapting it to accommodate changing conditions while preserving essential integrity.

"There's something else I'd like to share," Farrat said eventually, reaching into his messenger bag to extract a slim volume bound in simple cloth with an embossed geometric pattern. "The publisher sent advance copies of the threshold poems. I wanted you to have the first one."

He extended the book toward her—a gesture of offering without expectation, of sharing something significant without demanding particular response. Tauree accepted it with genuine appreciation, the weight of the volume in her hands representing tangible manifestation of their ongoing dialogue about architecture and poetry, about threshold spaces and emotional territories.

Opening the cover, she found a handwritten inscription on the title page beneath the printed dedication that already acknowledged her influence:

For Tauree—

Who helped create the threshold space where these poems could emerge.

With profound appreciation for the particular architecture we continue to build together.

—Farrat

The simple words carried complex meaning—acknowledging both past contribution and ongoing development, both professional influence and personal connection. Not excessive declaration or performative intensity, but authentic recognition of something valuable that deserved both celebration and continued evolution.

"Thank you," she said simply, the words encompassing appreciation for both the physical gift and the thoughtful spirit behind it. "This means a great deal to me."

"I hoped it might," Farrat replied, his expression warm with genuine pleasure at her response. "The poems exist because of our conversations about threshold territories, about spaces that permit multiple modes of engagement simultaneously. They represent the particular intersection of architectural and poetic perspectives that has emerged through our ongoing dialogue."

As evening settled more fully around them, the sun's final departure creating new patterns of illumination from streetlights reflected on the river's surface, they began their return journey along the riverside path. The conversation continued with that same surprising ease Tauree had experienced since their first genuine exchange, moving between reflection on their discussion of potential adaptations and more practical considerations about how such evolution might manifest in coming weeks.

Unlike their midnight walk months earlier, which had concluded with careful maintenance of physical distance despite emotional connection, tonight they moved with gradually decreasing space between them—not dramatic transformation, but subtle acknowledgment that physical proximity could reflect developing comfort with emotional closeness. Not conventional romantic performance, but authentic expression of the particular architecture they continued to build together.

When their hands eventually met—neither reaching with deliberate intent nor accidental contact, but mutual movement that created connection without requiring planning—the touch carried none of the awkwardness Tauree might once have anticipated in such moments. Instead, there was a curious rightness to the gesture, a natural extension of the understanding they had developed through months of careful conversation and selective disclosure.

The fog remained present, as always, that persistent gray filter through which she experienced the world. But something had shifted in how she navigated within it—not dramatic transformation or sudden clarity, but gradual evolution in her relationship to its varying densities. She had discovered new landmarks within the familiar gray, reference points that allowed orientation even when visibility remained limited.

And in Farrat's rainfall—that melancholy that moved through him in its familiar patterns—she had found weather that somehow complemented rather than complicated her own internal landscape. Not dramatic dispersion of either condition, but curious interaction that created their particular microclimate, where different atmospheric states could coexist without overwhelming each other.

"I've been thinking about the community center expansion," Tauree said as they approached the point where riverside path would return them to city streets. "The additional wing they've proposed for educational programming. There might be opportunity for literary events in the reading nook—perhaps featuring threshold poems and architectural writing that explores similar concepts from different perspectives."

The suggestion—professional collaboration emerging naturally from personal connection—represented exactly the moderate adaptation they had discussed, the thoughtful evolution that maintained essential balance while allowing further development.

"I'd like that very much," Farrat replied, genuine interest engaging with the possibility. "Creating physical manifestation of the conceptual territory we've been exploring together—a space where different disciplinary approaches can engage without requiring conformity to single perspective."

Their hands remained loosely connected as they walked, neither clinging with anxious intensity nor separating with deliberate distance. The physical contact mirrored their evolving relationship—present without dominance, connected without constraint, a threshold territory that existed between conventional categories of touch and separation.

When they finally reached the intersection where their paths would diverge—Tauree toward her apartment in Westwood, Farrat toward his in Riverside—they paused in that familiar moment of transition that had characterized so many of their partings. Yet tonight carried different quality than previous occasions—not conclusion requiring future initiation, but temporary pause in continuing development.

"May I suggest something?" Farrat asked, his tone maintaining that careful balance between offering and expecting that had become foundational to their connection.

"Of course," Tauree replied, curiosity genuine.

"Dinner tomorrow evening," he proposed. "At that small restaurant near the harbor we discovered during our day trip to Seaview. They've apparently opened a location in the city, maintaining the same focus on local ingredients and unpretentious preparation. Perhaps followed by the architecture lecture at the university—the visiting professor discussing threshold spaces in urban planning."

The suggestion—combining shared meal with intellectual engagement—represented perfect manifestation of the moderate adaptation they had discussed. Not conventional date with romantic performance as primary purpose, but thoughtful cultivation of both personal connection and professional interest in complementary rather than competing arrangement.

"I'd like that," Tauree said, the decision emerging without calculation or performance. "What time?"

"Seven for dinner?" Farrat suggested. "The lecture begins at nine, which should allow comfortable transition between experiences."

"Perfect," Tauree confirmed, appreciating both the specific plan and the consideration behind its arrangement. "I'll meet you at the restaurant."

As they prepared to conclude their final walk along this particular riverbank—not last meeting but last encounter in this specific configuration before evolutionary adaptation—Tauree found herself experiencing an unfamiliar sense of anticipation without anxiety. Not dramatic emotion or conventional excitement, but quiet appreciation for thoughtfully developed possibility, for carefully considered adaptation that respected existing architecture while allowing necessary evolution.

Their parting included a brief embrace—another threshold crossed, another boundary adjusted rather than abandoned. Not conventional performance of affection, but authentic expression of the particular connection they had established through months of careful conversation and selective disclosure. The contact lasted exactly as long as felt appropriate to them both, neither extended beyond its natural conclusion nor shortened by discomfort.

"Until tomorrow, then," Farrat said as they separated, his expression reflecting the same quiet appreciation Tauree felt for this carefully navigated transition.

"Until tomorrow," she echoed, completing their exchange with similar attention to balanced connection.

As they moved in their separate directions—temporary divergence rather than permanent separation—Tauree carried with her both the physical volume of threshold poems and the intangible understanding they had developed together. Not conventional relationship defined by social expectation or romantic tradition, but custom architecture created through careful attention to both individual needs and mutual possibilities.

The fog remained present, as always, that persistent gray filter through which she experienced the world. But it no longer represented barrier to navigation or obstacle to meaningful connection. Instead, it had become familiar element of her internal landscape, acknowledged without denial while prevented from defining her entire experience.

The careful architect of precise spaces had discovered that the same principles that guided her professional work could structure personal territory as well, creating relationships with the same thoughtful balance of containment and expansion, of guidance and freedom that characterized her physical designs. Not despite the fog, but within its varying densities—not overcoming depression through miracle or medication, but learning to construct meaningful experience while acknowledging its continued presence.

As she walked toward her apartment through the quiet evening streets, Tauree found herself contemplating the curious trajectory that had brought her to this moment. From professional detachment and emotional isolation to the particular architecture she and Farrat continued to build together—neither conventional relationship nor casual acquaintance, but custom structure designed for sustainable habitation according to their specific needs and capacities.

A threshold space, deliberately constructed, constantly evolving, uniquely theirs.

Act 3: The Resolution and Bittersweet Conclusion

Chapter 12: The Farewell

Winter arrived with unexpected gentleness, the harsh transition from autumn that Tauree had anticipated softened by mild temperatures and occasional sunny days that created golden islands of light amidst the season's typical gray. Three months had passed since their final walk by the river, where they had navigated that significant threshold from implicit to explicit understanding, from metaphorical to direct acknowledgment of what existed between them.

The adaptation they had discussed that evening had unfolded with the same careful balance that characterized their entire connection—gradual evolution rather than dramatic transformation, thoughtful development within established framework rather than wholesale reconstruction. Their weekly meetings had expanded to include both the original Wednesday evenings at Serendipity and occasional weekend activities that combined intellectual engagement with personal connection. The architecture lecture they had attended that first night had led to similar events—exhibitions that explored threshold spaces through different artistic media, performances that navigated territories between conventional categories, conversations that developed their shared vocabulary while maintaining separate disciplinary perspectives.

More significant still was the collaborative writing project they had begun—an exploration of threshold territories through complementary architectural and poetic approaches. Tauree's theoretical articulations of spatial liminality alongside Farrat's creative responses created a dialogue on the page that mirrored their ongoing conversation, each illuminating the other's perspective without requiring merger into single viewpoint. The architectural journal that had commissioned her individual work had expressed interest in this joint exploration, recognizing its unique contribution to understanding spaces that existed between defined categories.

Their physical relationship had evolved with similar thoughtfulness—touch becoming more frequent without performance or calculation, proximity developing comfortable familiarity without demanding conventional progression. Their first kiss had occurred during a walk through the university sculpture garden, where an installation exploring threshold spaces through intersecting planes of glass and steel had created perfect environmental context for crossing another boundary in their carefully constructed architecture. The moment had carried none of the awkwardness or expectation Tauree might once have anticipated, instead offering the same quality of thoughtful exploration that characterized their intellectual exchange—authentic expression of developing connection rather than social performance or romantic obligation.

Yet throughout this evolution, they had maintained the essential balance that made their relationship sustainable—connection that respected independence, proximity that honored distance, shared development that preserved separate identity. Neither had abandoned their fundamental nature in service of conventional relationship standards, neither had compromised necessary requirements to accommodate the other's expectations. Instead, they had continued building custom architecture designed specifically for their particular needs and capacities, a threshold space uniquely their own.

The fog remained present in Tauree's experience, as it always did—that persistent gray filter through which she perceived the world. Depression wasn't something that disappeared through personal connection or romantic fulfillment, whatever conventional narratives might suggest. But her relationship with the fog had continued evolving alongside her relationship with Farrat, developing from hostile territory that prevented navigation into familiar landscape that permitted meaningful engagement despite its varying densities. She had discovered new reference points within the grayness, landmarks that allowed orientation even when visibility remained limited.

And Farrat's rainfall—that melancholy that moved through him in its familiar patterns—had maintained its presence as well, neither dispersed by their developing connection nor forced upon her as emotional burden. His relationship with this internal weather had similarly evolved, from isolation within its downpours to shared understanding that acknowledged its reality without allowing it to define their entire experience. They had created, somehow, a microclimate where different atmospheric conditions could coexist without overwhelming each other, where fog and rainfall interacted without requiring either to transform into something it wasn't.

Today, however, brought unexpected disruption to the careful architecture they had constructed together. Tauree had received the news yesterday—an invitation to lead a significant international project, designing a cultural complex in Singapore that would implement her threshold concept on unprecedented scale. The opportunity represented professional recognition beyond anything she had previously experienced, potential development of her architectural vision with resources and scope that simply didn't exist in her current practice.

The complication lay in timing and distance—eighteen months on the other side of the world, with only brief returns possible during the project's most intensive periods. Not permanent relocation, but substantial separation that would require fundamental reconsideration of the relationship architecture she and Farrat had been developing with such care.

They had arranged to meet at the community center rather than their usual café—Tauree's suggestion, offered with the recognition that this conversation required different environmental context than their regular exchanges. The reading nook that had been so central to their developing understanding of threshold spaces, that had inspired some of Farrat's most significant poems and informed their collaborative writing, seemed the appropriate territory for navigating this unexpected transition.

She arrived early, wanting time to experience the space alone before Farrat joined her. The community center had been operating successfully for months now, the reading nook functioning exactly as she had designed it—a threshold territory that existed between public and private, between structured learning and organic discovery. Regular programming now included literary events featuring local writers, including an upcoming presentation of Farrat's threshold poems alongside architectural discussion of the space's design principles—the professional collaboration they had envisioned during their final riverside walk now approaching concrete realization.

Tauree settled into one of the carefully positioned chairs that offered both prospect and refuge, observing how winter light created different patterns across the floor and walls than the autumn illumination that had characterized their previous visits. The space remained fundamentally unchanged, yet its experiential qualities shifted with seasonal conditions—precisely the adaptive stability she had intended in its design, the capacity to maintain essential character while responding to changing circumstances.

Her thoughts returned to the international opportunity and its implications for the relationship architecture she and Farrat had been developing. Unlike previous experiences where potential separation triggered immediate withdrawal or anxious calculation, this situation engaged her problem-solving capacity directly—architectural approach to emotional challenge, structural thinking applied to personal territory. Not dramatic dissolution or binary choice between professional opportunity and personal connection, but thoughtful consideration of how existing architecture might adapt to new conditions without compromising essential integrity.

"You're deep in thought," came Farrat's voice, interrupting her reflections as he approached through the reading nook's open threshold. He moved with that quality of attentive presence she had observed since their first genuine conversation—aware of his surroundings without being distracted by them, engaged without being scattered.

"Yes," Tauree acknowledged simply as he settled into the chair positioned at right angle to hers—their habitual arrangement that created comfortable conversation while maintaining independent sightlines to the surrounding space. "Architectural considerations of various kinds."

"Professional or personal?" Farrat asked, his perception as acute as ever in identifying her current preoccupation without requiring elaborate explanation.

"Both," she replied, appreciating the directness that had become characteristic of their communication. "They've become increasingly interconnected."

Farrat nodded, understanding without need for further elaboration. This had become one of the hallmarks of their connection—the ability to grasp the essence of each other's experience without requiring exhaustive articulation, to recognize the underlying patterns in each other's thought without demanding constant translation.

"Something's changed," he observed after a moment, not a question but a recognition. "Not in your fundamental orientation, but in circumstantial conditions that require navigation."

The precision of his perception—identifying external change rather than internal transformation—created that familiar sense of being truly seen, of having her particular nature understood without requiring elaborate explanation. It was this quality, perhaps more than any other, that had allowed their connection to develop despite her typical wariness of emotional entanglement.

"Yes," Tauree confirmed, deciding to approach the situation with characteristic directness rather than careful preparation. "I've been invited to lead an international project—a cultural complex in Singapore implementing threshold concepts on significant scale. Eighteen months, primarily on-site, beginning in February."

She presented the information without emotional elaboration or apology, respecting both the professional significance of the opportunity and Farrat's capacity to receive complex information without requiring careful management of its delivery. This had become foundational to their relationship: the assumption of perceptiveness rather than the need for emotional cushioning, the recognition of each other's analytical capabilities without requiring protection from potential implications.

Farrat received this news with the thoughtful attention she had anticipated—neither immediate emotional reaction nor performance of supportive enthusiasm, but genuine consideration of both professional opportunity and personal implications. His expression revealed processing rather than response, assessment rather than reaction—exactly the quality of engaged thinking that had drawn her into increasingly deep conversation with him.

"That's extraordinary recognition of your architectural vision," he said finally, his voice carrying authentic appreciation without artificial excitement. "The opportunity to implement threshold concepts at cultural complex scale would allow exploration of relationships between different types of liminal territories—how various threshold spaces interact within larger architectural ecosystem."

The immediate engagement with professional significance rather than personal impact reflected exactly what Tauree valued in their connection—Farrat's consistent ability to recognize what mattered most in any given situation, to address core issues without being distracted by peripheral concerns. Not ignoring the personal implications, but acknowledging the professional opportunity's genuine importance before navigating relational consequences.

"That's what drew me to the project," Tauree confirmed, relief warming her voice at his immediate understanding. "Not just expanded scale of individual threshold spaces, but relationships between different types of liminality—transitions between transitions, thresholds connecting thresholds. Architectural metacognition, in a sense."

"When would you leave?" Farrat asked, moving toward practical considerations rather than emotional exploration—another aspect of their communication that had made discussion of challenging topics more accessible for Tauree's particular approach to relationships.

"Seven weeks from now," she replied. "Enough time for transition in current projects but not excessive delay given the complexity of international relocation, even temporary."

Farrat nodded, integrating this information with what she had already shared. "And the eighteen-month timeline? Is that relatively fixed or subject to significant adjustment based on construction realities?"

"Reasonably fixed for my involvement," Tauree explained, appreciating the specificity of his inquiry. "The project continues beyond that point, but my primary design implementation would be complete, allowing return to domestic practice with occasional consultation as needed."

As she provided these details, Tauree found herself increasingly aware of what this conversation was not—not desperate emotional negotiation or anxious relationship processing, but thoughtful exchange about changing circumstances and potential adaptation. The architecture they had constructed together over these months had created foundation for navigating precisely this type of transition without resorting to conventional relationship patterns or dramatic emotional performance.

"And you've decided to accept," Farrat observed, not a question but a recognition of decision already reached through careful consideration. There was no accusation in his tone, no suggestion that her independent choice represented betrayal or abandonment—only acknowledgment that professional opportunity aligned with her architectural vision in ways that merited acceptance.

"Yes," Tauree confirmed, appreciating his perception that this wasn't a point of negotiation but a decision already determined through her own assessment. "Though not without recognizing significant implications for the particular architecture we've been developing together."

The directness of this acknowledgment—bringing their relationship explicitly into the conversation without either emotional excess or clinical detachment—represented another evolution in her communication patterns. Not strategic planning or performance, but authentic engagement with what mattered most in this unexpected transition.

Farrat nodded, his expression thoughtful rather than dismayed or resigned. "Eighteen months represents substantial separation," he acknowledged. "Not permanent division but significant distance that would require fundamental reconsideration of our current structural approach."

The architectural framing—continuing their shared vocabulary even in this challenging conversation—created familiar territory for navigating unfamiliar emotional landscape. Not conventional breakup script or relationship negotiation, but collaborative analysis of structural challenge requiring thoughtful resolution.

"I've been considering potential adaptations," Tauree said, architect discussing design options with respected colleague rather than romantic partner proposing relationship compromises. "Different approaches to maintaining connection across geographical separation, each with particular advantages and limitations."

"As have I," Farrat replied, surprising her with this evidence of parallel thinking. At her questioning glance, he explained: "Your current projects have been approaching conclusion for some time, your professional trajectory suggesting international possibilities. While this specific opportunity wasn't predictable, some evolution in your practice seemed increasingly likely."

Once again, Tauree found herself appreciating the particular quality of attention he brought to their connection—observing patterns without imposing expectations, recognizing likely developments without demanding specific outcomes. This perceptiveness without presumption had been consistent throughout their relationship, creating space for authentic development rather than performance of predetermined scripts.

"What adaptations have you considered?" she asked, genuinely curious about his perspective rather than merely setting up presentation of her own proposals.

Farrat organized his thoughts with characteristic care before responding, his expression reflecting analytical consideration rather than emotional reaction. "Three primary approaches, similar to our previous discussion of relationship adaptation—conservative, moderate, and more significant modifications to existing architecture."

Tauree nodded, recognizing the consistent framework they had established during their final riverside walk. "Please elaborate," she requested, creating space for his complete articulation before offering her own assessment.

"The conservative approach," Farrat began, "would involve maintaining similar connection patterns across geographical distance—regular communication through digital means rather than physical presence, continued exchange of professional observations and personal reflections, shared intellectual engagement despite spatial separation. Essentially preserving existing architecture while substituting technological mediation for physical proximity."

The clear articulation of this option—its specific mechanisms and underlying principles—reflected their established approach to relationship navigation: explicitly defining possibilities rather than relying on implicit understanding, creating shared vocabulary for assessing potential directions.

"The moderate adaptation," he continued, "would acknowledge more substantial transformation of our connection during separation period—maintenance of foundational relationship with recognition that certain elements require redevelopment upon eventual reunion. Not suspension of connection but strategic focusing on aspects that translate effectively across distance while accepting temporary diminishment of elements requiring physical proximity."

Again, the precision of his articulation—neither catastrophizing the separation nor minimizing its impact—created that sense of being engaged in genuine problem-solving rather than emotional performance. Not conventional relationship drama, but collaborative architectural challenge requiring thoughtful resolution.

"And the significant adaptation?" Tauree prompted, completing the framework they were constructing together.

Farrat paused slightly longer before this final articulation, his expression revealing more complex consideration. "Would involve fundamental reconfiguration of our connection during separation period—explicit acknowledgment that eighteen months represents substantial portion of our relationship's current duration, that geographical distance introduces variables neither of us can fully anticipate, that personal and professional development may proceed along unexpected trajectories in different environments."

"You're suggesting a more complete separation," Tauree observed, neither accusation nor alarm in her tone—simply recognition of what his careful phrasing implied.

"Not separation as conventional relationship paradigm would define it," Farrat clarified, maintaining their consistent rejection of predetermined categories. "Rather, thoughtful recognition that attempting to preserve current architecture across significant geographical distance might create unnecessary structural strain. Not abandonment of connection, but intentional release from expectations that might prevent authentic development during transitional period."

Once again, Tauree found herself appreciating the particular quality of thinking he brought to their relationship—the capacity to consider challenging possibilities without defensive withdrawal or emotional manipulation, to articulate difficult options with both precision and compassion. Not conventional boyfriend suggesting "break" to avoid commitment, but thoughtful partner recognizing genuine complexity of approaching transition.

"And your assessment of these options?" she asked, neither accepting nor rejecting any specific proposal until their exploration had been fully articulated.

"I find myself drawn toward elements of both moderate and significant adaptation," Farrat replied after careful consideration. "Maintaining meaningful connection while releasing unnecessary expectations, preserving essential relationship architecture while allowing evolution that geographical separation will inevitably create. Not conventional 'taking a break' with its implicit permission for disconnection, but thoughtful acknowledgment that eighteen months of separate development will necessarily transform what exists between us."

Winter light continued its gradual movement across the reading nook as they talked, creating shifting patterns of illumination that highlighted different architectural elements throughout their conversation. Not dramatic transformation, but subtle evolution that maintained essential character while responding to changing conditions—exactly what Tauree had designed into the space, exactly what they were attempting to navigate in their relationship.

"Your perspective aligns remarkably with my own considerations," she acknowledged, the parallel thinking another confirmation of their particular compatibility. "Though I would frame it slightly differently—not as release from expectations but as recognition that different architectural forms serve different environmental conditions."

Farrat nodded, immediately grasping the distinction she was articulating. "Adaptation to circumstance rather than abandonment of structure," he suggested, developing her architectural metaphor. "Designing appropriate form for temporary conditions while maintaining essential principles that could support reconstruction upon environmental change."

"Yes, exactly," Tauree confirmed, appreciation warming her voice at his immediate understanding. "Not relationship as predetermined form that either survives or collapses under changed conditions, but architectural principles that can manifest through different structural expressions while maintaining fundamental integrity."

This reframing—shifting from conventional relationship categories to architectural approaches—created cognitive territory where both could engage authentically without resorting to emotional scripts or social performances. Not dramatic breakup or desperate attempt to preserve unsustainable patterns, but thoughtful design challenge requiring creative solution.

"So what would this look like in practice?" Farrat asked, moving from conceptual framework to specific application—another quality that had made their conversations consistently productive rather than merely theoretical.

Tauree considered this practical question with the focused attention she brought to all architectural challenges, her mind naturally organizing possibilities according to functional requirements and structural principles.

"Regular communication without obligation or performance," she suggested, beginning with fundamental elements. "Sharing significant developments and meaningful reflections when authentically motivated rather than according to predetermined schedule or relationship expectation."

"Maintaining intellectual connection through continued engagement with threshold concepts," Farrat added, building upon her foundation. "Not collaborative writing requiring consistent coordination, but parallel exploration that might occasionally intersect through shared observations or complementary insights."

"Freedom to develop new connections without artificial constraints," Tauree continued, approaching the most challenging aspect with characteristic directness. "Not conventional 'seeing other people' with its implication of replacing existing relationship, but recognition that meaningful engagement in separate environments may include connections that cannot be fully anticipated or categorized in advance."

This explicit acknowledgment—that eighteen months in different countries might involve relationships neither could currently envision—created a moment of genuine vulnerability between them. Not emotional performance or dramatic declaration, but authentic recognition of real possibility that required thoughtful navigation rather than avoidance or denial.

"With understanding that such connections would develop according to the principles we've established together," Farrat suggested, neither threatened by the possibility nor dismissive of its significance. "Not abandonment of what we've learned about sustainable relationship architecture, but application of those principles within different environmental contexts."

The clarity of this mutual understanding—this aligned approach to navigating challenging terrain—created another moment of profound connection between them. Not despite the approaching separation but because of their thoughtful engagement with its reality, their refusal to resort to either dramatic emotion or artificial detachment when addressing genuine complexity.

"And upon my return?" Tauree asked, architect considering not just immediate adaptation but longer-term developmental sequence.

"Intentional reassessment," Farrat replied without hesitation. "Not assumption that previous architecture can simply be reconstructed after significant environmental change, nor expectation that temporary adaptations would necessarily become permanent arrangements. Rather, thoughtful evaluation of how separate development might inform shared understanding moving forward."

"A new threshold to navigate together," Tauree suggested, drawing on their established vocabulary. "Neither guaranteed continuation nor predetermined conclusion, but deliberate exploration of what might exist between those conventional categories."

Farrat nodded, appreciation evident in his expression. "Precisely. Not conventional relationship with its binary outcomes of continuation or termination, but architectural approach to changing circumstances—thoughtful assessment of what forms might best serve authentic connection given new conditions."

As they continued developing this framework together—architect and poet creating structural understanding of emotional territory—Tauree found herself experiencing that familiar clarity of perception that had characterized their most significant exchanges. The fog remained present, as always, but it had evolved from obscuring barrier into navigable medium, its density varying but its fundamental character now familiar enough to traverse with increasing confidence.

And in Farrat's thoughtful engagement with this challenging transition, she recognized once again what had drawn her into deeper connection with him—his consistent ability to approach emotional complexity with both intellectual precision and authentic presence, neither retreating into detachment nor descending into drama. Not conventional boyfriend performing expected role, but genuine partner navigating real territory with characteristic attention and care.

"This represents significant departure from conventional relationship patterns," she observed, neither criticism nor concern but recognition of their particular approach. "Most would either maintain unsustainable connection through technological substitution or conclude relationship entirely given geographical constraints."

"We've never adhered to conventional patterns," Farrat replied, a small smile warming his features despite the serious nature of their conversation. "Our entire connection has developed in threshold territory between established categories—neither traditional friendship nor conventional romance, neither casual acquaintance nor formal partnership. This adaptation merely continues that architectural philosophy under changed environmental conditions."

The observation struck Tauree with its accuracy—they had indeed constructed something unique through their months together, a custom architecture designed specifically for their particular needs and capacities. This approaching transition, challenging as it might be, represented opportunity to extend that philosophical approach rather than retreat into predetermined scripts or conventional categories.

Outside, winter light had begun its early transition toward evening, shadows lengthening across the community center's interior spaces. The reading nook's carefully positioned lighting activated automatically in response to changing natural illumination, creating that perfect balance of functional necessity and aesthetic experience Tauree had designed into every aspect of the environment.

"When would you want to implement this adaptation?" Farrat asked, moving toward practical timeline with characteristic attention to transitional sequence.

"Not immediately," Tauree replied after thoughtful consideration. "The next seven weeks represent valuable opportunity for deliberate engagement before geographical separation. Not desperate attempt to compress relationship development into artificial timeline, but thoughtful appreciation of remaining proximity while preparing for approaching distance."

"Agreed," Farrat said, his expression reflecting similar assessment. "Neither ignoring upcoming transition through pretense of continuity, nor prematurely implementing separation before geographical circumstances require it. Balance between present engagement and future preparation."

Another silence fell between them—not awkward absence of communication but shared processing of significant exchange. This too had become characteristic of their relationship: the space to consider complex ideas without requiring immediate response, the recognition that some realizations deserved careful reflection rather than reflexive reaction.

"I have something for you," Farrat said eventually, reaching into his messenger bag to extract a small package wrapped in simple paper. "I had planned to give this during our collaborative presentation of threshold poems next month, but this conversation seems more appropriate timing given approaching transition."

He extended the package toward her—a gesture of offering without expectation, of sharing something significant without demanding particular response. Tauree accepted it with genuine curiosity, the weight suggesting book or similar object rather than conventional gift.

"May I?" she asked, indicating the wrapping.

"Please," Farrat replied, his expression revealing that characteristic blend of vulnerability and composure she had come to associate with his most meaningful disclosures.

Unwrapping the package with precise movements, Tauree discovered a handmade book bound in deep blue cloth with geometric pattern embossed on its cover. The craftsmanship was evident immediately—not commercial production but artistic creation, each element carefully considered and executed with remarkable attention to detail.

"Open it," Farrat suggested quietly.

Inside, she found collection of her architectural drawings reproduced alongside Farrat's poems—their separate creative expressions arranged in dialogue rather than mere juxtaposition.

Each page spread presented one of her threshold space designs with corresponding poem that engaged with its structural principles through complementary verbal exploration. Not illustration of architecture nor visualization of poetry, but genuine conversation between different expressive forms.

"This is remarkable," Tauree said, genuine appreciation warming her voice as she carefully turned pages to examine the thoughtful pairings. "Not just aesthetically, but conceptually—the relationship between spatial and verbal expressions creates another type of threshold territory, neither architecture nor poetry exclusively but something that exists between those categories."

"That was the intention," Farrat acknowledged, pleasure evident in his expression at her immediate understanding. "Artist's book as physical manifestation of the threshold concept we've been exploring together—object that exists between conventional categories, that permits multiple modes of engagement simultaneously."

As Tauree continued examining the book, she noticed that several spreads toward the end remained empty—reproductions of her architectural drawings without corresponding poems alongside them. Before she could inquire about this apparent incompletion, Farrat explained:

"The final sections represent spaces I haven't yet responded to poetically—your Singapore designs among them, which I've only seen in preliminary form. I thought perhaps..." He paused, organizing thoughts with characteristic care before continuing. "Perhaps our communication during your time abroad might include occasional poetry responding to your developing work there, gradually completing the conversation this book has begun."

The suggestion—specific mechanism for maintaining meaningful connection across geographical separation—created that familiar warmth in Tauree's chest. Not desperate attempt to preserve unsustainable relationship patterns, but thoughtful proposal for continued engagement that respected both distance and connection, both separate development and shared exploration.

"I would like that very much," she said simply, the words carrying deeper appreciation than their brevity might suggest. "Both the book itself and the continuing dialogue it might facilitate during separation."

"I hoped you might," Farrat replied, his expression warm with genuine pleasure at her response. "Not as obligation or performance, but as potential framework for meaningful exchange when circumstances allow."

As evening settled more fully around them, the community center's ambient sounds gradually diminishing as regular activities concluded for the day, they continued developing practical aspects of their approaching adaptation—specific considerations about communication methods and meaningful rituals that might facilitate connection across geographical distance without creating unsustainable expectations or performances.

Unlike conventional relationship discussions with their emotional intensity and dramatic declarations, this conversation maintained that quality of thoughtful problem-solving that had characterized their most productive exchanges. Not denial of emotional significance, but refusal to allow emotion to prevent effective navigation of genuine complexity. Architect and poet approaching transition as design challenge requiring creative solution rather than emotional crisis demanding dramatic response.

When they finally rose to leave, their planning complete but not exhaustive—framework established while allowing flexibility for unforeseen developments—Tauree found herself experiencing that curious blend of sadness and appreciation that seemed appropriate to their particular situation. Not devastating heartbreak nor detached acceptance, but authentic recognition of both approaching separation and meaningful connection, both challenge and opportunity this transition represented.

Outside, winter evening had fully settled, streetlights illuminating their path as they walked together through the community center's exterior plaza. Unlike previous partings with their characteristic threshold between connection and separation, tonight carried quality of continuity despite approaching distance—not conclusion requiring future initiation, but ongoing development entering new phase rather than terminating entirely.

"Seven weeks," Farrat observed as they paused near the plaza's center, neither immediately moving toward departure nor suggesting further extension of their evening. "Sufficient time for thoughtful transition rather than abrupt separation."

"Yes," Tauree agreed, appreciation warming her voice at his characteristic focus on constructive possibility rather than limitation. "Not desperate countdown but intentional preparation, not compression of relationship development but thoughtful engagement with approaching change."

Their embrace carried that same quality of authentic connection that had characterized their physical relationship throughout its evolution—neither performance nor restraint, but genuine expression of what existed between them. Not desperate clinging in face of approaching separation, nor premature detachment in anticipation of distance, but present engagement with current reality while acknowledging future transition.

"Until Wednesday at Serendipity?" Farrat suggested as they separated, maintaining their established pattern while acknowledging its approaching adaptation.

"Until Wednesday," Tauree confirmed, completing their exchange with that attention to balanced connection that had become characteristic of their relationship.

As they moved in their separate directions—temporary divergence rather than permanent separation—Tauree carried with her both the physical artist's book and the conceptual framework they had developed together. Not conventional relationship defined by predetermined scripts or binary outcomes, but custom architecture designed through careful attention to both individual needs and mutual possibilities.

The fog remained present, as always, that persistent gray filter through which she experienced the world. But it no longer represented insurmountable barrier to meaningful connection or significant development, merely element of her internal landscape requiring navigation rather than elimination. And in Farrat, she had found someone who neither demanded its dispersal nor pretended it didn't exist—who simply acknowledged its reality while engaging with the person who existed within its confines.

The careful architect of precise spaces had discovered that the same principles that guided her professional work could structure personal territory as well, creating relationships with the same thoughtful balance of containment and expansion, of guidance and freedom that characterized her physical designs. Not despite approaching separation but including it within larger developmental sequence—another threshold to navigate rather than obstacle to avoid or crisis to manage.

As she walked toward her apartment through the quiet winter evening, Tauree found herself contemplating the curious trajectory that had brought her to this moment. From professional detachment and emotional isolation to the particular architecture she and Farrat had constructed together—neither conventional relationship nor casual acquaintance, but custom structure designed for authentic engagement according to their specific needs and capacities.

This approaching international project represented not conclusion to that development but evolution within it—not ending of significant connection but adaptation to changing circumstances. The framework they had established together created possibility for both meaningful professional opportunity and continued personal development, neither sacrificed for the other but thoughtfully integrated within larger architectural approach to life's complexities.

The Singapore cultural complex would allow implementation of threshold concepts on unprecedented scale, exploration of relationships between different types of liminal territories within comprehensive architectural ecosystem. The adaptation she and Farrat had designed would permit continued connection across geographical separation while allowing authentic development within different environments, neither constrained by unsustainable expectations nor abandoned through convenient detachment.

Both represented threshold territories navigated through architectural thinking—neither conventional career advancement nor traditional relationship management, but thoughtful design responding to genuine complexity with creative solutions rather than predetermined scripts. Both honored the particular balance she and Farrat had established throughout their connection—development that maintained essential integrity while adapting to changing conditions, evolution within consistent framework rather than abandonment of fundamental principles.

A threshold space, deliberately constructed, constantly evolving, uniquely theirs—even across international distance.

Act 3: The Resolution and Bittersweet Conclusion

Chapter 13: The Starry Night

Eighteen months passed like the gradual transformation of a building under construction—foundation giving way to framework, structure emerging through persistent attention, final form revealing itself only through patient development rather than immediate manifestation. Singapore had embraced Tauree with its unique blend of precision and organic growth, a city-state that somehow embodied the threshold concepts she had been exploring throughout her architectural career. The cultural complex had evolved from theoretical designs into physical reality, her vision of interconnected liminal territories manifesting in steel and glass, concrete and light, creating experiences that existed between conventional categories rather than adhering to predetermined classifications.

February had become June had become December and then another August, seasons changing with subtle shifts in rainfall patterns rather than dramatic temperature variations. The equatorial climate created different relationship with temporal passage than she had known in more temperate environments—change manifested through quality of light and atmospheric moisture rather than falling leaves or winter snow. Time itself seemed to function differently here, simultaneously more measured in its professional precision and more fluid in its cultural rhythms.

The fog had remained her constant companion, as it always did—that persistent gray filter through which she experienced the world. Yet something curious had happened during these months abroad: the fog had begun interacting with this new environment in unexpected ways, creating different patterns of density and translucence than she had known in more familiar territories. Not dispersing exactly, but adapting to different atmospheric conditions, developing new behaviors within changed circumstances.

Her communication with Farrat had evolved exactly as they had architecturally designed during those careful conversations before her departure—not desperate attempt to maintain unsustainable patterns across geographical distance, but thoughtful engagement that respected both connection and separation. His poetic responses to her developing work had arrived at irregular but meaningful intervals, each engaging with specific architectural elements she had shared through photographs and drawings. The empty spaces in the artist's book he had given her gradually filled with these verses, creating continuing dialogue between their separate creative expressions despite physical distance.

Their personal exchanges had maintained similar thoughtful balance—neither performance of conventional relationship nor complete disconnection, but authentic communication when genuine significance warranted sharing. She learned of his visiting professorship at a prestigious east coast university, of the threshold poems receiving literary recognition beyond initial publication. He followed her professional development through the cultural complex, offering perspectives that engaged with architectural principles without presuming technical expertise.

Neither had attempted to compress the fullness of daily experience into artificial connection, recognizing the impossibility of truly sharing separate environments through technological mediation alone. Instead, they had focused on meaningful moments and significant developments, creating points of genuine engagement rather than simulated proximity. The architecture they had designed together had proven remarkably effective—maintaining essential connection while acknowledging necessary distance, preserving fundamental principles while adapting structural expression to changed conditions.

And now, after eighteen months that had simultaneously passed with surprising quickness and appropriate duration, Tauree stood in Singapore's Changi Airport awaiting her flight home. The cultural complex had been completed two weeks earlier, opening ceremonies conducting thousands of visitors through the threshold spaces she had designed with such care. Critical response had been overwhelmingly positive, with particular attention to how the interconnected liminal territories created experiences that transcended conventional architectural categories—neither purely functional nor merely aesthetic, neither traditionally Asian nor distinctly Western, but thoughtfully developed territories that existed between established classifications.

Her carry-on bag contained the completed artist's book, its final pages now filled with Farrat's poetic responses to the cultural complex's culmination. She had received the verses three days ago, his words engaging with the finished architecture through characteristic precision and unexpected insight, identifying relationships between elements she had consciously designed and emergent patterns that had developed through the building's completion. The book had become physical manifestation of their continued connection despite geographical separation—not desperate preservation of previous patterns, but thoughtful evolution of shared exploration through different structural expression.

The announcement of her flight's boarding came through airport speakers, prompting movement toward the designated gate with professional efficiency that had become second nature during these months of international work. Singapore had appreciated her architectural precision, her attention to detail and procedural thoroughness, even as it had gradually influenced her own patterns through its unique cultural rhythms. She had maintained essential integrity while adapting to environmental conditions—exactly the balance she and Farrat had envisioned for both professional development and personal connection during their thoughtful planning eighteen months earlier.

As the aircraft ascended through tropical atmosphere, Tauree watched Singapore recede beneath her—the distinctive skyline gradually diminishing into comprehensive urban pattern, individual buildings losing definition while larger organizational principles became increasingly apparent. The metaphor wasn't lost on her: how distance could simultaneously obscure specific details while revealing broader relationships, how separation might diminish particular moments while illuminating overarching structures.

She didn't know exactly what awaited her upon return—neither desperate reunion nor complete disconnection, but thoughtful reassessment of what might exist between them after significant separate development. They had maintained communication without obligation, connection without performance, shared exploration without artificial proximity. The framework they had established had effectively supported eighteen months of geographical separation while allowing authentic evolution within different environments.

The agreed mechanism for their reunion maintained similar architectural thinking—not dramatic airport encounter with emotional intensity, but thoughtful meeting after appropriate reacclimation to her return. Three days to resettle in her apartment, to readjust to temporal and atmospheric differences, to transition from international project back to domestic environment. Then Wednesday evening at Serendipity—their established pattern providing structural continuity while acknowledging significant development during separation.

The flight passed with that curious quality of suspended animation that long-distance travel often created—hours measured in artificial cycles of meal service and cabin lighting rather than natural progression of sunlight and darkness. Tauree used this liminal period between departure and arrival to review her Singapore experience with professional thoroughness, documenting final observations and significant learnings that might inform future projects. Not merely technical specifications or procedural improvements, but conceptual developments in her understanding of threshold territories—how different cultural contexts created different relationships with liminal spaces, how architectural principles manifested through varied structural expressions while maintaining essential integrity.

When the aircraft finally touched down, temporal dislocation became immediately apparent—departing evening in Singapore to arrive same-day morning after crossing multiple time zones and the international date line. A threshold crossed not just geographically but temporally, another liminal territory navigated through thoughtful attention rather than passive experience.

Her apartment welcomed her with that peculiar quality of familiar space temporarily uninhabited—everything precisely where she had left it eighteen months earlier, yet somehow different through absence and return. The skylights she had designed continued tracking sunlight across floors and walls with mathematical precision, creating patterns of illumination she had experienced only through memory during her time abroad. The environment remained structurally identical, yet her perception had evolved through separate development—another threshold territory navigated through architectural thinking rather than conventional emotional response.

The next three days passed in methodical reacclimation, professional thoroughness applied to personal transition. Tauree organized materials from the Singapore project, established initial communications with domestic clients about potential new commissions, and readjusted to temporal and atmospheric differences between equatorial city-state and temperate urban environment. The fog maintained its presence, as always, but continued demonstrating the adaptive qualities it had developed abroad—different patterns of density and translucence than she had known before departure, familiar in essential character while evolved in specific manifestation.

Wednesday arrived with unexpected clarity—one of those rare winter days when sunlight penetrates seasonal clouds to create precise illumination, shadows sharp-edged against light-washed surfaces. Tauree approached her appearance with characteristic attention to both aesthetic and functional considerations, selecting clothing that acknowledged international influence while maintaining essential consistency—architectural approach to personal presentation rather than performance or calculation.

The walk to Serendipity took her through familiar neighborhoods transformed by both seasonal conditions and perceptual evolution—streets simultaneously exactly as she had left them and remarkably different through changed observation. Singapore had influenced not just professional development but personal perspective, creating subtle shifts in how she experienced familiar environments. Not fundamental transformation but meaningful adaptation, essential character maintained while specific perception evolved.

Serendipity Café welcomed her with unchanged warmth—the wood paneling, mismatched but comfortable furniture, and walls lined with thoughtfully curated books creating that perfect balance of intellectual engagement and physical comfort she had appreciated since her first visit. Malcolm nodded from behind the counter, his acknowledgment carrying no surprise at her return—as if eighteen months represented merely expected absence rather than significant separation.

Farrat was already at their usual corner table, a steaming mug of what she knew would be her preferred coffee waiting across from his chai. His appearance carried subtle evidence of the passing months—perhaps slight additional silver at his temples, certain lines more defined around his eyes, his bearing reflecting continued development rather than dramatic transformation. He rose as she approached, his expression revealing that characteristic blend of attentiveness and composure she had valued throughout their connection.

"You came," he said, completing their traditional greeting ritual with the same words they had exchanged since their first genuine conversation.

"I said I would," Tauree replied, settling into the chair opposite him. The familiar exchange created immediate sense of continuity despite eighteen months of geographical separation—not denial of developmental distance, but acknowledgment of structural consistency beneath superficial change.

His smile reached his eyes with genuine warmth, creating that familiar flutter in her chest that neither time nor distance had diminished. "How was your flight?" he asked, beginning with practical consideration rather than emotional intensity—another aspect of their connection that had made challenging transitions more accessible for Tauree's particular approach to relationships.

"Long but uneventful," she replied, wrapping her hands around the coffee mug with appreciation for both its heat and the thoughtfulness it represented. "Temporal dislocation remains the most significant challenge of international travel—crossing multiple time zones creates curious relationship with experiential continuity."

"Threshold territories navigated temporally rather than spatially," Farrat observed, immediately engaging with conceptual significance rather than merely practical details. This capacity for intellectual connection alongside personal engagement had been foundational to their relationship from its beginning, neither sacrificed for the other but thoughtfully integrated within larger architectural approach to meaningful interaction.

"Exactly," Tauree confirmed, appreciation warming her voice at his immediate understanding. "The international date line creates particularly interesting examples—geographical boundaries that manifest temporal consequences, spatial transitions that produce experiential discontinuities."

As they continued sharing their separate developments—Farrat's academic positioning and literary recognition, Tauree's international implementation of threshold concepts and cultural adaptations—a familiar pattern emerged in their exchange. Each translated their individual experiences into terms the other could access and appreciate, creating bridges between territories that might otherwise remain disconnected. Not performance of artificial proximity, but authentic sharing of significant developments through their established vocabulary of meaningful communication.

"The artist's book has been completed," Tauree observed, removing the volume from her bag and placing it between them on the table. "Your final verses arrived just before my departure—perfect timing for bringing the project to appropriate conclusion."

"I hoped they might," Farrat replied, his expression revealing pleasure at this convergence of separate timelines. "The photographs you shared of the completed cultural complex provided necessary completion to the architectural narrative—the threshold spaces fully realized rather than merely designed."

They examined the book together, its pages now completely filled with the dialogue between her architectural drawings and his poetic responses. Not merely chronological documentation of separate development, but thoughtful conversation between different expressive forms—visual and verbal explorations of threshold territories creating another liminal space through their interaction on the page.

"This represents something significant," Tauree observed, her attention focused on the completed volume. "Not just professionally for each of us, but conceptually in its manifestation of threshold thinking—object that exists between conventional categories, that permits multiple modes of engagement simultaneously."

"Indeed," Farrat agreed, his expression reflecting similar appreciation. "Neither architecture nor poetry exclusively, but thoughtful exploration of territory that exists between those established classifications. Another manifestation of the principles we've been developing together, despite geographical separation."

The clarity of this mutual recognition—this aligned understanding of both artistic achievement and conceptual significance—created a moment of profound connection between them. Not despite eighteen months of separate development but because of how that separation had allowed individual evolution within shared framework, both maintaining essential principles while adapting specific expressions to different environments.

"And now," Farrat said eventually, his tone shifting slightly to indicate transition to more personal territory, "we approach another threshold together—neither complete reunion nor continued separation, but thoughtful assessment of what might exist between those conventional categories."

The directness of this acknowledgment—bringing their relationship explicitly into the conversation without either emotional excess or clinical detachment—created space for authentic engagement with the question they had intentionally deferred during geographical separation. Not dramatic declaration or performance of predetermined scripts, but genuine exploration of what might develop through thoughtful consideration rather than automatic response.

"Yes," Tauree confirmed, matching his directness with characteristic precision. "The architectural approach we designed before my departure proved remarkably effective for maintaining connection across geographical distance. The question becomes whether similar principles might guide whatever develops now that physical proximity has been restored."

"I've been considering various possibilities," Farrat offered, architect discussing design options with respected colleague rather than romantic partner proposing relationship progression. "Different approaches to potential reconstruction, each representing different relationships between previous architecture and new development."

"As have I," Tauree acknowledged, their parallel thinking another confirmation of continued compatibility despite separate evolution. "Would you care to elaborate your considerations?"

Farrat organized his thoughts with characteristic care before responding, his expression reflecting analytical consideration rather than emotional pressure. "Three primary approaches, maintaining our established framework—conservative, moderate, and more significant adaptations to existing architecture."

Tauree nodded, recognition of the consistent vocabulary they had developed for navigating relationship transitions. "Please continue," she requested, creating space for his complete articulation before offering her own assessment.

"The conservative approach," Farrat began, "would involve essentially reconstructing our pre-separation architecture—weekly meetings at Serendipity, occasional weekend activities combining intellectual engagement with personal connection, collaborative writing exploring threshold concepts through complementary perspectives. Effectively resuming previous patterns with minimal acknowledgment of separate development."

The clarity of this articulation—its specific mechanisms and potential limitations—reflected their established approach to relationship navigation: explicitly defining possibilities rather than relying on implicit understanding, creating shared vocabulary for assessing potential directions.

"The moderate adaptation," he continued, "would maintain essential structural principles while acknowledging significant evolution during separation period. Similar foundational architecture but with thoughtful modifications reflecting how separate development has influenced individual needs and capacities. Not dramatic reconstruction but intentional renovation based on current rather than previous conditions."

Again, the precision of his articulation—neither minimizing the impact of eighteen months' separation nor catastrophizing its developmental consequences—created that sense of engaging in genuine architectural challenge rather than emotional performance. Not conventional relationship negotiation, but collaborative design problem requiring thoughtful resolution.

"And the significant adaptation?" Tauree prompted, completing their established analytical framework.

"Would involve fundamental reconsideration of relationship architecture based on how separate development has transformed individual requirements," Farrat explained, his tone maintaining careful balance between directness and sensitivity. "Not abandonment of essential principles, but recognition that eighteen months represents substantial portion of our connection's total duration, that significant separate evolution might necessitate completely new structural approach rather than modification of previous patterns."

As he completed this framework, Tauree found herself appreciating once again the particular quality of thinking he brought to their relationship—the capacity to consider challenging possibilities without defensive withdrawal or emotional manipulation, to articulate difficult options with both precision and compassion. Not conventional performance of expected role, but genuine partner exploring real possibilities with characteristic attention and care.

"And your assessment of these options?" she asked, neither accepting nor rejecting any specific proposal until their exploration had been fully articulated.

"I find myself drawn toward elements of the moderate approach," Farrat replied after careful consideration. "Maintaining essential principles that have served our connection effectively while acknowledging how separate development has created different circumstances than existed before geographical separation. Not desperate attempt to reconstruct identical architecture, but thoughtful renovation reflecting current conditions rather than previous requirements."

Winter light continued its precise movement through Serendipity's windows as they talked, creating shifting patterns of illumination across their table that highlighted different aspects of the artist's book between them. Not dramatic transformation, but gradual evolution that maintained essential character while responding to changing conditions—exactly what they were attempting to navigate in their relationship.

"Your perspective aligns with my own considerations," Tauree acknowledged, the parallel assessment another confirmation of their particular compatibility. "Though I would frame it slightly differently—not as renovation of previous architecture but as new construction informed by established principles. Similar foundation supporting potentially different structural expression."

Farrat nodded, immediately grasping the distinction she was articulating. "Implementation of consistent architectural philosophy through fresh design rather than modification of existing structure," he suggested, developing her metaphor with characteristic precision. "Maintaining essential principles while allowing complete reconsideration of how those principles might manifest under current conditions."

"Yes, exactly," Tauree confirmed, appreciation warming her voice at his immediate understanding. "Not relationship resuming previous patterns with minor adjustments, but thoughtful development of connection reflecting who we have become through separate evolution, not merely who we were before geographical separation."

This reframing—shifting from conventional reunion narratives to architectural approaches—created cognitive territory where both could engage authentically without resorting to emotional scripts or social performances. Not desperate attempt to recapture previous connection nor complete abandonment of established understanding, but thoughtful design challenge requiring creative solution appropriate to current conditions.

"So what would this look like in practice?" Farrat asked, moving from conceptual framework to specific application—another quality that had made their conversations consistently productive rather than merely theoretical.

Tauree considered this practical question with the focused attention she brought to all architectural challenges, her mind naturally organizing possibilities according to functional requirements and structural principles.

"Perhaps we begin with essential elements and develop more complex relationships gradually," she suggested, architect proposing construction sequence rather than relationship partner negotiating expectations. "Weekly meetings continuing but potentially in different locations reflecting changed perspectives. The collaborative writing evolving to incorporate international influences and separate developments. Shared experiences selected for current significance rather than previous patterns."

"Creating framework for authentic engagement without predetermining specific manifestations," Farrat suggested, building upon her foundation with characteristic insight. "Not prescriptive arrangement but flexible structure allowing natural development through ongoing interaction rather than predetermined expectations."

"Exactly," Tauree confirmed, genuine appreciation in her voice at how precisely he had articulated her architectural intention. "Designing process rather than product, establishing principles rather than specific forms, creating conditions for authentic development rather than imposing predetermined outcomes."

As they continued developing this framework together—architect and poet creating structural understanding of emotional territory—Tauree found herself experiencing that familiar clarity of perception that had characterized their most significant exchanges. The fog remained present, as always, but it had evolved from obscuring barrier into navigable medium, its density varying but its fundamental character now familiar enough to traverse with increasing confidence.

And in Farrat's thoughtful engagement with this reunion transition, she recognized once again what had drawn her into deeper connection with him—his consistent ability to approach emotional complexity with both intellectual precision and authentic presence, neither retreating into detachment nor descending into drama. Not conventional partner performing expected role, but genuine companion navigating real territory with characteristic attention and care.

"There's something else I'd like to share," Farrat said eventually, his tone shifting slightly to indicate change in subject. "A development during your time abroad that seems particularly relevant to our current considerations."

"Please," Tauree invited, genuine curiosity engaging with this unexpected direction.

"I've been offered permanent position at the east coast university where I held visiting professorship," he explained, his expression revealing careful assessment rather than either excitement or concern. "Director of new interdisciplinary program exploring relationships between different creative expressions—literature engaging with architecture, visual arts interacting with performance, technology intersecting with traditional craft. Essentially academic manifestation of the threshold concepts we've been exploring together."

The information registered immediately as significant—not just professional opportunity but potential geographical implications that would necessarily influence whatever relationship architecture they might develop moving forward. Not dramatic complication but genuine factor requiring thoughtful consideration rather than emotional reaction or automatic adjustment.

"That's extraordinary recognition of your academic vision," Tauree observed, professional appreciation engaging before personal implications—exactly the response pattern that had characterized their most effective communications. "When would this position begin?"

"Next academic year," Farrat replied, providing precise information without emotional coloring. "Approximately seven months from now, allowing appropriate transition from current university commitments."

"And your inclination regarding this opportunity?" Tauree asked, seeking his assessment rather than immediately calculating potential consequences for their relationship.

"I'm genuinely drawn to the position," Farrat acknowledged, his honesty characteristic of their established communication patterns. "The interdisciplinary nature aligns precisely with my academic interests, the institutional support for threshold thinking represents significant opportunity for developing these concepts within educational context. The geographical considerations create obvious complications, but the professional alignment seems remarkably appropriate."

The clarity of this articulation—acknowledging both professional opportunity and relational implications without allowing either to completely determine response—created that familiar sense of genuine dialogue rather than emotional performance. Not conventional relationship weighing priorities through comparative valuation, but thoughtful consideration of authentic development across multiple domains simultaneously.

"Another threshold to navigate together," Tauree observed, neither dismay nor denial in her tone—simply recognition of genuine complexity requiring thoughtful engagement rather than automatic response. "Different geographical considerations than Singapore presented, but similar questions about relationship architecture across spatial separation."

"Yes," Farrat confirmed, appreciation evident in his expression at her architectural framing of this potential challenge. "Though with significant differences from your international project—permanent relocation rather than temporary assignment, domestic rather than international distance, regular travel possibilities rather than occasional visits."

"Creating different design parameters for potential relationship architecture," Tauree suggested, approaching this new information through professional vocabulary rather than emotional reaction. "Different structural requirements based on specific conditions rather than generic separation."

"Exactly," Farrat agreed, visible relief in his expression at her analytical engagement rather than emotional response. "Not insurmountable obstacle but genuine design challenge requiring thoughtful navigation rather than predetermined solution."

As they continued exploring this potential development alongside their reunion considerations, Malcolm approached their table with the unobtrusive attention that had characterized his café management throughout their relationship. The elderly former professor carried a small plate of pastries, which he set between them with a warm smile.

"Welcome back," he said simply to Tauree. "The café has missed your architectural perspective these past months."

"Thank you, Malcolm," she replied, genuine appreciation warming her voice at this understated acknowledgment of both absence and return. "It's good to be back in this threshold space you've created—territory that exists between public and private, between intellectual engagement and physical comfort."

"The best environments honor both structural precision and human experience," the former professor observed with the quiet wisdom of his years. "Much like the best relationships, I imagine."

After he had departed with a gentle nod, Tauree found herself considering his observation—the parallel between architectural environments and relationship territories, between physical spaces and emotional landscapes. This had been fundamental to her developing understanding with Farrat: the application of architectural principles to personal connection, structural thinking extended beyond professional practice into private experience.

"We've navigated geographical separation effectively once before," she noted, returning to their consideration of Farrat's potential relocation. "Different circumstances would require different specific arrangements, but similar architectural principles could inform whatever structure might develop."

"Creating framework that acknowledges both professional opportunities and personal connection," Farrat suggested, developing this approach with characteristic insight. "Not sacrifice of either domain but thoughtful integration within larger architectural approach to meaningful development across multiple territories."

Outside, winter sunlight had begun its early transition toward evening, the quality of illumination shifting toward golden hour that photographers prized for its particular relationship with architectural forms. Not dramatic transformation but gradual evolution, essential character maintained while specific manifestation responded to changing conditions—exactly what they were attempting to navigate in their relationship.

"There's something I'd like to propose," Tauree said eventually, her decision emerging through careful consideration rather than emotional impulse. "Not comprehensive solution but potential approach to current threshold—structural thinking applied to immediate possibilities rather than attempting final resolution of long-term considerations."

"I'm interested," Farrat replied, creating space for her complete articulation without interruption or presumption.

"These next seven months before your potential relocation represent valuable opportunity for deliberate engagement after significant separation," she began, architect presenting design concept to respected colleague rather than partner proposing relationship arrangement. "Not desperate attempt to compress connection before approaching distance, but thoughtful development of understanding that might inform whatever architecture we create for geographical separation if your academic position materializes."

"Using current proximity to establish framework that could adapt to potential distance," Farrat suggested, immediately grasping her architectural intention. "Not ignoring approaching transition through pretense of continuity, nor preemptively implementing separation before geographical circumstances require it. Balance between present engagement and future preparation."

"Exactly," Tauree confirmed, appreciation evident in her voice at his precise understanding. "Combined with regular assessment of developing conditions rather than rigid adherence to predetermined expectations. Architectural approach to relationship navigation rather than conventional emotional response to potential separation."

"This represents significant departure from standard relationship patterns," Farrat observed, neither criticism nor concern but recognition of their particular approach to connection. "Most would either commit to geographical adjustment regardless of professional implications or conclude relationship entirely given approaching separation."

"We've never adhered to conventional patterns," Tauree replied, a small smile warming her features despite the serious nature of their conversation. "Our entire connection has developed in threshold territory between established categories—neither traditional friendship nor conventional romance, neither casual acquaintance nor formal partnership. This approach merely continues that architectural philosophy under evolving conditions."

The clarity of this mutual recognition—this aligned understanding of both current situation and preferred approach to its navigation—created another moment of profound connection between them. Not despite potential separation but because of their thoughtful engagement with its possibility, their refusal to resort to either dramatic emotion or artificial detachment when addressing genuine complexity.

As evening settled more fully around them, Serendipity's characteristic lamps creating pools of warm illumination throughout the café, they continued developing specific aspects of this approach—practical considerations about communication patterns and shared experiences that might facilitate both current connection and potential preparation for geographical distance. Not conventional relationship planning with its emotional intensity and dramatic declarations, but thoughtful architectural development of framework that could accommodate authentic engagement across various potential conditions.

"Would you like to walk for a while?" Farrat suggested as they completed this phase of their planning. "The evening is clear, and there's something I'd like to show you—a particular quality of winter stars visible from the university observatory that seems relevant to our current considerations."

The invitation—offering continuation without expectation—maintained that careful balance they had established throughout their relationship. Not demand for extended engagement nor pressure toward particular outcome, but genuine sharing of meaningful experience without predetermined significance or required response.

"I'd like that," Tauree replied, the acceptance natural rather than calculated. "The evening is pleasant for walking despite the season."

Outside, winter night had fully settled, stars emerging with remarkable clarity against the backdrop of cold, dry atmosphere. They moved together through the quiet streets, their pace unhurried, conversation continuing with that same easy flow that had characterized their exchange throughout the evening. Not desperate attempt to recapture previous patterns, but authentic engagement with current reality—neither denying separate development during geographical separation nor requiring complete reconstruction of previous architecture.

The university observatory occupied highest point within campus grounds, its dome visible against night sky from considerable distance. As they approached, Tauree noticed that formal facility appeared closed, but smaller observation deck remained accessible via exterior staircase winding up the building's side. Farrat led her upward with confident familiarity, suggesting previous visits during her absence.

"I discovered this place during particularly difficult period last winter," he explained as they ascended. "The rainfall became temporarily overwhelming—combination of seasonal darkness, academic pressures, and geographical separation creating perfect conditions for emotional deluge. This elevation provided necessary perspective, both literally and metaphorically."

The acknowledgment—that her absence had created genuine challenge despite their careful planning and maintained communication—carried none of the manipulative guilt or emotional pressure Tauree might have expected in conventional relationship. Instead, it represented simply honest disclosure of significant experience, authentic sharing without expectation of particular response or unnecessary responsibility.

"The fog manifested differently in Singapore," she offered in return, similar honesty emerging without calculation or performance. "Tropical atmosphere creating different patterns of density and translucence than familiar environments—not fundamental transformation but meaningful adaptation to changed conditions."

The parallel acknowledgments—that both had experienced their respective forms of depression despite geographical separation and continued communication—created another moment of genuine connection between them. Not performance of emotional proximity, but authentic sharing of significant internal landscape without requiring identical experience or particular response.

They reached observation deck's summit, open platform beneath winter stars providing spectacular view of both astronomical display above and city lights below. The elevation created perfect vantage point for appreciating both celestial patterns and human development, natural and constructed environments simultaneously visible from this particular threshold between earth and sky.

"The winter constellations create different relationship with observer than summer arrangements," Farrat observed as they settled onto bench positioned for optimal viewing. "Orion dominating southern sky with geometric precision, Taurus and Pleiades creating more organic patterns nearby, Gemini and Canis Major completing winter hexagon that provides fundamental orientation during coldest months."

Tauree followed his gesture toward these stellar arrangements, her architect's eye immediately engaging with the spatial relationships between different celestial bodies. Not random scattering but complex organization, patterns emerging through both actual positioning and perceptual interpretation—another manifestation of how structure revealed itself through careful observation rather than immediate appearance.

"Different cultures perceive different patterns within identical stellar arrangements," she noted, professional interest engaging with this astronomical manifestation of threshold thinking. "Western tradition seeing hunter where Eastern perspectives identify administrative official, same exact stars interpreted through different cultural frameworks to create distinct meaningful patterns."

"Threshold territories manifesting astronomically," Farrat suggested, developing this observation with characteristic insight. "Identical physical arrangement permitting multiple interpretations simultaneously, neither exclusively correct nor comprehensively definitive but authentically meaningful within particular perceptual frameworks."

The parallel to their relationship architecture emerged without explicit articulation—how identical connection might manifest through different structural expressions while maintaining essential integrity, how separate perception could create distinct yet equally valid interpretations of shared experience. Not contradiction requiring resolution, but threshold territory permitting multiple meanings simultaneously.

As they continued observing winter constellations together, their conversation flowing between astronomical observation and philosophical consideration, Tauree found herself experiencing that rare clarity that had characterized their most significant exchanges. The fog remained present, as always, but it had evolved from obscuring barrier into navigable medium, its density varying but its fundamental character now familiar enough to traverse with increasing confidence.

And in this particular moment—seated beside Farrat beneath winter stars after eighteen months of geographical separation—she recognized something fundamental about their connection that transcended conventional relationship categories or emotional classifications. Not desperate reunion nor tentative reacquaintance, but genuine continuation of architectural development that had proceeded separately yet remained fundamentally aligned through shared principles rather than identical experiences.

"I have something for you," she said eventually, reaching into her bag to extract small package wrapped in simple paper. "From Singapore—object that seemed particularly relevant to our ongoing exploration of threshold territories."

She extended the package toward him—gesture of offering without expectation, sharing something significant without demanding particular response. Farrat accepted it with evident appreciation, unwrapping with careful movements that preserved paper rather than destroying it in hasty revelation.

Inside was architectural model she had created personally rather than through professional fabrication—miniature reproduction of the cultural complex's central atrium, where multiple threshold spaces intersected to create particularly significant manifestation of liminal territory. Not commercial souvenir but artistic expression, each element carefully considered and executed with remarkable attention to detail.

"This is extraordinary," Farrat said, genuine appreciation warming his voice as he examined the model's precise construction. "Not just aesthetically, but conceptually—the physical manifestation of threshold thinking through architectural miniaturization, the relationship between actual building and representational model creating another type of liminal territory."

"That was the intention," Tauree acknowledged, pleasure evident in her expression at his immediate understanding. "Model existing between conceptual design and physical construction, neither purely theoretical nor completely actual but threshold territory permitting engagement with architectural principles through different scalar relationship than either drawings or completed building."

As Farrat continued examining the model, attention moving between different elements with characteristic perception, Tauree found herself contemplating the curious trajectory that had brought them to this moment. From reluctant attendance at social obligation to thoughtful navigation of potential geographical separation, their connection had consistently developed through architectural thinking rather than conventional emotional patterns—threshold approach to relationship rather than predetermined scripts or established categories.

"What strikes me most about our reunion," she observed, the insight emerging without premeditation, "is how neither geographical separation nor potential future distance seems to fundamentally threaten what exists between us. Not because distance is insignificant or separation inconsequential, but because the particular architecture we've constructed seems remarkably adaptable to different environmental conditions without compromising essential integrity."

"I've had similar recognition," Farrat acknowledged, his attention shifting from model to their broader consideration. "The principles we've established have proven effective across significant geographical separation, suggesting similar approach might navigate potential future distance with equal effectiveness. Not because connection transcends physical reality, but because architectural thinking provides framework for adaptation without fundamental compromise."

The clarity of this mutual understanding—this aligned recognition of both current situation and potential development—created another moment of profound connection between them. Not despite geographical complications but because of their thoughtful engagement with spatial realities, their refusal to either ignore practical considerations or surrender to conventional limitations when addressing genuine complexity.

"It seems we're approaching another threshold together," Tauree suggested, drawing on their established vocabulary for navigating significant transitions. "Not between connection and separation exclusively, but territory that might permit both proximity and distance simultaneously—relationship architecture designed specifically for navigation across geographical variation rather than dependent on consistent spatial conditions."

"Exactly," Farrat confirmed, appreciation evident in his expression at her precise articulation. "Not conventional long-distance relationship with its implicit compromise and expected strain, but custom architecture incorporating geographical considerations as design parameters rather than external obstacles."

As they continued developing this understanding together—architect and poet creating structural framework for emotional territory—the winter stars continued their precise movement across the night sky above. Not dramatic transformation but gradual evolution, essential positions maintained while specific manifestation responded to ongoing temporal progression—exactly what they were attempting to navigate in their relationship.

The observatory platform had grown colder as night deepened, prompting eventual descent toward campus grounds below. Unlike previous partings with their characteristic threshold between connection and separation, tonight carried quality of continuity despite approaching considerations—not conclusion requiring future initiation, but ongoing development entering new phase rather than terminating entirely.

Their embrace carried that same quality of authentic connection that had characterized their physical relationship before geographical separation—neither performance nor restraint, but genuine expression of what existed between them. Not desperate clinging in face of potential distance, nor premature detachment in anticipation of separation, but present engagement with current reality while acknowledging future possibilities.

"Wednesday at Serendipity?" Farrat suggested as they separated, maintaining their established pattern while acknowledging its potential adaptation.

"Wednesday," Tauree confirmed, completing their exchange with that attention to balanced connection that had characterized their relationship throughout its development.

As they moved toward her apartment through the winter night, stars continuing their celestial patterns overhead, Tauree carried with her both the artist's book and the understanding they had developed together. Not conventional relationship defined by predetermined scripts or binary outcomes, but custom architecture designed through careful attention to both individual needs and mutual possibilities—threshold space that permitted multiple modes of engagement simultaneously, that honored difference while establishing genuine understanding across it.

The fog remained present, as always, that persistent gray filter through which she experienced the world. But it had become familiar element of her internal landscape, acknowledged without denial while prevented from defining her entire experience. And in Farrat, she had found someone who neither demanded its dispersal nor pretended it didn't exist—who simply walked alongside her through its varying densities, sharing his own rainfall in an exchange of understanding that had created, somehow, a microclimate uniquely their own.

As they reached her apartment building, another parting point in their ongoing navigation, Tauree found herself experiencing that curious blend of completion and continuation that seemed appropriate to their particular situation. Not devastating attachment nor detached independence, but authentic recognition of both meaningful connection and necessary autonomy, both shared understanding and separate development.

"I've been thinking," she said as they paused outside her entrance, "about the nature of constellations we observed tonight."

"In what sense?" Farrat asked, his interest genuine rather than perfunctory.

"How distance creates both limitation and possibility simultaneously," she explained, architect articulating conceptual insight rather than emotional declaration. "From Earth's surface, we perceive two-dimensional patterns in stars that actually exist in three-dimensional space separated by unfathomable distances. The patterns are simultaneously illusion created by perspective and genuine reality of human perception."

"Threshold territory between objective arrangement and subjective interpretation," Farrat suggested, developing her astronomical metaphor with characteristic insight. "Neither exclusively physical fact nor purely imaginative construction, but meaningful territory that exists precisely at the intersection of different perceptual frameworks."

"Yes," Tauree confirmed, appreciation warming her voice at his immediate understanding. "And it occurs to me that geographical distance might function similarly in relationship architecture—simultaneously creating separation in physical proximity and possibility for new perceptual frameworks that might not develop within consistent spatial arrangements."

Farrat considered this with thoughtful attention, his expression revealing active engagement with her conceptual proposition rather than automatic acceptance or dismissal. "Distance as creative constraint rather than merely limiting factor," he suggested, developing her architectural thinking. "Separation requiring innovative structural approaches that consistent proximity might never necessitate."

"Exactly," Tauree acknowledged, genuine excitement at this shared conceptual development overcoming her usual emotional reserve. "The Singapore project would never have materialized without willingness to navigate geographical separation. Your potential academic position represents similar opportunity that wouldn't exist without spatial flexibility. Perhaps relationship architecture might develop through similar engagement with distance as creative parameter rather than merely limiting condition."

The clarity of this mutual insight—this aligned recognition of potential transformation in how they conceptualized geographical considerations—created another moment of profound connection between them. Not despite spatial challenges but because of their thoughtful engagement with locational realities, their refusal to either ignore practical considerations or surrender to conventional limitations when addressing genuine complexity.

"Another threshold to navigate together," Farrat observed, the phrase carrying the weight of their shared vocabulary for approaching significant transitions. "Territory that exists between conventional categories of presence and absence, proximity and distance, that permits multiple modes of engagement simultaneously rather than requiring exclusive classification."

"The careful architect of emotional spaces meets the thoughtful poet of structural understanding," Tauree said, rare metaphorical expression emerging without calculation or performance. "Continuing to construct something neither conventional relationship nor casual connection, but custom architecture designed for our particular ways of being in the world."

Their farewell carried that same quality of authentic engagement that had characterized each significant threshold they had crossed together—neither performance nor restraint, but genuine expression of what existed between them. Not desperate clinging nor premature detachment, but present connection with current reality while acknowledging future possibilities.

As Tauree entered her apartment and Farrat continued toward his own residence through the winter night, each carried the understanding they had developed together—not conventional relationship defined by predetermined scripts or binary outcomes, but custom architecture designed through careful attention to both individual needs and mutual possibilities. A threshold space that permitted multiple modes of engagement simultaneously, that honored difference while establishing genuine understanding across it, that recognized distance as potential creative parameter rather than merely limiting condition.

The fog remained present for Tauree, as always, that persistent gray filter through which she experienced the world. The rainfall continued moving through Farrat in its familiar patterns, neither dispersed by their reunion nor intensified by approaching considerations. But something had evolved in how they navigated these separate weather systems—not dramatic transformation or miraculous cure, but gradual development of increasing skill in moving through varying atmospheric conditions with authenticity and purpose.

Above them both, though now observed from separate locations, the winter stars continued their precise movement across the night sky—different constellations visible from different vantage points, identical celestial bodies arranged into varied patterns through distinct perspectives. Not contradiction requiring resolution, but threshold territory permitting multiple interpretations simultaneously, each authentic within its particular perceptual framework while maintaining fundamental integrity across different observational positions.

The careful architect and thoughtful poet had discovered, somehow, a structural approach to connection that transcended conventional limitations without denying physical reality—that acknowledged geographical considerations without surrendering to spatial determinism, that recognized distance as creative parameter rather than merely limiting condition. Neither traditional romance nor platonic friendship, neither casual acquaintance nor formal partnership, but custom architecture designed specifically for their particular needs and capacities.

A threshold space, deliberately constructed, constantly evolving, uniquely theirs—even across potential geographical separation.

Epilogue: The Starry Night

Five years had passed since Tauree's return from Singapore, since that winter evening beneath observatory stars where she and Farrat had recognized distance as creative parameter rather than merely limiting condition. The architectural approach they had developed during that reunion had proven remarkably effective—not merely surviving geographical separation when Farrat accepted his academic position on the east coast, but genuinely evolving through the creative constraints that spatial distribution had imposed upon their relationship structure.

The book they had published together—"Threshold Territories: Architectural and Poetic Approaches to Liminal Spaces"—had received significant recognition across multiple disciplines, its exploration of spaces that existed between conventional categories resonating with readers who found themselves navigating similar territory in various domains. Not merely academic achievement but conceptual breakthrough, the volume had created framework for understanding threshold experiences that transcended specific professional vocabularies while honoring particular disciplinary insights.

Tauree's architectural practice had evolved in parallel with this theoretical development—her designs increasingly sought after for projects requiring thoughtful navigation of complex social and cultural intersections. Not merely aesthetic achievement or technical excellence, but genuine innovation in how built environments could create experiences that transcended conventional categories—spaces that existed between public and private, between structured guidance and organic discovery, between historical reference and contemporary function.

Farrat's academic position had similarly flourished, his interdisciplinary program becoming model for educational approaches that bridged traditional departmental boundaries. Not merely administrative achievement or institutional prestige, but meaningful transformation in how knowledge could be organized and transmitted—educational structures that permitted multiple modes of engagement simultaneously rather than requiring exclusive disciplinary classification.

Their personal relationship had developed through consistent application of architectural principles to emotional territories—not conventional romance with its predetermined scripts and binary outcomes, but custom structure designed specifically for their particular needs and capacities. The geographical distance between their primary residences had necessitated thoughtful consideration of when physical proximity served their connection most effectively, when technological mediation provided sufficient engagement, and when separate development required individual space rather than shared experience.

They had established seasonal patterns that balanced proximity and distance according to professional obligations and personal requirements—extended periods together during academic breaks and between architectural projects, regular visits during less intensive work phases, technological connection maintaining engagement during necessary separation. Not compromise diminishing both professional achievement and personal fulfillment, but thoughtful integration creating sustainable balance across multiple domains simultaneously.

On this particular evening—the fifth anniversary of Tauree's return from Singapore—they stood together on the rooftop terrace of her latest architectural achievement: a public observatory and education center built on the exact site where they had observed winter constellations during their reunion. The university had commissioned the project after their book's publication, recognizing potential for physical manifestation of the threshold concepts they had articulated together.

The building itself represented perfect embodiment of their shared architectural philosophy—structure that existed between conventional categories, that permitted multiple modes of engagement simultaneously, that created experiences transcending traditional classifications while maintaining functional precision. The central dome housed professional-grade astronomical equipment for scientific research, while surrounding spaces offered educational programming for various knowledge levels and observational platforms accessible to general public.

Most significant was the rooftop terrace where they currently stood—circular platform intentionally designed to recreate their experience from five years earlier, when winter stars had illuminated potential for understanding distance as creative parameter rather than merely limiting condition. The space existed between professional research facility and public educational environment, between structured astronomical observation and organic personal experience, between architectural precision and poetic interpretation.

"It's remarkable," Farrat observed as evening gradually deepened toward night, first stars becoming visible against darkening sky. "Not just professionally accomplished, but conceptually significant—physical manifestation of threshold thinking through architectural implementation of principles we developed together."

"The most meaningful aspect wasn't planned initially," Tauree acknowledged, professional humility balancing justified pride in significant achievement. "How the central structural elements create patterns of light and shadow that track celestial movement across interior surfaces. The architecture itself becoming astronomical instrument rather than merely housing such devices."

Farrat nodded, understanding immediately what she described—how the building's carefully positioned apertures and reflective surfaces transformed incoming starlight into meaningful patterns across interior walls and floors, creating temporal map that connected architectural experience with astronomical reality. Not merely aesthetic feature but conceptual manifestation, physical embodiment of threshold territory between built environment and natural phenomenon.

"Another manifestation of how constraints generate creative possibility," he observed, developing her architectural insight through their established pattern of complementary perspective. "The structural limitations necessary for supporting observation equipment becoming opportunity for transforming starlight into interior experience."

"Exactly," Tauree confirmed, appreciation warming her voice at his immediate understanding. "Not despite necessary structural elements but precisely because of them—the constraints becoming creative parameters rather than merely limiting conditions."

Around them, the evening continued its gradual transition toward night, more stars becoming visible as darkness deepened. Unlike their reunion five years earlier, when winter constellations had dominated northern sky, tonight's summer arrangements created completely different celestial patterns—Cygnus spreading wings across zenith, Scorpius curling across southern horizon, Summer Triangle creating perfect navigational reference overhead.

Different stars, different season, different patterns—yet observed from identical location by same individuals who had stood there years earlier. The astronomical metaphor wasn't lost on either of them: how identical physical position could provide completely different perceptual experience based on temporal context, how same relationship could manifest through varying experiential qualities while maintaining fundamental structural integrity.

"I've been thinking about fog and rainfall," Tauree said eventually, rare direct reference to their established metaphors for respective forms of depression. "Not as conditions to overcome or obstacles to navigate, but as particular atmospheric qualities that create specific relationships with surrounding environment."

"How so?" Farrat asked, his interest genuine rather than perfunctory.

"Singapore's tropical climate produced different relationship between atmosphere and architecture than temperate environments typically generate," she explained, professional observation extending into personal territory through their established pattern of translating between domains. "Buildings there don't merely resist moisture but engage with it—creating intentional interactions that transform potential obstacle into meaningful environmental feature."

"Architectural engagement with inevitable atmospheric conditions rather than futile attempt at their elimination," Farrat suggested, developing her metaphor with characteristic insight. "Design that acknowledges weather patterns as environmental reality requiring thoughtful navigation rather than problems demanding solution."

"Yes," Tauree confirmed, appreciation evident at his immediate understanding. "And it occurs to me that our respective internal weather systems function similarly—the fog and rainfall not conditions to be eliminated through medication or relationship, but environmental realities requiring thoughtful navigation and occasionally generating unexpected creative possibility."

The observation struck perfect balance between professional insight and personal disclosure—neither clinical detachment nor emotional excess, but authentic engagement with significant understanding that transcended conventional categories of professional accomplishment and personal development. Not therapy disguised as architectural theory, but genuine recognition of how similar principles operated across different domains of experience.

"Which might explain why conventional approaches to depression often prove inadequate," Farrat suggested, extending her thinking with characteristic perception. "Attempting to eliminate atmospheric conditions rather than developing architectural strategies for meaningful engagement with inevitable environmental realities."

"Exactly," Tauree acknowledged, genuine excitement at this shared conceptual development overcoming her usual emotional reserve. "Not miracle cure or pharmaceutical solution, but architectural approach to psychological navigation—creating structures that permit meaningful experience within particular atmospheric conditions rather than requiring their elimination as prerequisite for significant engagement."

As they continued developing this understanding together—architect and poet creating conceptual framework that transcended conventional categories of professional theory and personal experience—the summer stars continued their precise movement across the night sky above. Not dramatic transformation but gradual evolution, essential positions maintained while specific manifestation responded to ongoing temporal progression.

Other visitors moved across the observatory's rooftop terrace—students engaged in astronomical assignments, couples enjoying romantic setting, families introducing children to celestial observation. The space functioned exactly as Tauree had designed it—threshold territory permitting multiple modes of engagement simultaneously, architecture creating framework for various experiences without requiring exclusive classification or predetermined outcomes.

"There's something I've been wanting to share," Farrat said eventually, reaching into his jacket pocket to extract small package wrapped in simple paper. "Not conventional anniversary gift or emotional token, but object that seemed particularly relevant to our ongoing exploration of threshold territories."

He extended the package toward her—gesture of offering without expectation, sharing something significant without demanding particular response. Tauree accepted it with evident appreciation, unwrapping with careful movements that preserved paper rather than destroying it in hasty revelation.

Inside was antique astronomical instrument—brass armillary sphere representing celestial movements through interlocking rings arranged according to different orbital planes. The craftsmanship was extraordinary, each element precisely calibrated and beautifully decorated while maintaining functional accuracy in depicting astronomical relationships.

"This is remarkable," Tauree said, genuine appreciation warming her voice as she examined the instrument's complex construction. "Not just aesthetically, but conceptually—physical manifestation of how different reference systems interact while maintaining independent integrity. Multiple frameworks existing simultaneously within single structural representation."

"That was what drew me to it," Farrat acknowledged, pleasure evident in his expression at her immediate understanding. "Instrument creating physical manifestation of threshold thinking through astronomical representation—different reference planes intersecting without requiring reconciliation into single system, multiple frameworks maintaining independence while creating meaningful relationship through structural interaction."

As Tauree continued examining the armillary sphere, attention moving between different elements with characteristic perception, she recognized perfect embodiment of the architectural philosophy they had developed together—structure that existed between conventional categories, that permitted multiple modes of engagement simultaneously, that created framework for meaningful experience without requiring predetermined outcomes or exclusive classifications.

"It reminds me of something I've been considering," she said, her tone shifting slightly to indicate transition to more personal territory. "How the different residences we maintain might function similarly to these intersecting rings—separate reference systems maintaining independent integrity while creating meaningful relationship through structural interaction."

Farrat's attention focused with that characteristic quality of genuine interest she had valued throughout their connection. "In what sense specifically?" he asked, creating space for complete articulation without presumption or interruption.

"The geographical distance between our primary residences has functioned as creative parameter rather than merely limiting condition," Tauree explained, architect presenting design concept to respected colleague rather than partner proposing relationship arrangement. "The separate spaces maintaining independent development while creating meaningful interaction through thoughtful navigation. But I've been wondering if there might be value in establishing third location that would function as dedicated threshold territory between our separate environments."

"Intentional liminal space rather than merely alternating between distinct territories," Farrat suggested, immediately grasping her architectural intention. "Not replacement for existing residences but complementary environment specifically designed as threshold territory between established locations."

"Exactly," Tauree confirmed, appreciation evident in her voice at his precise understanding. "Not conventional move toward 'living together' with its implication of surrendering separate development, but architectural approach to creating designated space for shared experience while maintaining independent territories for individual evolution."

"Another manifestation of threshold thinking applied to relationship architecture," Farrat observed, developing this concept with characteristic insight. "Not compromise between autonomy and connection, but structural innovation permitting both simultaneously through spatial distribution rather than temporal alternation."

The clarity of this mutual understanding—this aligned recognition of potential development in their relationship architecture—created another moment of profound connection between them. Not despite geographical considerations but because of their thoughtful engagement with spatial realities, their refusal to either ignore practical considerations or surrender to conventional limitations when addressing genuine complexity.

"I've identified several possibilities," Tauree continued, moving from conceptual framework to specific application with professional thoroughness. "Small residence approximately equidistant between our primary locations, accessible with relatively equal travel requirements from either direction. Not urban environment but natural setting with meaningful astronomical visibility—location where celestial observation would provide continuation of significant shared experience."

"Creating physical manifestation of the threshold territory we've been developing conceptually," Farrat suggested, building upon her architectural foundation. "Space designed specifically for our particular relationship rather than adapted from conventional residential models or predetermined social scripts."

"Yes," Tauree acknowledged, genuine enthusiasm emerging through her usual professional composure. "Custom architecture in both physical and metaphorical senses—structure designed according to specific requirements rather than generalized expectations or standardized patterns."

As they continued developing this possibility together—architect and poet creating physical manifestation of the conceptual framework they had established over years of thoughtful exploration—the summer stars continued their precise movement across the night sky above. The observatory Tauree had designed tracked these celestial bodies with remarkable precision, its architectural elements transforming external astronomical movements into internal experiential patterns.

Around them, the public continued engaging with this threshold space according to their various interests and capacities—researchers conducting professional observations, students completing educational assignments, families sharing intergenerational experience, couples creating romantic memories. Not despite these different engagement modes but precisely because architecture permitted their simultaneous existence without requiring exclusive classification or predetermined outcomes.

"It strikes me as particularly appropriate," Farrat observed as they concluded their initial planning for this potential third location, "that we're discussing this architectural possibility in this specific environment—building that physically manifests the threshold concepts we've been developing together, that creates territory existing between conventional categories while maintaining functional precision."

"The location has additional significance beyond its architectural embodiment of threshold thinking," Tauree acknowledged, rare direct reference to emotional meaning emerging without calculation or performance. "This specific geographical position represents important transition in how we conceptualized distance as creative parameter rather than merely limiting condition."

The recognition—that physical location carried both conceptual significance and emotional meaning—created another moment of authentic connection between them. Not performance of conventional romantic narrative, but genuine acknowledgment of how intellectual understanding and personal experience had developed together through their particular approach to relationship architecture.

As night fully claimed the sky, observatory's professional equipment began its programmed observation sequences while public areas continued supporting various engagement modes simultaneously. The building functioned exactly as Tauree had designed it—threshold space permitting multiple experiences without requiring exclusive classification, architecture creating framework for meaningful engagement without predetermining specific outcomes.

Their conversation continued its natural flow between professional consideration and personal reflection, intellectual exploration and emotional recognition, separate perspective and shared understanding. Not despite geographical complexities that would resume when each returned to their primary residence, but precisely because their architectural approach had transformed spatial distribution from limiting condition into creative parameter.

Above them, summer constellations continued their celestial patterns—different arrangements than the winter stars that had illuminated their reunion five years earlier, yet equally meaningful within their particular seasonal context. Not contradiction requiring resolution but natural variation within consistent system, different manifestation of same fundamental principles operating through distinct temporal conditions.

The careful architect and thoughtful poet had discovered, somehow, relationship architecture that transcended conventional limitations without denying physical reality—that acknowledged practical considerations without surrendering to predetermined scripts, that transformed potential constraints into creative parameters rather than merely limiting conditions. Neither traditional romance nor platonic friendship, neither casual acquaintance nor formal partnership, but custom structure designed specifically for their particular needs and capacities.

A threshold space, deliberately constructed, constantly evolving, uniquely theirs—even across geographical distance, even through professional development, even within their respective atmospheric conditions that remained present without defining their entire experience. Not despite the fog and rainfall that continued moving through them in familiar patterns, but somehow incorporating these atmospheric realities into environmental conditions requiring thoughtful navigation rather than problems demanding solution.

As they eventually prepared to depart the observatory terrace—Tauree toward temporary accommodation near her latest project site, Farrat toward visiting faculty housing during his summer teaching assignment—their farewell carried that same quality of authentic connection that had characterized their relationship throughout its evolution. Not desperate clinging nor casual dismissal, but genuine acknowledgment of both meaningful engagement and approaching separation, both profound connection and necessary independence.

"Until our next constellation," Farrat said, the phrase carrying particular significance within their established vocabulary for navigating transitions between proximity and distance.

"Until then," Tauree confirmed, completing their exchange with that attention to balanced connection that had characterized their relationship throughout its development.

As they moved in their separate directions—temporary divergence rather than permanent disconnection—each carried both the antique astronomical instrument and the understanding they had developed together. Not conventional relationship defined by predetermined scripts or binary outcomes, but custom architecture designed through careful attention to both individual needs and mutual possibilities—threshold space that permitted multiple modes of engagement simultaneously, that honored difference while establishing genuine understanding across it, that transformed geographical distribution from limiting condition into creative parameter.

Different stars would illuminate their separate skies that night, different constellations visible from different vantage points. Yet identical celestial bodies would create these varied patterns, same fundamental reality perceived through distinct observational positions. Not contradiction requiring resolution, but threshold territory permitting multiple interpretations simultaneously, each authentic within its particular perceptual framework while maintaining essential integrity across different geographical locations.

Above them both, though now observed from separate positions, the summer stars continued their precise movement across the night sky—eternal yet evolving, consistent yet dynamic, structured yet fluid in their celestial choreography. Not unlike the particular architecture Tauree and Farrat had constructed together over years of thoughtful development—relationship that existed between conventional categories, that permitted multiple modes of engagement simultaneously, that created meaningful connection without requiring either complete merger or artificial performance.

A threshold space, deliberately constructed, constantly evolving, uniquely theirs—across geographical distance, through professional development, within respective atmospheric conditions that remained present without defining their entire experience. Not dramatic transformation or miraculous cure, but sustainable architecture designed for authentic habitation according to their particular needs and capacities.

The fog and rainfall continued moving through them in familiar patterns—acknowledged without denial, navigated without surrender, occasionally transformed from limitation into unexpected creative possibility. Not despite these atmospheric conditions but somehow through their thoughtful integration into environmental realities requiring architectural engagement rather than problems demanding elimination.

The careful architect of precise spaces and thoughtful poet of structural understanding had discovered, somehow, approach to connection that transcended conventional limitations without denying practical realities—threshold territory between established categories that permitted authentic development without requiring predetermined outcomes. Neither traditional relationship nor casual association, neither complete merger nor rigid separation, but custom architecture designed specifically for their particular ways of being in the world.

Beneath separate skies yet observing same stars, Tauree and Farrat continued navigating the particular architecture they had constructed together—threshold space deliberately designed, constantly evolving, uniquely theirs.

THE END

www.ingramcontent.com/pod-product-compliance
Lightning Source LLC
LaVergne TN
LVHW052242200926
848481LV00002B/248